STORGY®
BOOKS

Cover Design by Rob Pearce

First Published in Great Britain in 2017 by STORGY Books

1st Print

Copyright © STORGY Books 2017

London

Published by STORGY BOOKS Ltd
London, United Kingdom, 2017

10 9 8 7 6 5 4 3 2 1

www.storgy.com

Printed and bound by Page Bros, Mile Cross Lane, Norwich NR6 6SA

A CIP catalogue record for this title is available from the British Library

Trade Paperback ISBN 978 1 9998907 0 4
eBook ISBN 978 1 9998907 1 1

"What the caterpillar calls
the end of the world,
the master calls
a butterfly."

- Richard Bach -

...EXIT EARTH...

CONTENTS

FOREWORD

EXIT EARTH

EXIT EARTH EXTRA

FOREWORD

So, here we are. The EXIT EARTH Anthology. We made it.

Some of you may have read our previous anthologies, or the short stories we publish on our website, or experienced the work of our artists, and may even know a little about who we are and what do. For those of you who haven't, and for whom this is your first STORGY BOOK, welcome.

I feel no greater urge than to express our immense gratitude to an array of talented and dedicated people with whom we have worked on EXIT EARTH. Whilst it is most common to give thanks as the finale of a book, this is our beginning, and we begin with thanks and praise.

Thank you to everyone who has ever submitted their writing for our consideration, whether it was selected for publication or not. Each and every story we have read has enriched our lives and taught us lessons beyond the craft. Thank you to everyone who has read the short stories we publish and visited our website. Your continued encouragement and support is truly treasured.

Thank you to all our regular writers and reviewers who continue to offer their words for our - and your - consumption. The list is long, but each of you has enabled us to keep the faith. We would not exist were it not for your commitment to our cause. Your contributions have been - and will hopefully remain - invaluable to us and all our readers. You have helped to keep the dream alive.

Thank you to all the artists who have worked with us on EXIT EARTH and all our previous e-books; HarlotVonCharlotte, Amie Dearlove, CrapPanther, Rob Pearce, and Henry Davis. Your phenomenal artwork never fails to enhance the quality of our books and working with each of you has been an immense privilege.

Thank you to all the writers contained within this anthology; Rachel Connor, Duncan Abel, Joseph Sale, Erik Bergstrom, Francisco González, Tomas Marcantonio, Richard Lee-Graham, Virginia Ballesty, Michael Bird, Jessica Bonder, Philip Webb Gregg, Robin Griffiths, Guy Smith, Paul Turner, M. R. Carey, Toby Litt, James Miller, Courttia Newland, and David James Poissant. This book would not exist without your amazing words.

Special thanks to Diane Cook for judging The EXIT EARTH Short Story Competition and for helping us choose the stories you will soon discover.

Thank you to everyone who pledged their hard-earned money to our Kickstarter campaign. Publishing a print book has long been a dream of ours and each of you helped to make it finally come true. What you now hold in your hands is a product of your passion and faith in STORGY and all our authors and artists. You have enabled us to print EXIT EARTH and enter the publishing world, a world in which we plan to stay.

Thank you to the incredible team at STORGY. Alice and Tabitha you have both enlightened me with your endless enthusiasm and determination. Without your hard work we could not have published EXIT EARTH. I feel blessed to have met you, friends.

Lastly, thank you to Anthony Self and Ross Jeffery. From the very beginning of EXIT EARTH you have never wavered in your commitment and dedication. STORGY would not exist in all its forms were it not for your fervent belief in everything that we are and aim to be. I will never forget this unbelievable journey. Thank you for making it fun.

Finally, thank you to all our family and friends and thank you to you for buying this book. The only thing we ask is that if you enjoy EXIT EARTH, tell others about it. Encourage them to buy a copy, or give yours away. Take photos of the book or the stories or artwork contained within and share them on social media; #exitearth. We hope you enjoy it as much as we have.

Right, that's it from me.
No back-story or bullshit.
This is EXIT EARTH
...welcome...

Tomek Dzido

Illustration by Amie Dearlove

HOW TO CURATE A LIFE
by Rachel Connor

It has taken a week to harvest the girl's life. Jesse's device is connected to hers by a flex that curls across his desk like an umbilical cord. She was haphazard in her digital existence. Over six months of life-log footage, none of it edited. All that's left of her now, though, is powder; food for some memorial bush. The anachronism of a freshly-dug bed in winter. The garden of her parents' house, suburban, detached, red brick. He remembers, as they sat in the kitchen, the father's rolled-up shirt sleeves, his tanned forearms. The easy way he slid the notes across the chestnut counter.

Jesse couldn't remember the last time he'd seen real cash. It was stacked in piles, centimetres from his bag. It would have been easy to scoop it up and leave, bargain struck. The urge to touch it was strong. No wonder transfers were the sanctioned means of exchange. Less messy that way, no coins or paper rubbing against fabric, or flesh.

'They'll want to know where it came from.'

'They won't ask,' the father said. 'Not at my bank.'

The wife, opposite, with her indolent eyelids. The warm spiced smell, churning out from the vent: cloves and cinnamon. It made him think of a distant December. Hands around a mug, feeling the heat spread across his palms and his mother's face, eyes closed, satiated by the moment.

'More than a hundred times its electronic value.' The father caught his eye.

Jesse would become a man with capital; the owner of a box held deep in the innards of a building. He'd heard about those who visited their bank just to touch it. He imagined the texture of ink against his fingers, the pattern in relief of some long-dead monarch.

'I don't have the authority,' Jesse said. 'Not without a will. Your daughter's digital estate — it still belongs to her.'

'We're her parents.' The mother's voice was stretched tight like a rubber band. 'Surely we have a say?'

'Legally she was an adult. There's no loophole. I can't just —.' He looked at the father.

'We hoped you'd consider it. Discreetly of course.' The mother nodded at the money.

Jesse had only once pressed delete. He didn't know if he was ready to do it again. He looked at the sister. She didn't want this, he was sure. 'If your daughter had come to me —'. He opened the laptop. 'Look, I can still collate her data.' He clicked open the tab and angled it towards them.

3

'Why don't you take a look at the designs?'

'If she were alive, we wouldn't need you.'

At the mother's words, there was an intake of breath from the sister. She turned sharply away. He saw, through the window, a bird table in the centre of the lawn. The ground was strewn with rotting leaves.

The mother sat forward, back ramrod straight. 'Have you ever lost anyone?'

'My parents,' Jesse said. 'Both of them.' He realised they were waiting for more. There was silence and a blast of warm air from the room conditioner as they sat staring at each other: the sister, the mother, the father, and him.

'Then you'll know. You'll know what it's like. You're online and her face pops up. Photos you didn't know existed, maybe even one you've taken.' She looked at him. She was in the hard phase of grief, he could see, the angry part. The echo in Jesse's ears, the words he wanted to say. That once it is done, there's no going back.

A movement across the partition makes him look up: Sal sliding from one end of her desk to the other, the sound of casters on the hard floor. She initiates a FaceTime and he hears her caffeinated laugh, thinks of the freckles in that dip below her throat. Some days, when it's hot, he sees the sheen of sweat on her skin, a suppressed urge to taste it again. That last time on her kitchen floor. He'd had a sense, even as she opened the door, that she was going to end it. But that word — *passive* — jabs at him even now.

'You plan on taking a break this month?'

Django's voice behind him, at the entrance to his booth. It's almost violent, being wrested away from the world he's been populating, the world of the dead girl. Footage of summer days, light cutting across the lens, the fizz of orange and yellow at the periphery of vision. Insta images. Haystacks in a field, perfectly spaced.

'Lunch?' Django sticks out his thumb and motions to the door, a hitch-hiker in an old movie.

Jesse opens the drawer to retrieve his cards, turns to the window to assess the day. Bright winter sunshine. He pockets his sunglasses. They walk down the corridor together, Jesse trying to match Django's pace. He follows him down a flight of stairs to the ground floor until they push through the automatic doors and into the light.

It's just about mild enough to sit in the quad, the central square of green that is subdivided by wooden decking and bamboo grass. They pick up soba takeaway from one of the coloured trucks parked at the entrance. A runner in a fluorescent vest laps the perimeter, tracking his progress on a watch.

'So.' Django's mouth is full of noodles, sauce dripping onto his chin. 'The file you're working on. Want to tell me about it?'

Jesse is aware of the knot of office girls sitting nearby. They've brought those thin, plastic-backed travel rugs with them. Even wearing coats and cardigans, they stretch out their legs to catch the sun. One of them has her eyes closed. He wonders if she is listening.

Jesse nods towards them. 'Best not.' He tastes tofu and peppers, a sharp hit of chilli. 'Anyway — you know the pact. It's lunch.'

Django turns to look at him. Wide open eyes, fringed with black lashes. Jesse sees why women go crazy for him. 'I checked the drive. You haven't set up a template.'

He feels a prickling at the back of his neck, that cold clamminess he's experienced before. A flash of his father's dying face. The rasping breath. The hand on top of the sheet that everyone expected Jesse to hold. But he couldn't bring himself to do it.

He focuses on the action of his chopsticks. He needs to be careful, even with Django. 'The parents haven't come back on the design yet.'

Django leans into him. 'They made you a deal, didn't they?'

Raucous laughter erupts from the office girls. One holds her hands over her mouth and the others are ribbing her about something.

'In your job, it's always going to happen. It did to Rasmus. Remember him?'

'The Danish guy?'

Django nods. 'The client's husband was cheating on her. When he died, she got Rasmus to —.' He makes a cutting gesture across the throat. Jesse checks to see if the office girls are watching.

'He made a will, though, right?' Jesse whispers. 'The husband?'

Django shakes his head.

The runner has stopped, stands with hands on hips, face contorted.

'How do you know this stuff?'

'I keep my eyes on the drive. You start to see the patterns.' Django takes a swig of water and offers the bottle but Jesse thinks of the black bean sauce residue, shakes his head. Django looks back at him. 'I don't see what's taking you so long.'

The office girls are on their feet, shaking out their rugs, collecting the remains of their lunch. Django darts a look at them, then turns to Jesse.

'If you're going to delete everything,' he hisses, 'why bother to collate it?'

There'd been very little of his father. A few scanned-in photos with a thick white border, taken in his sporting days. Rows of young men with long hair and green jerseys, those at the front squatting. His father in the middle, the grinning and victorious captain, the ball by his feet. When Jesse hit delete, he erased the photograph. But he couldn't forget the smile.

Django reads something in his face and his laugh reveals disbelief, frustration. 'You haven't decided.'

'I've got 'til the end of the week.' Jesse can't tell his friend that he hears the dead girl breathing. He knows her. 'I just think — ' The runner is lying on the ground, legs vertical, stretching his hamstrings. 'They might change their minds.'

'You're insane. You know that?' Django gathers up their detritus — the empty cartons, drink bottles — signaling the end of lunch. The way he dumps it in the canister makes Jesse's irritation rise.

By Friday afternoon, he's gone through everything but the video content. She preferred Polaroid Swing, so her YouTube is minimal. In the first film, she's in a park; a dot moving amongst the trees, so far off that he wonders if it's her at all. A face comes into the frame. A boy. Downy hair on his cheekbones catching the light. He is smiling, confident in the knowledge that, even across the distance, he has her in his grasp. Jesse can trace the boy's movements, the sensation of grass under bare feet. Then the screen goes dead. What happened? Did the boyfriend grab her? Did they collapse on a blanket, his hands on her hot skin?

Jesse clicks on the Polaroid folder. He hadn't watched them when he was collating, just used the still of the first image as an index. There are so many images of her at parties, gardens in the dark, fairy lights strung in the background; girls wearing too much make up. He hovers over the icon, risks being pulled in to the memories of places she's been. Travels around Europe; festivals. It's not so long since he was doing the same, and he remembers the American backpacker in Prague. The hostel's musty sheets. The way the ends of her hair felt against his chest and thighs.

The file has somehow opened. Jesse's fingers are on the mouse. A still of the girl's face: dead but very much alive. She's laughing, pulling back a strand of blonde hair. It must be hot because she is wearing very little. There is the whisper, underneath her shirt, of a bikini; cornflower blue. It brings out the colour of her eyes. She is looking at him. He activates Swing and the image becomes real; a woman's body moving in time and space, the hand settling the hair back into place. She turns away but, over her shoulder, her smile, broadening.

Jesse is mesmerised. He's there, on the sand dunes; the prickle of marram grass against his legs, gritty sand in his mouth. She is soft. The heat of her midriff under the shirt. He closes his eyes as she hoists herself on top of him, because he knows what will happen next. She will touch him. He will grow hard. Hidden in the hollow of the dune, the heat on their backs; he'll feel her breasts brush against him. He will enter her gently and she will be wet, making it easy to work inside her.

He feels overheated, pushes back his seat. In her cubicle, Sal is staring at her screen, earbuds jammed in. Across the way, Django grins. In the toilets, Jesse closes his eyes but can't prevent the images replaying. He splashes his face with water and looks at himself in the mirror. How is it possible to feel desire for a dead girl? He can't believe she isn't here, laughing, dancing, having sex. He swears he can feel her mouth on his neck.

He leans over the basin, breathes into his lungs: the biological function that keeps him alive. It stopped, suddenly, for her. He never asked how she died. There are photos of her grinning from a kayak, helmeted, paddle in hand. He imagines her slipping under the surface, her foot catching on a reed or a piece of metal on the riverbed, toiling and fighting to break free and finally relenting, everything slowing down. The last thing she would see: her boyfriend's face.

Jesse looks at the scar under his left eyelid; the stubble on his chin. Signs of the body being alive, trying to heal itself. He turns the tap on again, washes his hands. He remembers the first time his father took him to visit his mother in hospital, the chemical smell, her tight smile, welts across her wrists: her only means of escape. Only later did he realise how persistent she must have been.

Back at his desk, Jesse puts his headphones on and selects a soundtrack. Deep Focus. He'll need it for what he's about to do.

By the time he's finished, everyone has gone. As he leaves the office, the sensor lights activate and the corridor twitches into life. He feels, momentarily, like an actor on stage. The muscles in his legs ache from the strain of clenching them at his desk. He longs for the rhythm of the tram and a few minutes' sleep before he's spewed out of the station and onto the streets.

At reception, the reflections in the windows make it difficult to see where the outside begins. Starkey is in his usual seat, head down, staring at a tablet. Jesse recognizes the porn site. His dick twitches, involuntarily. He thinks of her.

Starkey closes the cover of his tablet. 'A late one for you.'

Jesse nods, hands over his staff ID and Starkey files it away with the others. 'No devices tonight?'

Jesse smiles. 'Giving myself the weekend off.'

He pushes his bag through the X-ray scanner and pictures what the machine won't pick up: a piece of paper. A handwritten letter that he'll deliver to the girl's parents tomorrow.

Jesse wants to be outside, to feel the evening cold against his skin. The revolving door is slower than usual and he waves as he goes through: see you next week. There's no need for Starkey to know. He'll find out soon enough when the email reaches Jesse's boss on Monday with news of a job elsewhere. He wonders, briefly, if Sal will miss him.

The bag is so light. The girl no longer exists. But what he's done is much more creative: a new template, a record of her life. He has managed her online presence, locked it away so no one can retrieve it. No one — not even her parents — will know she's there. The data is encrypted. She's indelible, anyway, for him; stored in that part of his brain he vaguely remembers from his ancient science class. The limbic region. The hippocampus.

Jesse thinks about tomorrow, how he'll sleep until late, watch movies in bed and eat takeaway from the carton. At some point, he'll cross the threshold to run along the river, altering his route to take in the suburbs. The sun will set slowly. He'll breathe as he runs, inhaling water vapour, the girl's molecules; her biological traces.

1st PRIZE
HOW TO CURATE A LIFE
by Rachel Connor

Rachel Connor is a novelist, dramatist and short story writer based in Yorkshire, where she teaches creative writing at Leeds Beckett University. In addition to writing plays for stage and site-specific performance, she has published short fiction and is the author of a novel, *Sisterwives*. Her debut radio drama *The Cloistered Soul* was broadcast on BBC Radio 4 in 2015 as part of their Original British Dramatists season. She is currently exploring how technology can facilitate powerful experiences of immersive storytelling. Rachel is on Twitter *@rachel_novelist*.

AFTERWORD

There is something fascinating about imagining a future we cannot yet see or know, just as we might reconstruct a past that is out of our reach. 'How to curate a life' began as an idea from something I found online about careers that will be ubiquitous in the future. It is predicted that, some day, there will be a job for people overseeing the digital estate of a person after death: a digital death manager. This prompted so many questions. When we die, who owns the self in virtual form — the deceased person, or the next of kin? Are we ever truly dead if there are traces of the self in images and our exchanges online? And where, in all this, is the soul? Once the body has expired, is our online footprint a repository of the soul, a means of achieving immortality?

Of course, there are no answers. Being human is a mystery that has puzzled us for millennia and will surely continue to, whatever era or cultural context we exist in. 'How to curate a life' is my attempt to explore the fundamental needs we have, as humans, to connect, to touch and be touched, physically and emotionally; to matter.

And, there's the thing. We *are* matter: simply collections of atoms, cells and stardust. But the human condition can also contain, if we allow it, the feeling of something bigger; something that is both burden and gift. Our connection to other beings makes us, in the end, weightier than bodies, more powerful than the constellations of energies clustered in the stars.

Illustration by HarlotVonCharlotte

DON'T GO TO THE FLEA CIRCUS
by Duncan Abel

We were dying of hunger. Uncle Horatio had been the first to go. I wanted to draw him as he lay there, cold and bone-thin in just his underpants. Mumma wouldn't let me. She said we had to bury him before the Circus came for his body. But that was yesterday.

This morning, in the kitchen, Grandpa was ripping the tongues out of my school shoes.

'There's nutrients in the leather,' he said. 'Did you know that, Ely?'

'They're my only pair, Grandpa.'

He continued hacking at them with his penknife.

I looked past him, through the frayed curtains to the snow-covered street below. People just walked past the bodies that lay on the pavements now. There were too many to bury. No one had the strength.

I took what was left of my shoes from Grandpa and sat on the cold linoleum to pull them on.

The front door clicked and Mumma came in, the bottom of her coat wet from the snow.

'How's the broth?' she said.

'It's getting there,' Grandpa said, 'Hey, Ely?'

'Yes, Grandpa.'

He dropped the shoes' tongues into the pot, along with a tangle of leather belts, which really we needed because our trousers had all grown too big.

'I managed to get this piece of carrot and a sachet of sugar,' Mumma said.

She was shivering beneath her coat, tensing her shoulders as if to hold her bones together.

'Drop 'em in the saucepan, then,' Grandpa said. 'We'll eat today. Like kings, we'll eat.'

I side-stepped to the door, hoping neither of them would notice.

'Where are you going, Ely?'

I looked back to him, to both of them. There was a feeling these days that the last time you saw someone, it might be the last time for good. I did a mental sketch. They were both a mismatch of skin, bone and ragged clothing. I suppose I was too.

'I'm going for a walk,' I said.

I could see Mumma weighing up whether to say it or not. Grandpa spoke for her. He was serious now. Moral.

'Don't you go to the Flea Circus.'

Outside, people moved slowly and silently. Oversized coats drooped over their curved spines and dragged in the snow. There were fewer people each time I came outside, and those left had grown so pale they were almost transparent. I kept my eye out for the men from the Circus. But I didn't really know what they looked like. I only knew the rumours.

Across the street from our tenement, I saw Mr Henry coming out of his house; he used to be my art teacher before the Big Starve. His suit hung from his bones as if he were a scarecrow made of broom-handles and old coat hangers. He still wore the flower on his lapel.

'Good God, Ely. It's wonderful to see you alive,' he said, the creases in his face turning almost to a smile. 'Where are you going?'

I found the strength to shrug.

'Are you still drawing?' he asked.

'Doesn't seem much point if we're all going to die.'

'We were all going to die anyway, Ely. You must draw what you see. Leave something so people will learn about all of this.'

He cast his hand out at the streets. It made me see it all anew. Ransacked buildings. Looted shops. Decayed limbs poking out of the snow. Up on the hill, you could see the high fences the government erected to keep us in – or was it to keep us out? I couldn't see any of the border-guards patrolling them, though. But they were there. We knew that.

'How's your family?' he asked, and then lowered his voice, 'I heard you had all...'

'Mumma and Grandpa are still alive,' I said. 'And I'm still here. How have you been managing, sir?'

He took too long to answer, and I could see it in his eyes.

'You haven't been going to the Flea Circus, have you, sir?'

'These are difficult times, Ely.'

I thought of Mumma and Grandpa – what they would say if they knew what I was thinking? But these days I mostly thought with my stomach. I whispered, as if to prevent my own conscience from overhearing.

'Will you take me with you?'

'The Circus, Ely. It's not a place for children. Not anymore. I bet you don't even have any money, do you?'

I put my hands in my pockets, my fingers prospecting for any coins I might have forgotten about. All I could feel was my leg. Bony. And cold.

'I have this watch.'

'No one's keeping time, here, Ely.'

'But what's the point in money?' I said. 'You can't eat it, and there's nowhere to spend it.'

But something in what I said seemed to snag his ear. His yellowy eyes searched for whatever secrets he thought my own eyes might be hiding. But there were no secrets here anymore. Women had stopped dyeing the grey out of their hair, stopped shaving their legs. And the men, once proud and private, had become beggars on street corners. Hunger had made us equals. Starved out our hidden truths the way a poacher smokes a rabbit out of its warren. Mr Henry held his stare.

'You don't know about the Bottleneck?'

'Is it a way out of here?' I said, but he didn't answer, just began walking down the street, my footprints in the snow a pace or two behind his.

In the doorway of what used to be the library, two men in long, grey coats were loading a stretcher with the frozen corpse of a young woman. A blue-lipped smile frozen to her face. She almost looked happy. They stopped when they realised I was watching, and met me with a stare that remained unbroken, even when a swirl of wind flecked their beards and eyebrows with snow.

Mr Henry pulled my shoulder. 'Come on, Ely,' he said, his eyes remaining on the men in grey coats. An understanding between them to which I was not privy.

'Are they from the Flea Circus?' I said, glancing back. They were still watching me. 'Are they the men from the Circus, Mr Henry?'

'Look, if you're coming with me, please, Ely, don't ask questions.'

The Flea Circus used to be an old flourmill before the river that ran through here grew to a trickle and then to a puddle and then to nothing at all. The wheels and gears of the grain mill were rusted together and the wooden structure had rotted to a sagging skeleton, but the stone structure remained mostly intact.

Candlelight wobbled as Mr Henry and I stepped inside; the shadows took a moment to settle back into the sunken eyes of the men and women who hunched in silence. The place reminded me of the opium dens I once read about in Victorian stories of London, Bangkok and Burma. In the corner, a lady was quietly shushing a baby, the tired hint of a lullaby on her breath. She pulled from her cardigans a breast, floppy and empty. She put it to the child's lips and tried to wring out the last drips of milk. No one spoke. Mr Henry patted the seat next to him.

Before The Starve, Jonah and I used to go to the Flea Circus after school. We'd save our lunch money to buy the Madame's honeycomb and chocolate covered raisins. Some people said she used dead flies instead of raisins, but I could never tell. She would wind up an ancient pipe organ and, on the millstone-stage, command her fleas to perform their tricks. They would walk across a tight rope, score goals with tiny footballs, pull chariots through a maze. Once, I saw a flea pedalling a tiny Penny-farthing. I had once tried painting what I had witnessed at the Flea Circus, but I always found it difficult to draw from memory, and Mumma never liked those paintings. She said there was something sinister in the fleas that scared her. Mr Henry said he liked the way I pulled a darkness out of primary colours. I gave one of my paintings to the Madame once, hoping she would display it in the auditorium. I never saw it again.

A dust sheet lay over the pipe organ now, silence the only accompaniment.

Soon, a curtain swung open, and the Madame entered.

'I thought your family was too good for us,' she said.

I went to speak, but she didn't care for it.

'Everyone ends up at the Flea Circus one way or another,' she said. 'Did anyone follow you?'

'It's just me and Ely, here,' Mr Henry said.

'How much have you got?'

Mr Henry held out his hand to show her a few coins. She sighed.

'Is it for both of you?'

'Ely's starving, Madame.'

'Everyone's starving,' she said, and pocketed the money before disappearing behind the curtain. Mr Henry and I sat together on a small bench that was church pew cold. I couldn't stop myself from looking at him. Funny how teachers looked so different out of school. He was almost like a real person. Sad. And tired. His eyes stayed forwards, and his nerves made me nervous.

The Madame returned with two steaming bowls of soup.

'Are you sure no one followed you? Not the police? None of those border-guards...'

'Quite sure, Madame,' Mr Henry said.

She handed us the bowls and pulled two spoons from her apron. The lady who was nursing the baby looked up, but when our eyes met, we both looked away.

I balanced the bowl on my knees and stared into the soup. When I brought a spoonful to my lips, a thought of Mumma made me hesitate.

'Don't deny yourself, Ely,' said Mr Henry. 'We have no choice.'

But it was as if he were convincing himself as much as anyone else – his conscience made easier by spreading the immorality out among us all. There was no going back.

I had heard people say that human flesh tastes like chicken, but in the weak, thin soup it tasted of nothing at all. No sooner had we begun eating, it was nearly all gone. I slowed to make it last. Not just the food, but the damp warmth of the Flea Circus. The heat from the pot-stove. I could feel my body coming back to life as if it had been a deciduous tree, clenched against winter. Mr Henry stood to leave. The Madame appeared from behind her curtain.

'See you again,' she said.

I had never been inside Mr Henry's house, even though we were friends long before The Starve. He had always let me stay after school to use the art equipment, while he marked students' papers or planned his lessons. My friends said it was weird that I wanted to spend time with him. Grandpa said it was weird that he wanted to spend time with me. I just thought he was friendly. Mumma said he was lonely.

His house was a jumble of bric-a-brac, and the damp air made the dust stick thickly to everything. The walls were covered with paintings.

'Did you paint these, sir?'

He hesitated. The look on his face was one I hadn't seen before. Embarrassment, I think.

'Just that one,' he said.

I positioned myself in front of the painting. Maybe even tilted my head. The colours were such an intense mix of greys and dirty whites that, at first, I thought it was a just a pattern, some expression of monotony or disillusionment. But a closer look revealed figures, people so faded that they were almost invisible within the heavy brushstrokes. It was very ugly, and I didn't know how to compliment him on it.

'Can I see more of your paintings?'

He didn't answer, just lit the fire and set a brass kettle over it. He dropped some nettle leaves in two mugs and added the water when the kettle boiled.

'Let it absorb the nettles' nutrients for a minute,' he said.

I held the cup in my hands the way Mumma did when she was trying to warm herself. Mr Henry sat in a high-backed chair and spread a blanket over his legs. I stood with my back to the fire, the warmth crawling up my spine. It became so hot that it burned, but I wanted to somehow store the heat in my bones for later.

'You won't tell my mumma that I've been to the Flea Circus, sir?'

He sipped his nettle water. I copied. It was nice. I wondered about asking Mr Henry if I could take some nettles home for Grandpa's next batch of broth.

'How on earth is she sustaining you all, your mumma?' he said.

'Grandpa survived the last starve,' I said. 'He finds calories in all sorts of things.'

'I don't know how they've managed to keep such a tight grip on their morals. God knows, Ely, I tried not to go to the Flea Circus. I resisted for so long, but hunger – it's a kind of madness, isn't it?'

I thought of Grandpa, eating postage stamps because he said there was nutritional value in the glue.

'I thought I'd go, just the once,' Mr Henry said, 'just to get my head clear so I could make some kind of plan. But once you cross that line... God knows, I've sat next to people down there, Ely, people I've known all my life. They don't acknowledge you. They don't even look up. No one wants to admit to being there. Even to themselves.'

'Grandpa said it's illegal, what the Madame does down there?'

'Of course. But I've seen police officers eating with the rest of us. The laws we make are only ever as robust as those who enforce them. No law will stop us trying to survive.'

Mr Henry swirled the nettle leaves in his mug and slurped.

'Have you ever wondered, sir, how long it will be before there's just one person left, having eaten everybody else? Just one huge person surrounded by bones and old clothes.'

He thought for a moment, his hands together like a steeple. 'Perhaps that's the subject of your next painting. Here, have some more water.'

'What's the Bottleneck, sir?'

He added a few nettle leaves to my cup.

'A secret is what it is.'

'But what is it, actually?'

Mr Henry's smile sagged in defeat.

'There's a bridge. You know where the river used to bottleneck through the woods.'

'But the army fenced right around those woods. I went there on my bike when everyone was making a run for it.'

'Some of the guards who work that section, they smuggle one or two people out every night. Sold to the highest bidder.'

'So why have you not bought your passage, sir? You have money, don't you?'

'I've tried. God knows I've tried. I'm outbid every time by one of the Madame's family, and the days when the bids are low, I've been so mad with hunger that I've spent my money at the Flea Circus. We all inch closer to death as the Madame and her family, one by one, find their way out.'

We fell quiet then. A renewed futility crept in. If survival was bound to wealth, there was no hope for Mumma and Grandpa and me. We had sold anything of value, and we'd even begun burning our furniture for warmth. We were the ones for whom the fences were built, that was clear.

Days passed. And then weeks. Each morning I made an excuse to go to Mr Henry's house. I told Mumma that we were drawing, and that he was showing me his paintings. I'd take my sketch pad and brushes, but each day we'd go to the Flea Circus.

Back at Mr Henry's house, we did draw. Even though the energy used was a cost. He worked on a sculpture using dried twigs. He said they looked like bones and was the only medium he wanted to work in. I began composing sketches for my picture, 'The Last Survivor'. We worked together in a busy silence. We enjoyed each other's company. Treated each other as equals. His sculpture began to take life. A contorted human being, knee deep in bones. My composition was ready to transfer to canvas. But there was no end to The Starve.

Rumours that aid was on its way were met with counter-rumours. We stopped believing anything. We had been abandoned. That was all there was. It was each for his or herself. Each town for itself. Each country for itself. Grandpa grew weak, but it was Mumma who died first. I hadn't realised that whatever morsels and rations she had, she had been giving to Grandpa and me. The world was growing silent.

Once Grandpa died, I stayed at Mr Henry's. In time, we noticed that the portions at the Flea Circus had grown smaller. The dead were so skinny that even human meat grew sparse. The men in grey coats were waiting on people to die. Stalking us. We couldn't go on like this. The end was near. I could see it in Mr Henry's eyes, hear it in his dusty cough. He knew he was on his way, and maybe that meant that I was too.

He looked peaceful in his chair, the morning I found him, his head resting on his shoulder. The room had a different smell. Quietly, as if he might wake up and catch me, I looked through his belongings. His own paintings were hung on his bedroom wall. Mostly nudes of a young man. For a moment, I thought it was me, but most of them had been painted before I was born. I missed him even more for knowing this about him.

I was on my own. And yet, I still believed that things would change. I'd lost everything, but still wanted to survive.

The Bottleneck was my only hope. I ransacked Mr Henry's drawers, looking for anything of value – a few coins, bits of old jewellery. Each night, I went up to the bridge to watch the bidding, pleading, and the greed. The bids fluctuated over the days, growing too high and then crashing. I had collected coins from wherever I could but money was of increasingly low value. The global markets had crumbled. Currencies were failing. People wanted tangible items like food, clothes, medicine. The true value of gold and silver had been revealed – it was just metal. I broke into unoccupied houses and grabbed tablets, tools, matches – items of intrinsic value.

My rucksack was filled with everything I thought valuable, but I was growing weaker and had to fight myself from trading it all in down at the Flea Circus. Just hold on, I told myself, the bids were decreasing; I would soon be there.

The night for me to travel had come. It was now or never, I could feel it. But the hunger. I couldn't control it. If I just spent a few pennies at the Flea Circus. Just a…

I wrapped myself up like an Arctic explorer. It was so cold, each step through the snow heavier than the last. I was so weak that my vision blurred, but I was close… so close… the Flea Circus… a small piece of food, just to get me to the bridge, and then…

I don't know when I fell, but there I was. I hadn't the strength to stand and, like someone drowning, I lost all sense of up, down, left, right. Was this really it? The end. The spot where I would die. I knew of hypothermia and the insidious way in which it gives the impression of warmth, tricking you into giving up the fight. So, I fought to stay awake. Wait for someone to see me. But my eyes… my eyes kept…

I didn't know how much time had passed, but I could feel someone moving me. Was I really still alive? I could see the blurry grey shape of two men. I tried to speak, but my voice was numbed by the cold. I put every remaining scrap of strength into swallowing, trying to clear a passage for my words. My eyes were too weak to open, but in the cold blackness I heard my voice, as if in a dream. 'Please, please… Take me to the Flea Circus?'

The bag zipped up over my head. And a strange warmth.

'Yes, Ely,' said one of the grey coats. 'We're taking you to the Flea Circus.'

2nd PRIZE
DON'T GO TO THE FLEA CIRCUS
by Duncan Abel

Duncan Abel's short stories have been published by Unbound Press and Spilling Ink. His short story, "A Good Son", was performed at London Lit 2012. His novel, *The Way Home*, was shortlisted for the 2010 Luke Bitmead Award. Duncan Abel has written for BBC Radio drama; his Afternoon Play, *When I Lost You* (co-written with Rachel Wagstaff), was broadcast in 2013. His monologue (also co-written with Rachel Wagstaff) based on the life of Isambard Kingdom Brunel was performed and recorded by Hugh Bonneville, for Sing London. For the stage, Duncan Abel is currently under commission to The Original Theatre Company and Marion Theatrical Productions.

AFTERWORD

I've always been struck by the fact that we live in a world where a great number of the population is dying from starvation, while a similarly great number is dying from over-eating. "Don't go to the Flea Circus" came from the concept of mass starvation. I took some inspiration from accounts of those who had survived the Leningrad Blockade, the Blockade of Germany and from survivors of shipwrecks, and the lengths to which they went in order to stay alive: cooking their shoes, licking the glue from envelopes and, in the end, eating human meat.

With this story's post-apocalyptic vision, I felt that an unspecified time, place and 'event' would allow the reader to project and recognise aspects of their own town, their own country, and not consider it to be a story about a problem faced by "other" people but, rather, a potential problem faced by us all.

Illustration by Amie Dearlove

WHEN THE TIDE COMES IN
by Joseph Sale

We knew exactly when it was going to happen because they told us, so we went down to Nauru Coast to watch the sunrise.

We set out at 3:00am and clambered down the dust-slick cliffs, using palm trees as handholds. We found our usual perch, an old World War II bunker, the red sun flag scrubbed off through erosion and buried under layers of crude graffiti.

Hidetaka brought two crates of *Asahi* and a cooler. We swigged it like westerners, watching the darkness in silence. The sky was moonless and starless, deeper dark touching the rippling mirror of the ocean. Ayako wore a short white skirt of all things; it shone like a luminous, giant lily. I imagined the goosebumps on her legs from the cold. Her hair shone that kind of purple-black, making her shoulders look like they were draped with a mantle of night itself.

After a while, Hidetaka broke the spell.

'If you could have sex with one person right now, who would it be?'

Ayako didn't hesitate.

'Solid Snake.'

'What?'

'He's fictional,' I reminded her.

'So? There weren't any rules about that.'

'Okay, explain your reasoning,' Hidetaka grinned like a talk-show host. He had hair that looked like a mop and was always falling in his face. His teeth were slightly yellow from all the sugary sweets he loved. From a distance, I imagined he'd look something like a scarecrow – all gangly limbs, clothes dangling from a wire frame. I guess all three of us must look like scarecrows. There was no one else around.

'He has a perfect body,' Ayako started, putting a finger to her lips playfully. She could be a model, a magazine cover-girl, a stripper, a superstar, anything with those looks, but she is just the world's most-tipped hotel receptionist.

'The best that computers could render in 2008.' Hidetaka nodded.

'And it's that gravelly voice too. David Hayter's so sexy.'

David Hayter was the American-born actor living in Japan who voiced Solid Snake in the *Metal Gear Solid* video-game series for 20 years. Ayako is an avid gamer. Another reason most men go crazy over her.

'You prefer him to the Japanese guy?' Hidetaka was incredulous.

'Definitely. Something about him. I think Kiefer Sutherland made a good

Snake too. But nowhere near as good as David Hayter. I think there's something boyish about his voice which makes him cute. You know. He's all rugged but also like a child. It pushes all the buttons.'

Hidetaka stuck out his lower lip and nodded.

'Okay, Ryu, what about you?'

In my head I said: *Ayako, Ayako, Ayako and only Ayako.*

Out loud, I said:

'Natalie Dormer.'

'You're both traitors!' Hidetaka cried, throwing his hands in the air. 'Bloody westerners taking the hearts of our best and brightest.'

'But isn't she really old?' Ayako said, raising an eyebrow.

'She's thirty-five.'

'Ancient!'

'Ayako's right. She's too old for you, Ryu.'

'She doesn't look it though, does she?'

'Well...' The expression in Ayako's eyes was hard to read in the dark.

'You see, my theory is, Natalie Dormer is one of those people whose beauty comes down to bone structure. Therefore, she's not really going to age. She's just going to mature into her looks. I guess the same way men do.'

'It's true, old men are hot.' Ayako nodded fervently.

'So in choosing Natalie Dormer I play the long game,' I concluded, raising a beer. 'To Margaery of House Tyrell!'

Ayako laughed. The sound was like sea foam rushing up my body, the cold a secret, balmy blessing. Hidetaka chinked his beer bottle next to mine, downed it, and threw it out onto the beach. It hit the sand with a dull thud.

'Hidetaka!' Ayako shouted. 'The environment!' She pointed a stern finger and narrowed her eyes.

We all froze for a moment, then burst out laughing.

'Come on Hidetaka, you tell us yours now.'

Hidetaka put his chin in his hand, doing his best impression of Socrates pondering some weighty question about reality.

'Hmm, hmm, hmm, this needs some thought.'

'Come on!' Ayako poked him in the ribs. He yelped and swatted her hands away. She tickled him, digging her fingers beneath his armpits. Hidetaka squealed and rolled around, batting her hands away as though they were hornets. I watched, drinking, wishing I could have such easy physical contact with her. Ayako never starts this kind of thing with me. I wonder if it's because she knows I couldn't handle it, that I would think it meant something more.

'Okay, okay, it would have to be Lucy Liu!'

Ayako opened her mouth in shock.

'You're a traitor too?'

'At least she's Asian!'

Ayako crossed her arms and turned away from Hidetaka.

'Unacceptable.'

She winked at me and giggled. My heart attempted to beat regularly, but ended up cascading, like a fall of blossoms, shed all at once.

'So the truths are out,' Hidetaka exclaimed. 'That's all. That's all I wanted.'

We laughed, finished our drinks, got new ones, then settled into silence again. I checked my watch. It was 4:00am. The cold deepened to stinging point. There was still time.

'What happens when the tide comes in?' Ayako stared out at the water. There were grey rock formations a few hundred meters out that looked like gravestones, casting sundial shadows over the waters. I wasn't sure what she was asking, what she could possibly mean. I'm not even sure she knew what she was asking, just talking to fill the void.

'I guess all the tourists just pack their bags and leave,' Hidetaka said.

I nodded in agreement.

'High tide puts the whole beach under, right up to the treeline.'

We shared contemplative silence again.

'You ever been skinny dipping?' I couldn't believe the words spilling from my mouth, but then, things were different now we knew.

'What's skinny dipping?'

'Sounds western.' Hidetaka couldn't hide his suspicion.

'It's when you swim naked in the sea.'

'You crazyman!' Ayako grinned, her teeth eerily like the Cheshire cat's, two frightening sickles. I wondered if she'd had whitening. 'I'm cold enough already. Don't need to get any colder.'

'It won't be cold once you get swimming.' I lied. 'Besides, the sea is always two months behind the weather. It should be ok now.'

'Who told you that?' Hidetaka looked a little bit like The Rock, his eyebrows at mathematically impossible angles.

'Natalie Dormer.'

They both laughed. Laughter can be like a drug. You get addicted to hearing it, until you want it after everything you say.

'So how about it?' I stood up, gesticulating wildly and shouting about the wonders of skinny dipping, half of it made up and the other half incomprehensible; I felt like I'd never felt before, some kind of religious leader with ideology and purpose. The reality was just some drunk trying to get his friends to run butt-naked into the sea with him.

'Okay, okay! If you won't shut up about it!' Hidetaka stood up and threw his beer into the sand (a little pile of brown beer bottles had formed at this point). He ripped off his T-shirt, exposing a body entirely without musculature or fat.

Seeing his bare chest made me realise it was real, and a terrified shiver ran through me. I remember studying abroad in England for 3 years and going to London, seeing St Paul's Cathedral for the first time, standing beneath the magnificence of that art, its colossal, dwarfing architecture like something from the realm of the *shinigami*, striking down those unworthy to look upon it. *No wonder*, I'd thought, *westerners walk with a hunch when they have to live beneath such terrible structures*. I was filled with awe but also fear. I understood, I thought, their God, and heaven and hell, and righteousness, as I stared at the gold-plated Christ, writhing in agony amidst this helical, Gothic wonder. The shadows of that place were deep, but the light, incredible. I felt so nervous then, as if I might be crushed any minute by sheer awe. Buddhism has nothing like that. There is awe, yes, to stand beneath the Emerald Buddha, but Faceless Compassion does not carry with it the destructive omnipotence of their holy, tortured God.

Hidetaka whipped off his belt, dropped his pants, showing thick black tights.

I burst out laughing.

'It's cold!' he exclaimed. 'It's cold, alright? So I wore tights.'

Ayako pushed him and he tumbled from the bunker, falling into the sand with a squawk. She stood, pulled off her top like there was nothing in the world to be afraid of. I had to fight not to stare, so tackled my own T-shirt, but I could barely get it over my head, I was sweating so profusely, fingers weak.

I felt her hands on mine. She yanked and the T-shirt came loose. We stood face to face. I don't know what my eyes showed, but Ayako's expression was cool as ice. She winked again. I almost fell off the bunker myself.

'Hey, come on! I don't want to be the only one naked here!'

I looked down at the beach and saw Hidetaka, fully nude, cupping his hands over his groin.

'Where the hell's your pubic hair, Hidetaka?'

'I shaved it off! The ladies love it!' He threw up his hands, realised he had revealed all, then quickly covered his penis again. 'Whoops!'

Ayako threw her bra at Hidetaka, covering her breasts with the other arm. They looked a lot smaller out in the open. She must have been wearing a bra with padding in it. That didn't change a thing.

'Look away you perverts!'

I turned my back to her, blushing red as a cherry blossom. I kicked off my trousers and dropped my pants, cupping my groin at all times. I had a second wave of terror at the thought of getting an erection. It was bitterly cold but for some reason that was only making it worse. The wind on my balls was like that awful peppermint shower-gel.

'Okay you can look now!'

I looked over my shoulder and saw Ayako, one hand over her chest, the other between her legs. It reminded me of a painting I'd seen in a museum in London: Aphrodite, or as the Romans called her, Venus, emerging from the clam, shrouding her sex, the mystery of it so evocative, so primal. I think, sometimes, there is an honesty in western work that is mistaken by people like Hidetaka as primitiveness. By the same token, westerners do not understand the expressive nuance of eastern art and thereby think it is all the same, or else, repressed.

Ayako stepped from her pile of shed clothing, legs supple as the deer that roam Nara; she looked unearthly. Nothing like the painting. Her skin was tanned, not white. Her hair was black, not red. Her bust was small. But she looked – to use a western word – like heaven.

'Okay go!' Hidetaka roared.

We ran, the sand like cold rice beneath our feet. As we touched the water, all three of us let out a scream. A wave came in, slapping our knees out from under us. We toppled in, yapping like wild animals, foam washing over us. This was a different cold, a cleansing, cold that made me think of draughty temples, of silence, of something understood.

Yet, we were not silent, but screaming with delight. Hidetaka shook his hair like a shaggy dog and sprayed our faces with freezing water. I felt every droplet, as though I was perceiving the world in slow motion. Ayako splashed him back with both hands, no longer concerned with covering herself up. What was there to cover? We are all human.

I was rock-hard beneath the water. My erection fears had come true. I swam out, crawling through the waves, feeling the pull on my back muscles, tasting the salt, the richness of it, thinking of a thousand delicious meals in that moment. I plunged my head beneath the water, letting the cold engulf me, feeling held in that dark place, feeling my mother again in the *shushing* of the waves above, heard only dimly, as though through the veil of a dream.

When I emerged, the others were calling my name.

'There you are! We thought you'd drowned!' Hidetaka splashed towards me, put his hands on my shoulders. I prayed my erection did not touch him beneath the water.

I gripped his shoulders in return.

'Ikigai!' I bellowed it at the top of my lungs.

'Ikigai!' He and Ayako chorused me. I threw Hidetaka into the water. Ayako waded out to us, began splashing us with flecks of foam. I dived under, re-emerged, threw water at her. We played like children until light crept across the ocean, banding the glistening water with incomplete halos. The sea turned translucent, the sand beneath shimmering like undiscovered gold.

'Ikigai,' I said again, this time just to myself.

'Let's get back.' Ayako beckoned to us. We ran as fast as we could for the shore (thankfully my erection had finally died down), towelled ourselves off, then dressed again, sheepish as children. I became aware of Ayako, as though seeing her for the first time; her beauty, as the sun stripped away all shadow from her, was as complete and holy as *tanku*. I imagined, somewhere far off, a bell tolling, once for each of the 108 illusions, my addictions and vanities being stripped from me, until there was only the contemplation of that which was perfect and beatific.

We sat, shivering a little, opening the last beers. We cheered in the European fashion and drank. The Asahi had been left out of the cooler and so was lukewarm but we were glad of it.

'Pin,' Hidetaka said, slowly.

Me and Ayako shared a look. Ayako was sitting to Hidetaka's left, between us.

'Pon,' she said.

'Pan.' I pointed at Ayako.

'Pin.'

'Pon,' I chimed.

'Pan.' Hidetaka pointed at me.

'Pin!'

Ayako cried out 'Pon', being the first to miss the pattern. Together, me and Hidetaka chanted *iki iki iki* even though we weren't drinking Ikis. She downed her drink.

'Wuhoo!' Hidetaka roared, rocking back on his butt, balancing with his two legs in the air, like a freeze-frame of someone falling off a roof. 'Who needs video-games, eh Ryu?'

'Yep. I never could have made a better game than Pin Pon Pan.'

'*Kuso!* Now I don't have a drink left!' Ayako pulled a pouty face.

'Have mine.' I handed her the Asahi, stood up, and dusted my hands of sand. 'Hidetaka, can I talk to you for a second?' I winked at Ayako. 'Boy talk.'

'Ooohh.' But she didn't ask. Again, I thought about whether she already knew.

Hidetaka got to his feet, outrageously lurching. He looked like a parody of drunkenness: Jackie Chan in the *Drunken Master* movie. He put an arm around me, his head lolling onto my shoulder almost like a tender nuzzle. I could feel his breath on my skin, the warmth of it. It was almost more than I could bear.

'I have something to tell you,' I said, when we were a good distance from Ayako. The beach was deserted. There was a time when it would have been flooded at this hour in the morning, filled with tourists and couples and dogwalkers. Fishermen too in *wasen*. But now we were the only ones. I guessed because none of us had much in the way of family left.

'Me too,' Hidetaka said.

My heart shrank in my chest.

'You too?'

'What?'

I closed my eyes.

'No, me first!' Hidetaka said, words rushing out one after another, making me think of a cat chasing its own tail. He took a steadying breath, wiped the mop of hair out of his face. His eyes were dark, still and deep. 'I love you.'

I felt as though I'd been hit with a freight train.

'Excuse me?'

'I love you.' He grinned, his eyebrows, the ones that were so expressive, flexing upward into two semi-circular arcs. 'Weird huh? So many better-looking guys. But, it's true.'

'I didn't even know you were gay.'

As it sunk in, my heart expanded again, the tremors died down, I was filled with elation like the delayed onset of the drug. I'd thought he was going to say he loved Ayako, which would have been a terrible, crushing thing. This was weird: it's not every day your best friend reveals, after twenty years, he's secretly gay and has a crush on you. But it was so much better than the alternative.

'Well, it's not exactly easy to come out, is it? Not in our society.'

'No.'

I didn't know what to do, so I grabbed him and pulled him into a hug. I even gave him a manly pat on the back. I'm pretty sure it's not what he wanted, but it's all I had to give. I couldn't love him in that way, couldn't see him like that.

'I'm sorry.'

'It's okay. I know you're not gay. You're in love with Ayako, aren't you?'

'Yeah.'

Hidetaka laughed and we broke apart. He wiped a tear from his eye. Briefly, it caught the light, flashing like a beacon, as though somewhere out to sea someone was trying to signal to us.

'We're all fucked then, aren't we?'

I laughed.

'No. Not really.'

'You going to tell her?'

'I guess it's the time for truth, isn't it?'

'What's the time?'

I checked my watch.

'Seven.'

'Now or never.' Hidetaka put an arm on my shoulder and shook me. He smiled, cheeks puffing like a blowfish, a rosy tint to them. I may not have loved Hidetaka like a boyfriend, but I loved that yellow-toothed smile of his.

We walked back to where Ayako sat on one of the towels. She had finished the last Asahi.

'Ayako.' My throat felt like it had a noose around it.

'I'll give you some space.' Hidetaka took off down the beach, picking up stones and shells, lobbing them out to sea like a child that'd only just discovered their ability to throw things. 'I'm going to hit those graves!'

'Ayako,' I repeated, tongue stuck to the roof of my mouth. She leaned forward, a question in her face.

'Ryu?'

'I...'

Somewhere out in the deep there was a noise like tectonic plates colliding. The smell of the air changed. The waters stopped lapping, became frighteningly static. It was as though the tides had been powered by a great machine and that machine had been turned off. Dark spots appeared on the sun.

We all turned to face the sunrise, the water. Ayako took my hand and held it warmly in her own. Hidetaka took hers, and we stood, the three of us holding hands, like the last protesters at a Flower Power rally in 70s America, another world.

'This is it, isn't it?' Hidetaka said, his voice flat, as though spoken in closet, the invisible world shrinking around us.

'Yes,' I whispered.

They emerged from the sea in rank upon rank, a black and inevitable wave. The percussion of the first shots shattered our eardrums. The sand rushed backwards with the shockwave of detonations, away from the ocean, as though through the body of an hourglass.

They came at exactly the appointed hour and we met them there on the shore.

When the tide comes in, you just have to pack your bags.

And leave.

3rd PRIZE
WHEN THE TIDE COMES IN
by Joseph Sale

Joseph Sale is a novelist, writing coach, editor, graphic designer, artist, critic and gamer. Born in Bournemouth by the sea, he studied English with Creative Writing at the University of Birmingham. His first novel, *The Darkest Touch*, was published by Dark Hall Press in 2014. Since, he has authored Seven Dark Stars, Across the Bitter Sea, Orifice, The Meaning of the Dark, Nekyia and more.

He is the creator of *†3 Dark*, a unique publishing project born in 2017 showcasing the work of 13 writers including Richard Thomas and Moira Katson; each story is accompanied by original concept art from Shawn Langley and with cover art by Grand Failure. The first issue, *Dead Voices*, was funded via IndieGoGo in June 2017, and soon became InDemand. He writes features and reviews for GameSpew, where he talks about his love of video-games as art.

His short fiction has appeared in Silver Blade, Fiction Vortex, Nonbinary Review, Edgar Allan Poet and Storgy Magazine. In 2014 he was nominated for the Sundress Award for Literary Excellence. In 2017, he was nominated for the Guardian's "Not The Booker Prize".

In his spare time he plays badminton, watches Two Best Friends Play and puts on his DM hat, concocting fiendish dungeons for his friends to battle through.

AFTERWORD

I spent a long time thinking about a story for Exit Earth. Hours went into meticulously plotting a story with multiple perspectives and complex socio-political points. When I finished the story, I handed it into my partner, Michelle, the constant support and love of my life. She read it, with the beautiful attentiveness she always gives, and when I asked her for feedback she said something that utterly shocked me: 'This story isn't you, *at all*. The characters are just so cold. I can't relate to any of them.' As with most things, she was right. Completely bang on. I'd written a story using my head and nothing else, and as a result, it was academic, distant and, ultimately, powerless. I'd ended up tied up in political and environmental points – which I'm not saying aren't valid – but which didn't really come from the heart.

So I went back to the drawing board, and thought: *What does Exit Earth really mean to me?* beyond the frightening political and environmental situations we find ourselves in. And then, half-dreaming, it clicked. *Exit* Earth. It was a stage direction, a Shakespearean farewell. It was the moment your favourite character, the electric Mercutio or the rebellious Johnny Byron, says goodbye, shuts the door, walks off-stage, seemingly forever. At that moment, the story welled in me, like a tide rising up. It came out in one evening in one fluid hit. This time, it was *all* about heart, about what it would feel like for everything to just be swept away, like a sandcastle under a wave. I've always been connected to water, having grown up on the coast. The tides, the ebb and flow of things, has always been a core way my family has thought about life. We have lows when everything seems to be rushing in at us, and highs when we can swim so far out it seems we're able to touch the buoys, which was a common trial-of-manhood when I was a kid. It was only natural, then, to me, that the end would be nothing grand, nothing unusual, just a rushing in of the tide. This time, for good.

I found these three characters Ryu, Ayako and Hidetaka in my own personal experience: the wonderful friends I've had the good fortune to know, and the great times we've had. I imagined what it would be like to share this moment, this *exit*, with them, what truths might come out, what games we might play. I was also heavily inspired by the works of Haruki Murakami and Ryu Murakami. The beauty of Japanese prose, and the poignancy it can elicit, is a force to be reckoned with in the modern publishing world. I also drew inspiration from Hideo Kojima, the legendary game-developer who worked on the *Metal Gear Solid* video-game series, mentioned early in the story. The *Metal Gear Solid* series was a key part of my childhood and identity – the vibrancy of its characters was something I hoped to capture in Ryu, Hidetaka and Ayako.

Ultimately, *When The Tide Comes In* is a story about friendship, heart, joy. It's about how we find beautiful meaning in even the most seemingly stupid and little things.

And it's about goodbyes.

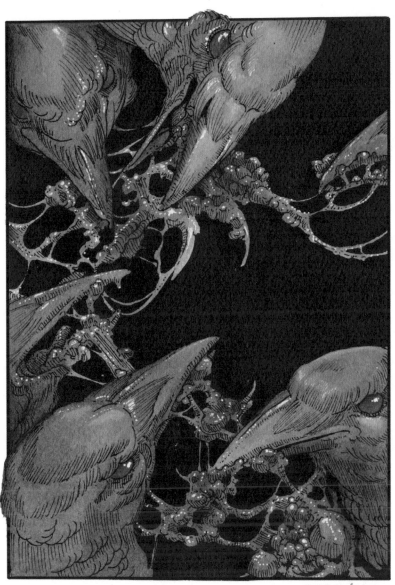

Illustration by Crap Panther

CROW RIDES A PALE HORSE
by Erik Bergstrom

When the murder returned last winter, they found only cockroaches and us. Those thousands of crows hovered like a cloud of gnats in the always-night, sometimes circling around each other, sometimes suspended in place, and always looking down at what we did to the earth.

This used to be a homecoming. An annual get-together in the sprawl to scavenge for winter scraps and protect each other from bigger, hungrier birds. This year they came with a delayed duty to give us the warning our ancestors wrote about.

It's true that they're omens of approaching death. But they came to eat the dead, too. Pecking at eyeballs, tearing at bloated skin, turning scattered corpses into dots of scarlet red over a landscape covered in gray ash.

Ash: that's my brother's name. Short for Asher. He was born before everything happened, but not by much. He's eight now, and he loves to kiss everything.

That's what he was doing in the empty store where we found the food and water for Momma: sitting in the corner, kissing the bag of rice and box of Stove Top stuffing and whispering "thank you". I was walking up and down the aisles, looking for anything left behind, and I could hear him from that back corner of the store, whispering.

It's because the world got quieter after everything happened. We could hear things without wanting to listen. I heard Ash whispering, heard the sound of his lips smacking the cardboard covering Momma's food. I heard the crows making noise from the broken window, looking for us.

"Ash? Will you get up off your butt and help me?" The kid annoyed me sometimes, but how I said it came completely from fear. I was feeling surrounded and closed-in-on.

The cases of water were all gone like I expected, though I was small enough then that I could squish and shimmy my way in between the empty shelves and an old ATM. I found a couple of stray bottles behind the machine, back where nobody else could look. I twisted and contorted myself a few different ways before I could reach, wriggling my fingers and tickling the plastic until the bottles rolled into my hand.

Stuck like that is where I heard Ash saying my name. Whining it. His voice sounded far away, farther than what made sense.

"Faye? Faye?" Over and over so I knew he was in trouble. He's sounded like that before, like the one time I locked him in the closet when those strange men came around. "Faye?"

"Coming!" I intoned confidence, mainly to let him know I'd heard him. But I was afraid, too. I just didn't have the luxury to show it.

I found him still hugging Momma's food, trying hard not to look at the crow strutting towards him. Behind it was another one, and another one after that.

"Get up." I held out my hand. "Come on Ash, let's go!"

He shifted. The bird puffed out its chest and opened its wings wide, cawing something shrill that got Ash crying. There was a stack of cellophane-wrapped paper plates next to me, and so I grabbed the pack and flung it at the bird, missing by a mile but close enough to scare it back. I yelled at Ash to get up one more time and he listened.

We ran to the doorway of the shop and looked out. The crows were everywhere. They filled in the dead branches of trees and made them look alive again. They lined up on the edges of old buildings like hungry gargoyles, swaying side to side.

"Where did they all come from?" Ash asked.

I didn't have an answer. All I could think about was how far away Momma was: all the way on the other side of the city, sick and thirsty and alone. We had to get back to her at all costs, no questions asked. And I'd have to do everything I could to make sure Ash never became one of those dots of red in the sprawling gray.

It used to be that every year when winter came, the cold would just seep in. By the end of the season, most of us were steeled to it enough that we could spend more and more time outside without freezing.

That's how it was the day Ash and I stood outside the door of that convenience store. Steeled to it. It didn't matter that we were wearing tattered jackets and beanies, or boots a size too big or small. We were ready for it, ready for each year that fell a couple of degrees more on the thermometer.

Some things remain. The buildings we left behind are still around, stretching up to a charcoal sky that never goes away. There's cars and trucks, too; some that are still drivable. I know there's people nearby when the air is cold and I can smell the exhaust from cars with families huddled inside, cranking the heat to stay warm, even if getting gas is a little more difficult these days than just pulling a lever on some pump. That's something I still hadn't figured out then. All I could do was drive a car until it couldn't go any further. Then I'd leave it sitting in the street, parked however it wanted to be parked, and keep going.

Another thing that was left behind, that got a lot more popular after people crawled back out, was the shopping cart. That's what I was looking for after we left the doorway with our rice and stuffing and potato flakes. Ours was parked right where I'd left it, hidden behind the store. We loaded it up. As much as I wanted to crack the top of that bottle and splash my face with clean water, I left it closed, for Momma.

"Where we going next?" Ash asked.

"That's enough for right now," I said. "We better get back." He loved these little adventures, but I felt like I was aging another eight years each time we left Momma behind. It was even worse that day, after all those birds came back.

"Will we find a car?"

"Maybe. Most likely not." I'd stopped lying to him about two years ago. I used to think it was the right thing to do, to shield him from mostly everything. I used to think this life was all he'd ever known, so it was okay to lie about why things had to be a certain way. But then, he'd flash a surprising memory from before it all happened. That's when I figured lying was a rotten thing to do.

The cart rattled over the pockmarked road. Steam came up from the sewers, and the smell that seeped out was like a hot day in July—except this was December. Once in awhile I'd catch Ash peering through the small hole in the manhole cover, though I don't know what he expected to see. Maybe a mutant ninja turtle? We could've used one that day.

Most times the crows would scatter when we steered into them, though I always felt them behind me. And I never, at any time, felt like I wasn't being watched. Crows are patient animals, even when it comes to something impatient like revenge.

We walked like that for a while, to the point where I had to start thinking about where we might stop if we needed a place to sleep. There'd been a few abandoned cars along the way, but without the ability to start one, not just for the heat but also for a quick getaway, it was like sleeping in a mink trap. Somebody might find us, sneak up on us, and steal all our food. Or worse.

Ash was running along the curbs of the street, smashing the glassy parts of ice under his boots, when suddenly he looked up into an alleyway and shouted: "Woah!"

He ran towards a shadow between the two buildings. A scattering of crows flew out, noisily cawing. I stood with the cart in my clutches and yelled his name, having a hard time letting go of it. I yelled his name two or three times more before I had no choice but to follow him in.

I pushed the cart up onto the sidewalk and tried to get a clear look into the alley. Ash stood next to a plastic garbage bag that was hunched over at the side of a dumpster. I saw an assortment of colors, pinks and greens and browns and whites, and I knew what was inside. Something I'd even told Ash about before.

"Are those donuts?" I asked. He was in such a trance that I doubt he heard me. And I doubt he noticed the birds at his back, curious, stepping around him as he examined the bag.

"Donuts! Donuts, donuts!" He looked at me and said, "Can we have them?"

Of course I wanted to say 'yes'. But I couldn't deny how it looked. Fresh donuts tossed out next to the trash? Who could have put them there? And why?

Instead of answering, I stepped closer. The plastic was ripped, likely by the crows, and some of the food was chewed. I reached into the bag and grabbed a donut. I smelled it, tasted it. The bread crumbled apart in my hand. I couldn't tell how long they'd been out there, but otherwise couldn't find anything wrong with them. Yes, they were stale, and they weren't nutritious, but...they were donuts.

Ash started kissing the bag, whispering 'thank you' again and again.

"Stop that."

"Can I have one? Please?"

I breathed in deep before saying 'yes', just to show part of my concern. He knelt down, dug in, grabbed one covered in chocolate icing and bit into it. Donut pieces crumbled through his little eight-year-old fingers. One brave crow stepped in and pecked near his feet. Ash giggled, mouth full of food.

"Look at that." I cracked a smile.

"I want another one," he said. I nodded 'okay'. After the day we were having, he earned it.

Soon he was surrounded in a little halo of donut crumbs. There were at least four crows near him, all feasting. One of them, the one that'd been at his feet earlier, got a little too close and pecked at the donut in his hand. He shrieked and dropped his food.

"Okay, Ash. I think that's enough. We'd better let them alone."

"No!" he shouted. His little fingers trembled near the crow's head.

"Leave it. Just grab the bag and we'll have the rest later."

I'm sure he would have sat, pouting forever, if he hadn't looked up. If he hadn't looked past me to see a horde of crows darkening the alley's entrance. His eyes bulged. I turned and looked back. The birds cut into any clear opening we might've had. They were five rows deep, at least. When I looked the other way, same thing. A battalion of crows, having gathered unseen, were marching, slightly out of step, in our direction from the darker part of the shadow.

"Get up," I said. Instead of standing, Ash curled into himself. "Come on, get up," I tried again, frantic. But Ash is a smart kid, and he knows when he hears terror in his big sister's voice.

The crows at the front stuck out their chests, flapped their wings, and made a clicking noise with their beaks. Soon enough it dawned on me that they weren't talking to us.

I wrapped Ash's coat in my fingers and pulled. He was a rock, and I wasn't as strong then as I am now. He budged a little, but he wasn't moving.

The crows were close enough for me to hear their miniature claws on the pavement. Close enough where I could see our reflection in their glassy eyes. Where I could see us five minutes into the future, on our backs, covered in red.

I was curled up about as tight as Ash, whispering something to calm him, when a commotion occurred. One crow, not much bigger than the others, ran in a straight line across that first row. Her wings were spread wide and she was making a noise I'd never heard before. The others shouted back at her, fumbling around while she bombarded them.

She darted at the group blocking our exit. Several of them flew off. The others parted in front of us. Ash looked up to see what was happening, and so I pulled on him again. This time he understood. Sometimes, especially while out on a run, we communicated best this way.

We ran. I never let go of him, even when he wanted to stop and look back. Our momentum carried me into the cart and I almost tipped it sideways when we jumped off the sidewalk and back into the street. I could still hear them— heard them for maybe another mile, the cart rattling under my fingers, us out of breath and trying to suck in the cold air, and our bellies rumbling from having eaten hardly as many donuts as we'd wanted.

"Faye...Faye..."

"What?" I asked, my head on another planet.

"How much farther?"

I looked down the road as far as I could see. It never ended. I could tell it was later. The clouds were a dimmer shade of gray, with the sun giving up on another attempt to break through.

"I don't know. Try not to think about it." He looked like a lumbering, sad penguin the way he moped in his heavy winter coat. "You want to push the cart for a bit?" I offered, like some kind of reward. He agreed without answering.

We walked that way for a while. Ash complained about being tired. Being hungry. I had to remind him about Momma, about how she'd been tired and hungry all those days she let us eat the last bite of food.

In the end, I gave in. I'm still his big sister. I let him have a Pop Tart with chocolate frosting.

When it got to be real dark, too dark to see the block in front of us, I started looking for open cars or buildings. After everything happened and we got back out again, every other car we ran across still had keys in the ignition and gas in the tank. It stayed that way for a while, simple like that, so that we didn't even need to rely on dumb luck to find one.

It'd been almost two months since I'd found a car with keys. And I still didn't know how to hotwire one. Sleeping in a car without keys is a trap, indeed, but at that point it felt like there were worse things to leave to chance. I told Ash to start looking for some open doors, too.

I was waiting for a scattering of crows to move out from the front door of some laundromat when I heard his echo shouting for me. Panic and dread, or a dizzying cocktail of both, set in. First I heard it one way. The next time it was somewhere else, bouncing around from all directions. Fooling me. I finally found him standing next to some old Dodge station wagon, the driver door swung open wide. The part of his face that wasn't covered by hat or scarf looked happy and proud. I cracked a smile, a great big one filled with relief.

The car was in the perfect spot: wedged in behind an old brick pizza shop and a tall wooden fence. I might've never seen it if I wasn't following an echo, especially in that kind of dark. "Nice," I said.

"Look, there's blankets in it and everything!" said Ash. Something dropped in my gut. He could see it. "What?"

"This is someone else's," I said. "We can't have this one."

"How do you know?"

If he'd only been older, I wouldn't have had to explain. I tried, anyway.

"I don't want to keep looking!" Ash whined. I hated having that power; the one where I can turn an eight-year-old's carefree jubilation into the worst despair in the world. He slammed the door and walked to the other side of the car, away from me, his back turned.

I looked up, way up at the ozone layer where the effects of what we did still glowed above the clouds. Crows were crossing overhead, dimming the brighter spots for a fraction of a second. A group of them gathered on the awning over the back door of the restaurant. Their heads jerked around almost like they were pretending to ignore us, even though I was smart enough to know we were all they wanted.

"Get the food in the car," I said. Ash didn't move. "Come on. Hurry up." He turned around, maybe wanting to see my face to know that I meant it. "I'm serious!"

I popped the trunk and we started throwing our rations inside. The compartment was empty when I looked at it, which I thought was a good enough sign. Maybe Ash was right not to worry about it. Maybe I was still too young myself to need to care about such things.

"Okay, get in," I ordered. Right then a crow landed just behind my heels and cawed something. I know it wasn't right to kick at him, but that's what I did. Then I leapt into the car, the same way I used to jump into bed after shutting off the light.

It was the 'thump' that jolted me awake. I must have been dead tired. Leaning back in the passenger seat like I was, it took me a few seconds to realize the car was even moving. I was suspended in that place where a dream still has a hold, which is why, when I turned and saw the bearded man next to me, I sat up and screamed.

Ash was up in the backseat right after, screaming too. We must have scared him, because he shouted back and lost control of the car for a second.

"Who are you?" I shouted.

"Who am I? This is my goddamn car you're in!"

Ash yelled for me, saying my name over and over. The man told me to shut him up. "Ash, shhh, it's okay." That time I had to lie.

"Thanks for stocking me up," he said, smiling on one side of his face. "Couldn't find food for shit yesterday." He swerved into a gathering of crows, scattering them.

"That's our food!" shouted Ash.

"Thought I told you to quiet down!"

"Where are you taking us?" I asked.

He peeled the car around a corner. That's when I knew we were in the heart of the city, on Third Avenue, the road leading back northeast to Momma. The river bridge was up ahead. It was the only one still standing.

Once he levelled the car out, I asked him again. He looked at me and all I could see was a full and sickening smile spreading across his hairy face. "That's for me to know," he said, jumping the car over one of those red blots in the road, "and for you to find out."

"Are you taking us home?" said Ash.

He smiled at me again. "You could call it that."

Just as we were coming up to the bridge, I spotted a woman on the sidewalk, trying with some difficulty to get her shopping cart over a curb. It wasn't full with food, but it was enough worth protecting.

I couldn't see much of her, covered up as she was, but she moved like an older person would and was caught in a small assault of crows trying to get at her rations. She batted them away with her right hand and tried to lift the cart with her left.

The car slowed. I clutched the door handle tighter. The man stopped and shifted into park. Then he said, "Just a minute. Looks like she needs a little help."

The old woman kept fighting with the birds, probably didn't even notice we were there until he was right up next to her. She was startled, naturally, backing away and pulling her coat tighter around herself. The man kept his hands up and approached slowly. I couldn't hear what he was saying, but I felt the low vibrations of his voice from inside the car.

Behind me, Ash whispered, "Look...", pointing ahead. I peered through the windshield. "No." He tapped my shoulder, then pointed again. I saw it that time. He was pointing at the keys, still in the ignition. The car was still running.

"So what?" I said. A little whimper came out of him. I breathed a heavy sigh. This is what big sisters were for, I guess.

I lifted my left leg and moved slowly over the console between the seats. That's when I saw the grungy man reach out and grab the woman at her shoulders. He had her turned towards us, her head pulled back. I saw the glint of a blade in his fist, right at her throat.

I don't remember seeing the blade slash. I think it's because all I can remember, all that takes up space in my mind now, is the quick and heavy stream of red down her neck.

"What's that?" Ash said.

"It's okay." I turned around to face him and block his view. I don't know why I said it was okay. It wasn't. It's just a trick Momma played on me, once.

I let a few seconds pass before I slid the rest of the way into the driver's seat. I had to make my move. Now or never. I pulled the shifter down like I had hundreds of times before and floored the gas pedal.

I still missed him by a mile.

I think it was the curb that slowed me up and shifted the car so far to the left. We were stuck on it. When I saw his blur in the passenger's side window, I got a sick feeling in my gut of knowing it was all over for us.

It's probably why I didn't put up much of a fight when he tied me up. I knew if I did that I'd be the next one with a birdbath of blood around me. I had to stay alive for Ash, and so I knew that meant letting him put his hands on me, put the rope around my feet and wrists, probably tie a little tighter than he had to, giving me a hurting that wouldn't go away right after.

He kept me in the passenger's seat. I suppose it'd been a long time since he had anyone to talk to. He had to tie Ash up too, but he didn't keep my little brother's mouth free like he did with me.

When he was done with the dead woman's food and with tying us up, the bearded man slumped back into the driver's seat, put it back into gear, and said, between heavy breaths, "Where were we?"

He backed the car off the curb, out onto the street, and hit the bridge, weaving around the piles of bodies left there, some of them fresh enough to be breakfast for the crows. I looked down the river, near the crumbled Stone Arch Bridge, and I saw a collection of floating bodies bottlenecked there, with black dots of birds hovering above, stalking and swooping in every so often for a taste of soft, bloated flesh.

I sometimes wondered how we weren't down there with them. What made us so special? We weren't healthier or smarter than these people. We all made it through what happened so many years ago.

In the back of my head, though, I knew. It was in the back of my head because I didn't have to ever think it. And it stayed alive because it was the thought that put me out there, on those always-night days, scavenging and trying to turn my little brother into a man. It was Momma.

Right when we got to the end of the bridge there was a loud SMACK against the windshield. Crooked lines cobwebbed out from the point of impact. The car swerved and went up onto the sidewalk, with the greasy bearded man shouting curses all the while. Quick as it was, everything felt like slow motion as we crashed into that lamp post.

There was a jolt, with lights brighter than I'd ever seen, and the loud crinkling of metal. When I came to, I don't know how long after, I looked at the man and noticed the way he was slumped over the wheel, bleeding from his mouth. One of his teeth hung out on his fat lip. Ash was in the backseat, crying.

I rubbed my temples. I remember there being a loud wheeEEeeeEE noise, but I couldn't tell if it was from me or the car. Steam poured from the hood, which looked very much like a warning sign. I told Ash it was time to leave. Problem was, we were both still tied up. That's what I thought, anyway.

When I felt Ash's cold and wonderful hand on my face, it didn't register at first. Once I figured it out, I turned to face him, and I don't know why but I cried. He looked worried and still fresh from crying himself, but he told me, "It's okay," and I was grateful that he was young enough then that it wasn't a lie.

He got out of the car, came around to my side, and he untied me as fast as he could with his eight-year-old fingers. Once I was free I told him to run far away from the car. I needed to stay behind to pop the trunk and get whatever we could out of there.

Leaning over and reaching in front of the bearded man to find the lever felt like the longest ten seconds of my life. My heart was racing. My fingers trembled. I kept my eyes on his face, on his fat lip and dangling tooth. After stumbling for a bit and thinking I could see his eyes moving beneath their lids, I finally found the lever and pulled. I heard the trunk pop open.

I leaned back to breathe and looked out the windshield. I don't know how I saw it, maybe it's because I was simply meant to, but right where the cracked glass met the hood, cradled next to the windshield wipers, was a walnut.

Once I was free, I called Ash back and instructed him to pull the food and water out from the trunk. I walked around the front of the car, past the lamp post it was wrapped around, and I grabbed the walnut. I looked to the top of the next post over, the one where the bridge ends, and I saw a big, black bird up there. I swear to this day that I recognized it from some time in the past.

We didn't have our shopping cart anymore, but Ash found a skateboard near one of the benches in the park. We also found some rope that I tied around the axle so I could pull it. On the skateboard we had our bag of rice, four water bottles, two boxes of pasta, and a can each of beef stew and ravioli. We had to leave the Pop Tarts and the lady's peanuts behind. All in all, not a bad day's work.

The path home was a lot clearer than when we were in the city. After an hour or two of walking, I noticed a single crow over our heads, hopping from lamp post to tree to awning. It was the same bird from the bridge.

When I had a moment, and when Ash wasn't humming to distract himself, I pulled the walnut out of my pocket and showed it to him. I wasn't sure if he'd ever seen a walnut in his life.

"What's that?" he asked.

"It's a present," I said. "From her." I pointed to the crow, just ahead of us, perched on the edge of a two-story apartment.

I thought he'd be his normally curious and puzzled self and ask how I found it. But he just took it from me, eyed it for a couple of seconds, whispered "thank you" and kissed it, and then put it away in his coat. He looked up at the crow and did the same thing, blowing his kiss in her direction.

Later, when we were at home with Momma and I was boiling some rice on the stove, I thought of Ash's question about where all the crows came from. I thought of telling him that they were always here, and that we only just noticed them now when we needed them most. I was thinking of the best way to put it when I heard Ash and Momma murmuring in the other room.

I turned and peeked through the doorway. They were sitting on her mattress on the floor, Ash on Momma's lap, greyish-white light coming in through the window. He was showing her the walnut.

I'll never forget how Momma smiled when she told him a story from before it all happened, when Ash still had to crawl through the backyard where she threw peanuts and hardboiled eggs to a family of crows. She always wore tinsel in her hat so they'd know it was her, and she always performed the same sign language—a "thank you" and a kiss—so that they'd always come back again.

SHORTLIST
CROW RIDES A PALE HORSE
by Erik Bergstrom

Erik Bergstrom lives and writes in Minneapolis, MN.
By day he works as a copy editor for an automotive marketing company.
Nights and weekends, he writes gloomy stories. You can follow him on
Twitter @erikbbergstrom and read his weekly fictions at
https://erikbergstromwrites.tumblr.com/

AFTERWORD

Minneapolis has its fair share of tourist traps, though if you really want a sight to write home about, you'll come up sometime in late November/early December for the mega-murder. A gathering of crows, thousands deep, all meet in the same section of town each year. Looking for what? Who knows. Who wants to?

I started writing "Crow Rides a Pale Horse" after riding the city bus past the crows last winter. The more I learned about the bird's amazing memory and ability to identify specific humans, the more I needed to write a story about them. As I struggled with the title, I came across Sherman Alexie's poem, "Crow Testament", and I couldn't get the last verse out of my head for days. I can only hope I did him, and the beautiful birds that inspired both of us, justice.

A lot has led to me getting here with my first published story. I often trace it back to reading "Catcher in the Rye" the summer before my own "coming-of-age" at college. I should also give credit to my parents, who entrusted me with their undeveloped artistic genes. My dad often wrote poetry to my mom while he crossed the country in his 18-wheeler. She had her own story she carried in her head, whiling the days away as a nurse. She shared it with me one night, a smile on her face and her voice trembling like she was telling a secret, and I knew it was a very prideful moment for her. She passed away with that story in her head, and that's when I knew it was "now or never" for me.

I choose to be a minimalist in life, and so the same goes for my writing. My favorite part with each draft is picking a word count, writing double the amount, and then cutting that extra fat anywhere I can. It's just one of the techniques I've taken from writers I admire. Dialogue, my favorite to write, comes from writers with expert ears; people like Salinger, Hemingway, and Faulkner, but also Joyce Carol Oates, David James Keaton, and Stephen Graham Jones. Constructing a world without suffocating the reader with details is also important, something I've taken from writers like Gemma Files, Laird Barron, and Brian Evenson. And the most important thing, the power of a well fleshed-out character, comes from my admiration of Stephen King, Chuck Palahniuk, Emma Cline, and Carmen Maria Machado.

And of course, there's my dad, who now sends his poetry to me.

Illustration by Amie Dearlove

SONGS THAT ONLY SQUIRRELS CAN HEAR
by Francisco González

I always thought of Grandfather as a sweet old man. *My* old man. The villagers saw things differently, of course. Most of them thought he was vaguely menacing, perhaps certifiably insane. Which he was. Certifiably insane, that is. And totally menacing, not vaguely menacing—not at all vaguely. Grandfather had a special place in his heart for me, though. I was his adopted child. He took care of me, did right by me.

He had a special place in his heart for the squirrels, too. Maybe the dark, festering, slimy part, where a spirochete of outrage takes root and squirms and whines. The grove was thick with squirrels, and the old man hated them. He refused to accept that "those filthy animals" should crawl all over *his* pecan trees, stealing "precious nuts," gnawing, scurrying, defecating, and "without the slightest bit of respect!" I'd giggle. Squirrels . . . defecating . . . respectfully— it was *funny*.

But in all seriousness, it gave him immense satisfaction to shoot them. If I'm being honest, he got an even crueler satisfaction out of skinning them. Also—if I'm being even more honest—he thoroughly enjoyed eating them.

So did I, for a time.

*

In the beginning, he hunted the squirrels with his shotgun, which would shred them with a bang.

"Dramatic," he called it, "and magnificent."

That was decades before I met him, when the trees were young. By the time I came along, he was more fastidious, more refined. Trial and error had made a virtuoso out of him.

Grandfather loved me more than anything, but he loved those pecan trees more than anything else. "The shotgun was too much," he explained. "The blast cone's too wide, see? Too much collateral damage to my grove. When you're going after the *bad*, you don't want to hurt the *good* in the process." So the old man put away his shotgun. He strapped it under the dining room table, still loaded, "just in case." And there it stayed. Mostly.

The rifle completed him. "My plus-one," he'd call it, with a fond chuckle. Or, "the little lady." His .22 was a precision instrument, an extension of his will. Most of the squirrels were smart enough to understand the danger. They knew

55

what was coming when Grandfather leveled the barrel at them. They'd hop around like mad. They'd vault from branch to branch, trying to elude him. They'd cry out in desperation.

Grandfather didn't reserve any pity for them. No quarter was granted, no quarry was spared. Some of them were fast, but none were nearly fast enough. And some of them seemed to be a different breed altogether: boars, tougher than most, bigger than most, fiercer and more wicked than the average rodent. But that didn't make their demise any less inevitable. Or any less painful.

It was bound to happen every few days or so: one or another of those hard-boiled types would take the bullet *and* survive the fall—and the fall was eighty, ninety, a hundred feet or more. They'd writhe on the ground, shattered. They'd advance a few inches toward an imagined deliverance. A non-existent salvation.

Such is the spirit of a squirrel: it is a creature of pure courage. A squirrel never gives up. It will fight to the very end. But valor never saved them once they were on the ground, sputtering blood, mutilated, draped in the long shadows of the pecan trees.

The old man would stroll over to them with his butterfly knife. He'd close in on them, and he'd hum a tune to no one in particular. A simple, wordless lullaby, tender enough that his voice was obscured, now and again, by the sighs of dense leaves in the wind. And Grandfather's strides were easy. His footfalls were relaxed and unconcerned, as gentle as his song.

Every squirrel has a tiny soft spot on its skull, and Grandfather knew exactly where to find it. He'd stop them in mid-squeal. He kept his knife keen. They'd only shudder for an instant.

*

On my eighth birthday, Grandfather brought my present into the kitchen: a small, wooden footstool. When I stood on it, I could reach the counter and the stove.

"Look at you! You're nearly a grown man!" he declared. "And I'm a used-up, dried-up *old* man," he laughed, with a touch of lamentation. "I'll tell you what: you're going to clean them from now on. It's easy! I'll show you how."

I was clumsy at first, even though I'd seen him do it countless times. The squirrel was on the cutting board. I removed a Winchester knife from the rack, but Grandfather grabbed my wrist before I could begin.

"Forgetting something?" he teased. "Unless you want hair all over your lunch, you'd better get that squirrel good and wet." He motioned to the earthen bowl next to the sink. "Give him a nice bath for a minute. Keeps fur out of the equation."

He nodded approvingly.

"Good, now make that opening slice at the base of the tail, like you were about to do. Try not to dig into the meat. Work your way into the skin. Careful, now! Whatever you do, *don't cut that tail off*. You'll need it to pull the hide. Good . . . very good! Now hold it upside down. Make a couple of slits on the hind legs—yes, just so. Next, you want to really sink your fingers into those slits. Work the skin loose . . . work it from the meat. Ha! Tricky, right? Don't be ashamed. It was tough for me, too, when I was your age. It gets easier, believe me . . . there, you got it! So now I'm going to hold this flap you've made—you can do it yourself next time—while you pull the hind legs. Pull hard . . . good boy! Keep it going. Now we work it from the arms—I'll hold it again, you pull. Go, go, go! Nicely done! Ok. Here, let me take care of this part. Hand me that cleaver. We have to remove the head—like so . . . and . . . the feet—like that. All set. Now I'll put him on his back, so you can empty him out . . . give him a good vertical slice there and . . . you've got nice, small hands—reach in there. Go ahead. Don't be shy. Yeah, pull everything out of there and toss it. Wait, wait, wait—not those. Take a good look: that's the heart, and that's the liver, remember? Your favorites! They're tasty and we can fry 'em up. Wow . . . nice and clean. See, what was that? Three minutes, tops? We made good time!"

*

He could make sixty-seven dishes. "No two are the same." That was his boast. Grandfather would slather them with truffle oil, or a few dollops of shallot brown butter. Or he'd whip up some roasted red pepper lime cream, which could almost carry the meal on its own. On a cold night, he might dust off his "Madagascar" recipe: firecracker chili, butter, and a touch of shaved dill. He'd stuff the whole thing with Fontina, a cheese with melting properties so exquisite that it borders on witchcraft.

Then there was "ardillas a la diabla," if he was feeling ballsy and bold. He'd concoct a devil of a marinade: mounds of garlic, chiltepín, lemon zest, and lemon juice. He'd ornament the meat with fried capers and chorizo. Heirloom salad on the side. Often, we'd have grilled sourdough bread as a clincher. "You only live once," he'd tell me, with a roguish grin.

My personal favorite was nothing fancy. A pound and a half, maybe two pounds of boned squirrel, depending on my appetite. A bit of plum tomato and basil on the body. Some sliced pancetta, or lean bacon if possible. A pinch of guajillo flakes. Not too much, just enough to give the squirrel a little stinger. Throw a sprig of cilantro on the side, because it's refreshing (plus, it looks pretty). Sea salt, with a few teaspoons of olive oil to bring it all together. And the Pernod cream, of course. Consistency is crucial.

In the kitchen, as in all things, he was the general; I was his lieutenant, his sous chef, his apprentice, his heir. Even now, I can close my eyes, and all those hours roar back into my consciousness: a symphony of spices and disparate flavors, distinct yet unified. Grandfather's unconcealed pride, as I mastered one recipe after another. And the sense that I was part of something grand and joyful. Something important.

At Grandfather's insistence, we often ate dinner at the edge of the grove. "God shat them into this world to make my life miserable. Now let the living ones see us and learn a lesson," he'd proclaim. He wasn't joking.

I was nine years old when he said that. It never crossed my mind back then, but I can't help but wonder: what lesson *would* the living ones learn? They'd observe their fallen comrades from high up on the interwoven branches. They'd watch, and maybe they'd hope for something like a spectral chitter. A brief twitch. The rekindling of once-bright eyes.

*

The man I called "Grandfather" told me the story of the pecan trees. He'd planted them half a century before I was born. He watered and nourished them with his future-wife when they were both ten years of age, scarcely more than children.

The boy and girl leveled the soil. They dug into the silt and loam in late autumn: one hundred holes, sixty feet apart, one arm deep and two hands wide. The kernels came from strong northern stock, and the youngsters felt the thrill of the shells splitting, the ground swelling, the buds and shoots emerging into daylight. They lugged buckets from the cool brook in mid-summer, when limbs grow and roots thirst. They protected the infant trees.

And so the saplings burgeoned into a sturdy grove, standing witness overhead as the youths fell in love. The foliage absorbed their muted laughter, their whispers and murmurs, the first flush of their pleasure. And the wedding took place beneath the placid, vibrant verdancy of trees, which by then were sixty feet in height or more. At long last, the boy—now a man—knew that he was home. His home was not built upon the earth; it was built upon a woman.

One year later, Grandfather brought his wife and newborn son home from the hospital. All alone, he took them to the grove, concealed in their white shrouds. He laid them to rest in the shade of the trees.

*

"Grandchild."

"Grandfather?"

"Tonight, for your thirteenth birthday celebration, we'll make 'squirrel with apricots and pecans'—one of the most elegant dishes I know. It's a special occasion. And you're ready for it."

"Is that why you bought garam masala at the marketplace?"

"Yes, child. Good eye. You were watching me carefully."

"So it's like a curry?"

"More of a casserole, really. Go ahead and pull the masala out of the spice cupboard for me, will you? Thanks. Now let's gather the rest of the ingredients ... red onions?"

"Check!"

"Tomatoes?"

"Check!"

"Garlic?"

"Double-check!"

"Pecans?"

"Fistfuls of them!"

"Dried apricots, white wine vinegar, vegetable oil, ginger?"

"All systems ... go!"

"Good. Then there's only one missing ingredient."

"What is it, Grandfather?"

He takes the .22 rifle from its place of honor on the dining room wall. Smiling, he hands it to me—the one item I've never been allowed to touch. Stunned, I take hold of it for the first time.

An extraordinary feeling manifests in my body. It happens first on my left hand, which grips the stock of the rifle. Then it's perceptible on my right hand, which grasps the barrel: a unique sensation crawling up the fine bones and muscles of my fingers, migrating up my forearm, spreading all the way up to my shoulder, continuous and prickly, and as I hold the .22 there is an element of warmth involved, throughout my body. It's too hot. I'm too hot. I feel as if I'm standing perilously close to a bonfire, near enough to be set ablaze. I'm paralyzed. I'm terrified? My heart, I realize, is racing. My forehead glistens. I don't understand why. I can only hope that Grandfather won't notice.

"Grandchild," he whispers. "It's time now. For thousands of years, young men like yourself have reached a certain age, and older, wiser folk have sent them out to hunt. Because a real man takes care of his own. And taking care of your own means *feeding* your own.

"Out there," he points in the direction of the village, miles away to the southeast, "the old ways are fading. Things were different when I was your age. My people gathered together, and they sent me off. They sent me into the wild—and it was much wilder back then than it is now. But they didn't give me a gun. All they gave me was this blade," he pats the sheathed butterfly knife at his waist, "and a machete. And these words, from ancient scripture:

'When a man dies, people are frightened by his bones. But one's essence is not lost. It remains whole. The faces of lords, warriors, artisans, and orators are neither extinguished nor destroyed, for they will leave their children. Now I have done the same through you. Climb up to the surface of the earth; you will not die. Take my wisdom. So be it.'

"They told me not to come back without meat. Two weeks later, I returned with a jaguar."

*

"The jaguars are all gone now—the great beasts are extinct—but you can still do your manly duty and show me that you can *provide*. Make an old man happy. Because there will be a time, Grandchild. There will be a time when I am dust. How soon? I can't say. But if you bring meat to our table, then I can leave this world in peace. So use your gift wisely. Take care of her. Respect her. Love her for what she is, and the hunting will be good. Take up my weapon—she's yours now. My reflection rises out of your face. As you see yourself, I once saw myself; as you see me now, you will be seen."

Grandfather sighs. I can't tell whether it's proud, or bittersweet, or both, or neither. The rifle seems to shift in my hands, of its own accord. It's such an astounding gift that I still can't think of anything to say. Perhaps Grandfather sees this. He chooses his words. He reassures me,

"Don't worry. You don't have to say anything right now. Just get me a big one—one that feels heavy in your hand. Heaviness means *ripeness*. And ripeness," he adds with a renewed grin, "means flavor."

*

As I step out the door, the grove appears closer to our house than ever before, and the rifle is heftier than I imagined. Grandfather sits on the porch, watching me, and I know that he's unsheathing his butterfly knife, just in case. The crowns of the pecan trees dance in a passing zephyr, and they teem with squirrels. Oddly, they are unfazed by my approach: father squirrels and mother squirrels, baby squirrels and ancient squirrels. Brooding squirrels, crafty squirrels, bereaved squirrels, pensive squirrels, brawny squirrels. Entire families, entire bloodlines, entire gene-pools of squirrels, who outnumber the leaves on trees that are more squirrel than tree.

"Why are you not running?" I ask them, under my breath, disengaging the safety of the loaded weapon—of *my* loaded weapon. I'm close, so terribly close. My heart pounds, and foul sweat oozes from my pores. Does the heart of a squirrel beat like my own? Even now, their footing is sound, their breaths untroubled as they frolic, as they amuse themselves with the games squirrels play. I take aim, and it strikes me that their fortune is great. I will live out a tortured existence, as all men do, cut short by an ignominious demise. But they will never suffer the madness of possession, the grief of betrayal. They will never sense the lure of vengeance.

Time, in the guise of a squirrel, slows to a crawl. Grandfather is waiting; he must be smiling. I know I won't miss. I could take this shot a million times and it would always find its mark. Still, I am all but overcome by this anxiety, this fever. I struggle to steady myself. And the hearts of squirrels, and their deft movements, are reduced to an afterthought as I focus on my "duty."

But sometimes an afterthought grows and looms large in the fullness of years, leaves of gold, fronds of green, blooms of spring, roads and days, where even a thing so small as a heartbeat of a squirrel takes on a life of its own. The silence of astonished flesh, and then the cries. A creature of the grove that staggers, falls, untethered from its canopy, coming to an end on the ground below. And there it sleeps. There it slumbers, dreamlessly, against the hard earth, as its carefree soul drifts away with the same breeze that stirs the treetops.

SHORTLIST
SONGS THAT ONLY SQUIRRELS CAN HEAR
by Francisco González

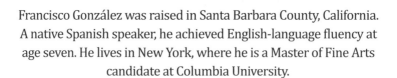

Francisco González was raised in Santa Barbara County, California. A native Spanish speaker, he achieved English-language fluency at age seven. He lives in New York, where he is a Master of Fine Arts candidate at Columbia University.

Illustration by Crap Panther

THE SUPERHERO
by Tomas Marcantonio

Kids in the street think I'm a superhero. Adults stand and stare, eyes glazed over, dissecting me from head to toe. But none of them see me. They can't see the wrinkle on the bridge of my nose, or the arc of my eyebrow; the lines of concern on my forehead or the lights of my eyes. I'm a shadow on the streets; a ghost in the last city of the world. To men I'm a mystery, a challenge, an exotic fantasy to mock and fear. To women I'm a threat, a lost soul, a disfigured object of pity. They're all right, and they're all wrong, but I prefer the kids' idea. The superhero.

The doctors said I could take the mask off after three months once the wounds were healed, but I came to like the mask. It made me feel invincible, became a part of me. More than that, it defined me. I stopped wearing suits and blouses and skirts to work because they weren't me anymore. Neither was my job. Black is my colour now, and lots of it. My hair soon followed. No more little buns and flowery hair clips, no. Now it's long and wild and bushy, and only I can tame it, and no one will ever tame me. And that's me: an outsider, anonymous, free.

I spend my time in the old town; fish market at the centre, a thousand spider web alleys spiralling out, alleys and lanes of hole in the wall bars, of old crones with hard faces and fish at their feet. Tanks of crab, eel, squid, shrimp, and plastic bowls of clams and mussels and animals I don't recognise. Rubber pipes of running water, cobbled floors shining wet, and more hard faces. Follow the silken threads in any direction and you'll find fortune tellers, gamblers and dealers, subtle handshakes, rats in cages, crows in cages, clotheslines weaving wall to wall, squalid gutters showered in piss. An intricate web of life, entangled at the end of the world.

But it's only when the black curtain falls that you can truly see, for the sun exposes nothing here save for the red vessel explosions in commuters' eyes and the violent yellow of urine against white walls. The night illuminates us all, when lanterns glow and neon signs throw hawkers into shadow and puddles paint illusory mirrors of a better world than that in which I live. Businessmen stutter in spotless suits, their faces tinted red by hanging neon lies and drunken dreams, narrow alleys dwindling as day goods disappear and ghost bars stir with conquered wooden stools. Broken umbrellas lay crushed by polished shoes as sacks of waste await collection, the air consumed with secrets, lies and whispers, and the sour sound of spirits dribbling into shot glasses.

Fumiko is in her usual spot on the corner of The Cross, the glimmer of girls in windows flickering behind her as alleys fork further off into the seedy night. Her face is dark and wrinkled and she doesn't acknowledge me. She never acknowledges me until she has no choice.

'Let them go,' I say, my eyes flashing to the windows.

'I've given them a life,' she croaks, her usual bitter answer, black eyes barely meeting mine.

I wait for a moment and watch the shadows move behind her. The girls are young and soft like melting wax, oblivious to the hideous choice they've made. But maybe they *do* know and they're simply denying it, the same way *I* deny it when I'm not watching them and their sleek grey silhouettes.

'I'm getting those girls out of there,' I say to the old lady as she smiles a toothless smile, lips wrinkled and warped by age and a life of immorality. She nods slowly as though she approves, but I hate her *and* her ancient face. How I'd love to have her killed, if only my mask meant what the kids thought it meant.

Head down, I shuffle past the basement bars and brothels and the lonely counters of noodle holes and darkness, into the cover of fading neon signs and black and crooked walls.

I'm going to see Ganzo, a chubster who runs a sushi joint which is open til dawn and often beyond. He makes a fortune because his customers are drunk and eager to pay to eat beyond their bellies. Everywhere round here's open all night. People call these lanes The Pulse, because they *always* pump, even as the world slowly withers and fades away. But The Pulse is firm and fast, and come four bodies litter the ground, backs against walls and mouths dribbling over gutters.

Ganzo's place is down ten wooden steps behind a black metal railing and a bamboo plant. A little bell rings when I push the door open but Ganzo's the only one who glances up when I slide in. It's a tiny place, with sloping walls and a ceiling held together by paper lanterns and old newspaper cuttings. Three suits sit on bar stools, shot glasses on their right and bowls of wasabi on their left, salmon tongues clamped between their chopsticks and soy-drowned grains of rice streaking their ignorant lips. A young couple are down in the corner, the girl's face innocent and blissful, the boy proud to be a part of the last underground world. Ganzo's standing behind the bar in his white hat and apron, his clean, bare hands, which for the sake of perfect sushi he insists he'll never glove, sharpening a sashimi knife.

'Quiet tonight,' I say, pulling out a stool next to the suits. It looks like there's barely room for anyone else, but I've seen this place full and this is nowhere near.

'It's not one o'clock yet,' Ganzo says, his button eyes unworried. He specialises in the post-club crowd, the twenty something's with pockets full of cash and fears of reaching home before midday, or the end of the world, whichever comes first. 'Busy night?'

'Always,' I say.

He doesn't ask me what I want because he already knows. He sets to work, first with the shot glass, twisted black letters printed across the front. Next the porcelain bottle, turquoise and purposely crooked, like the building itself, filled to within a millimetre of the brim with hot sake. The final touch; three immaculate pieces of Ganzo's art lined up on a white plate hardly bigger than my palm. Yellowtail with jalapenos, shime saba, and basashi for the finale. Ganzo's round face is fully concentrated as his fingers glaze over his masterpiece. With the plate in front of me, he glides off to wash his hands.

I eat slowly, pouring myself sake and listening to the drunks next to me. They're going to cheat on their wives tonight, and their wives are probably grateful. I'm silently willing Ganzo to poison them, but the big pug doesn't have the heart. Ganzo only cares about his art, his knives, and me, and I'm a very distant third judging by the way he looks at those knives.

The businessmen are soon stumbling up the wooden steps, leaving behind a wad of crumpled notes and leftover plates of chaos. The young man in the corner puts his arm around the girl in this new quiet created by their absence.

'What do you want?' I ask Ganzo, my plate and bottle empty and my patience gone with them. Ganzo only ever invites me here when he needs something. A very distant third, for certain.

Ganzo sharpens his knives and watches me. He pours me another sake and one for himself.

'They're closing me down.' He doesn't meet my eyes.

'Why?'

'I didn't pay off all the people I was supposed to.'

The bags beneath his eyes are darker than usual.

'You need money? I can get you money.'

'That's not it. It's Ume. She's taken over The Pulse and she knows you're a friend of mine. She says you're to stay out.'

'Stay out of The Pulse? That's half the city.'

'The worst half.'

'And the better half. Where does she expect me to go?'

'She's dangerous.'

'Then I'll go to the police. I've done nothing wrong.'

Ganzo tilts his head to one side and exhales. I know where this is going. 'You remember the fire, Ani,' he says. It's not a question, so I don't offer an answer. 'I'd say you've done plenty enough.'

'Jurors confirmed it was an accident,' I say, caressing the sake bottle.

'They *said* it was an accident because my money told them to. I can't afford to save your skin again, not this time. I've got enough of my own to worry about now.'

The knives are sparkling next to the pink tongues of tuna.

'Is that all?' I ask.

Ganzo looks at me with those panda eyes; he's too soft for this city.

A crowd bursts through the door and the little bell jingles as each person bundles in; a group of rich kids with too much confidence in their eyes and booze in their bellies.

'I'll be leaving then,' I say, finishing the sake and leaving my bar stool wobbling behind me. The youngsters are swarming the bar before Ganzo can say a final word.

I sweep back out into The Pulse and the darkness and rippling neon puddles comfort me. That's my real world, down there, somewhere on the other side, where no one falls in love or suffers scars from self-ignited flames. As I head for the narrows two drunks pass me, and one of them eyes me up and down, so I throw my full weight against his puny chest and send him clattering into a doorway. His friend yells foul words after me but I'm already in the shadows and they're already forgotten.

So what if it's Ume? She's too young to take over the racket on The Pulse. Can't be twenty yet, and isn't vicious enough. I watched her during the trial; sixteen and fragile, her girlfriend dead, eyes dull and blurred and lacking the life that everyone fell in love with. And I saw the way she looked at me, my face wrapped in bandages, and the way she couldn't even muster any hatred for me. No, nowhere near ready to take over The Pulse.

I walk the web, aimlessly and with all the purpose in the world, looking for someone to save, searching for a fire, a drowning rat, anything, but there's nothing but drunks in disarray. It's the hour between two and three, the hour of lost hope and new hope, the hour The Pulse is truly alive. The Drowning Hour. I pad through the darkest arteries like a cat, sliding up against walls, disappearing in doorways, watching the dogs and their loud, lewd barks.

Down to another basement. Nakata's place this time. Smaller than Ganzo's and darker, with even more people. The walls are lined with black leather and the air smells of leather and smoke, but it's just smoke from the machine in the corner because not even Nakata can get hold of real cigarettes anymore. The tables that fill the place are hardly bigger than the round stools that hold up my fellow shadows, and there are several of them, and they're all awake and fox-eyed and not as drunk as they should be at this time. Nakata's behind her long marble bar and she watches me with her big black eyes. Her hair is still short but it's dyed blood wine. Most people wouldn't have noticed it through the dim light and smoke, but I have.

'They're closing Ganzo down,' I say, leaning an elbow on the bar. 'Espresso.'

'And Ume's after you,' Nakata says, her voice deep and throaty like a man's.

'She shouldn't be,' I say. 'I've done nothing.'

Nakata slides the espresso in front of me and turns around. She takes a fresh record out of its sleeve and lifts the needle on that old record player of hers. With steady hands she removes one record and slips in another before replacing the needle. It's her favourite, Ray Charles, I Can't Stop Loving You, and no one else reacts because no one remembers it, or no one's ever heard of Ray Charles. But I know it because I've spent too much time in the artificial smoke-clouds of Nakata's basement, and the song is my song for solitary nights in The Pulse, and the end of the world.

I can't stop loving you. I've made up my mind,

To live in memories, of the lonesome times...

'You burned her girlfriend alive,' Nakata whispers, her straight face fixed on me as I swirl the glass. Nakata has the largest eyes in the city, and there is nothing more attractive than large black pupils and short hair on a dark night with puddles outside. 'You do remember that, don't you?'

'It was an accident,' I say. 'Look at this mask. I lost my face in that fire.'

The other customers are perched on their stools drinking slowly in the smoke, and there are amber ales on tiny tables and froth on the top lip of the pretty girl in her business suit with her makeup, and there's a moustache on the man opposite her with his sad eyes. Then there are shot glasses in front of the old couple who have run out of words but are still here trying nonetheless, and there's a closed book - a real book - on the table in front of the lonely man with his meandering thoughts. And there's a group of four fresh from a club, loud and merry, and the talk flies between them like there's electricity on each pair of lips, and them being in the bar makes everything okay.

...They say that time, heals a broken heart.

But time has stood still, since we've been apart...

'You're a good person,' Nakata says, almost to herself. She takes a fresh glass and slides it in front of me. 'You know that, right?' She pours the clear sake and leans on the bar.

'I saved that girl,' I say. 'I saved that girl, Ume. I saved her from that basement, from those men paying for her thirteen-year-old body. I haven't forgotten that.

I gave her a life.'

I take the shot and Nakata watches me, unblinking.

...So I'll just live my life

In dreams of yesterday.

The song ends and Nakata turns and removes the next record from its sleeve. This time it's Sam Cooke, A Change is Gonna Come. There's a moment of stillness as the needle searches and scratches until the black disc whirls into life, the violin commencing its old and forgotten hymn.

I was born by the river, in a little tent.

And just like the river, I've been running ever since...

'We loved each other,' I say.

'No,' Nakata says gently. She puts a hand on mine and shakes her head. I turn around and look at the amber ales and smoke.

'Ume was just a girl, and you were the only person who cared for her. She saw you as her saviour and nothing more, and that broke your heart. She never loved you, not in the way you wanted.'

The foursome in the corner are joking and laughing because they have ale and smoke between them and they can always order more ale.

'You burned that building down, Ani. You killed that girl because Ume loved her and she never loved you. You remember that, don't you?'

'Another,' I say, holding up my glass.

...But I know a change gon' come, oh yes it will.

Nakata watches me with her wine-dyed hair and large pupils before reaching for the bottle behind her, but I'm already a shadow in the smoke, back in the blackness of The Pulse, my heels clipping the cobbles and the countless worlds in puddles waiting for me.

Most people have no idea what it takes to save another life, what it means to rescue a child from absolute misery, and the love and care it spawns. I'm walking the web again, back in the centre where fish heads lay lifeless on the floor and another shower is beginning. The raindrops prickle my cheeks and fall in my bushy hair and I don't care if it's acid rain like everyone says it is, because I like the way it feels, and there's nothing better than the sight of the prancing puddles in The Pulse.

I don't know how long I'm standing there before Ume appears from the darkness. Her hair is wet and strands are stuck to her cheek, and the tattoos on her arms and neck are glistening in the rain, and it looks like she's crying but really her face is set and hard like it was the very first time I met her. She's as beautiful and heartbreaking as she is every time I see her.

'You have to leave,' she says. 'I can't go on knowing you're still here, skulking around like you've done nothing wrong.'

'I *have* done nothing,' I say, not knowing how she can't understand. *I* was the one who saved her from Fumiko and that basement of seedy men with their money and fetishes and their slow destruction of the world.

Ume takes a step closer to me and I can see her ferocious eyes drilling into mine and it's as though we're one being, one soul. Then in a flash everything changes. Before I can blink Ume's hands are on the back of my head, her fingers in my hair dragging me to the floor until I'm on my knees gasping for breath.

'Look at yourself!' Ume screams. 'Look!'

She holds my head above a puddle and I see myself there in the world on the other side, the mask and dead eyes and the lights of a world without love and the screams of burning girls. Ume rips the mask from my face and throws it in the gutter before releasing me to shiver and shake, on my hands and knees, the superhero disgraced. I stare at my superhero face, but it belongs to the woman on the other side. Her nose is deformed, her eyebrows gone and the skin from nose to brow is waxy and wrinkled and hideous. It is not the face of a superhero but the face of the villain, wretched and callous.

'Do you see?' Ume says, her voice calm and controlled. Still defeated, both of us. You're going to live with that, like I live with the pain of what you did - and I'll always live with it - no matter what happens, and I'll never, ever, forgive you.'

The hideous face is staring back at me from the other world, my own face trembling and lost and afraid... and I'm lost... I don't know who I am.

'Get out of here. Out. Start again and live with your scars, and stop hiding from what you did and become who you used to be.'

Tears are showering the puddles, but they can't be my tears because heroes don't cry. It must be the rain, passing through my very skull, because I'm not there anymore. I'm not the person who did that terrible thing. I can't be.

'You were good once. I remember. I remember the woman who tore through Fumiko's and dragged me out by the wrists. I remember the look on your face when you saw me in that short skirt and all that makeup, and your hair was in a bun and you were wearing a grey suit, and you looked like you didn't belong there any more than I did. You saved me. I was thirteen, and you, you were sent from heaven. Go back to being that woman. Please. And leave.'

I tear my eyes away from my reflection and look up at the young, hard, ruined face of the girl in front of me. She looks the same as the lost thirteen year old, but now she's crying, and I'm at her feet like a dog, a drooling dog pawing at her ankles, begging to be dragged in from the rain. But she turns and leaves and I wonder how she doesn't just collapse after everything she's been through. And soon she's gone and I know I'll never see her again, and I deserve it. I don't deserve anything, even the right to skulk in these poisonous alleys like a disgraced cat. I can't bring myself to stand, not yet, and I linger on my knees and look up, the rain falling on my healed skin for the first time, and it's cold and terrible and new.

I stand slowly, shaking, and my hair is soaked and stuck to my face, and I breathe and banish new tears. I stare at the darkness between faint neon and ancient timber signs, and there's Ganzo and Nakata busy in their basements... but they'll never see the maskless me... and I search for more but all I see is darkness. If I keep going I'll find my way out of this web I've been trapped in for so many years. This is the last city and midday may never come, but somewhere, somewhere out there, there's a place where no one knows me, or what I've done. *I* know... and I'll always know... but hero or villain... finally... I can live with it.

SHORTLIST
THE SUPERHERO
by Tomas Marcantonio

Tomas Marcantonio is a writer and English teacher from Brighton, England. He graduated from the University of Sussex with a degree in English Language and Film, and he has since been travelling widely. His travels have influenced much of his writing, which includes travelogue *Gift of the Gap*, and his first novel, *The Leap of Grebes*. He is currently based in Busan, South Korea, where he teaches English and writes whenever he can escape the classroom. You can follow Tomas on Twitter @TJMarcantonio for more of his published work.

Author photo by *Seung-Jin Yeo*

AFTERWORD

I've always been attracted to the backstreets. The dystopian city in *The Superhero* owes a lot to some of my favourite areas in Korea and Japan. Wandering these back alleys at night, it's impossible not to be drawn into the stories that surround you. When every dark passage can be home to a dozen restaurants, bars, and unknown establishments, all home to crooked characters drinking on stools, stories tend to leap out at you. Sometimes, at the end of a night when drunks are stumbling home and the streets start to fall quiet, it really does feel like those futuristic, dying-world metropolises seen in the likes of *Blade Runner*, *Akira*, and *Ghost in the Shell*.

While many Westerners who travel or relocate to Asia comment on receiving stares or special attention from locals, I've always experienced an overriding feeling of anonymity as an expat. As someone who tends to avoid social interaction, there's something appealing about this feeling of being unknown. In this respect, the idea of skulking around a bustling, neon-lit city in a mask all night is something of a fantasy. There's nothing new about this idea; the appeal of masquerade balls is that wearers are granted the freedom to act as they please without judgement or consequence. However, masks also allow a person to escape from their true identity.

For the protagonist in *The Superhero*, the mask is both the symbol of her terrible past, and also the means to hide from it. I've always enjoyed complex characters, and that's why this was never intended as a story about heroes and villains; it's about facing up to who you are. For people with social anxiety in particular, the idea of hiding away in shadow is undoubtedly attractive, but it's easy to get sucked too far into the hole. Accepting your flaws and past mistakes is vital to owning yourself, and sometimes taking off that mask and entering the stark light of day is one of the hardest things you can do.

Illustration by HarlotVonCharlotte

THE EUTH OF TODAY
by Richard Lee-Graham

Nathan's terror evaporated. He tossed back his last powdery sip of coffee and inhaled the clean air that filled the featureless, white room. Across the desk from him sat a shaven-headed man in his twenties, glowing with five-a-day health and the neck muscles of a racehorse. The man wore a white lab coat to denote his authority. White coats had been proven to coerce greater obedience in subjects such as Nathan – Nathan knew this fact, yet found it impossible to ignore the young man's *obvious* authority.

'Are you comfortable?' asked the man in the white coat.

'I can honestly say, I've never felt such an absence of discomfort,' said Nathan, searching for dregs in his paper coffee cup.

'Good. We have your results.' The man would only refer to himself as, "we", and Nathan couldn't resist the feeling he was being addressed by an entire army of men.

'We can confirm you've been referred for Euth.'

'Oh. I see,' Nathan's insides dropped. 'But I've only *just* turned fifty.'

'We've run the tests, examined the data. There's no doubt. Your contribution and efficiency levels are well below threshold. The Algorithm is never wrong.'

'I just thought I *was* contributing. I'm going to be part of Gov's "Culture Festival" — my paintings have been exhibited at the National Gallery, you know?'

'*Terribly* inefficient building. All that wasted space.'

'Wasted space?'

'Unfortunately, Mr. Gardner, the arts are now considered a *minor* contribution.'

'I never heard — since when?'

'Your Euth appointment is entirely voluntary, of course. But I do recommend you read this pamphlet before making your decision.'

The man handed Nathan a perishable screen. *Do Your Bit!* it read.

'Do my bit,' said Nathan, holding the pamphlet in resignation.

'The waiting times for walk-ins at the Euth Centre can be lengthy. It's advisable to book. Shall we say next week? When's good for you?'

***

Nathan stepped out from the Euth Assessment building into the congested street. His lungs were rudely awoken by the impure air and they ordered up a wet cough in protest. A winter gust blew into his face — it was so cold it made his teeth ache. Nathan looked for an opening in the laboured crush of bodies, bulked with thick coats and woolly hats. There was no gap. There might *never* be a gap. The shuffling humans were bonded like atoms, moving towards efficient and contributory matters. Nathan was thankful the wall of waddling flesh moved in the direction towards home. He wedged a flat palm between two bodies and prised their chemical bonds apart to join the crowd.

'Scuse,' said Nathan.

'Scuse,' said the man in front of him.

'Scuse,' said the woman behind him.

'Scuse,' said a pocket of humans a few metres in front.

This was the sound of the world. The constant hiss and murmur of a single syllable, as men and woman politely offered their apologies for their unavoidable proximity. *Scuse*: efficiently shortened from the archaic, 'Excuse me, please.' Decades ago, through intention or accident, a newspaper had released a single-syllable edition. *Each word read as just one sound.* The paper was hailed for embracing the government's mandate for a more efficient future. Certain news outlets were already ahead of others in this art, but eventually everyone followed suit, given the rise in sales and parliamentary plaudits. In order to sustain this monosyllabic trend, longer words had to be shortened, phrases were acronymed, and a new, super-efficient version of English evolved. '*The Sun's* English' now sat at the heart of the national curriculum.

Nathan lumbered amongst the padded bodies, staying alert to the shifting currents. A ripple of uncertainty passed through the herd and Nathan hesitated before the weight of the crowd shoved him forwards again. He arrived at the source of disruption: a young woman was being trampled. No one could stop to help or else they would join her on the icy concrete. She screamed as her bones were cracked and flattened like a discarded chicken carcass. 'Scuse, scuse, scuse,' replied the crush.

Nathan was carried past a coffee-shop that had a line snaking out of the entrance. The queue was a thriving micro-economy, with independent sellers positioned at intervals, hawking substandard coffee from makeshift stalls to those who could be tempted to win back some moments of their lives. Towards the back of the queue the coffee was not fit for consumption. You had to get near the front for the good stuff. It was rare to make it inside the coffee shop, which could charge whatever it wanted. The earthy smell of coffee spiking the air made Nathan's skin prickle against his wool jumper.

This moment of inner happiness was punctured by the sight of the local Euth Centre: a white cube structure that looked the same as any other modern building, except for a chimney, which billowed white smoke into the heavens. Outside, the resident protestors huddled together in sleeping bags, their spirits quietened by the constricting temperature.

Placards with familiar anti-Euth slogans were scattered on the ground: *YOU HAVE USE: SAY NO TO EUTH. EUTH IS SIN. EUTH: FUCK OFF.* A hooded protester sat on his haunches smoking something resembling a pipe. His bearded face was in shadow as he eyeballed the passing crowd. He nodded at Nathan and raised a fist in camaraderie. Nathan looked at the ground and continued towards home.

***

Nathan's flat was part of a large, multi-story cube. Most of the city lived in 3D-printed buildings just like it. It doubled as his studio, where he spent most of the day on his work. Nathan was one of the few artists in the world who was still considered a master of the near-extinct medium of oil painting. His workspace was a time-capsule to the lost era of analogue art: oily rags, curled up paint tubes and colourful Pollock-splatters were sown on the floor around his easel. He'd tried virtual painting, but it just felt better to hold a brush, smell the turps and hear the horse-hair graze the canvas.

His doorbell rang and he was quick to answer. He was always glad to have company.

'Hello, Alex', said Nathan, greeting his next-door neighbour with surprise. They spoke rarely.

'Hi, hi,' said Alex, standing with both hands in his pockets.

'Is everything all right?'

'Yes.' Alex looked down the corridor towards his flat and nodded with bulging eyes. 'We got a Euth note — re: you.' He turned to Nathan and presented a perishable screen from his pocket.

'Oh,' said Nathan.

'I... I hope you'll do your bit?' said Alex. 'My kids — think of them.'

'Yes, but...'

'Think of what's-his-face down the hall. He'd a chance to do his bit.'

'That was very sad.'

'It was *right*. If you don't do your bit...' Alex hesitated. 'You get lynched.'

Nathan took a step back from the doorway, 'It *is* voluntary, you know?'

'We've got too much shit on our streets,' said Alex, in a rehearsed manner. '*Do your bit*, Nath-Gar.' He turned and marched down the hall with a new-found confidence. Nathan saw Alex's wife standing by their open door, listening covertly. He watched them disappear inside their flat.

Nathan soon heard muffled shouting vibrating through the thin walls. A few moments later, there was a gentle tapping at his door. It was Alex again, his shoulders now drooping a few inches lower.

'Scuse, I meant to ask - can we have your leftover art?'

'I didn't know you were interested in my work?'

'Well, they might be worth a few bob, once… you know.'

***

That night, Nathan stood before a blank canvas and began to mix some paint. He wanted to create something that would prove his work had value — that art had value. As he stirred a whirlpool of crimson and black he thought about the children he'd never had, not wanting to burden the world with more flesh and bone. He considered the lovers who'd come and gone — Nathan could never sustain love alongside his devotion to his work. He'd put his life into painting. Today he'd been told that made him worthless. He dipped a brush into the dark, red paint and with rare hate and anger he flicked it at the blank canvas, again and again, filling the space with thick clods and bloody rivers which coursed down the terrain of the white fabric. He took a deep breath to calm his feelings and stood back to view his work.

He wept. It was a terrible painting.

***

The next morning, Nathan dressed and left the house without breakfast. He piled up some recent paintings outside Alex's door in the hope they might provide his family some happiness. Or money. Nathan wasn't sure of the difference any more.

It was early, and the human crush was not yet at its peak. On arriving at the Euth Centre, Nathan loped around the tents housing sleeping protestors and joined the back of the queue. He'd made his decision: there seemed little point delaying his fate.

A hairless man in a white coat was making his way down the queue, scanning fingerprints and handing out synapse-tingling coffee. The woman in front of Nathan held rosary beads and was silently bidding farewell to her teenage son, who laid his head on her shoulder before he had to leave for school. He couldn't afford to be late, or else The Algorithm would register it as a permanent stain of inefficiency.

Nathan remembered the day he'd come to the Euth Centre with his own mother. He'd been so young. She'd towered over him wearing a hard, stoic countenance and reminded him he *had to do her bit*. Then Nathan realised he wasn't remembering his mother at all, but an actress he'd seen repeatedly on an advertisement. Nathan now struggled to recall his own mother's face.

A burning miasma wrestled Nathan's senses, and a cloud of white smoke surrounded his head like a halo. Nathan presumed it was the fumes from the Euth Centre's chimney blowing into his face, but then he was tapped on the shoulder.

'Nathan Gardner?' It was the hooded protester from yesterday, puffing and puckering at his wooden pipe with rigour.

'Christ,' said Nathan. 'Is that *tobacco*?'

'Yep. Best in town. Want some?'

'God, no. That stuff kills you.'

'Yep. Does it a lot slower than this place though,' he lowered his hood and squeezed his features together in a warm smile, pointing at the building with his eyes as the pipe bobbed up and down from the side of his chapped mouth. 'Smoking *is* voluntary, you know?'

Nathan had never seen a face as old as the one the man revealed. His skin was weathered and cracked, with deep valleys running from feature to feature. His wispy beard was unkempt and lopsided, flat on the side he must have slept on, protruding like a cumulus formation on the other.

'You're Nathan Gardner, the painter. Right?'

Nathan hesitated, 'Nath-Gar to the kids.'

'What?' The man stopped puffing his pipe. His overgrown eyebrows sprouted from his face like the bristles of one of Nathan's old paint brushes.

'Nath-Gar,' Nathan repeated. 'In *The Sun's* English.'

The man shook his head with his eyes shut, 'Please — let's not speak in that pygmy tongue.'

'All right,' Nathan shrugged. 'Yes, I'm a painter... *was* a painter. How on Earth would *you* know?'

'I'm a great art fan, of course.' He opened his callused palms and raised his shoulders in wonderment. 'You're a hero.'

'I doubt that.' Nathan considered the idea of being a hero. His eyes were drawn to the man in the white coat handing out steaming coffee near the front of the queue.

The old man came closer to Nathan and his voice became stern, 'You haven't had any of that coffee have you?'

'Um, no,' said Nathan. 'Not yet.'

'Good,' he barked. 'Don't — ever again.' The man wrapped a smoked arm around Nathan's shoulder and his geniality returned. 'You *must* come with me. This place isn't for you.'

'Apparently it *is*. The Algorithm said so.'

The man removed his pipe from his mouth to release a bleat of laughter. 'There is no Algorithm. That's just a word they use to bamboozle. Come with me. I've a wonderful place to show you – a place where art has *value*.'

Nathan's eyes widened. 'I don't know... I'd sort of made up my mind.'

'Come, brother,' he said, steering Nathan away from the queue. 'If you don't like what you see, you can come straight back here and I promise you'll be floating up through that chimney before midday. My name's Terry.' Nathan shook his hand, which was as hard and rough as pumice. 'Terry Rorke.'

***

Nathan was led down a side street, not far from the Euth Centre. Terry had tied their wrists together with coarse rope so they weren't separated in the crush. It burned Nathan's skin, but he'd felt too anxious to mention it.

'We're here,' said Terry, removing the rope from their arms. The relief from the pain was blissful to Nathan, who rubbed his raw wrist and looked around the quiet alley. A rare thing backed up onto it: a building of bricks and mortar, hidden like a forgotten blemish amongst the featureless modern architecture.

Terry started down a concrete staircase, steadying himself with an iron handrail. 'This way,' he beckoned to Nathan. 'Come and meet your brothers.' Nathan followed with trepidation, running his fingers along the worn brick wall.

They arrived at a wooden door, rotting at the edges and flaking black paint. There were no markings, not even a door-handle. Terry pounded it with his fist. 'It's Terry, you lazy shits. I've got a guest.'

The door was wrenched open and a warm glow spilt out with the din of loud chatter and raw, imperfect music. Piano and guitar and accordion and flute — Nathan heard them all. He followed Terry inside. The smell of tobacco consumed everything and Nathan's wet eyes stung in the haze. The small basement room was crowded with men and women, hunched awkwardly on makeshift tables and chairs — crates and church pews and upturned buckets. Some groups were locked in debate, with bearded men pointing angrily at the heavens. Others sat in silence, eyes closed, swaying, bouncing their knees, letting the jaunty music trickle into them. The languid musicians strummed and squeezed and exhaled from a cramped corner, nudging each other with stray elbows, often missing notes.

Terry turned to Nathan, removed his pipe and opened his arms out wide. 'Welcome to "The Chimney,"' he said, baring his remaining teeth with a triumphant smile.

Nathan quivered with adrenaline and hunger. 'What is this place?'

'This is where the dead come to *live*, brother,' said Terry, ushering Nathan to a bar constructed from stacked fruit-and-veg boxes. 'Even the *beer* is dead here. Two *halves* please!' he screamed at the withdrawn barman who launched into action, avoiding Nathan's gaze. Terry leaned into Nathan and grunted, 'It's still morning, after all.' Nathan felt unable to tell him he found all varieties of beer revolting, regardless of the time of day.

'Come. Sit with me,' said Terry, patting the filthy surface of a nearby table. 'I'll tell you about my little establishment here.' He stuffed his pipe with fresh tobacco and used a candle to puff it alight. Nathan sat on an upturned bin, his stumpy legs dangling above the floor.

'Everyone you see here has been in that same queue for the Euth Centre, Nathan,' he pointed around the dimly lit basement. 'Artists, writers, musicians: the heart of humanity — just left to go up in smoke. Poof!' he exhaled a smoke signal. 'But, *I* saved 'em,' he grinned.

'Old Terry here has friends on the *inside* of those Euth Centres. I've sneaked these brothers and sisters out through the backdoor before they were turned into fumes. It's the chimney, or The Chimney,' he gestured at their surroundings with an exuberant waft. 'Most choose to stick with me.' Terry's twang travelled the British Isles, with rolled Cornish vowels rubbing against the rasping consonants of the Highlands. 'No one comes looking for 'em. The records say they went to their Euth appointment, and it's the records that matter these days. You're drinking with *ghosts*, Nathan.'

Nathan pretended to sip his stale beer, 'And you're dead too?'

'I was never *alive*,' Terry let out a phlegmy chuckle which developed into a coughing fit. He spat on the basement floor. 'No one has a record of old Terry Rorke. No birth certificate. No National Insurance number. No family. Nothing. I never *was*, you see?'

'I don't understand,' said Nathan. 'Someone must have raised you?' He held his nose and took a gulp of the warm liquid. The bitterness assaulted his mouth and he couldn't prevent his face from contorting in violent displeasure.

Terry released a gargantuan laugh and his pipe fell from his mouth. The musicians missed a beat and fumbled to re-establish their rhythm. 'You get used to it,' said Terry, downing his glass and scooping his pipe off the floor. 'We brew it ourselves — we do our best.'

'No, no. It's delicious,' Nathan wet his upper lip with a theatrical swig.

'I never got to know my parents,' frowned Terry. 'I'm one of the "lost-children" — after the one-child policy came in — cast off to fend for myself before I could be found by Gov.' He watched the smoke rising from his pipe. 'I moved from place to place, and I've changed my name many times. But that doesn't matter now. What matters is, I learnt all I know from you lot.'

'Us lot?'

'I didn't go to any school, you see? Libraries and galleries were my playground. I learnt all I need to know from writers, poets, artists: the very soul of this here planet.' He pointed upwards, as though the entire crust of the Earth lay above their heads. 'You people are my fathers, mothers, brothers, sisters and teachers.' He put a heavy hand on Nathan's shoulder. 'My brother,' he said.

Nathan cleared his throat, 'Yes. Brother.' He raised his glass and took another ghastly mouthful. 'So, what does everyone *do* here? I mean, it looks fun. But what, you know, happens?'

'This is a place for art to *grow*, Nathan. Talk about life, love, the masters of old. Whatever you want. You can stop thinking about being *efficient*. Stop wondering if you're *contributing*. Just be the genius you are. That's what *happens* here. I'm saving humanity. Don't you see?'

'I do. I do see. It's a wonderful thing you're doing. Wonderful!' But Nathan didn't see much art going on. The clannish patrons sat like disgruntled passengers waiting for their train to be repaired. It was like the men and women really *were* ghosts, and Nathan was trespassing in purgatory.

'The world is broken, Nathan,' said Terry, a bottomless crevice forming between his brow. 'I can't just let people like you get tossed on the rubbish tip. The world has to fucking see. It has to open its eyes and *fucking* see.'

There was a heavy silence between them. Nathan downed his beer.

'So,' said Nathan, wiping his mouth and stifling a shudder. 'Am I dead now too?'

'No, brother,' replied Terry, his embittered mind releasing its hold on his scowl. 'We need you *alive*.'

'Oh? Why's that?'

'You're part of Gov's "Culture Festival", yes?' Terry presented a semi-perished screen from his pocket. *CULT-FEST: NEW WORK FROM ART MAN, NATH-GAR* it read, with a mugshot of Nathan's round face.

Nathan looked at the flyer. 'Well, I was, yes...'

'— Excellent. I have a plan,' he leaned closer to Nathan. 'Together, we're going to open their eyes like never before, brother!' He grabbed Nathan's blistered wrist and squeezed it in his powerful grip. 'The papers are going to have to bring old words out of retirement for what we've got planned. And I give you my guarantee, if you do as I say, you'll live until you're an old man, like me — and art will be *important* again. Are you ready to be a hero?'

***

Before Nathan was allowed into the Euth Assessment room, he was asked to make a selection: *NATH-GAR, PLEASE CHOOSE SUN-ENG OR OLD-ENG(LISH).* He selected old-English by nodding to the right of the screen. The screen flashed *INEFFICIENT SELECTION* in response. *Another black mark*, he thought. *Not that it matters any more. GO IN.*

'Please sit, Mr. Gardner,' said the man in the white coat, looking younger and even more radiant than before. 'Are you comfortable?'

'I'm fine,' replied Nathan.

'Good. What can we do for you?' He leaned forward. 'We booked you in for Euth next week. Would you like to bring your appointment forward?' He began flicking through a scheduling chart on his desk-screen. 'We've had a cancellation for tomorrow morning?'

'Er... no. That's not why I'm here. I need more time.'

'We don't understand.'

'I'm going to present a final work at the Culture Festival. It will be my...' Nathan looked at the scrawled ink on his palm. 'My masterpiece.'

'Does this mean you want to *postpone* your appointment?' The man fiddled with some dials and a steaming cup of coffee rose up from inside the desk. 'We really do advise against leaving it too long. Please, enjoy a coffee on us.'

'Well, I suppose... just a sip,' Nathan wrapped his hand around the hot paper cup.

'You need to do your *bit*, Mr. Gardner — face the music.' The music. Nathan remembered the rambunctious, dysfunctional music and smelled the ghost of tobacco living in the fibres of his woollen jumper. He remembered Terry's frightening words: *Don't drink the fucking coffee.*

'No,' said Nathan.

The man raised his brow high enough to crack a single, maiden wrinkle across his forehead. 'No?'

Nathan put down the coffee cup. 'I'm revealing my masterpiece at the festival next week,' he said, focusing on the message written on his hand. 'You lot will be there won't you?'

'Us lot?'

'Yes. All of you lot in the white coats.'

The man rolled his eyes. 'Yes. Gov wants us there. Good PR,' he shrugged.

'I'm going to reveal a work dedicated to The Algorithm.' Nathan viewed his palm again. 'It'll be my last work before my Euth appointment. I'd like The Algorithm's disciples present for the unveiling. Will you join me on stage? It'll be *great* PR.'

'We'll have to check with Gov. What is this *painting*?'

'It's called: "The Algorithm's Portrait."'

***

Trafalgar Square was brimming with bodies like a bubbling cauldron. Most people were just attempting to pass through, but a handful had gathered for what had been fervently billed by The National Gallery as the 'art event of the decade', which to most citizens was considerably less exciting than the opening of a new coffee shop. Incidentally, the day prior to the event, Gov had quietly announced that it would be the last annual "Culture Festival" (until further notice).

At the steps of The National Gallery, which loomed over the square at one end, a stage had been erected. Nathan stood on the platform along with a suited representative from The Gallery, a lectern, and a giant, blood-red curtain which concealed Nathan's masterwork. Also on stage were four hairless men in white coats, standing impatiently as beacons of health and efficiency, each of them worthy of permanent residency on the plinths at each corner of the ancient square.

The gallery representative spoke into a microphone at the lectern and his voice echoed across loudspeakers positioned around the square. They had been set up by some tech-novice from the gallery, and as such, the feedback made his voice almost unintelligible. He continued admirably, showing no signs that he might be perturbed by the shoddy sound engineering of a young intern, who had *sworn* he knew what he was doing. 'Nathan Gardner, AKA... A... A', he paused for effect. 'Nath-Gar... Gar... Gar.' There was a smattering of light applause from the sibilating crowd.

Nathan stood to one side in a state of deep-rooted anxiety. He held his arms behind his back and picked and peeled any dry skin he could find around his fingernails. He'd insisted there was no need for him to say anything, but The Gallery man beckoned him to the microphone. Nathan made his way to the lectern despondently. The men in white coats were monitoring instruments, tutting and shuffling their feet. At all times, at least one of the men was looking at his watch, as though it was a synchronised agreement between them.

Nathan had begun speaking, '... my final work... k.... k.' He looked at the man from The Gallery, who stood next to a dusty golden rope attached to the red curtain. 'My masterpiece,' said Nathan, nodding at the man. '"The Algorithm's Portrait... trait... trait."' The rope was pulled and the curtain dropped to the ground like an unzipped ball-gown. An enormous canvas was revealed, obstructing the view of The National Gallery's grand entrance. Nathan turned to regard it eagerly — he'd not seen it since Terry Rorke had presented it to him, just a few days ago.

The hissing and mumbling of the crowd stopped as they absorbed what they were seeing. The loudspeakers crackled and distorted with intermittent wails and the four men in white coats looked at the artwork in utter bewilderment.

The canvas was blank. Not a single drop of colour blemished the clean white slab, which towered like an unearthly monolith at one end of the grey square. Nathan was wilting under the weight of silence.

'I don't get it,' said one of the men in white coats, gawping at the wall of nothing.

'Nor me,' said another.

Another simply said, 'No.' And it was clear, that was all he would be saying today. The men shook their heads and began prodding and swiping at instruments, no doubt satisfying The Algorithm deity.

A hooded Terry Rorke stood to the side of the stage and was glowering and gesticulating at Nathan. 'Get off the stage *now*, you idiot,' he said. Nathan remembered his instructions and quietly slid away.

'I don't think they understood,' said Nathan to Terry, who was frantically groping for something in his pockets.

'Of course they didn't,' said Terry. 'Their eyes aren't open yet.'

'I understand... stand... stand.' The voice of The Gallery representative boomed through the air. Nathan stopped to listen, but Terry urgently dragged him away from the stage. The man stood at the lectern, surrounded by the white-coats, who observed him with intrigue. He continued to speak, 'This is clearly post-modern existentialism in the style of the mid twentieth century minimalists depicting the very nature of what it means to appreciate life expressed through the medium of two coats of white emulsion applied with a roller... ller... ller,' he paused for breath. The puzzled white-coats nodded in agreement and stroked their cleft chins. The crowd nodded too. The Gallery man cleared his throat to continue...

An explosion. An eruption of limbs and sinew. An excruciating noise that made Nathan aware of every nerve ending lying dormant in his inner-ear. The crowd recoiled and swelled in harrowed panic.

Smoke from the blast cleared. The lectern had been replaced by a jagged hole in the stage, gaping like the jaws of a nightmarish beast. The artwork was no longer blank, but covered in miscellaneous flesh, hanging body parts and blackened blood which dripped red streaks down to the sickening, offal-strewn steps of The National Gallery.

Terry leaned in towards Nathan's ringing ear, 'Your masterpiece,' he whispered, before disappearing into the chaotic horde. A fine spray of bloody shrapnel showered Nathan's skin and discoloured the granite plinth which he'd found shelter by.

The caw of sirens approached. Nathan was rooted to the spot, dumbfounded by the apocalyptic scene. The artwork — a sheet of metal that Terry had scavenged from a scrapyard and painted white — still stood as tall and true as before. It was smeared in ferocious streaks of blood and carbon, like the brushstrokes of an angered god. It was a symbol of such brutality, it couldn't be ignored. A violent expression that would never be forgotten.

Nathan wept. *It is a masterpiece*, he thought.

The police sheared through the crowd, deflecting civilians from their path like determined snowploughs. Nathan was brutally tackled to the ground and restrained. 'Scuse,' said one officer, punching him in the kidney.

Nathan was dragged away, his face distorted in shock. 'It was Terry Rorke!' he screamed. 'Terry Rorke did this! Terry Rorke!' It was all he could say, over and over, like the echoing voices he would hear for the rest of his life. 'Terry Rorke!'

***

BANG!

> Huge bomb went off in town. Lots dead. Art man called Nath-Gar did it. Bad man. Scum. But brave Cops got him. Good Cops.
>
> Man who lived next to Nath-Gar said, 'He was strange, lone man who would not do his bit. But he made nice art which I can sell for good price.'
>
> There are calls to bring back the rope to hang Nath-Gar. But Gov said no. 'We live in fair and just place. We do not kill our own.' Good Gov. Nath-Gar will die old man in jail.
>
> When caught, Nath-Gar told Cops why he did it: 'It was Ter-Ror,' he said. 'Ter-ror. Terror (sic).'

SHORTLIST
THE EUTH OF TODAY
by Richard Lee-Graham

Richard Lee-Graham studied creative writing at Central Saint Martins in 2012 and has completed a writers workshop at City University of London. He's also part of a local writers group in London, Tooting, called Chalk the Sun.

Common themes in Richard's work are death, time, and life's misfits — but it's not all glum — he likes to try and find humour where possible. Richard also has a BSc in Psychology, giving him a firsthand insight into why people choose degrees they don't end up using. His greatest influences are the novels of Kurt Vonnegut, the journalism, fiction and poetry of *The New Yorker*, and the music of David Bowie.

As well as short fiction, Richard writes poetry and satire. You can find more of his work on his blog, rlgwrites.com or get in touch on Twitter: @RLGwrites

AFTERWORD

The question I had in my head throughout writing *The Euth of Today* was: what does art contribute? If you're reading this, that may seem a strange question, because you'll appreciate the virtues of reading, writing and the craft of story-telling. But the wider world doesn't always place much worth in the arts. Expression can be viewed as one of life's luxuries; a pastime, a frivolity. So, why then, when the financial rewards are likely to be scarce, are we so compelled to create?

I like Kurt Vonnegut's view (I like his view on most things): "*I say in speeches that a plausible mission of artists is to make people appreciate being alive at least a little bit. I am then asked if I know of any artists who pulled that off. I reply, 'The Beatles did'.*"

Not many could argue with that.

As I was working on the first draft of *Euth*, news broke that President Trump was proposing to scrap all funding for the arts across the United States. "America First, Art Last", as *The New Yorker* put it. I wish Kurt Vonnegut was still around so he could write a letter to Mr. Trump about the dangers of devaluing human expression. I suppose *The Euth of Today* is *my* letter to Mr. Trump. I even wrote some of it in monosyllables, so he might understand it.

On the other hand, the art world can often seem excluding and stuffy. The Gallery representative's breathless monologue about the meaning behind 'The Algorithm's Portrait', is a little joke about this. People in the art world can find meaning in just about anything (I know, because my partner is an art historian).

I'd be delighted to hear what meaning people extracted from *The Euth of Today*. But, more than anything, I hope those who made it to the end garnered some enjoyment from it – at least a little bit.

Illustration by Amie Dearlove

CAKE
by Virginia Ballesty

Antoinette swiped left across the halo screen. She lounged indolently, her lithe body stretched across the length of the couch. It was an old-world piece of furniture; re-upholstered and stuffed with down. An extravagance by anyone's imagination but hers. She cast her gaze my way, her mouth turned down in an attractive pout. I pretended not to notice, for all the good that would do. What Antoinette wanted, she always found a way to get, whether it be my attention or more likely, my discomfort. I didn't need to look up to see her eyes narrow into calculating slits. I tensed, feeling her perusal, her disapproval, slip over me.

"What do you think of this one?" She pinched the halo and with an easy flick of her wrist cast it onto the 3D-imager. Another extravagance, but Father would only have the best for Antoinette.

The light in the imager blinked and settled into a white dress. It was long and frothy, layers of lace on silk. It had a vaguely old world look to it, and not just because of the precious natural materials it was made from. The cost of the dress... I did the calculations quickly in my head. Enough to feed a dozen polyblend families for a year.

She stood slowly, drawing herself upwards. There was nothing overtly provocative about it and yet the way she stretched was undeniably sensuous. She had the look of a cat in the cream. Antoinette knew she had my attention. She always had it when she wanted it. She stepped onto the imager. The dress blinked again as the 3D-imager processed her shape and height, then it settled around her. She looked down, surveying the bodice and the way the skirt fell around her legs.

"Well?"

"It's very pretty," I said, my voice neutral.

Her eyes narrowed and mouth twisted. The sneer lasted only a second. Anyone else may have thought they imagined it; the look of disgust that flickered across her perfect face so quickly. Then her brows smoothed out and her eyes widened. She gazed at me with pure blue innocence and my gut twisted in anticipation.

"Maybe you're right," she mused. "The lace and frill... and what's with these skirts? It's much too conservative. After all, this will be the wedding of the century. Maybe you'd prefer I walk down the aisle in something a trifle less dowdy?"

She pinched her halo screen again and threw another dress onto the imager. It wound around her body, the holograph sliding like silk along her legs and up her abdomen. I felt my face flame and a warm heat settled into my belly. I cursed and looked away, but the image was already in my mind. Sheer lace clinging to her hips and breasts...

"Be serious, Antoinette. You're not getting married in that," I snapped.

She laughed, mocking my unease. I glanced back. A mistake. She was stripping her shirt off under the holograph. Her skin was creamy beneath the lace. She smoothed her hands over the halo, running them languidly up her flat stomach and breasts. A finger traced the opaque design across her chest and then trailed down as it tapered back to sheer and opaque again across her pelvis. It was barely a nod towards modesty. Barely an inch of her was left to the imagination and mine quickly filled in what the dress barely hid. I sucked in an uneven breath and she smiled.

"And why shouldn't I? Isn't this why we're marrying? Don't you want to show off the goods that Daddy purchased for you?"

I had no answer to that and she knew it. She turned and twisted, watching herself in the mirror. The room felt too warm and I was red up to my eyebrows. This was what she wanted. My discomfort. I watched her as she preened, refusing to look away again. I wouldn't give her that much satisfaction.

"They're all jealous, you know. There isn't one of your friends that wouldn't take your place if they could."

I had no answer to that either.

She took my silence as the agreement it was and continued, "Do you want to know which ones have come on to me... and what they promised me in return?"

"Who comes on to you or doesn't and what you do or don't get out of it isn't my concern," I replied harshly.

She turned to face me, arching an eyebrow. "Isn't it? After we're married, you won't mind if I keep company with others? Is it so long as I keep it under wraps... or maybe just so long as I don't bear anyone's children but yours?" She ran her hands over her stomach again. "That would make the wedding a mite more interesting, wouldn't it? Put a brat in me today and marry me six months knocked up. A show of your prowess, one might say." She cast her long gazed sneer at me.

I broke first, looking away again though I'd sworn not to. She was beautiful, my fiancée. Perfectly shapely, in face and eye, leg and arm. Antoinette was cast in the mold of old world beauty. None of the polyblend nonsense found in the common population where they interbred until everything was the same color of muddy brown. And none of the cellular diseases caused by intra-breeding among the Pures, the old world gentry who kept their lines clean and skin light, but at a high genetic cost.

Antoinette couldn't be compared with either of those extremes. Neither could I. Like her I was made to old world specs. Just similar enough that we could meet the standards of the Pures, but not so similar that our marriage would be incestuous. The best geneticists had selected our make-up, the best labs had grown our eggs. Mother did carry us to term, though she died shortly after. And Father raised us. Just like any other family... only Pure, he was fond of reminding us.

The whirring sound of a hover chair echoed down the hallway. As if mere thought could summon the devil himself. Antoinette spun to the door expectantly, posing as our Father passed through the threshold. She smiled brightly at him. "Daddy, what do you think?"

I held my breath, waiting. He was the one person capable of bending Antoinette to his will, the one person she didn't dare stand against. I shouldn't have expected him to chastise her though. He liked nothing better than when she showed her body off. His reminder that money could buy anything, even perfection. Antoinette swished her hips and he smiled, his eyes grazing over her appraisingly.

"Very nice, darling." His voice rasped through the ventilator. The hover chair lurched forward, circling her in entirety before he stopped it by me. Papery white skin, fragile to the touch. I barely contained my flinch when he patted my smooth hand with his mangled one. "There's not a man in the pews that won't be envious of you, son. You're going to be a very lucky man." He winked and leaned in. "You're welcome."

I jerked back and stared at him, but his eyes were on Antoinette. She stared back, not at him, but at me. Her eyes were icy and accusing. One eyebrow lifted, as if she were waiting for me to deny the truth of my father's congratulations. The perfect bride had been created for me, just as the perfect husband had been made for her. We were the products of our Father's insane obsession; the culmination of years of genetic meddling.

I couldn't hold her eyes now any more than I could before. There was something uncomfortable in the depth of her. She was poised, as if waiting for something. As if she expected something from me. I didn't know what she wanted. Instead I turned back to father.

"We have an interview with the Public Comm today. They want to talk about the Infinity Engines."

Father had never been healthy -- very few of the Pure were -- but there was a time when nothing slipped past him. He was still sharp, most of the time, but more and more he was leaving the details to me. His rheumy eyes fixed on Antoinette, still preening in front of the mirror.

"We can talk in my office."

"Are you coming?" I snapped at her, pushing myself out of the chair.

Father waved a hand weakly. "Leave her alone boy. She's got a wedding to worry about. No reason to fret her over minor details of the business."

Minor details? I thought, following him down the hall. Since when had Antoinette not been interested in the details of Manson Enterprises? And since when did the launch of the Infinity Engines count as minor details?

"Antoinette should be here. She's part of the interview." I closed the door and sat myself in front of his desk.

"She has her part to play and you have yours, boy. Don't forget it. Now, did you get a list of questions for the interview?"

"It's general. They want it to play conversationally. But there's been some rumors about the launch and the selection process for the civilian crew. A few tabloids are calling it an exodus."

"Conversational... hmm, I'm sure they do. Hope they can trip you up, boy, get you to admit to some wrong doings. Be sharp and don't rise to the occasion."

I nodded. He wasn't saying anything I didn't know already. "When is the government going to release the details of the evacuation?"

"Evacuation, what on earth are you talking about?"

I glanced at him sharply. He was forgetting details, but nothing so important... but no, there was a glimmer of humor in him. His shoulders shook with ill-held laughter. I frowned. It wasn't a laughing matter. Earth wouldn't be sustainable for carbon-based life much longer. Already the light from the sun burned orange-hot, searing through even UV protected glass shields. I understood keeping it under wraps while we finished the Infinity Engines. There was no reason to panic the population when we didn't have a ready solution, but the engines were finished now. They'd been tested and refined, and tested again. Enough were in production to take a full half of the population off Earth before it was too late. In the meantime, other precautions could be taken. It wasn't the sun exploding that would kill us, nor would it swallow our tiny planet whole. No, it was the radiation. The cancerous rays that would eat away at cells and skin; dangerous to myself and Antoinette, but twice as dangerous to the inbred Pures. Ironically, the polyblend commoners would live the longest.

"You can't be serious. The government is going to announce the danger, of course?"

"They'll hold a draft for volunteers to go on an exploratory mission. After the main personnel and priority passengers are selected, of course." It wasn't an answer, but enough of one.

I opened my mouth to argue, but he shook his head sharply. "Don't think to question the government, boy. Or me. You may be handling some details, but I am still Manson Enterprises. Stay on topic and if they ask uncomfortable questions, let Antoinette handle it."

I bit back an angry retort. His shoulders shook a little and I knew he was laughing at me. Two of a kind, my father and Antoinette. I slammed the door on him as I left.

#

I tried to remember when the change in Antoinette started. She hadn't always been like this. As children we'd been close. It never occurred to me that I'd spend my life with anyone but her and that thought never bothered me, growing up in our house together. It happened softly, the change. So slowly that I didn't notice it until she was too far from what she once had been. But... no. That was a lie I told myself and now, facing forever with her, I couldn't tell it anymore.

That first time I came back from studying abroad she'd been quiet, distant. I noticed, but hadn't pressed. I told myself it was the natural growing apart of children into adults. It wasn't as if I abandoned her, after all. Father had a list of finishing schools a mile long, each dying to enrol the famous Antoinette Manson. She had her choice of the best in the world, but chose to stay. She wanted to learn about Manson Enterprises from the knee of our father. Her choice. So why now, looking back at those years, did I feel like I'd missed something important?

She sat across from me, head tilted and attention a million miles away. Moments like this it almost felt like before. I could crack a joke and she'd turn with her brilliant smile and her laughter would hold joy instead of derision. I let my eyes linger on her in a way that I rarely dared. Her shoulders, pale and delicate, exposed under the lace shift she wore. The hover came to a slow stop and she turned to look at me.

"Smile, Anthony," she whispered. It sounded sad. It sounded like my Antoinette.

She opened the car door and stepped out. A cacophony of welcome greeted her. I didn't need to look at her to see what they saw, although I watched nonetheless. She charmed with her whole body and they loved her for it. Like moths to a flame, and the way I watched her, I was no different.

The Public Comm had done an excellent job with the crowd. They were primed to believe the lies that were about to drip from Antoinette's perfect pink lips. I surveyed the stage set-up. It looked almost like a tea room, with three chairs in a mini circle around a table and a fake rug beneath. The reporter was already in the centre chair. His eyes passed over me and settled quickly onto Antoinette, his smile wide and confident. Antoinette dropped gracefully into the chair on his left, her hands smoothing down her skirt, arranging it as she sat. His eyes lingered, dropping to follow the lines of her body. I felt my hands begin to clench and just as quickly relaxed them.

"Welcome! Welcome!" His voice reverberated through the room. "We're so glad you were able to join us today."

The crowd echoed his sentiment, the noise enveloping the room. A sea of Pure faces, welcoming the symbols of their genetic supremacy.

"Our pleasure...?" Antoinette lay a hand on his, her fingers stroking a lazy design across the back of his hand.

"Crispus." His smile widened to a smirk.

Stupid polyblend. It took a confident -- and foolish -- man to be this cocky with my sister. He saw only the pretty girl on the surface and not the piranha that lurked below. She'd already noted his dark eyes and his dyed hair, just like I had. He was Pure enough to pass on camera maybe, but not close up. Somewhere in his background was a genetic diversion. Even were I not here and our wedding not public, she'd never lower herself to him. But she would enjoy making him think otherwise. She was playing with him, just like she did everyone.

"We've been promised an update on the Infinity class ships and Launch Day. Your father assured us that you two are just the people to provide such an update."

"Well, Crispus, we have only good news to report. Manson's engineers have finally found the missing ingredient to stabilizing the engines." Antoinette had a lovely speaking voice. Her cadence and pitch were perfect. The crowd fell silent, hanging on her every word. "It's a difficult timetable that he's set for his employees, but we're confident that the ships will be ready for Launch Day."

"Why don't you tell us what's still to be done? With the engines working, there's no chance of moving Launch Day up?"

"The hardest part is over, but there's still a lot to be done before the ships are inhabitable long term," I heard myself say. The script tripped easily off my tongue. "Hydroponics need to be installed and living quarters finished. The ships are functional, but not comfortable, you might say."

"Most will happen over the next month or two," Antoinette added. We were a well-oiled PR machine. "Each of the ships will be taken on a short test voyage, just to be sure it's in working order. While they're in the sky our builders and mechanics will be working double time on the final stage."

"Sounds like your father has it all figured out."

"He likes to think so." Antoinette smiled conspiratorially. "But it certainly doesn't hurt to have the best and brightest working under him."

The crowd chuckled at that, as they were supposed to. She basked in their adoration, her eyes half lidded in pleasure.

"Some are calling Launch Day, Doomsday instead, you know. The launch is being called an exodus of the wealthy and Manson Industries has been labelled a genocide machine by many of the liberal factions. Do you have an official comment on that?"

"A genocide machine?" I laughed easily, "That's a bit far-fetched, don't you think? We're not killing anyone, we're simply spearheading an exploratory mission for the government. There is a lottery-based system for volunteers, and while it's true some cabins are open for purchase, it's how we're funding the mission. A necessary evil; wealth and advancement have always walked hand in hand."

"But what about the reports that Earth's viability is limited?"

"Podcast nonsense," I retorted. "It's true there's studies that the sun is slowly expanding, but don't you think that if there were any real and present danger we would know? Besides which, it's exactly why this exploratory mission is so vital. We're too crowded, too cramped to continue to grow here. The re-plantation of so many to the ships will leave room for the next generation, and the plans my father leaves for the Infinity Engine and ship designs will ensure future generations can follow us if they wish."

"And what of the accusations that this is not in fact an exploratory mission, but an exodus?"

I opened my mouth to answer, but Antoinette beat me to it. Her burble of laughter was so authentic, I almost believed it myself. "An exodus, really Crispus? And what are we fleeing from? Don't you think the population would know if there was anything untoward happening? Manson Enterprises is government-contracted."

He smiled back at her, leaning in just a little. "Don't blame the reporter, Miss Manson. The question had to be asked."

"Did it?" She replied, but there was humor in her voice. "And please, call me Antoinette. There have been conspiracy theorists throughout history and largely they've been wrong. This is no different."

"Well and true," he admitted. He dropped a hand to her knee, and leaned closer. It was casual-looking, almost innocent. As if he were a confidant and the crowd wasn't watching. "If there's no comment from Manson Enterprises on the mission, maybe you can assuage our curiosity on another front. Everyone wants to know about the wedding and you've been so secretive... will you give us an exclusive, Antoinette?"

She laughed and with a wink replied, "Maybe, but it's hardly an exclusive if we do it here... is it?"

He settled back, satisfied with the suggestion in her smile and Antoinette led him merrily down another line of conversation. It was easily done, as I predicted. She always did know how to play a fool.

#

We sat silent in the hover after the interview. Antoinette clicked expensive heels against the floor. She was lost out the window again, her face in an easy repose.

"What happened?" I asked. The question that burned on my tongue for years, the question I choked down again and again because I couldn't -- wouldn't -- face her derision over asking.

It sparked life into her.

I'd seen her mocking and cold many times over the years. I'd seen her bitterness and her derision; all the things she held from the world, she held for my view only. I suddenly realized that I'd never seen her angry. Not like this. Her shoulders tensed. Graceful and delicate, they clenched hard enough I thought she might shatter. Her jaw clicked, teeth ground together then released. It was fascinating. Then she relaxed and when she turned to face me there was nothing but easy mocking in her eyes.

"What do you mean, darling?"

"Don't play games, Antoinette. What happened while I was gone?"

"Which time? You're so rarely around these days..."

"Fine," I snapped. "Don't tell me if you don't want to."

She laughed. She mocked me. "So easily dissuaded? You don't want to know. You're happy in your ignorance."

"I wouldn't ask if I didn't want to know. What happened to the girl who used to laugh without irony? What happened to the Antoinette who wanted to run this company?"

The hover stopped, it's engines idling as the driver waited for us to step out. Neither of us moved.

"You really don't know..." It was almost a revelation to her. "All these years, I thought you wanted to be ignorant, but no. You really are clueless."

My stomach twisted at her words. All those times that we'd paused in our animosity, when she'd looked at me with expectation, waiting for something. She was right, I wanted to be ignorant. I reached a hand out to brush hers. "Tell me."

She flung the door open, following it as far from my touch as she could get. "Don't. Don't suddenly pretend you care just because we're marrying." There was a disgust in her voice that I couldn't countenance. I knew our marriage was a charade, a joke to her. My father's grand plan for Purity after Earth. A new life, with a new set of genetics; a Pure set of genetics.

It was always his idea, his vision for the future. His children, raised by him but not related, groomed for their place in the Empire he was building. We always knew we would be wed one day. We'd never talked about it, but she'd never sounded like that before either.

"Do you not want to marry me?" I asked. It was the first time I thought to.

"Does it matter?"

"Of course it does. You've never said you didn't want to."

"And you've never said you don't want to run the damn company. Who is going to stand up to him? Who is going to say that we won't marry and breed him an army of Pure heirs? You?" The way she said it made her thoughts on the matter clear.

It stung that she wasn't wrong. "If you want me to," I said quietly. "I won't force you into this, Ann."

If the use of my childhood name for her had any effect, she didn't show it. "And then what?" she asked. "If you don't marry me, where does that leave me?"

"Running the company by my side." I was surprised she thought she would end anywhere else. "The way we always planned."

She shook her head. "That was never the plan."

"Of course it was."

"It was our plan, never his. Why two children, Anthony? Why a boy and a girl?"

"Because mother wanted two."

"Mother wanted whatever he wanted. You're so stupid. You think he made this to run his damned company?" she gestured at herself, sweeping her hands over her body with disgust. "You think he ordered this to be made, so I could sit in a chair and order around men? That's not the point of a pretty body, is it?" Her voice descended to a hush, "Not the point of breasts or hips or a finely curved ass."

She shook her head at me again. "You never understood it growing up.

Gods, you're lucky that he's old and has to die someday or he wouldn't need you either. You think he's spent all these years mourning mother? Some old woman who was as defective and diseased as him? You're lucky perfect genetics are his plan or he'd be as liable to plant his seed in me as to let you. And you think he'll let you waltz in there and tell him that you don't want to run his company but I do and he should let me? You think if you tell him that you're not going to father his perfect generation in the perfect fucking incubator that he made you, that he'll just nod and say 'OK, son, whatever makes you happy'? You're an idiot, Anthony. A fucking idiot."

I backed away step by step. The bile in her voice poured over me, washed into my ears and down through my gut. It boiled in my stomach until I thought I'd be sick and I remembered the way his gaze lingered on her and her comments about my friends. The perfect laugh when she let Crispus touch her and she steered him away from the conversation we didn't want to have. My father's voice echoed in my ears, And if they ask uncomfortable questions, let Antoinette handle it.

I wanted to tell her that she was wrong. That I wasn't an idiot and that father loved her as he should love a daughter, and me as he should love a son. She huffed at me, rolling her eyes. She turned and walked away. I hurried down the corridor after her. I wasn't ready to let this argument go. I wasn't going to let her brand me with the same label she did our father. I wasn't him.

"Antoinette!" I yelled after her.

"You're back already? Come in here, boy." Father called as I passed his office. I paused, hovering between him and the retreating backside of my fiancée. "What are you two arguing about now?" his voice carried down the hall and she stopped. Neither of us dared to ignore his summons.

She smiled sweetly when she turned and retraced her steps towards me. The bitterness was well concealed behind it. "A wedding date, Daddy. I want Launch Day, but Anthony thinks it's too much of an imposition."

"Launch Day!" he coughed the exclamation. "Wonderful idea. Capital!"

I stared at her, taken aback by the sudden turn of topic. Before I could think of the right response, she continued.

"Wonderful. I'll give you the list of personnel. Officiant, photographers, caterers, florists, stylists, and of course the guest list."

I spun around, aghast. "Antoinette, you cannot be serious."

"And why ever not?" She blinked at me with perfect blue-eyed innocence. The look she gave me when she wanted me to hurt.

"Every person we add is a person that has to be removed from the lottery. This is... it's... it's inhumane. How are we to choose who gets left behind? And what about families? Some of them may have families here or on other ships. This mission isn't exploratory, Antoinette. It's an exodus."

She chuckled. "Of course it is, darling. And those lucky enough to participate in our nuptials, should be blessed with life, don't you think? Our gift to the common population."

I glanced at Father for support, but he was eying my sister appraisingly. "Will that suit then, my dear? If your perfect wedding happens on Manson Enterprises' flagship with a view of the Old World as your backdrop?"

She tapped a manicured finger against her porcelain cheek as if thinking about it. It suited her, of course. People's lives rearranged to fit her whim, chaos at the flick of her finger.

She liked it.

"Father," I turned to appeal to him, "You can't honestly be considering it."

"Why not? The lottery winners are just that... from the lottery. It's all luck and chance anyways and most of them are poor. They won't be able to afford to bring their families. Maybe it's best if they stay. We're taking a difficult choice and making it for them. If they knew, they'd probably thank us."

Next to him Antoinette was nodding. Her voice was sweet, but her eyes hard as she said, "We'll have to be sure to invite your college buddies, Anthony. You'll like having them close after the nuptials."

"And their families," Father added. "The more Pures the merrier, I always say!"

She walked over to the windows and looked down. Hundreds of floors below us people walked beneath UV panels. They blended into each other, the polyblends, the commoners. I knew she was angry. I knew she was bitter and for the first time I understood why. I could even understand how she ached for control over something, when control over her own life was so thin.

I tried one last time. "You're playing with people's lives, Ann. The people who you force onto our ship, they'll never see their families again. And the ones who could come, but get left behind... what of them?"

She stared down at the UV panels, down at the people so far below her; common polyblends with so much more in their lives than she'd ever had. Anyone else might have thought she was being playful or didn't know the weight of her words. I wasn't fooled though, I knew my twin. Viciously smart and honestly, just vicious.

She waved her hand at the window dismissively. "Honestly, Anthony, who cares? Let them eat cake." Antoinette grinned at her own quip as if it were a great joke between us and with a wink she added, "Wedding cake," and walked away.

LONGLIST
CAKE
by Virginia Ballesty

Virginia Ballesty is a writer based just outside of New York City.
She works in the city in marketing and writes in her in-between hours.
She originally wrote "Cake" for an Apocalypse themed anthology, but at the
end of the day couldn't bring herself to write the destruction of Earth. It sat
on her back shelf for years until Exit Earth. The minute she saw the anthology
theme, she knew it was a perfect fit for Cake. She has one other short story
published in the Almond Press' anthology "Broken Worlds." When she's not
writing, she likes to climb, hike and generally enjoy the outdoors.
You can follow Virginia on twitter at @Vballesty

AFTERWORD

One of the things I love about short stories is you can give this intense and intimate snapshot of a person or a conflict and then just as quickly it's over - leaving what's next up to the reader. Although Cake ends on a down note, there's so many possibilities still open. Sure, maybe nothing changes and Anthony and Antoinette follow their father's plans through, *but what if they don't?* What if a tragedy befalls Manson Tower, taking the family with it? Is it an accident, or the act of an angry population? What if it compromises the ships and the plans, as well as the Pures living in the tower? Could one act of fate, or of hate, destroy everyone's chance to escape?

But what if instead, Anthony defies his father? He steals the Infinity Ship plans and puts them in the hands of a polyblend engineer. When he finally leaves Earth, it's not as the heir to his father's doomed empire, but as a member of new Earth. What if in his absence, Antoinette overthrows her father and takes the Pure's fleet over? She becomes the brilliant leader she was always meant to be; she never learns to be soft, but she does learn to be fair. Does her leadership change the misogynistic culture of the Pures? And what if the fleets meet in the distant future? Are they doomed to pick up where they left off, or instead do they finally find what they need in each other; the Pures have the provisions and the resources, but the Polyblends have the genetic stability and strength. Does leaving Earth leave room for redemption?

Personally, I'm a fan of the last scenario. I like to believe that hope lies in people's ability to make a different decision tomorrow than they did today.

I know that lends the question; if that's the ending I like to believe, then why isn't that the story I wrote? Truthfully, Cake is a far cry from my normal fare, which tends more towards the optimistic than the doom and gloom future I portrayed here. I sat on this story for a long time trying to figure out exactly where it came from and what it meant, until I finally submitted it to Exit Earth. Since that submission, I've had several emails back and forth with Storgy on the themes and the meaning of Cake. Through those conversations, I was finally able crystallize where it all came from.

It's no surprise that short stories are reflections about many things; hopes, dreams, possibilities, fears – and that Cake is largely about fear. What is the next step for a world where *Black Lives Matter* is met with *All Lives Matter* (completely ignoring that white lives aren't at risk)? Where the Trump Presidency – the Presidency that my country somehow elected – screams from its pulpit about Muslims and terrorism and fake news, until it becomes just noise. Welcome to the new status quo. Where birth control for women is less important than controlling women. Where our bodies and the rights to them are just another subject for debate. Where sexual assault and rape are still the fault of women, because we shouldn't [wear those clothes, be in that part of town, talk that way, exist].

Antoinette is indisputably the antagonist of the story, and even Anthony is debatable as a protagonist, yet in a dystopia full of fears (sexism, racism, hate), these are the fears that I can speak to personally, viscerally: that even as a woman who is educated, affluent, and admittedly privileged, I can still be disenfranchised. That someday the only descriptor of me that might matter is woman, and that there are already extremists in the US and outside of it that do not hear equal, when they hear female.

However, Cake is also an acknowledgment that there are other fears. I cannot speak in the same visceral fashion to the fear that a person of color feels when they are pulled over by a cop. To the fear of a Muslim when they are aggressively approached on the street or the subway, or the fear of the LGBTQ community that all they've fought for in the past decade could be taken away in little less than 4 years' time. These are not experiences I can claim, and I wouldn't want to presume to do so – however they are present in Cake to the extent that I could make them in 5,000 words because they are no less valid for that. The fear is no less present, no less connected to the same fears that I feel and the culture that is driving so many of our problems today.

Cake is a dystopia based on what may happen if the worst of the worst prevails: a world in which not all white men are bad, but all white men still reap the benefits of a system rewarding race, gender and sexuality. And that you don't have to be bad to participate – you just have to be silent.

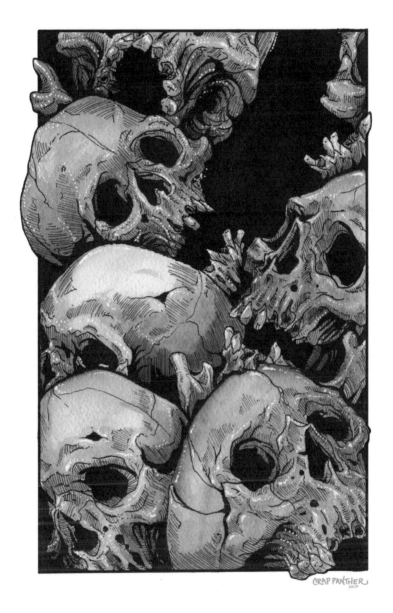

Illustration by Crap Panther

FALLOUT
by Michael Bird

I was looking at the houses on Harcourt Avenue. They had arched roofs and were divided into two homes, with a tiny fence between. People called them semi-detached and would say: "I live in a semi-detached". It was like they were willing to lend half of what they owned to a neighbour. All my friends lived in a "semi-detached". If you lived in a "detached" you were rich and mean, and if you lived in a "terrace" or an "estate" you were poor. I had nothing against poor people, but they weren't my friends.

I had never really looked at these houses before, because they were just there, weren't they? Why take an interest in something that never changes? Because it *had* changed. After I saw that film last night. Now I wasn't sure these houses would be here much longer. And I missed them. I was looking at them, and I missed them.

Walking up the drive to Ginny's, I rang the bell. Through the frosted glass of the front door, I could see the shape of her Mum. The door opened and she was wearing a plastic apron, loose white shirt and slippers.

"Ginny's not on top of the world today," said her Mum.

I needed to talk to someone. Ginny would understand. We had to get into a deep conversation. She came into the front hall, her jacket off one shoulder, the straps of her backpack falling to her elbows.

"Don't forget to take your lunch money," said her Mum.

"I don't want food," said Ginny.

"Why not?"

"Does it matter?"

Her Mum held out two shiny one pound coins.

"If I have to," sighed Ginny, yanking the cash from her Mum's palm.

We walked down Stanhope Road and over the zebra crossing to the crossroads at Eastern Avenue. Ginny kept her head bowed and her pace steady. I looked up at the sky. The bank of clouds a light shade of grey.

"Last night did you watch *Threads*?" I asked her.

"I don't want to talk about it," she said. "There's nothing more to say, is there?"

The film's images were echoing through my head. The grey blocks of Sheffield. Smoke from its factories. A man and a woman plan to have a baby. But their parents tell them they are too young and haven't been together long enough, so suggest the couple should have an abortion. At the same time, the

Soviets and the Americans are fighting over Iran. On the radio and TV the announcers talk about the "costs" for everyone, but they all carry on their normal lives. The sirens sound. Panic in the city centre. The people shopping and pushing their prams don't know where to run. The bomb drops. Sheffield is on fire. Britain is on fire. People are killed by falling buildings, or cry in basements, vomiting until they die. The Government tells everyone to "remain calm". There is a kid, Michael, who sits in the corner of an aviary, clutching his pet birds. His parents call him into a shelter made from a door and mattresses, but he stays with the birds. Days later, when they leave the shelter and walk through their collapsed house, they see the broken pieces of chicken wire and wooden slats of the aviary, covered in bricks and dust. From the rubble pokes out a leg, a foot, an Adidas trainer.

"Millions will die," I said. "70 per cent of the country."

"I've had it with mankind," said Ginny.

"We have to do something."

"What can we do?" she said. "Make a plan in the twenty minute break between Maths and Combined Science?"

"What if it was me," I said, "having that child?"

"You and Jakob Anthony?"

The name cut me.

"Shut up, Ginny!" I said.

"Tell me to shut up, and I will shut up. But silence won't help you. Won't help you and Jakob Anthony and your radioactive baby."

We arrived outside middle school, five minutes before our tutor group began. Bill was there. He was always first. With spikey short hair and a blue v-neck jumper, he was seated on a small brick wall with his head in his hands. Sandie - the biggest girl in our class - was standing, watching a space between the school buildings, where we could see down the hill to the new houses. Jane, her shorter and thinner friend, was walking in circles nearby. These two were always chatting together. But today it looked like they had been arguing.

Jakob shuffled over to us, his jacket sleeves rolled up, his tie loose, shirt out of his trousers, and his hair standing up in a wave. I was excited and nervous. Guilt. How could I feel desire when millions were at risk? He had come early. None of his friends were here. He had no one to speak to. Sandie was too weird. Jane too silent. Bill too square.

Just remember, I said to myself, you must talk to Jakob in complete sentences. Put feeling in your words, sound confident, and laugh at his jokes.

"What's up?" he said.

"Monday," I shrugged.

"The last Monday," said Ginny. "The last ever Monday."

I was sure Jakob hadn't missed *Threads*. His parents were teachers. I saw them at demos in the city square wearing donkey jackets and badges with a smiling red sun, surrounded by the words: 'Nuclear power? - No thanks'. I was about to ask him. But what did I think I was doing? Was this how to chat up boys?

"Ah," said Jakob, "you both saw that film, right?"

Yes! *Threads* was cool! I was about to say more, but Jakob kept talking.

"You know we just gotta make peace," he said, "make peace with the Russians, with the Americans, make sure everyone just starts getting on - because there's no other way, is there?"

"Peace is super!" I said.

Damn! This sentence sounded so pathetic! I had to add something else. Make another comment. A smarter point. Show to Jakob how similar we were! I could talk about Iran or even Libya. I could try at least. Before I could go further, Craig ran up to us and grabbed Jakob's scalp, messing up his hair.

"Stop it, you bender!" shouted Jakob.

Craig was broad-shouldered with a near skin-head, and talked with slow and precise words, like an adult giving instructions.

"Are you guys all coming tomorrow?" he said. "You gotta be there. You gotta support me."

We didn't reply.

"The trials! After school. Four PM. At the field. I'm playing left-back."

Jakob nodded slowly.

"I can do it this time. I can make the team."

"And what happens when you're sick?" said Ginny. "When you're throwing up your organs?"

The two boys were silent. They were looking at something behind us. I turned around. Alice Havers was walking past. Blonde hair in a pig-tail, her eyes dark, skirt a centimetre above the knee. She was always told off for pulling up her blouse and knotting it around her belly-button, revealing her flat stomach.

Now she untied the blouse, tucked it in her skirt and walked into the school building. Craig and Jakob turned back to me and Ginny.

"Like I was saying," said Craig. "Four PM. Tomorrow."

Our tutor group. Mrs Brooker stood in front with her big black curly hair and tortoiseshell glasses. Craig was leaning back in his chair listening to Jakob describe the plot of *Threads*. He was going "wooah!" and "wow!" and "will they repeat it?". Bill was sitting next to Craig, his eyes welling up. Before the teacher began to speak, he ran out of the room.

"Where are you going, Bill?" said Mrs Brooker. "It is time for the register."

The door slammed shut.

"He's crying in the toilets," said Jakob.

"Oh, I knew this would happen," said the teacher.

"He's only expressing himself," said Alice Havers, "about how we all feel!"

What - she saw the film? No. This wasn't possible. And now she was defending Bill? No one defended Bill.

At lunch break, we queued for the canteen in silence. I picked up a plate of luke-warm ravioli in tomato sauce. I sat down next to Ginny, Jakob and Craig, and stared at my food. No one else was eating.

"We have to look on the bright side," said Craig.

"Are you kidding?" said Ginny. "Isn't our fate clear to you?"

"It's not happening yet."

"But that makes it worse, doesn't it?" said Ginny. "When it happens, it happens. We get sick. We die. Hey-ho. That's what we expect. But until then... we have to wait."

Ginny pierced her meat pie with a knife, and watched the gravy pour onto her baked beans and chips.

She put down her cutlery, leaned back in her chair and folded her arms.

"If there's a war, you know what I would do?" said Jakob. "When that siren blares, and we have to stay at home, I would take my bike. I would ride it from Barrington Close to Western Road, down London Road and off to the new estate on Chipplefield Close. And there I would knock on the door of Alice Havers's house. And her Mum would answer. Or her Dad. He'd be home, I guess. And I would say 'Alice Havers - I am in love with you and I want to spend the last moments on this planet with you'. We would sit down on her roof and watch the horizon. It would be red. There would be planes flying across the sky. Maybe we would see the mushroom cloud in the distance. Over London. Or over Sheffield. And I would kiss her on the lips. She would respond. And it would be worth it."

"Oh God!" I said, my voice high-pitched. "You only think about yourself!"

Everyone on the table turned to me.

Blushing, I looked down at my cold ravioli.

"War," said Craig, "is a total bastard."

It was double English, and our tutor took the lesson. Sandie laid her head on her desk, and her arms covered her face. Jane was next to her, slouched and pouting. Bill was seated near Craig and his eyes were welling up again, while Craig threw his hands in the air, gesturing to Jakob that he didn't know what to do with his desk-mate.

On every table were worn and battered school copies of *The Silver Crown* by Robert C. O'Brien. Mrs Brooker held up a hardback edition, which she prepared to read aloud. I had the book open at the page we reached the week before. But others in the class were looking out of the window, or picking at the cover of the book. Bill stood up, pushed his chair back quickly, and ran out of the class without asking permission.

"OK people, change of plan," said Mrs Brooker. "We will not be reading *The Silver Crown*." There was caution in her voice, as though she was afraid of our reaction. "Today we are going to write a poem."

A groan rose up from some boys at the back of the class, but not as loud as when Mrs Brooker usually mentioned the word 'poem'.

"This will be different," she said. "We will not sit in silence for an hour and write our own composition. Instead we will do this together. We can only finish the poem if we all agree on a final version."

There were no complaints, as many of the less talkative kids thought they wouldn't have to do much. I didn't want to say anything more, but knew that because I had won a poetry competition the year before, there would be pressure on me to make a contribution.

"Because many of us saw a film yesterday that affected us," said Mrs Brooker, "the theme of this poem will be war."

I tensed up on the last word. It was as though someone had shone a light on my private pain. I wanted to help. I had ideas. But I also didn't want to burst into tears like Bill. Or get too angry. Especially around Jakob.

Ginny sat with her arms crossed. Her eyes staring in the direction of the blackboard, but not at the blackboard - it was as though she were looking at a distance far further than the wall. Bill came back into the room, walking slowly, his head down, his face red, and sat next to Craig.

"To me the first part of the film was more scary," said Jakob. "The fear. Before the bomb came."

"People began to realise what was going to happen, but they didn't understand," I said. "They were naive."

"They tried to buy all the food in the shops and knock down parts of their houses to build a shelter," said Bill. "Then the phone lines went dead. And the roads were closed."

"We have an idea," said Mrs Brooker. "Different things that happen. Different things that we lose."

"That could be the poem," I said. "A list of those things."

"Or," added Jakob, "we could make a list of what we lose before the bomb drops - and then a second list of what we lose after."

I looked around to Jakob, and smiled at him. He picked up a pencil and shook it at me, like a call to action. Ginny coughed and I turned back to the teacher.

"Who would like to offer some suggestions?" said Mrs Brooker. "You do not need to have seen the film."

The other kids shouted ideas. Buses. Trains. Cars. Shops. Pylons. Food. Supermarkets. Mrs Brooker told us to think smaller, that it did not matter how tiny this loss was, as unimportant things gain significance when they are put in peril. They act, she said, like a metaphor for us, and our own helplessness. We learned about metaphors the week before, so this was a chance for her to revise the subject. The teacher moved around the class to make sure everyone contributed - even Sandie, who shouted out something without raising her head from the desk. Alice Havers said the words "love between a man and a woman", and I saw Craig leaning back and nodding to Jakob. I was filled with rage. Why hadn't I said this? I was thinking it. I was. I really was. God - I hated her.

On the blackboard appeared a long list. It was so long that Mrs Brooker had to write the final parts in tiny letters, cramped at the bottom of the board.

What we lose before the war

School
Tinned food from shelves of shops
Bus routes
Fire engines
Confidence
Family ties
Electricity
Water
Gas
Dogs, cats (run away)

What we lose after the war

TV
Peace
Light
Heat
Hair
Skin
Milk floats
Faith in God (debatable)
Biscuits
Our lives (up to 70 per cent of the British people)
Flats, houses, bungalows
Cars (no petrol)
Hospitals
Government
Birds (dead)
Money
Flowers
Crops
Cuddly toys (burnt)
Love between a man and a woman
Babies (deformed)

"We can mix up this list with the statements the Government makes in the film," said Jakob.

"That is an interesting idea," said Mrs Brooker. "Can anyone remember the announcements?"

Some of us put on a posh and bland accent similar to the man who read out the weather forecast on the radio.

"*Remain calm,*" said Jakob.

"*In an air raid attack, you are better off at home,*" said Alice Havers.

"*Stay underground!*" I said.

"They didn't say that," said Jakob.

"It's what they did," I said. "They hid in the basements."

"That sentence wasn't in *Threads.*"

I didn't want to argue. No - I didn't want to. Not with him. I had only one comment to add.

"And you can remember every bit of the film?"

"Yes," said Jakob, "because it was very important to me."

He was so annoying! How I hated this! It was important for me too. Even more so! But I couldn't say this now, could I? It would be like I couldn't think for myself.

"*The symptoms of radiation sickness and panic are identical,*" said Bill.

"*Do not stay outside,*" said Alice Havers.

"*When you hear the attack warning, you must take cover,*" said Jakob.

Mrs Brooker asked us to help turn these single words into phrases that could become lines in the poem. Bill wanted something on religion, because he went to Church every week and knew about it. Jakob said that the birds were an "important motif" in the film. That was a cue for Mrs Brooker to teach us what a 'motif' was, which she liked doing. After that, Jakob kept talking. He suggested a line about birds who caught fire and died, and how a phoenix would rise from these flames. Mrs Brooker had to tell everyone what a phoenix was. Everyone except me - because I knew already. But then she told Jakob that, although she was pleased with his suggestion, she felt that incorporating the phoenix myth was "too imagistic" for this poem. Jakob sighed but didn't argue because, I think, he didn't know what 'imagistic' meant. Ginny was happy to get in a comment on how money didn't mean anything, while I wanted to say something about what would happen to flowers in a nuclear war. As soon as my idea came out, I could hear some of the boys wincing.

This was what Mrs Brooker called "our first draft".

The schools are closed, the shops are empty
The lines are down, the roads are blocked
The doors are stripped, the dogs have scarpered
Remain calm!
The birds do not know where to fly
Now the sky is full of fire
In the case of an air raid attack,
you are better off in your own home!
My skin is black, my hair is gone,
My son is dead, the milk float has crashed
The symptoms of radiation sickness
and the symptoms of panic are identical
Do we still believe in our lord?
Why hast thou forsaken us?
The horses have died, the hospital steps overflow with blood
And money means nothing anymore

Even if it did before
Those who can work have access to more food
And the more people who die the more food there is
And the flowers no longer reach for the sun
They wait, they wilt for it to come again

"I don't think the milk float works," said Craig.

"It was in the film," said Jakob.

"Even so, it seems a bit funny there," he said. "I mean - my hair and my skin are burnt off, a kid is dead, and then you talk about a milk float?"

"It is a contrast," said Mrs Brooker.

"*That's* why it doesn't work."

"No, no, Craig," said Mrs Brooker. "Contrasts are seemingly different things that work well together."

"But this contrast doesn't work."

Mrs Brooker looked at the blackboard for ten seconds.

"Is anyone especially attached to this milk float?"

Everyone in the class shook their heads. With a dirty white cloth, the teacher wiped it away.

We started on a second draft. Ginny asked to have her line changed. She said she wanted to get rats into the story. Mrs Brooker was sceptical about this, and rejected the idea as 'too graphic'. I thought I had to refine my line on the flowers, and Jakob asked if he could put his phoenix theme in once more, but as a metaphor. Mrs Brooker said that there were not many 'metaphorical' phoenixes in a nuclear war because nearly everyone died, so not only was the idea too imagistic, but it was also inaccurate. Jakob slumped in his chair and folded his arms. I had sympathy for him. I wanted to say: 'Poetry is about feeling, not accuracy', but I was still angry with Jakob for having a go at me earlier, so I shut up. Mrs Brooker cleaned up the lines, making sure they 'scanned' and had 'stresses' in the right places. At this point she didn't explain what she was doing. We talked among ourselves, although Ginny wouldn't say anything. She just stared at the blackboard. After five minutes, Mrs Brooker turned back to the class.

"We need a name for the poem," said the teacher.

I had an idea. I'd thought about it earlier and it fitted with the theme and the images, but also had another meaning. I was sure Mrs Brooker would like it.

"*How about Lost Property?*" I said.

"Interesting!" said the teacher. "I can see where you are going with that. Very clever."

"Call it *Fallout*," said Alice Havers. "You know what fallout is?"

Of course I knew. I wanted to put my hand up, but I didn't want to get into a debate with Alice Havers.

"My Mum told me," she said. "After the bomb hits, everything is on fire. But even if you escape the fire, you may not escape what happens next. All the ash and the dust that remains is radioactive. It's like poison. The wind blows this everywhere and makes the whole world toxic. But it's silent. You can't tell which dust and ash is deadly, and which is safe. Only if it rains do you know. Because fallout turns the rain black. Like the night is splitting apart and falling to the earth."

"What if we add that?" said Mrs Brooker. "*The night splits apart and falls to the earth.* And we need a line before, to set it up."

"We could say..." added Jakob, "debris shuts out the heat and light."

"Yes," said Alice Havers, turning to Jakob and putting on a serious voice. "That is very beautiful."

"*The* light," said Mrs Brooker. "Debris shuts out the heat and *the* light. This way the stresses fall better. And we can add it at the end."

No - what was this? They could add it where? Not after my line!

"I think it is a more powerful climax," said the teacher.

!!!

Mrs Brooker fiddled with a few more words and added a couple of rhymes to pad out the entire poem. She asked the class if she could get rid of the official warnings from the film as she felt they interfered with the flow. Everyone agreed, except Jakob, who muttered something about 'censorship' and 'fascism' that none of us really understood. While Mrs Brooker finished, the class started talking loudly again, except Ginny. She was leaning forward, her back arched, and was silent, examining the teacher at work.

Fallout

School gates are locked, the shelves they stand empty
All roads are blocked, we're told for our safety
We strip off doors, we hide in the darkness
The dogs run free, but us we are helpless
A sound, a light, birds know not where to fly
Now the fire up above fills out the sky
My skin is black, windows are all broken

My hair is scorched, our houses have fallen
Mother, father, do you still have the faith?
Now He finally brought forth such waste
Money means nothing to us anymore
If it even meant anything before
And the flowers no more reach for the sun
They wait in hope for it to come again
Debris shuts out all the heat and the light
Rain turns to black, as the summer takes fright
We fear the day, our heart, our life, and birth
When night splits apart and falls to the earth

"Well done, class!" said Mrs Brooker. "Give yourself a clap!"

As everyone put their hands together, Alice Havers was looking pleased. She glanced at me and began to smile, but turned quickly towards Jakob and Craig. Bill was grinning through his tears. Sandie perked her head up and was looking at the words on the board. Only Ginny wasn't clapping.

"I don't like the last line," she said, as the applause petered out.

"Everyone else seems satisfied," said Mrs Brooker.

"I don't like it."

"So what do you suggest?"

"It's those words - *splits apart* - it doesn't fit."

Mrs Brooker looked over at the clock on the wall. It was almost 3:15.

"Well you have to come up with an alternative," said the teacher.

"I don't have a suggestion," she said.

"Then we will have to leave it as it is."

The bell rung. Everyone slammed their exercise books shut, packed away their pens and pencils in their cases, and threw them into their bags. They raced towards the door causing a bottleneck at the exit.

I had put away my stuff in my backpack and was ready to join them, but Ginny hadn't moved.

"Come on," I said.

"I don't know how to change it," she said, "but it needs to change."

I looked out of the window, where the other kids were talking.

"Your homework," said the teacher, "is to come up with a better phrase than *splits apart.*"

Outside Sandie was standing in the same place as this morning, watching the houses on the hill. Then I saw Alice Havers walking towards the gates, Craig and Jakob either side of her.

"*Fragments,*" I said.

Mrs Brooker was about to say something. I think she wanted to tell me it didn't scan. She was right. But she went to the blackboard, brushed off the words *splits apart* and replaced them with *fragments.*

"No," said Ginny. "It still doesn't do it for me. In fact, there are more problems. *Broken* does not rhyme with *fallen.* The line on God is odd. There is no story. It seems to be a bunch of lines from other poems chucked together."

Mrs Brooker put down her piece of chalk and picked up her folders and the hardback copy of *The Silver Crown.*

"Well, it is the end of the day," she said, "and we have to go."

"You're giving up?"

"Only you seem to have a problem with this."

"Because the others don't care. All they want to do is go home and play video games, and watch football, and eat their chips and beans, and listen to their tapes and get off with their boyfriends."

"The class is over."

"But don't you want it to be perfect?"

"It is an exercise."

"It's more than that," said Ginny, "it's real - and we have to take it seriously."

"Like I say," said the teacher. "You can continue it at home."

"On my own?" she said. "You're leaving all this to only one person?"

"Ginny, it is just a..."

"Let it *annihilate* you all. It's all you deserve. This is why our future will be only ashes. Because of people like you. Saying it doesn't matter. It's not important. We'll leave it up to someone else to solve. Don't you understand?"

Mrs Brooker put down her folders and book on the desk, and moved over to the blackboard.

"Would you prefer me to get rid of every line?" she said.

"Yes," said Ginny.

"Wipe all this away because it is not perfect?"

"We should do that."

Mrs Brooker took a cloth from the tray and quickly erased the title, then the first line. As we made no protest, she cleaned away the entire poem from the blackboard, making sure the trace of every letter vanished. Specks of chalk crumbled to the floor, leaving a clear dark space.

"Then let us start again," she said.

LONGLIST
FALLOUT
by Michael Bird

Michael Bird is an award-winning investigative journalist and writer mixing multimedia elements, verse, lyrics and website formats into fiction.

Based in Bucharest, Romania and London, as editor of in-depth journalism site www.theblacksea.eu, Michael has revealed how Sky News publishes false and dubious content in east Europe, how football super-agents fix the player transfer system, how drug addicts shoot up killer home-made drug Krokodil in tenements in Georgia, why Romanians and Ukrainians prostitute themselves on the streets of Naples, and why the HIV epidemic continues to thrive across the ex-USSR.

His work has appeared in dozens of publications worldwide, including the Independent on Sunday, Politico, Tagesspiegel, Mediapart, Ukraine Today, Design Week, the New Statesman, EU Observer, the Daily Express, Business Insider and Deutsche Welle TV, and he contributes regularly to BBC Radio 5 programme 'Up All Night'.

https://michaelbirdjournalist.wordpress.com/

AFTERWORD

In the 1980s - before videotape was widely used - sometimes over ten million people in the UK watched the same television programme at the same time. This was a collective experience undertaken privately in people's homes. The morning after, almost everyone in the office, factory break-room or at the school gates would speak about what was on TV the night before. No one needed to catch up, and no one held back on revealing spoilers - because you had either watched the show, and were part of the conversation, or you hadn't, and had to hope for a repeat.

Mostly the viewers would try to remember the lines of a comedy, or talk about the issues raised in a cop drama, or the shock revelations of a news investigation - but in 1984, the BBC broadcast a domestic drama about a young couple in Sheffield on the verge of marriage, called Threads, which descended into a graphic expose of nuclear war, spotlighting the visual horror and social disintegration of a potential holocaust.

This film shell-shocked a nation - and disturbed a generation of children. *Fallout* dramatises a group of teenagers' reaction to the film, but also how they manipulate this response for their own selfish ends. I wanted to show how the impact of a terrifying future could be integrated into the politics of the playground, with characters torn between their own personal desires and their fears for humanity.

The execution of the story faced two challenges: capturing a plausible teenager's voice from the 1980s, and building a narrative tone that was engaging and upbeat due to the misery of the subject matter. John Hughes, writer of The Breakfast Club and Pretty in Pink, and John Green show that integrity and respect are key to embodying a young voice. While Green's characters may be too precocious for some readers, he never patronises their thoughts, nor attempts to build an argot based on the fashions of the moment - with few superficial exceptions, kids have spoken the same way for the last fifty years.

For the story, I needed a tone that wasn't portentous - it had to be intimate, funny and uplifting - even in the face of impending disaster. So while I was writing, I pinned post-it notes to the top of my computer which read 'NO DYSTOPIA' and 'MORE JOKES'. In order to bring comedy and tragedy to a mundane setting such as a high school, the best writers to read are those who reveal the absurd and grave in the everyday - and for that, Anton Chekhov is instructive. On a grander scale, Roberto Bolaño is never afraid to encounter disaster with wit and irony, and the reader of his work is unsure if they should be laughing, crying or scared. This ambiguity of intention is key to creating a compelling narrative.

These 1980s fears have relevance today - as nuclear catastrophe no longer seems a relic of the Cold War, but a possible outcome of an unstable geopolitical battle between world leaders prone to egotism and nationalistic fervour. Now we see a new generation downloading 'Threads' from illegal torrent sites - and an audience revisiting the issues at the core of the movie, as the cold brutality of its message and imagery illustrate a contemporary paranoia.

Illustration by HarlotVonCharlotte

KEN
by Jessica Bonder

The white man with dreadlocks down to his butt asks if I can take his picture next to the effigy. I say sure, of course, I mean, it is *my* effigy. It's the least I can do. He unstraps the Polaroid camera from around his neck and hands it to me, jogs back apace, shouts at me is this good? Meaning: Is the effigy in the frame of the shot and also him? Not: Is it cool to be immolating a black pregnant lady, granted she's papier-mâché? I yell yeah no you're good, maybe a tad close, and I point to the point on my own butt where his dreads would end if I were him, like: Careful with the long hair, mon, don't catch it on fire. He nods/ understands, takes two massive strides away from the flames, shouts now we good? I give him a highly visible thumbs up, as in: Yes, Mr. Rastaman, now we good. I click the red button. The square tongue of film spits out. I pinch it along its thick white edge, the safe space at the bottom, sparing the memento's tender field.

I snap shut the camera. Shelve it atop my belly, boobs like bookends, holding it snug. The strap, I don't even need it. The added weight, it barely registers, like one of those symbiotic birds on the back of a rhinoceros. Eight months in, I'm huge. I look at the photo, undeveloped. Mucus clear. Hard to believe. Hard to believe anything will come of this. That from a void can emerge a mass. Or, what is a fetus I can't justify.

"Hey thanks!"

"No problem."

Mr. Rastaman jogs back, plucks the photo from me, then does a flamingo pose to pick something sharp out of his bare heel. Glass shard? Hypodermic needle? How can anyone go barefoot in Veterans Park, or, what is a tetanus shot for $200 Alex? Turns out to be a bottle cap, which when dislodged leaves a temporary tattoo, a ghost-white circle impressed upon flesh. Later getting corn dogs, Ken-that's dude's name-Ken tells me he doesn't believe in tetanus shots or any shots, certainly not those administering vaccinations to children he doesn't have. No children that he can conceive of, anyway. His swimmers can't swim. So long's you're clean, Ken goes raw dog. As far's his corn dog, make it the vegan.

"So how's it feel being America's most hated War Mom?" Ken says, shaking his Polaroid picture like it's a Polaroid picture. Like that song by that guy from eons and eons ago.

"It's a blessing," I say, rote, as I have been trained. War Moms like us've got a script. An arsenal of rehearsed answers for every imaginable question, every foreseen criticism. Boilerplate. This is what they teach us at The Center: Human beings think in patterns. Behave in sequences. Force of habit. History dictates. Nothing like the weather, consider mankind a two-headed coin. 100% predictable.

Take Ken.

Floored by my feel-good answer, just as I expected, Ken twitches, his face does, his reaction: gobsmacked! Like he just watched that video of that cat doing that trick. With the wee foam basketball? With the wee plastic hoop? Whilst wearing the wee blindfold? You know the one. You watched it at the office, you snorted bad coffee, you minimised the screen when Jerkface walked by.

This is what I mean, what we learn at The Center. It doesn't take a mind reader. Ken is like all the other Kens. Most of whom are here today, protesting me. The others-are not. Are at home, watching me burn on TV, like that Yule log at Christmas. Which is fine. I don't need to meet every Ken. I've seen the binder, read their profiles. I can know them without knowing them. That is what is funny. That is what is sad.

"Look, I know we're on different sides and everything but wow. What a great attitude!"

I say thanks, that means a lot to me. No really. It does.

"Yeah, I mean. I don't agree with what you represent at all, like not even in the sense that you're sacrificing for your country or whatever, but it's like hey, way to keep it positive!"

I say thanks, that means a lot to me. No really. It does.

"Like for you to even come out here today? Mad props."

Ken offers me a fist bump, all, look at us over here, building bridges! I accept, raise my knuckles to his, and play along. Otherwise he'll call me bitch. That is a Standard Response. Another is him staring at my chest. Oh silly me, his camera! I hold it out to Ken like, here take your shit, I don't want it. To free up his hands, Ken bites the photo, baring horse teeth, long and yellow. Dentists pushing fluoride, that's a conspiracy, too. Sedates sheeple, is the gist of it. Keeps them shopping, keeps them dumb.

Ken's full of theories. I'm sure I'm one of them. He could explain me to me.

Ken takes the camera. Checks it over like I did something to it. Casually wipes it with an edge of his flannel shirt. Snaps it open, polishes the aperture with a fully covered elbow. What I want to say is: Don't worry, homes. What I've got's not contagious. What I decide is: Don't. Just follow protocol. Pretend you're dead. Makes life easier.

Ken slips the strap around his neck, like a nylon noose. That's exactly how

I imagine it, a noose. Then I imagine a chair. A hard-backed chair, ramrod spindles like prison bars. Then I imagine Ken's dirty feet on it. Then I imagine me kicking it over, over and over. The chair. Then I imagine the hangman's not Ken anymore but me, me and the unborn, strangled. At the last second, the roles have reversed, the floor drops out, and there's nothing I can do.

A day at the park and this is where my mind goes.

"You okay? You don't look so hot."

"I think I need to sit down."

"Here, let's get you to a bench."

I feel upside down. Nauseated. Dizzy. This has been happening a lot lately. The intrusions, the swings. It is wrong to blame the incubation. To curse chemicals, hormones. I know my own body. This is something else. This is what I tell my Spiritual Adviser. That there is something growing inside me that is not the obvious. That I am starting to cultivate doubts about The Calling. That sometimes, I am ashamed to say, I slip into fantasies about breaking contract. About aborting the mission. About leaving The Center for good.

I'm scared. Scared of myself. Of my own potential. Just really, really scared.

My Spiritual Adviser says relax. My Spiritual Adviser says this is Normal. What *wouldn't* be Normal, my SA jokes, is if a War Mom *didn't* have thoughts like these! Haha! His point is, don't worry, all War Moms get this way. Feel real feelings from time to time. It will pass, believe him, a lab coat with a clipboard. He says have you been taking your Freogans. I say yes, all of them. Even the ones that make everything worse. Even the ones that do nothing at all.

Hmmm.

He reviews my chart. Says excuse me, he'll be right back. Leaves the room to consult with his supervisor. His supervisor, who I know is out there but cannot see, stands behind a two-way mirror, fashioned with lace curtains to create the look of "window." Lipstick on a pig, it's not fooling anybody. Two hours later, which I apply toward a vertical nap, my SA returns with a suggestion. Maybe the answer isn't more Freogans. Maybe the answer is I need to be reminded of just how bad things have gotten out there. Of just how few options exist for a person like me. Of just what horrors await should I decide to renege. Then maybe I will be more grateful. For The Center and all it has done for me. For giving me a reason to live, lead-free water to drink, Free Refill Fridays, etc. etc.

What do you think.

What choice do I have.

The answer is none.

Choice is an illusion.

My SA tugs my earlobe. Tells me hold still. Tags me with a permission chip to leave The Center. Ow. Eight hours, 9 - 5, a standard workday, that's all I've got. To execute the itinerary. To get an attitude adjustment. To wake up. My big day out, it's all by design. If time expires and I'm not back at The Center, my crystal carriage reverts to pumpkin. My dress to rags. My slippers, paper bags. In other words, my brain will explode.

It will not be pretty.

The product, though. The product will be saved. Will not go to waste. That would be stupid.

Upside is, I'm prepared. Can finally put all this training to good use. Who says it isn't practical? That wouldn't my Cultural Sensitivity Certificate make a great coaster?

"Check it out!"

Ken's sitting next to me on the bench we found, away from the crowd, beside a trashcan. There are soda bottles and bees. I forgot how much garbage the world is. Ken's excited. Ken's all about his photo. Colors! Shapes! See? It's him and the thing! Ken presents the image. He's not wrong, it's him and the thing. Ken and the thing that is more Mary Wilson to this mob than I am, the actual Mary Wilson. The actual Mary Wilson, they don't even see me. It's like I'm invisible. A phantom at my own funeral. Which, if I'm being honest, is what I'm used to. How people see me, how they've always seen me, even before I became a War Mom, is that they don't. Only when they need something from me, à la Ken. A photo or a sound bite, something quick and easy. They take from me and leave. Don't stick around to help. That would make them responsible. That would harsh their mellow.

A protest besides is way more funner. You and your friends can coordinate T-shirts.

"You should totally frame that."

"I know, right? God I love Polaroids. That whole digital movement? Nearly killed me."

This is why I became a War Mom. Why I was recruited in the first place. The War needs women like me. Women who expect no recognition. Women who, through no fault of their own, have nothing else going for them. Women who, in exchange for food and shelter and healthcare, consent to grow product exclusively for The War. The Center provides all the necessary materials; all you have to do is show up. Heavy sedation and a sharp pang later, and congratulations, you're filling the queue. Supplying The War with its future fighters. Everything starts early nowadays. Basic Training begins Day One. A snip of the cord and they're off to boot camp. Working on motor skills, assembling puzzles, guns. By age three, they're commanding drones. Dropping bombs. From their highchairs.

At The Center, they've got science down to a science.

Caveat is, in exchange for the good life, you have to promise. That you will never ask to see it. That you will never ask does it look like me, is it healthy, will it survive. That you will never ask, the one that took out that village, that hospital, that school, was it mine? Not even on your birthday, not even on your deathbed, if it is still alive, can you request to see it. You were given a job and you did it. There is a waiting list of women who would be thrilled to take your place. Lest we remind you. So don't ask. It was never yours to begin with.

But chin up, now. It's not all sturm und drang!

What *can* be yours, from the moment you sign the contract, is the life you've always dreamed of. A utopia, really, is what living at The Center is. Basic essentials, what some might call *luxuries*, are provided gratis. Or at least at wholesale. Let's just say, for things like oxygen, you will not be paying retail. Trust us, ladies. Life at The Center is not a fairy-tale. War Moms really can have it all. So heed The Calling today! Don't let dreams be memes.

Oh, GIF of Gene Wilder says, you haven't heard of The Calling? Let me show you the rock you've been living under.

The Calling is what they call it, this keystone of the War Mom brand, this selfless gift we give of ourselves. Also referred to as "our service." They say it makes us noble. They say it makes us special. That for us select few, The Calling is more than a choice. It is not, as media pundits routinely suggest, "a last resort" or "a band aid on a broken system." No. The Calling is that most precious of all things, that undeniable psychic groundswell, just as the name suggests: a calling. What saints and professional wrestlers had, back in the day. For farming out our lady parts, The Center thanks us with, among a host of other bennies, a world-class salad bar with all the fixin's Tuesday nights. All-you-can-eat. I admit it was a selling point. One does not simply resist bacon bits.

That is one side. Our side.

Then there is the other side. Ken's side.

Ken's side says we War Moms are evil. That for us, women they've never met, The Calling most definitely is a choice. That it is never defensible. That it makes us completely selfish. Lazy, even. Get a real job, bootstrap it like everybody else, ever heard of Horatio Alger? What if I told you there are women who pump out babies just to live in a day spa? And not even organic babies, *artificial* babies, babies not even necessitating the participation of men! Babies that are then, oh the humanity, shipped off to The War! This is the kind of bullshit enterprise our tax dollars fund. That is why it must be stopped. Not The War, because that would send the wrong message, that we basically are a nation of weak-kneed pussies, and seriously what could be worse than that, but us. War Moms. We are the problem. We who represent the worst of all things: single mothers.

I look over the crowd, over pumping fists, banners, bullhorns like giraffe heads. There she is, my giant doppelganger, ten feet tall, ablaze. Ten feet tall, that's like two of me. Two Mary Wilson's half this country loves to hate. The other half, by their resounding silence, I can only assume means they love me. Seems that, best way to show support, is to act like no support. See something, say nothing, that's a true friend. The co-worker at lunch who doesn't tell you you've got broccoli in your teeth. The houseguest who doesn't tell you you're out of toilet paper. Until after you've grinned at your boss. Until after you've dropped trow.

Allies are the ones that let you take care of your own problems.

A strand of cindering newsprint hair breaks off Big Mary, alights on a breeze, snags a tree branch, ignites an oak. The park's lone deciduous. What a goddamn shame. Someone, I hope, is filming this. There are so few left. How you can tell, is the real ones are flammable. Which is why they're doing away with them. They're fire hazards.

"Hey, want to grab a corn dog? I know the folks who run the truck. They're good people."

Ken thinks we're friends now. Let's see how long this lasts. This poor man's kabuki.

"One sec."

I squeeze my earlobe for a time check. In my head, I hear a woman's voice. Alexa. Pleasant. Alexa pleasantly updates me, says thirty minutes and twenty seconds, is how much time I have left before I am due at the next site, down at the Pier, where another protest of me is happening right now. After all, it is a Saturday. The busiest protest day of the week.

Then a flash of ancient memory. Of when I was growing up, shuttling back and forth on holidays between multiple sets of parents. A child, then, could not be two places at once. The technology did not exist yet; for pregnant mothers, it still is not safe. Thus today I'm taking Ubers. The Center gets a discount. I don't know how much. I'm guessing 10%.

"So what's the T?" says Ken, who apparently knows about Alexa. Of course he does. Everything about me, Ken knows. Fair enough. It takes two to war.

"Sure. I'm game. Let's get them corn dogs!"

Ken says cool, stands up, looks down at me. Lends me his arm tentatively like: Do you want help getting up or? Make a decision, woman. This offer is time-limited.

Looking up at Ken, it's like, I've just decided. Decided that, for whatever time I'm Out-Center today, I'm saying yes to everything. Living like there's no tomorrow. Because as far as I'm concerned, that's a legit possibility. What have I got to lose? That plus I threw up breakfast this morning. As I do every morning. And here we are, almost lunchtime. The pieces are all coming together.

What I'm trying to say is, I'm fucking starving.

For what is a corn dog, I take the enemy's hand.

***

To my surprise and once again, Ken is not wrong. The corn dog folks, gotta give it to Ken, are good people. Nice couple. Jeff and Mark. The food truck, it's their baby. Before this, they were corporate. Rich but not spiritually. Existentially bankrupt. Yadda yadda. So they quit their jobs, went to India, saw a corn dog in the clouds at the summit of Mount Dunagiri, and all was decided. Now they're so fulfilled! So happy! Best thing they ever did! Sure, a shared sleeping bag under the deep-fryer is what they call home, and neither of them can afford to get sick ever, and if either of them does they're like totally screwed, but so what. Beats working for the Man. Who's the boss of them now, what what! They do all the major protests. Rallies. Parades. High profile crime scenes. They say hope to see me at the next one, check their website for updates. South Street, Philly, I think is what they said. Where they expect to be next. The Right to Life (Sometimes) March. They anticipate a mediocre turnout. Unless a celebrity shows up. Or dies.

"That's one classic and one vegan, coming right up!"

This is Jeff. Jeff is eager to help us. He and Ken go way back. Mark's in the back, cooking. Mark says hello.

"Either of you care for a sweet-n-sour? Mark brines them himself. On the house!"

Ken, standing next to me, raises a pierced eyebrow. It's infected, oozing pus. He raises his nasty brow at me like pretty sweet deal, huh? Being friends with me? Me being friends with Jeff and Mark? Ergo all us being friends? Ergo pickles on the house?

It is. It's pretty sweet. And sour.

I nod for a pickle, as does Ken, which pleases Jeff way more than it should. He's way proud of Mark's achievement. He serves us each a sizeable dill via 16 oz. Solo cup. The red frat party kind. We stand there and crunch, chat it up with Jeff, wait for Mark to make our corn dogs. To order, from scratch. That's what makes their concept so different. At The House of Dog, everything's

133

cooked fresh.

"Tasty, right?" Jeff.

"Very tasty." Me.

"Glad you like it!" Mark, unseen, from the back.

I don't get it. What the fuck is going on here?

I mean, I find the whole thing rather disturbing. These guys, Jeff and Mark, sure they're nice, but *why*? Why are they being so nice to me? More than baseline courteous, they're above-average approachable. Dangerously close to friendly. Their behaviour, as observed, does not abide the Restaurant/ Eatery Scenario. They've gone off script, gone rogue. It catches me off-guard. Makes me feel unprepared, vulnerable. This is foreign territory-no Standard Responses in sight! Where's the ignoring me? The helping others first? The hoping I'll go away, the I'm not their desired image, the I'm repelling customers with desired image by just my standing here, existing? You know, optics?

I mean what the hell. Don't they know I'm Mary Wilson?

I mean Christ on a bicycle. Complimentary mustard?

I mean oh right never mind. I'm with Ken.

"How far along are you? Looks like you're about to pop!" is Jeff forever later, handing me my finally ready corn dog. For which Ken offered to pay. For which I accepted. Which is also troubling. I'm starting to feel cheap. Like a sell-out. I don't even know who I am anymore. What happened to all my training? To my hard-won identity? Never *Trust Nice Guys*™- isn't that what my tattoo says? The one I got on Orientation Day? The one burned backwards across my loins, burned backwards as a courtesy? So that in the lavatory mirror, when I'm checking for mystery bruises, the message reads straight, reads correct?

"Eight months." I graciously receive the corn dog. I say this looks delicious. I hate myself.

"Oh that's awesome. Congratulations!" goes Mark's face, butting into the service window, revealed. Mark's wearing a hairnet. On his beard.

Jeff gives Mark a little push on the shoulder. Get back there, you. There are oblong meats to be battered.

Mark gets back there.

Ken shakes his head, chuckles, oh fellas. Gets his alternative corn dog direct from the source. Reaches up, says thanks Jeff - and Mark too, obvi! Raises it to me, a toast. To tearing down old walls until one of us offends the other, in which case, restore walls, reinforce with chunks of old walls. I take a bite of mine, a big, disgusting, self-loathing bite. I swallow the dog. Hold my breath. Wait for the truth to hit me hard. Wait for reality to punch me in throat. Tell me, just tell me: What do you motherfuckers want?

"You know, Mark and I have been thinking about starting our own family," is Jeff to Ken, and to me, sorta. Mostly Ken? It's not clear. Jeff, for all I know, could be talking to himself. It's not unheard of.

"A family? Dude that's so genius! I would *so* do that myself but you know. Motility issues." Ken tips his head down, down to where the problem is, his dangling excuse.

Jeff directs his gaze at Ken. Okay. Now I understand. Jeff's talking to Ken. I am no longer here. Got it.

"Why not adopt? That's what we're considering. Overpopulation, isn't that what you're always banging on about?"

The question hovers.

Wat do?

Ken gnaws his ersatz meat, goes mute.

Meanwhile, I'm going deaf. Alexa is screeching in my hear drums. She is no longer pleasant. She is super pissed. *Alert! Exceeded allotted time by full hour! Missed deadline for arrival at Pier! Uber rental suspended! Good luck getting taxi! Good luck getting taxi in this neighbourhood, you black and pregnant, haha! Alert!*

Did Alexa just say that or was that me, my thoughts, my conscience? So much confusion, such dissonance. I can't even hear myself think anymore. Not that I'm passing the buck; I forfeited that right long ago. Voluntarily, signed it away. Still makes no sense to me. To forfeit something, you have to possess it first. To forfeit something, means you stood a chance to win.

Alert! Leave now! Leave now! Alert!

Goddamnit. Goddamnit for believing I could live for today. For believing I could turn my life around. For believing I had agency. For believing.

No atheists in foxholes, used to be true.

Mark pops back into the service window. He just can't help himself.

"Yeah, like, maybe getting one from *your* country."

I squeeze my earlobe, hard. Alexa, please shut up. Please. I can barely hear the guy.

"Beg pardon, what did you say?"

Mark wipes his hands on his apron. Puts his hands on his hips. Guess he's done frying. For now.

"Uganda, amirite? Where you're from?"

A stillness as the words land.

They all stare at me. Mark, Jeff, Ken. They want a reaction. They want it big. There is an art to this. It is centuries old.

"Close. Chicago."

They all look at each other. Then together they all laugh. Then together they all stop. Synchronization, it's the only thing they've got going for them.

Ken hands his corn dog over to Jeff. Ken steps toward me. Ken grabs my arm. Ken gets real close. Ken breathes on me. His breath reeks. Like hot rot.

"Don't play cute. We know you're not American."

Inside me, the article kicks. Kicks strong, resists. I concentrate on the kick-spot. Concentrate on what I have left to feel. Nothing in this world is mine, even mine. I try to pull away. Say excuse me, I have to go. Please let me go.

Ken does not let me go.

Ken slaps my corn dog out of my hand. It hits the asphalt, splatters mustard on my shoes. The only shoes I have. The ones The Center issued me. Made in Bangladesh.

"Where's the birth certificate, bitch?"

I turn my face away. From Ken, from Mark, from Jeff. From my effigy crumbling in the distance, from hate signs everywhere emblazoned with my likeness, with drawn-in devil horns, with star-spangled swastikas. I want to go home. I want for nothing in this world. These fuckers can take all of it. I surrender.

"Yes. Uganda. I'm from Uganda. Born and raised."

I say this with the conviction that it is true. I say it like I mean it. I die inside. I look up.

Their faces. The expression on their faces. When I give them what they want. When I fully disarm them. Who are we to bully now? is the expression on their faces.

Ken, for whatever reason, releases me.

Not whatever. I know the reason.

I served my purpose.

Threw myself on the pyre.

I am free to go now.

I am free.

LONGLIST
KEN
by Jessica Bonder

Jessica Bonder is an American fiction writer. She has published short stories and prose poetry in The Stockholm Review, The Lonely Crowd, The Honest Ulsterman, STORGY Magazine, Split Lip Magazine, Black Heart Magazine, The Bohemyth, Vending Machine Press, The Fiction Pool, and Unbroken Journal. Honors include: Longlisted for the 2017 Berlin Writing Prize; Honorable Mention in Glimmer Train's Fiction Open (March/April 2017); Longlisted for STORGY Magazine's 2017 EXIT EARTH Short Story Competition; Shortlisted for Short Fiction Journal's 2017 Short Fiction Prize; First Place in STORGY's 2015 Short Story Contest.

Her website is www.jessicabonder.com. Tweet her @jessbonder.

AFTERWORD

Artist Cindy Sherman did a series of photographs in which she arranged female mannequin parts in pornographic poses. One in particular, *Untitled #261* (1992), served as a source of inspiration for my writing 'Ken.' It became a ritual: Every morning I'd turn to this image—its colorplate bookmarked in my tome of women artists—and place it beside me as I wrote. Confrontational by design, it is a work that holds no punches. The assembled "woman" stares out at the viewer—her glass eyes popping cartoon-wide—her body foreshortened and upside down; she has no agency; she is at the viewer's mercy. Important to note, the mannequin parts are not Barbie-doll smooth, the neutered variety of a department store dummy. Rather, they are anatomically correct prosthetics, the type used for medical instruction. *Untitled's* breasts have nipples, her genitals labia. One more thing: *Untitled* has no legs; she cannot walk away. As such, the image aggressively challenges the viewer, holds them responsible for the captivity of this nameless woman. #261, just another number. To me the artist's message could not be more clear:

Women are nothing if not their parts.

I thought about this. Thought about the politicization of the female body. Thought about it as disputed territory, as a point of conflict in a much larger war. A battlefield. Then I thought about motherhood, about its public perception, about its idealization. Thought about it in the Christian context, about Mary the mother of Jesus. Mary as martyr, surrendering her son to serve a higher power. Did Mary have a choice? Could she have said no? I thought about that. Thought about choice and free will and opportunity. I'll say the word again: agency. How much agency does a woman have in America—and not just any woman. A not-rich, not-famous, not-connected, not-white woman. A Mary Wilson. How many options for her, in reality, exist. How many options, in reality, for any of us.

Just how free are we as Americans.

Philosophical questions—spiritual existential nihilistic—drove my story forward, gave it bite. Add to these questions a host of words/phrases/concepts I'd collected in my notebook during these tumultuous times: safe spaces, virtue signaling, special snowflakes, identity politics, meme wars, deplorables, sheeple, nice guy syndrome, white knights, cucks, social justice warriors, mansplaining, red pillers, feminazis, libtards, man whores, get woke, intersectionality, silent majority, welfare queens, white privilege, keep calm and carry on, microaggressions, code-switching, protest culture, makers vs. takers, the end of men, slut shaming, truthers...

It goes on.

And on.

And on.

What I have humbly attempted to do with 'Ken' is compose a story that operates like Cindy Sherman's *Untitled #261*. That is, goes balls to the wall. Confronts the reader with the truth. Says it right to their face, fearless, no apology.

In other words, says it like a man.

Illustration by Amie Dearlove

AND THE WAVES TAKE THE WORDS
by Philip Webb Gregg

She saw the lights again last night, far out in the east. The boom rumbled across the water, something like thunder but nothing like thunder. It shook the sand, and coconuts fell from above. She hugged her knees until dawn, weeping- wondering if tonight was the night. But no. No, not yet.

Today she cannot remember her name. It's a strange thing, to have a hollow in your self. As if the searing lights had burned away that scroll in her head that served to give language to an otherwise illegible script. She senses that she is losing it. All of it. Blistering away before her eyes. Her name is only the most recent casualty in the long list of things that are rendered worthless by the flames and the rumblings in the night. After all, where is the use in a name if there's no one to speak it? No one to whisper it close, or scream it in rage?

It's the monotony that hurts most. The unshifting repetition of empty routine. At sunrise each and every day, she wakes and looks around her, checking that the world is still spinning. Upon reaching the surprising conclusion that yes, she is still alive, she uses the whacking stick to bring down coconuts from the palms, and feeds herself. Then she sits on the beach. For hours. And hours. And hours. Sometimes she swims, or does exercises on the sand. But mostly her gaze is vacant and her heartbeat is slow. Waiting and expectant, she is forever astounded not to be reduced to smoke and ash by the time the evening comes. Silently, she eats again, and watches the sunset.

She thinks how once this life would have meant bliss. How people would have paid vast amounts to experience this level of solitude and rich stillness infused with sunshine. A fortune's worth of boredom.

She hates it. Every hour of every day she wants to scream. Often she wishes she were dead. Several times she has tried to kill herself, but it's difficult- there are no rocks to leap off, no carnivores to taunt, or spiders to swallow. All that this tiny island has to offer are palm trees and sand. There is the ocean, of course. And if she had pockets she would fill them up with stones and try to sink, but she doesn't. And no matter how much she wants to, she can't bring herself to swim and swim and swim until exhaustion takes her. She just can't.

So she wonders about the old world instead, tries to remember all the little things that made it beautiful. Worthy of love. All the tiny details that completed the picture, interweaving like cobwebs between clockwork.

She does not think of grand events, virtuosos, or magnum-opuses. No Shakespeares, Mozarts, or Picassos crowd her thoughts. All of that is just gloss. Just cream on the surface of a successfully rotting culture. She does not miss it. Instead she thinks about the smell of fresh coffee after a night of really good sex. The texture of fruit, apples and peaches in her palms, at a market busy with bodies. The brilliance of a hot shower after a long day. Being touched, softly, on the shoulder, or the upper forearm. A casual intimacy. She wants to hold a wooden spoon in her hand and think about all the events that have brought it to that moment. The seed that fell, the plant that grew. The wood that hardened and was cut. The whittling, by hand or machine, carelessly or with love. Then the transport. All the middle men. And finally her, in her kitchen, with the radio on and the air thick with the aroma of food in the pan. She aches painfully for a supermarket, just to wander the aisles in seamless anonymity. Close, yet sheltered from the throngs. All the struggling shapes. And she wants so much just to listen to speech, or music. Any music. Just to hear humanity's desperate re-interpretation of silence. Anything but the sound of the lights in the night. Anything but that.

*

The first item to wash up on shore is, ironically enough, a boat. A plastic boat, less than a foot in length, cheaply made; the word *CHINA* stamped in raised letters across its keel. She tries to laugh, or to smile at least. To see the mad comedy in all of this. The absurd stab and twist of life. But she can't. It's too painful.

Instead she takes the boat up to where the sand meets the palm trees, and hammers it in. Nose first. So that it looks like a cartoon ship, drowning in a pantomime desert; impenetrable dunes extending out in every direction. *Beached.* It seems appropriate. But still, she doesn't smile.

Reaching for the stick that sits beneath the trees, she walks back down to the water, with something like an idea whispering in her limbs. There is a curious sense of urgency in her movements. She stops at the place where the sand and the sea meet and tumble and pull away from each other. That continuous battleground of intentions; a relationship. She contemplates the earth, touched by the ocean, made damp and malleable. Suddenly the solitude and the sight of the boat seem the most important things she has ever known. More than that, it seems like she has never known anything else. Her loneliness is bigger than the ground and the sea and the sky all put together. She grips the whacking stick with a firm hand, and begins.

Somewhere in the Jiangsu province of Eastern China, a young boy of Mongolian descent walks out of his first ever science lesson and wishes he could grow up to be a physicist. Though he doesn't know it, he is the last in a direct line leading all the way back to Genghis Khan himself- who conquered half the known-world, and is the genetic father of 0.5 % of the Earth's population. Though none have such a sure claim to the bloodline as this one boy, who will spend the next two decades working in a slum factory and starving himself so that he can afford evening classes. When he presses his stamp to the body of the plastic toys, he daydreams of steppes and equations.

The stick drops to the ground. Something like a smile flashes across her lips as she moves back to the palms. Behind her, the sea presses forward, and the waves take the words.

*

All of the things in the world. All of the terrible and heart-breaking things. Stories of starvation, pillage, and plague. Tales of war and rape. Narratives of simple human nature. The spine that spans the length of history, since modern consciousness fell from the trees or stepped out of the cold. No longer. All of it going, going. Gone.

She counts pebbles in her palm, trying to untangle the numbness in her body. Sometimes she tries to pray, to any god that might be listening. Pressing her palms together, she looks up to the sky, or down to the ground, or out to sea. But she never knows what to say, what to ask. All that comes to her tongue are curses and cruel words. Statements of blame and abuse. And this is not what prayers are for. So she says nothing, and closes her eyes. She thinks it might be different if she could remember who she was. Some details about her past – a slideshow of emotions attached to a memory. But there's nothing. She is an empty page. Vacant. A dead calm, untroubling the surface.

Yesterday a tire washed up, from a bicycle. A child's bicycle. The rim was painted pink and purple, but the salt had eaten most of it away. Her muscles shivered as she dropped it by the boat, angling its bent frame so that the one supported the other. A crutch, to keep things standing. Or a metal, one-eyed creature, with its tail in the sand.

Today a boot. A perfect boot. As if the sea had never touched it, it might have come straight from the catwalks of Paris or New York. It doesn't look expensive, but there is a certain elegance to it, a functionality coupled with aesthetic. She is almost tempted to try it on. But no. After a moment she adds it to the others and calmly picks up the whacking stick.

The child's name is Cindy. Her brothers call her Cinders but Cindy is her name, short for Cinderella- the princess. When she grows up she wants to slay monsters. At twenty two she joins the New York Police Department, and three years later a bullet thuds into her chest cavity with a sound like a large storybook snapping shut. As she lies on the ground, she notices for the first time the elaborate design on one of her shoes, which has come off in the struggle and is now soaked in blood. She has never seen anything quite so beautiful.

Again a feeling that she cannot describe washes over her. Pleasant, nostalgic, and intense. When she returns the stick to its place, her eyes catch the objects, and for a moment she feels like a duty has been done. Perhaps, somewhere in her heart or her limbs, she remembers. Meanwhile down on the beach, the ocean yawns, and the waves take the words.

*

There is something in her chest. Something desperate. It crawls up her throat most evenings and sits, keening, on her tongue. At night she watches the lights. They colour the horizon like ink from a madman's brush, bleeding frantically into the dark. Some shine white, while others buzz red and gold; fireflies dancing over the surface of the water.

She has collected a small pile of items now, gifted from the sea. She calls them her raft. She stacks them and re-stacks them in the sand, finding interesting positions for them. She isn't the slightest bit aroused, but she cannot escape the thought that they're having an orgy. That somehow these random objects are taking obscene pleasure in the discovery of new angles, new patterns of connection, holes to fill and protrusions to swallow. She laughs about it. Alone as she is, it is nice to hear human laughter resounding amid the trees.

Among the items of the raft is a jacket, so stained and disfigured it can barely be called clothing anymore. Still, she focuses on it, and soon she is strolling down the beach, and reaching for the whacking stick.

A man wears the same suit every day for a year. This is an extremist act. He showers in it, and sleeps in it, and goes on holiday to the Amazon still wearing it. He walks through the jungle in his once shining shoes, and swipes at insects with his briefcase. He is making some kind of statement. Something about modern life and the demands of the workplace. He is an artist. After a long and interesting life, he will die of a heroin overdose. And as his loved ones file past his open coffin, they will note happily the bright pink pyjamas which contrast starkly with the pale and scared flesh of his body.

One of her favourite items on the raft is an ancient pair of dentures. Gapped and broken by years of storms and rubbing shoulders with shipwrecks. She focuses again, and moves across the sand.

An old woman, mad and joyous, talks endlessly to her houseful of adopted cats. Her home is tiny, little more than a ruin, but she feeds them steak and Foie Gras; on the weekends she spends hours shelling oysters for them. She talks about the news, the soap opera, the supermarket. Anything and everything. She has never been kissed by a man. She is perfectly happy.

She stops, satisfied, and the waves take the words.

*

It occurs to her early one morning, as the sky is blinking; all of the beautiful impossible things. The stories, not just of fact, but fiction. All of the full-blooded epics and gentle misdirections of truth. The lies that maintained a more solid reality. Suddenly they spin and boil behind her eyes. All gone. Burning somewhere among the bodies. As the sun rises across a careless ocean, she quietly weeps.

A box washes up on the shore. Slight and black, as if for a wedding ring. When she opens it she finds a cluster of tiny crabs, each one a different tint of purple and brown. They scatter over her fingers like plastic beads from a broken necklace.

In a high-rise flat in central London, a man and a woman wake together after an exhausting and vigorous night of love making – they kiss and stroll naked through the many windowed rooms. They make coffee and eat pineapple, giggling as they push small slices into each other's mouths. He is nearly fifty years older than her. They are thinking of starting a family.

She sighs. Somehow, it is not enough. And waves take the words.

Sometimes she runs about. Kicks the sand, boxes with the trunks of the trees. She shouts and howls. She dances. Movement is a form of relief for her. She can almost feel how her bones hold together, marrow on marrow – remembering how to live. She envies them.

She is not young but nor is she old, her body moves well when it wants to. Naked from the waist up, her small breasts are hardly a nuisance. Laughingly she gives thanks to her genes for a slight bust. Her cycle is a different matter. Amazed that it still flows, and the sight of the blood still shocks her – a reminder that, against all the odds, she is still alive.

One morning she pulls a flag from a knot of logs and seaweed. It is impossible to tell which country it once represented, but she wraps it around the whacking stick anyway, and waves it- once, twice, three times, for comic effect. It is not funny.

On the outskirts of Istanbul, three young brothers break into a zoo with the intention of liberating the animals. They imagine the beauty and purity of all those wild bodies spilling free. The first falls into the bear pit and is mauled to within an inch of his life. The second is caught by the police, and for two weeks he is repeatedly raped and beaten in the prison house. The third, however, escapes, having freed nothing more than a pair of parrots. He will grow up to become a world-renowned revolutionary, and seek emancipation for thousands of suffering citizens. His brothers, however, will never forgive him.

Even in the day the bombs are falling. They drop with distant thuds and booms, like so many coconuts. She can hear them as she turns her back on the sea, and walks to her raft. Behind her the ocean remains impartial, and the waves take the words.

*

This cannot go on. She is reaching the end now, she senses it. The air has begun to glimmer faintly, like the sheen of old meat. It tastes different too. Hot and oily in her lungs. She knows she is dying.

It is an interesting thing. She does not miss humanity as a whole. Not in the slightest. Humanity was largely cruel and indifferent, to each other and themselves. No. What she misses are people. Individuals and instants, unique, caught in the spiral of time and place. Made faultless by a maze of imperfections. Like the scattered flotsam she pulls from the swells, ruined beyond repair and indomitably free. Because really, doesn't the breakability of a thing show its true worth?

The last item she lifts from the water is a sign. *WELCOME TO*, it says. Its lettering is surprisingly unfaded, but the name of the town has been scratched away by something blunt. She holds the sign in her hands for several moments. Sturdy, but not heavy, she is pleased by its shape. She begins.

There was a town famed for its boredom. Everyone who went there said the same thing. Boring- boring- boring. The locals agreed, and the tourist office made a roaring trade out of this interesting phenomenon. One day a brilliant comedian came to live in the town, and vowed to liven the place up no end, but he barely lasted a year. The locals murdered him.

Using the flag as a makeshift rope, she ties the sign to the end of the whacking stick. Together they form something like an oar. She smiles then, and laughs. And the ocean laughs with her, and the horizon flickers with death, and the waves take the words.

*

Her raft is an impressive sight. Roped and strapped with rags and rubber thread, it tilts and sighs in the afternoon sunshine. She has packed it full of coconuts and is ready to leave. Before she does she steps back onto the beach one final time, and after a moment of thought, starts scribbling in the sand with the butt of her oar.

She writes for a long time. A story longer and more complex than any of the others. Replete with nuance and human complication. Dialogue, action, love and death. All squabble for space in the soft sand. She is writing her life. As she remembers it. As she wants it to be. She writes her name at the end, then turns away.

On the raft, she rows, and the tide takes her. She sets out into the east, toward the lights, while back on the beach, the island is perfectly peaceful; no coconuts fall, no sand shifts, no one screams or weeps. A heavy stillness settles like a silent goodbye, and the waves takes the words.

LONGLIST
AND THE WAVES TAKE THE WORDS
by Philip Webb Gregg

Philip Webb Gregg was brought up among a subculture of activists, nihilists and travellers. His work seeks to question established norms, both in the conflict of the individual, and the wilderness of wider society. Love, madness and nature are all major themes, but the overarching pursuit is nothing more than honest storytelling, pure and simple and filthy and complex.

He has previously been published in such places as: The Molotov Cocktail, Fictive Dream, Flash Frontier and Reflex Fiction. His plays have seen stages in London and Cambridge. His poetry mostly only ever sees the inside of a notebook, though they have been known to escape their bindings, every now and then.

He is a student of Cambridge School of Art who gathers his inspiration from eldritch galleries and high mountains. The work of Murakami, Ali Smith, Gabriel Garcia Marquez and Angela Carter also hold a very strong influence on his life and words.

AFTERWORD

I was sitting in the passenger side of a car, and we were talking about getting lost. The driver, a good friend of mine, casually said that if she was ever stranded on a desert island, she would need to tell herself stories to stay sane. It was one of those moments when an idea actually seemed to come alive in the space behind my eyes, like a match flaring in the dark, a striptease of writhing flame and charcoal. I searched frantically for a pen while the driver complained about bad map-reading and ruined compasses.

'And the Waves Take the Words ' is a story about stories. It's about the endearing qualities of our rancid species, and the strange things we do to stay sane in an insane world. I hope that it highlights the need for careful reflection in these careless times.

These days, we are bombarded from every angle by bad news and fresh catastrophes on a daily basis. As such, it's easy to be saddened or depressed by the magnitude of the global situation. But the truth is that the only problem is people, and as such, the only solution is people. If there is a will to change, then there will be change.

'And the Waves Take the Words' is a message in a bottle to anyone who needs it. It says: we are here. We are making a difference. It says: please be strong. The world is worth living for.

Illustration by HarlotVonCharlotte

EARTH 1.0
by Robin Griffiths

Sun low in the sky. A feeling of winter. Thin air and a pale blue backdrop upon which we are all reflected. Trees stripped of their warmth. I've learnt about Hygge from the Danes, but Earth winters can still be bloody freezing.

I wish I'd never volunteered for this mission, what was I thinking? Should have kept my head down, stuck to the Fast Track Admiral Program; why did I think I could save the Earth? No one here wants fucking saving. They want X Factor and takeaway pizza. Go back to bed humanity, here's your disposable life: Primark, Instagram, and Greggs. Get in your Ford Focus and drive to the packaging shop where if you're lucky you'll find some food amongst the plastic.

Earth 1.0 is drowning in itself, choking on its own vomit. The exponential age of shit.

'Ok Mags, we tried, we failed.' I'm finding this all incredibly depressing. 'Have you done Ship Check Protocol one through five?' I probably sound like every other officer at the academy, a bit posh, quite friendly.

'Yes sir,' says Mags in his high Remok estuary whine.

'And?'

'Well it's a good job I did it twice sir because Check five cocked up Check two.'

'Meaning?'

'I had to get the 3D printer to print out another 3D printer.'

'Well done Mags. So everything double checked?'

'Quadruple, captain.'

'So Mags...a year on Earth. What will you do back home?'

'I'm going to write a book and a screenplay, captain. "A Halçyonan's Year on Earth."'

This revelation feels completely congruent with Mags' personality.

'Also, sir, this spaceship alone is a fanny magnet, imagine when I'm a famous author doing readings and book signings at Stonewaters. I'll be beating them off with a shitty stick.'

Mags has always had a prodigious imagination. Earth women loved him. He's not exactly blessed with looks, short and hobbity, but the tales he span about intergalactic travel (which basically involves a lot of sleeping) had the girls magnetized. I was the captain for First Contact, but he was the rockstar.

I say, sighing, 'Shall we go, then?'

'Let's quit this crazy fuckhole,' says Mags.

We sit side by side in the cockpit, an opulence of brushed titanium, none of your used future. As I press the HOME button on the holotablet, a huge melancholia envelops me. We completely failed.

To activate the NovaNav requires both our biometric signatures, including pheromone detection, retinal scan and earlobe compliance.

'Cap'n Bob?' Mags sounds like a right pirate sometimes. But he also sounds quite serious at the moment. 'Why weren't they interested in saving their planet?'

I say, 'I think they thought it was too late,' as the NovaNav re-plots a route home avoiding toll wormholes.

Mags says, 'But they were so blasé about us even getting here. First contact and all that?'

'Too many sci-fi films I expect. Bloody sci-fi.'

I can tell by Mags' eyes that he's started playing a game on his internal net.

I say, 'Even President Amabo was pretty glib about it all wasn't he? I suppose they think Earth will just see out their own three score and ten.'

'But their kids?'

'Resigned to it. It's why none of them bother getting jobs and are constantly out of their heads. Impending annihilation has led to pure hedonism. Did you see the amount of drug and tattoo parlours? It's why they've legalised absolutely everything.'

Although it only really takes me to fly the ship, I wish I'd brought Patti along. She scares the shit out of me and I'm married to her. Bloody cutbacks. 2 crew maximum, and 1 had to be a Cosmic Support Officer, i.e. doing the same job as a fully qualified technician for half the pay.

Even on Halçyona, a Virtual Mirror Planet, we've envied Earth, jealous from a distance, amused by its evolution, like watching a child grow. The one thing we didn't predict was plastic. How Earth took to it. Plastic begat plastic. It was said that there was enough Lego alone on Earth to build a model of New York to scale.

Mags and I enjoyed some reverential tourism, although Glastonbury was a bit disappointing. It's a haven Halçyonans have always wanted to visit, once the cost comes down. Wait till I tell them it's full of shops selling Non-Potent Crystals, and drug addicts. I hope Earthers don't find the Full Power Crystals, which as far as I can locate are under a major international landfill site in Haiti. They could never handle the sheer brawn of them, and Earth 1.0 would be over even sooner.

'Come on Mags, stop playing with yourself and make me a cup of tea.'

'What sort, captain?'

'Blue Teal, please.'

I have this theory that Earth could avoid the logical conclusion of their rapacious behaviours, just, but it would take a massive cull. I have calculated that if 92% of humans were eradicated and global fuel, plastics, travel and waste were heavily restricted via an international legal body; Earth could stop and reverse impending Armageddon. Also with vegetarianism as a non-negotiable law.

So the question would be who lives? Well, for a start, no disabled, nobody over fifty, no adult who can't ride a bike twenty miles in two hours. Children of coding parents only. Invert the ageing population.

'Tea captain!'

'Thanks Mags. You know my Earthling Cull Theory? You can't ride a bike can you?'

'No sir. But I'm pretty good at pool.'

'Well you wouldn't make the cut. How would you feel about that; being culled for the greater good?'

Mags puffs air through his lips.

'Do I get a death row meal?'

'That's a good idea. What would it be?'

'Well, let me think.' It's surprising how much he sounds like an Englishman from the West Country sometimes.

'Arbuthian fried seagull, infinite cooked sky lettuce, and iced Günter plasma. Phwoar, I'm hungry now!'

'Well all we've got is Skoon porridge, so fill your boots. I wish we had a food manifester like on Star Trek. They didn't predict much right did they?'

Mags settles into the rarely used co-pilot's chair.

'No. Where are all the fit automatons wearing skin-tight uniforms?'

'Exactly. All I've got is you...and you're a scruffy bastard. Aren't you 15% female?'

'Technically sir.'

'So how does that manifest?'

'Well, I wear women's knickers.'

'What? I thought it was supposed to be a subtle behavioural divergence?'

'The knickers are usually quite subtle.'

I breathe in, deeply through my nose into my diaphragm. Mags is spinning in the co-pilot's chair, making laser noises. He really is a fuckwit.

'Should we give it another go, Mags? Try and persuade the Earth idiots?'

'They're never gonna go for it sir. A 92% cull? How will they police it, implement it?'

'We could offer to do it. Use the Dream Cannon. It would take five minutes, literally, particularly with the new semi-firmware.'

'These people voted a man that wears a Guinea pig on his head as the most powerful human ever. Do you think they are going to listen to cosmic reason?'

Mags picks his nose, observes his bounty and rolls it between finger and thumb until it is dry enough to flick back in to the galley corridor.

I sit silent.

'We could just do it anyway,' I say quietly.

Mags' eyes look wild.

'SIR! No! We haven't got the clearance for anything like that, the singularity law council would go mental.'

'But we'd be saving them from themselves and Earth would become a desirable holiday destination. A Planet of Outstanding Cosmic Beauty.'

We meditate on this for a moment.

'Fuck it,' I say, 'let's do it.'

To access the Dream Cannon I have to go through layers of security, but like all tech you just have to be tenacious.

Retinal scan. Check.

Thumb print. Check.

Voice recognition. Check.

Sphinctoral bypass pitch. Check.

For some reason I still can't access the software, and it isn't synced to my implant.

'Mags, do you know anything about this extra layer of security on the cannon?'

He looks at me reticently.

'I can't believe you're being so bombastic sir. And to quote word of the day, it's heinous. I don't want anything to do with it.'

'Ok, ok! Look I'm sending your moral aversion to it all on novamail now, by the time they get it, it will all be over. It is a sanction of my own doing. So, any ideas on the extra security?'

Mags looks pre-penitent. 'They did mention something at college sir, but I wasn't really listening. Something about neural access?'

'Ok. Thanks.'

I try to go through the system another way, rebooting my implant, resetting passwords.

Still nothing.

A message flashes up on the holotablet:

DREAM CANNON ACCESS
NOT AVAILABLE AT THIS SETTING

'There must be a way round it,' I say to Mags, 'there always is.'

'Oh so you've committed interstellar genocide before sir? This is a cataclysmic situation. It's not like that Earth film where he talks about shooting swamp rats on Tatooine - this is real!'

'Yeah, good film though.'

I tap a rhythm out on the knee of my space onesie. I wish I'd listened a bit more in those Space Ethics lectures. What was it Draagekreik said? The Universal Dictum: Needs of a planet outweigh needs of a species.

'Fuck it, let's do it!'

'You said that before sir.'

'Well let's really DO IT this time.'

I hold down the toggle switch on the Dream Cannon controls, simultaneously rebooting the holotablet, but this time I triple tap my net with an amygdala synapse. The Dream Cannon glows pink.

'Boom! We're in. We just had to use the most primitive part of our brain so the whole protocol, from basal cognition to hominids' highest ever tech becomes like a...like a...'

'A technical haiku sir?'

'Exactly! Wait a minute, what have you been reading Mags?'

'That Stephen Hawking geezer, the one that did a shamanic peyote ritual that transformed all his muscle tissue into brain mass. A heavy trade off but it worked for him. David Beckham did the opposite ritual.'

I feel something cold on my bottom lip and when I touch it I see blood on my finger. I've not felt this dizzy since I had that bout of space flu.

'Mags...I feel terrible.'

'Sir, your nose, there's some weird stuff coming out of it.' He sounds really concerned. I look in the cockpit mirror and the 'stuff' coming out of my nose is grey-white matter. It looks and feels like I'm bleeding brains.

The yellow triangle on the Dream Cannon is upside down and flashing. Somehow I rebooted the cannon in reverse.

I need to sever the connection, but how do you sever a connection that consists of your brain and an electromagnetic field?

I feel like Satan. I'm consuming all the bullshit humans have ever produced in a stream of ones and zeros, mainly zeros. My veins are turning black and there is an effluvium of rotting Ramis kebabs.

'Sir! Sir! What should I do?'

I feel my entire consciousness leap out of my head, it can't handle it in there. I realise in that moment, that I can take all the anthropogenic ecomisery, but it will be to another dimension, and I will no longer exist in the Prime Universe.

The only problem, (actually one of many) is I don't know 'where', although that word isn't really applicable, 'where' my consciousness will end up.

Well what's the worst that can happen? An infinite of pain and seclusion? An insanity never imaginable?

So I make the decision.

++++++

Sun

low

in

the

sky

LONGLIST
EARTH 1.0
by Robin Griffiths

Robin Griffiths has tried everything. Stand up comedy, acting, cartooning, poetry, busking, peripatetic charity performer (travelling clown) and wasn't that great at any of them. Writing has been the one constant. He makes a living in Bath as a guitar teacher. His partner Carol is his heroine.

AFTERWORD

I'm fascinated about the future, or potential lack of it. It's so unpredictable. Who would have predicted electronic fags? One of my great hobby horses is global population and I don't think it is debated enough. I hope that as writers we can highlight and address serious issues, but hopefully with a small dose of levity.

Illustration by Crap Panther

RECORDED INTERVIEW 3
by Guy Smith

Y ou're familiar with the concept of publication bias, Detective Connelly?'

'I am.'

Connelly's face bears a natural empathy that has stopped her rising further in the department. Thick dark hair frames her face. Quiet eyes sit amongst soft features, behind glasses that could belong to someone else. The cold light of the room glances off the man's watch on her wrist.

'It's the idea that pharmaceutical companies only publish results of trials that support positive findings regarding their drugs.'

'As I said, I know what it is.'

'Sorry, yes. You must see it all the time.'

'We do.'

'Does it make you uncomfortable?'

'It does.'

Silence. She watches Garner, wanting to allow this digression to break the unhappy rhythm of the interview. He is wiry, with strength in the frame of his shoulders and arms. His face is drawn but looks younger than its forty-two years. He has a habit of frowning before he talks, bringing creases to the edge of the eyes. A trace of a smile intermittently comes to his lips. Connelly recognises it as one that belies discomfort rather than amusement: the closest she has come to being able to read him.

'It's always seemed strange to me that there are drugs out there that have had eighty percent of their trial results suppressed.'

'It's a flawed system,' she agrees.

Garner's fingers form an arch under his chin. 'People are going to hear about this though, I suppose,' he says to himself. The grey eyes are fixed on the coffee cup on the table, the liquid inside long since cold.

She leaves him to his thoughts. She doesn't want to be here; the room feels oppressive, she is tired, the lights give her a dull headache. One of them is making a clicking sound. She is struggling to reconcile the magnitude of what she has been told this man has just achieved with the things he has done to achieve it. It is disarming to be confronted by him wearing the grey tracksuit of a prisoner. Every photo she has seen of him has shown him in a white lab coat. He looks incomplete without it.

'I want to get back to July last year, Dr. Garner.'

'OK.'

The voice is passive. The harsh light penetrates his pale skin.

'I want to remind you again that you're entitled to have a lawyer present.'

She knows he will not accept the offer, but makes it anyway.

'This is no longer just a Health Research Agency inquest. As you have deduced from my presence, this is now a criminal investigation.'

'No. I'm fine, thank you,' he replies. The voice is quiet.

'Alright.'

She gathers her thoughts.

This man has made the most significant medical breakthrough of the century. This man is a murderer.

***

We are in the small house in the hills. The one with the fig trees and the little terrace overhung with vines and the view down the valley that stretches to the sea. You are standing outside, framed by the open doors. There is a rhythmic sound as the warm rain falls.

I have been watching you for five minutes. Everything about you makes me feel something. The light is catching your hair. I want to walk over and stand with you but I can't break the picture.

Eventually you turn back towards the house and see me standing in the darkness.

'Oh, hello,' you say, with a sleepy smile. There is a detached look in your eyes that I haven't seen before.

When I think back to it, this will be the moment I'll identify as the first time I should have known something was wrong.

***

'Tell me again how you came to administer the third and fourth variations of the drug to trial subjects Milton and Ross, despite the phase two death of Mr. Hastings the previous week.'

Her voice is hollow in her own head. She can hear the echoes of hundreds of interviews that lie in her past, none of which have prepared her for this.

The man who sits five feet from her is not present in the room. Something childlike comes across his face and then is gone. He is quiet.

'Dr. Garner?'

These long silences will play out patchily on the interview tapes, which irritates her more than it should.

'Detective Connelly, can I ask you a question before I do?'

'Go ahead.'

A small nod of the head.

'If it works, do you think what I've done will have been worth it?'

***

In the early days, I will pretend nothing is wrong. Then, on the day they call me from your office, telling me that you seem confused, I will cry in the car on the way to pick you up. I will kiss you on the head and hold you in the car park. When we get home I will make you tea and will look out of the window to avoid seeing the cup shake in your hand. The garden will be turning to autumn, the grass covered in dark leaves.

***

'The disease is caused by the build-up of proteins around the neurotransmitters. Primarily the deposition of extracellular amyloid plaques and intracellular neurofibrillary tangles. We call those NFTs.' He has been looking down but now looks up at her reticently. 'Sorry, you probably don't need to go through all this.'

'Please, carry on.'

He pulls himself forward in the seat. 'Most Alzheimer's treatments to-date have only been symptomatic. They have helped to control the issues associated with the disease, and in some cases have slowed patients' declines, but they don't address the problem itself.'

'I see.'

'We have been looking for a disease-modifying treatment.'

'Meaning one that targets the root cause?'

'Yes. I was using an antisense oligonucleotide. A type of molecule that interferes with the formation of proteins.'

'That can treat the disease?'

'It has the potential to help. We've known that for some time. But no one has formulated a treatment using an oligonucleotide that actually improves the condition of patients.'

She crosses to the water cooler and fills two plastic cups.

'So you were trying to create a cure?'

A twitch.

'That is too simplistic.'

'OK, but a significant breakthrough in the treatment of the disease?'

'Yes.'

'And from what I've been told, you were successful.'

'With the compound administered to Milton, yes. It would appear so.'

'That makes this a monumental moment, doesn't it?'

She passes him the water.

'It would. But we will need to carry out more tests.'

Connelly watches the skin of his knuckles pull tight over each other as he works his hands. She returns to her papers on the table, finding the briefing note provided to her earlier.

'It has been verified independently. Mr. Milton is showing an improvement. The drug is working.'

He crosses his arms protectively across his chest. He says nothing.

***

As you get worse I will begin lying to you. I will tell you I go running in the mornings, but instead I sit on the bench by the woods - the one we used to sit on and talk about the things we were looking forward to. I will sit and think about what we won't now get to do together. I will let the rage pour out of me, into the snow.

I will tell you I am going to work, but when I get there I will be paralysed by my inability to make progress, and by the speed of your decline. I will tell you we are doing well with the research, when in fact we are travelling in ever-diminishing circles.

***

'The Head of R&D says he instructed you to cease clinical trials after the death of Mr. Hastings. Is that true?'

'Yes.'

'You were instructed not to move to a phase three trial?'

'Yes.'

'Is it fair to say it was obvious that Mr. Hastings' death was caused in part by the drug he had been administered in phase two?'

'It couldn't be confirmed immediately.'

'So there was no way of knowing?'

The eyes find hers.

'It was very likely.'

Her shoulders are heavy; she feels herself hunching over. She continues.

'But you still took the decision to proceed to a phase three trial of two more compounds on subjects Milton and Ross?'

'I did.'

'Without HRA approvals or a treatment plan?'

One hand reaches up and ruffles his sandy hair.

'Both Ross and Milton proceeded with informed consent. They knew how close we were. They knew how important it was.'

'Even if that was the case, Mr. Ross died whilst taking part in a completely unapproved biomedical trial. One that you decided to conduct.'

Another nod of the head.

'And it doesn't seem you're going to offer any defence?'

'What defence could I give?'

'You must want to put up some kind of rationale for your actions, other than blind ambition and a disregard for human life?'

She feels the heat rising in her.

'How much do you know about Jeffrey Ross?' he asks, after a moment.

'I have reviewed his file, that's all.'

'He is a stockbroker from Surrey. He has worked for the same firm for thirty years, lived in the same house for twenty of those. His wife Marie has been by his side through all of it.'

'OK.'

'They have three children.'

He is talking about Ross in the present tense but she doesn't correct him.

'Yes, I saw in the file.'

Another pause.

'As well as being a sufferer himself, Jeffrey carries single-gene mutations on chromosomes 21 and 14,' he says, before shifting in his chair. 'These same gene mutations were present in two of his children. They are the hereditary genes that can increase the chance of someone developing early onset Alzheimer's.'

'I see.'

'His eldest daughter was diagnosed with the disease two months before we began Jeffrey's phase three trial.'

***

One night, a year and a half in, I wake from a dream and you are sleeping next to me. For two perfect minutes, I forget that anything is wrong.

***

Connelly takes off her glasses and rubs her eyes harder than necessary. They have talked for over three hours.

'You realise that any sentence will be severe?

'I do.'

He blinks as if emerging from darkness into light. The gesture is one of tiredness, or of remorse, or of relief.

The room is quiet. The clicking of the light has stopped.

'I don't understand why you didn't just seek approval,' she says. 'From what I've been told, you would have got it.'

He looks at the watch on her wrist.

'Have you ever lost someone, Detective Connelly?'

'I have.'

'Would you have done anything if you thought you could have saved that person?'

***

It is June 21st 2019. I will first administer the successful drug only a month later. I am in the lab that morning when the hospital calls.

LONGLIST
RECORDED INTERVIEW 3
by Guy Smith

Guy is a passionate, enthusiastic and inexperienced storyteller. He works in the film industry in London, and this is his first published short story. He hopes to write much more across different mediums in the future. If anyone would like to get in touch with him (me) then they're very welcome to drop an email to guy.sants.smith@gmail.com.

AFTERWORD

I'm a child of the Jurassic Park era. That is how I would, very simply, sum up what I most value in storytelling. Sitting in a seaside cinema at the age of six (I know - questionable parenting) I was introduced to the boundless nature of stories, and to their potential to explore any version of the future their creators could dream up.

Stories can examine our past and imagine our future. In a world that is changing at a dizzying pace, one thing that remains constant is the ability of narrative to bring to life our greatest fears, wishes and dreams. For thousands of years, humans have used stories to help them process the changes happening around them. Above all else, they have used them to entertain one another, in good times and bad.

Something I am interested in doing in my writing - and that I sought to do in *Recorded Interview 3* - is to imagine the human issues, moments and interactions that will arise as we plunge into a future of advancements and discoveries. What personal cost will those at the forefront have to pay? How will their lives be affected? What hard decisions will they have to make?

I'd say there's plenty of material there to keep me going... I'm aware that I'm attempting to follow in the footsteps of some amazing writers who have been preoccupied with the same questions. If, over time, I can add in any tiny way to the storytelling tradition they have created, I'll be a very happy man.

Illustration by Amie Dearlove

NO STATE
by Paul Turner

NO STATE, NO CHOICE, it reads in dripping blood-red paint on the dusty brick wall of a dilapidated building, synonymous with this ongoing apocalypse. And I don't know if it's a protest or a political slogan. I just can't tell anymore. These words are written everywhere you turn, but I don't think anyone reads them. In this age of apathy, we're nothing more than homogenous clones in a time that seems to have come to a standstill.

I've finished work for another day, walking towards the subway with all the other rats. On any other normal day, I would join them as they are herded down the escalator to the subterranean platform and onto the slow-moving and over-populated train that would take me back to my high-rise home in Zone 6.

But not today.

Today, I am not going to do what is expected of me. Today, I will not be told what to do. And so I walk past the queue of rats as the sun begins to drop and night prepares its invasion. As I walk past, I stare at their glum faces as they patiently wait to be admitted into the station by the guard. The entrance is locked shut for their own safety. It's the early evening surge and the platforms are overcrowded already. They all wait outside in an orderly line, standing on the designated footprints painted in yellow on the pavement, telling them to WAIT HERE. Heads are dropped, but no one complains. This is just the way of things. I've stood and waited there many times before, but not today.

I work in the 'Records Transfer' department for a large financial institution. They're the child of a larger money-machine monopoly that formed after the last financial crash. The company I work for kept their name and, more importantly, their logo, but they're no different to anyone else. It gives the allusion of choice; something that no longer exists. I spend each day, sat third desk along on bank 'K', migrating all of the redundant, paper-based records into the digital archive. I am part of it all. I am complicit. I am a small cog that is responsible for the removal of any physical proof that we exist. I move it all into the virtual world. Lives are compressed into a few megabytes, stored on a server in a room on the other side of the world. We are trapped in webs with our heads in the cloud, whatever that might be. There's nothing left of any substance. You can no longer hold onto anything physical or real anymore. The world is paperless and that's a good thing. That's what everyone wants, isn't it? One-touch and there it is, all at your fingertips. Instant gratification is all that's required and nothing less will do.

I wade through the customer records that I retrieve from the file room – a room that they want to clear out and turn into a 'Recuperation & Inspiration Place', whatever that means. Every time I complete a job, I am given the next reference number on the list. Once I've located it, I accept the job and get on with it. I work through the letters, correspondence, the financial statements and balances. I manually type everything into the relevant screen in the 'Global Finance You-Space'. When I've finished, I shred the paper – with the scribbled signatures, tea stains, creased fold-lines...all evidence that this was handled by a real person – and I move onto the next one. I destroy all evidence of what really happened. The personal touch is forever lost, replaced by pixels accessed via the GFY-S online portal with a two-stage verification login process. I have the power to remove all evidence that someone ever existed. I could shred the files and no one would ever know.

I work on the tenth floor of the company headquarters. The office is set out like lines on a page, bank upon bank of desks. We sit side-by-side with no partitions, all looking forward, in front of flat screens that display our daily targets in the 'Rationalisation Project'. Signs hang from the dropped ceiling with the word SILENCE written on them in bold-red font on a white background. We are surrounded by floor-to-ceiling windows, but the blinds are always drawn and the flickering strip-lighting is always on. I work in silence, along with two hundred people that I don't know and never will. The only conversations I have are via the instant message pop-up screen, using approved abbreviations, acronyms and symbols...never words. Words can be misinterpreted. People have been fired for using the right words in the wrong way.

At five-thirty, assuming the daily target has been achieved, the rats all stand up as one, get their coats and head for the exit. They queue to leave the building. They queue for the lift down to the reception foyer. They queue as they walk towards the subway. They queue when they get there. They queue on the platform. The queue on the train. They queue to leave. No complaints. No words. No conversation. Nothing. And I'm no better. Every day that I've worked here – for nearly five years now – I've done the same thing. I have no idea what lies beyond the entrance to the subway and what exists in the periphery of the financial district. In the morning, when I exit the station, I've only ever turned left. I've never turned right.

NO STATE, NO FREEDOM, it reads above the entrance to the subway. And I know this must be part of the propaganda-machine of the new regime. It's glossy and stark. The letters are written in a blood-red font with no character, on a brilliant-white background. People don't look up, but I do. No one reads the words anymore. You don't need to, because everyone knows what it says. It's familiar, like a road-sign, or a company logo. A quick glance is all it needs and that's how I know that THEY have won. The NO STATE is in control. I read the words over and over in my head. I do this until they sound alien to me. I can't forget the words. It's the only thing we have left. The regime discourages 'words'. Words lead to panic. Words lead to lies and slander. Words lead to intolerance and hate crimes. Words are our enemy, as are the trolls who use them. They're replaced with symbols, logos or icons; pre-approved drop-down messages and predicted sentences that your device will choose for you... <select as appropriate> ... to make your life 'easy' when you're 'on the go'. Do not speak to people you do not know. Do not speak unless you have prior authorisation. Do not offend someone's race, gender or religion. Preferred method of contact: tap-tap-tap on the keyboard... instant message... instant reply. It's recognition rather than reading. We've de-evolved back to the time of Neanderthals and apes.

One grunt for YES and two for NO.

I'm thirsty. I want to find a coffee-bar that allows you to purchase and smoke a government-approved electronic vaping device. These places are all the rage in the new world, if you believe all you see on the monitored blogs... <message removed due to inappropriate content> ... and the attention-deficient television shows. The queue of rats is behind me. I dismiss the past and I look towards the future...the unknown. I take my device from my pocket and unlock it with my thumb-print, swiping to the third screen where I go to my 'LOCATIONS' group where my map and local services applications are, tapping the yellow thumb and selecting 'Coffee Bar' from the drop-down list of approved searches. I pass fifty, maybe sixty people who are coming the other way, all of them 'plugged-in' with the thin white wire drooping from the hand-held device and up into their ears, heads down, looking fifteen centimetres in front of their faces. My device tells me to walk five-hundred metres and turn right. It provides me the name of the place it is taking me to, but I have already seen the logo. I recognise it from the advertisements on television.

As I walk down the street, I feel as if I am caught in between two parallel universes. On the opposite side of the road, there are a series of grand, historic buildings with glass frontages. Inside, men and women and any other genders you'd care to list – I can't keep track – are all laughing and talking to each other. They are the social elite. They are the managing directors and the CEOs and the celebrities and the actors and the football players. They are the people we are told we need to aspire to be. They're in the club that we're all told we want to be part of. They are the people who can afford 'Social Licenses' and are automatically exempt from hate crimes. They can say, pretty much, what they feel like and we all just accept it, because we 'know' them. They're forced down our throats, through our television sets and the news blogs. They are the people to whom the rules do not apply. On the side of the street all of the shops are boarded up, the windows blacked-out and covered in protest posters. In this new age, if you want something, you just click your fingers and it will be yours. There's no need to go to a designated place to get what you want or need. Instant gratification. One click and all of your dreams come true. Forget the rest. That's how it works in the NO STATE.

I find the coffee bar. I recognise the logo. The window to the shop has seven other smaller icons that tell me everything I can expect from this place. Self-Serve. Free wifi. A number of social media symbols that will sync with your device and tell everyone that you're there. We've walked into a police state with our eyes closed. We have no idea where all this data goes and who sees it. I fear that I am the only one who knows all about this. Or am I just being paranoid? I need to talk to someone about it. I need a conversation. I can't go on like this; a daily migraine caused by staring at the flickering screen that is melting my brain... <approve... like... allow> ... I'm confronted with the self-serve screen that's as tall as I am. I select a coffee and skip all the options, prompted with pop-up messages with each skip asking me, 'ARE YOU SURE THAT'S CORRECT?' At the end, it asks me to verify my order, as if the machine's not been listening to me either. I select an e-VAPE, with a similar number of obstacles and warnings. At the end of it all, I am offered an animation of a device being presented to the black port at the side of the machine. I comply, following the instructions as played out to me, my account debited by ten-point-five credits. The e-VAPE drops as I am directed to booth '6', with a red, animated arrow pointing me left. And I start to wonder whether this saves any time at all. Wouldn't it have been quicker if I'd simply spoken to the person behind the counter?

There are thirteen people in here. They're all 'plugged-in' with their heads down. Homo-erectus just got shorter. I select the 'Telephone' icon on my device, despite it being disabled. I do this, every so often, just to check. Someone may have enabled it by accident… an administrative error. It prompts me to enter my 'Social License Identifier,' and so I close it down… <ARE YOU SURE YOU WANT TO DO THAT?> … No. But whatever. I scroll to my 'MESSAGES' group with my six message applications, and I really hope I've got a message from someone, because what else am I going to do if I don't?

My coffee has just appeared next to me and I don't know how it got there. I didn't notice. I wanted to say 'thank you' to the person who made it for me, but I was distracted.

I scroll through each message application. Three so far and no message. I lose track of who contacts me through what application and so I have to loop through them all… left to right… right to left. I select the green speech-bubble and I see the number '1' next to #Abby, who could be a boy or a girl, or neither… or both. I've been too afraid to ask.

The message reads, #NoStAtE and I have no idea what this means. It was sent nine minutes ago. I trawl through the conversation history to see if there's anything that I've missed that might give me a clue. I'm nervous. Is this a protest message? I don't want to get embroiled in something like that. The new regime disapproves of 'protests'. I know these conversations are monitored. I know there are eyes everywhere.

The conversations, to date, have been aimless. Much like all of my conversations with these people or machines… I can't tell the difference. The last three messages from #Abby were a laughing face in response to my thumbs-down, a thumbs-up in response to my picture of a train, and a grey cloud, sent yesterday at five o'clock as it started to rain. #Abby and I 'connected' a few months back when we both bought and liked the same product on the same market website. I received a private message with a thumbs-up and a question mark, asking how I was finding it. I sent a thumbs-down and an angry face, and this is how we've interacted ever since. This message has been like no others I've seen.

I respond with '?'.

The [...] flickers as #Abby writes a response. #NoStAtE, it reads. And I can't bear this any longer and so I type, 'wot r u trying to tell me?'

[...] '60 secs'

'?'

'#JoinMeInTheGutter'

'??????'

'#JoinUs'

I don't write anything else. I suck on my e-VAPE and drink my coffee that was cold when it arrived. No one can get anything right anymore.

'????'

No response.

'wot do u want me 2 do?'

<Arrow-Up> and <Arrow-Right>

I get up from my seat and leave the coffee shop and turn right, back towards the main road.

'ok??????'

<Arrow-Right> '100m'

I turn right up the main road, but my gaze is fixed towards the screen.

<Red-Cross>

I stop.

<Arrow-Left> '200m'

I comply. I don't know where I'm going.

<Red-Cross>

I stop. I look up. There's a young woman standing in front of me. She's the sort of person I wouldn't look at twice. Her hair's a mess and she's wearing too much mascara. Her nails are painted black, but most of it has peeled off or been chewed away. We're in a claustrophobic narrow side street in between two brick walls with no windows. She smiles at me, but says nothing. She walks up to me and kisses me, pushing her tongue into my mouth, covering my lips with saliva. She stops. She moves backwards, smiling, pushing her messy hair behind her ears.

I think I'm in love.

'Come with me to the gutter, Nathaniel,' she says. 'The gutter is where life resides, not up here with the machines with their spies and their stool-pigeons. We don't belong here.'

'How did you know I'd...'

'Be here? I've been following you.'

'I know you follow me,' I say. She's been following me for months.

'No. I mean, I have been following you. In real life. I tracked your GPS tonight. I've been waiting for the day that you walk past the station. You've been saying it for months.'

'I've not told you anything.'

'You didn't need to. I've observed your patterns. I've processed all our conversations through my algorithm. I've been waiting for this day and now it's finally here.'

She takes my hand and drags me down the side street, taking a can of blood-red spray paint from her bag and writing, NO STATE, NO LIFE on the dirty brick wall. And whilst I recognise this from before and now I know that this is a protest, I'm still confused.

She leads me towards a disused multi-storey car park. I'm lost in the maze of streets and so I pull out my device to see where I am, but it's telling me NO SERVICE. I shake it to try and wake it up and #Abby says, 'that won't work.' I ask her why and she says, 'it's a dead-spot. We've blocked it all. No signal. No wifi. Nothing. It's the only place where you can be free in the NO STATE.'

And whilst I have no idea what she's saying, it all makes sense.

We're in the basement of the car park. We're in the gutter. I look around the room. This place is 'un-plugged'. The thirty-or-so people in here are all drinking, laughing and smoking without a device in sight. In the gutter, I can become human again. There's a makeshift bar where #Abby introduces me to a keyboard-warrior and want-to-be techno-terrorist called Seward. He seems pleased to meet me, like he knows me already.

It's YEAR FIVE now. That's what Seward is telling me. No one knows this, but the regime reset to ZERO after the last financial crash. They needed a baseline, that's what he says. I'm handed a beer and a real cigarette. Seward lights it for me and I take a drag, practically fainting as I get an almighty head-rush.

God! I've missed it.

#Abby stands close by as Seward proceeds to tell me about an organisation called ASPHYXIA who control the world. 'They are everywhere and nowhere,' he explains. The walls of the gutter are covered in the propaganda of the regime and safety signs that help us not to think; compliance through subliminal recognition… SILENCE. HOLD THE HANDRAIL. NO SMOKING. STAND ON THE LEFT. These are the instructions we no longer need to read. The words have become pictures that we instantly recognise.

'The technology we have today was available twenty years ago,' Seward goes on. 'It's been drip-fed to us over time so we don't realise how they're taking control. We've slipped into a coma and now it's too late for us to wake up. We've passed the event horizon.'

They invented terrorism.

They financed the moon-landing and fuelled the space race.

They've started and ended wars for financial and political gain.

'It's a complex long-term plan that's centred around control. It's all it is. Most of it is pointless. They're just showing us who's in charge, whilst hiding in the shadows.' Their methods of communication are complex, run through numerous agencies, some of which I've heard of, others I haven't. But he's working on an algorithm to break their code. It's his life's work.

'They're getting lazy. They're becoming complacent. Since they upgraded to the latest operating system, there are more ways in.'

Seward sounds like the voices in my head.

While giving me a potted history of the significance of the last five years, Seward is distracted, mid-sentence, by two newcomers. They embrace and slap each other on the back and exclaim that it's been far too long. I look at #Abby, who seems withdrawn, nodding her head to the background music. She looks up at me and smiles and so I take this opportunity to find a corner and sit with her. I want to know everything there is to know about her. I take her hand and pull her to the other side of this concrete shell towards the worn leather couch that's covered in chunks of dried plaster.

'How long have you been coming here?' I ask her. And whilst I know that must sound like a really lame opener to a conversation, you have to remember that I'm out of practise.

'Since my eyes were re-opened,' she replies. And whilst I know she hasn't answered my question, I know exactly what she means. If someone asked me the same question, many years from now, then that's what I'd like to think I'd say.

I look down at my watch, trying to figure out what I'd be doing right now in my old life... up in my high-rise apartment... sixteenth floor... apartment 1601... disposing of the leftovers from my microwave meal that I'd shove through the garbage-shoot... checking out the latest dreary box-set that 'everyone's blogging about'... upgrading my device to the latest operating system... click-click purchase of the new to replace the old, like-for-like... new features... never-seen-before... set my alarm for another day that will be exactly the same as the last... staring down at the lines of red on the expressway below. It's no way to exist.

#Abby squeezes my knee and smiles as she moves in to kiss me. My heart races with the sensation of attraction; an intimacy that's not pre-defined. It's something new and exciting. I have no idea where this will go, or how it will end. I lean in to her and we kiss. Two bodies fusing together in a symphony of saliva. I want to tell her everything, but I don't know where to start. I'm not sure I can find the words, but I want to try.

NO STATE, NO FEAR. That's what I will spray on the wall of my high-rise apartment, if I ever decide to return. It's the state that tells you NO. It wants you to do what you're told. In the NO STATE, there is no choice. I've been reading it correctly all along. These people have shown me that. They've shown me how we are at war with ourselves. It's divide and rule. They tell us not to fear. They tell us not to hate. They preach intolerance towards intolerance. They pretend this is all for our own good. But it's all part of their plan to make us all the same. The homogenous ideal. They fear us. They fear our unpredictability. They don't want us to be human.

And whilst you may think I've painted you a picture of a dystopian future, I assure you that I have not. This is today. It's now. It's 2017. NO STATE, NO CHOICE. That's the message. That's what they want you to see. But I realise today that I do have a choice. This night has given me hope that this is true.

I take my device and I smash it on the ground. I'm not going to be part of this anymore. I've found the exit. And the people in the gutter cheer.

LONGLIST
NO STATE
by Paul Turner

Paul Turner lives in Oxfordshire with his wife, Victoria, and their cat, Kipper. With a degree in surveying, Paul fell into the energy industry by accident and into a career in IT building models and systems, making sure all the numbers add up. It is, therefore, unsurprising that he escapes into small worlds in his head. Paul has never been published, let alone long/short listed for a short story competition. This is his first foray into print and he hopes it won't be his last. Paul writes both short stories and short novels (mostly consigned to a shoebox in his attic study), but hopes that this will provide the spark to create and submit more. When not writing, Paul plays music with his band: *möbius* – and they're looking to gig soon! (Here's a link to their *Soundcloud* page: https://soundcloud.com/user-719005486)

AFTERWORD

For a long time, this idea was nothing but two words on the pages of countless notebooks, journals and scraps of paper where I'd list out all the titles of ideas that I wanted to write... one day. It was so long ago that I've forgotten the exact moment when *No State* came to me. All I can remember was seeing the yellow footprints painted on the floor telling me where to stand... I just don't recall where. It may have been triggered when I read *1984* again and reignited when I read *Infinite Jest* (and no, I didn't fully get it and I really do need to read it again) where my eyes were opened to a contemporary future gone mad. Or it could have been when I was looking to submit a different short story and found the STORGY Exit Earth competition and realised there was an outlet for this idea after all. Either way, it's all there in black and white and I can't change it now.

It was meant to be a novel, perhaps. It was meant to be a vision of a broken future. One of control, abuse of power and where technology rules us, rather than the other way around. It was meant to show the death of social interaction in a future that I wanted to predict, but never got around to... and then it happened. A glimpse into the future, or rather the present? I wrote the opening line about a hundred times and the rest just flowed. I didn't think about it too much. I just let it happen. My wife read it. She liked it. She helped me edit it and so this is all for her.

Within this story are other ideas that I hope to develop in whatever form that may take. Whilst I've been writing for some time, it's only recently that I have become confident enough to share. The themes of my writing and my ideas can be triggered by anything, be it a song I'm listening to on the way home from work, or an announcement on a train. Empathy is the foundation. Imagine a life-changing event... good or bad. An anti-hero coming to terms with being a killer, the loss of a brother during childhood, a search for absolution and meaning. I want to imagine a life that's not mine. I want to become the narrator. I don't want to write lists of titles anymore. No longer will I be a chronic procrastinator.

...EXIT EARTH...
EXTRA

Illustration by HarlotVonCharlotte

THE SONS OF TAMMANY
M. R. Carey

My name is Thomas Nast. I'm sixty-two years old, and to be honest I don't expect to be able to hold up my hand after another year's seasonal turnings and returnings to say I'm sixty-three. I'm dying, at long last. And death dissolves all the bonds of obligation except the ones I owe to God. That being the case, I feel like I'm free at last to talk about the events of August 1870, which formerly I had held back from doing on account of they implicate a whole lot of people in a whole lot of queasy doings, and I couldn't really back up what I was saying with anything you might count as actual proof.

But when a man's staring straight down the barrel of his *nunc dimittis*, and the writing's not just on the wall but on the face that stares back at him out of the mirror, he stops fretting about the legal niceties and starts to think about setting the record straight. Which is what I aim to do.

In 1870, I was residing in New York City and working as an artist and cartoonist on that excellent periodical, the Harper's Weekly, under the editorship of George Curtis. I counted Curtis as a friend as well as an employer. But when he called me into his office on the morning of August 13th of that year, he was wearing the boss hat rather than the friend one.

Curtis gave me a civil nod and gestured me into one of the two visitor chairs. Already ensconced in the other chair was a man of a somewhat striking appearance. Although, having said that, I'm going to show myself a weak sister by admitting that I can't really say what it was about this gentleman that was so singular.

He was a good deal older than I was, and he'd seen enough summers to get a slightly weather-beaten look around his cheeks and jowls. He was kind of short and dumpy in his build, which was neither here nor there, but he had one of those half-hearted little moustaches that looks like it's about to give up and crawl back inside, and to be honest that was sort of a point against him in my book. If a man's going to go for a moustache, he should go all-in for one, say I, and Devil take the hairiest. He was toying with a cane that had a carved ivory handle in the shape of a lion's head – an effete sort of a gewgaw for a man to be playing with. And he had a suit with a waistcoat, and the waistcoat had a pattern to it. In my experience, that doesn't speak to a man's moral seriousness.

I guess, thinking about it, it was the eyes that were the selling point. They were a dark enough brown to count for black, and they had a sort of an augur-bit quality to them. It was the most startling thing. Like when this gentleman looked at you, looking wasn't really the half of it, and maybe you needed a whole other verb.

"Tommy, this here's Mr. Dupin," Curtis said. "Visiting from Paris. Not the Texas one, the t'other one, over in France."

"Well, it's good to meet you, Mr. Dupin," I said, taking the collateral of the eyes against the rest of the stuff that was on offer. Curtis pronounced the name "*dupan*", which I estimate is French for "out of the pan", as in the thing you bail out from before you end up in the fire. Which wasn't a bad name at all for this particular customer, as things transpired.

"Only he ain't a Mister," Curtis added, scrupulous as you'd expect a good editor to be. "He's a *chevalier*."

"What does that mean?" I asked.

"Means he's got a horse stashed somewhere, as I understand it."

"Good job," I said. "With that waistcoat, he may need to access it in a hurry."

"Monsieur," the little man said in a waspish voice, "I speak excellent English, and I thank you for the compliment. I can, if you wish, give you the address of my tailor."

"Oh, that won't be necessary," I told him. "I think one of those things in the world at any one time answers the purpose pretty well."

The Frenchman surprised me by laughing at that – and it was a big, loud horse-laugh, too, not the little snigger you'd expect would come from underneath that lamentable moustache. "Perhaps you are right," he said. "One at a time. Yes."

And then Curtis got to the point, which was that Mr. Du Frying Pan wanted to see something of New York while he was here. What's more, he carried letters of introduction from a job lot of people who were (as you might say) the human equivalent of big guns on big limbers, and could blast Curtis and me and Mr. Harper and the subs' desk and Uncle Tom Cobley and all into the Hudson if we didn't show their friend Dupin a good time.

"So I thought perhaps he could come with you today when you go to sketch the bridge," Curtis wound up.

I knew that was where he was aiming at, so I took it in my stride. "I think that's a swell idea," I said. "Sure. Mr. Dupin, come and see my city. She's something to see. George, you want to come along?"

"Oh no," Curtis said hurriedly. "I'm tied up every which way here, and I won't see daylight this side of Tuesday. You guys go and have a good time. Lunch is on Mr. Harper, so long as you don't get into a second bottle. And you can take a cab to get down there." He waited a decent length of time – maybe a slow count of five – before adding "Trolley car will bring you back."

"And what is it you do, way over there in Paris, Mr. Dupin?" I asked, as we toiled down the stairs. The Equitable Life Building which they'd just finished building over on Broadway had its very own hydraulic elevator, but every time I mentioned that to Curtis he walked the other way.

"What do I do?" Dupin repeated doubtfully.

"Yeah. What's your motive and your métier? What's the singular thing that you pursue?"

"Ah." The little man's face lit up with understanding, but then it closed down again as he took that question over the threshold of his ruminations and worried it some. "The truth," he said at last. "The truth is what I pursue."

"Really? There any profit to be had in that?"

He gave out with that belly laugh again. "No. Not usually."

We waited for a cab on the corner of 41st Street right next to Peason's cigar store. Mr. Du Griddle Tray kept taking sideways glances at the cigar store Indian as though he might be looking to pick a fight. "That there is Tamanend, of the Lenape nation," I told him. "He's widely known in these parts, despite having turned up his toes back in sixteen-ought-eight."

The Frenchman's answer surprised me. "Yes," he said. "Of course. Because of the Society of St. Tammany, to which many members of New York's current civic administration belong."

I gave him a nod, and probably my face showed him that I was impressed. "One up to you, Dupin. That's the connection, all right. The Great Wigwam, they call it – the Tammany Hall, down on 14th Street. And it's got its share of famous patrons, like you say. Our illustrious mayor, Oakey Hall. Judge George Barnard, who doles out wisdom to the city benches. Hank Smith, who's the president of the Police Commission. Oh, there's a whole ring of them."

I didn't mention the Grand Sachem, William "Boss" Tweed, in the same way that you don't speak of the Devil – in case you turn around and find him breathing over your shoulder.

"Political corruption," Dupin mused. "It is a scourge."

And yes, it is. But this was my city we were lambasting, and I don't care to see my city, good-time girl though she may be, roughly handled by a stranger. So I changed the subject and talked about the bridge instead. And not long after that, we managed to hail a cab.

In deference to Du Sausage Cutter's hind parts I picked out a Duncan Sherman, which had a sprung undercarriage and a horse with something of an imperturbable nature. Truth to tell, we could have made better time walking – but you've got to push the boat out when you've got a guest to entertain, and besides it was setting in to rain a little. On a rainy day, Fifth Avenue is a lot more fun to ride down than to walk down.

As we rode, I carried on waxing lyrical about the bridge. "Over yonder," I said, pointing, "to the east of us, those buildings you see are not a part of the fair city of New York. They belong to our neighbour polity, Brooklyn, which like New York is a thriving metropolis, home to close on a half a million people. It's got just as many warehouses and factories and refineries as we do, and we'd like nothing better than to increase the ties of mutual amity and profit between the two cities. Only trouble is, there's sixteen hundred feet of water laying between them. It would need a bridge longer than any in the world to cross that gap."

"That would seem to be an insuperable problem," said Dupin, who knew what was required of a straight man.

"Well, sir, you'd think so. But Mr. John Augustus Roebling, of Ohio, drew up a plan for a suspension bridge whose spans would be supported by steel wires redoubled inside flexible housings. He died before he could start in to build the thing, but his son, Washington Roebling, took over. Then Washington got sick from the Caisson disease, and deputed his wife, Emily, to see the project to completion. Now the Brooklyn tower's mostly up and they're laying the foundations for the New York side. Hell of a thing to see, I'll tell you. When it's done, it will bestride the East River like a colossus."

"Remarkable," Dupin observed, dryly.

"Yes, sir, it is."

"And yet, dogged by ill fortune and tragedy."

I shrugged that off. I was a younger man, then, and more easily impressed by big dreams and big ideas. The misfortunes of the Roebling family didn't seem like such a big almighty deal to me. "Well, the salient fact is that this will be the biggest suspension bridge in the whole damn world. Biggest one right now is in Kentucky, and Roeblings built that too. America is a place where anything's possible, Mr. Dupin."

The Frenchman nodded solemnly. "Yes," he agreed. "I believe that is so. That is one reason why I wished to see it."

I was opening my mouth, about to parrot some more facts and figures about steel wires and three-way overlapping joists, when I realised that I'd lost my audience. Mr. Dupin was staring ahead down the street towards the Centre Street Pier, or rather just before it, which was where they'd erected the scaffolding for the tower on the New York side of the river.

"It seems," Mr. Dupin said, "that we have chosen a busy day."

And in truth there was a crowd milling in the street beside the pier, the like of which I hadn't seen since the draft riots. They didn't seem to be up to any mischief, but there was a lot of shouting and shoving of the kind that normally signals something unusual has happened, and – undeterred by that past tense – people are jostling to line up in its wake. A few city police were trying to keep some kind of order, along with a crew or two from the new paid fire service which had replaced the volunteer brigades a few years back. They were having a lively time of it.

I paid off the cab and we pushed our way through the crowd, my press badge making little difference to the citizens but winning me a little headway with the cops and the firemen. Finally we got through the police line and into the building yard. In front of us was the massive, complicated apparatus known as a caisson – the chief aid and comfort of bridge builders everywhere, and (sadly) the scourge and terror of their workers. It only showed six or seven feet above the ground, but it extended a great long way beneath us.

Normally, this building site was such a humming pit of industry that you had to duck and weave as you walked along, leading with your elbows like a forward in the Princeton University Football game. Today, though there were a lot of workers around, nobody was actually working. Most of the men were sitting around looking unhappy or sullen. The rain was coming down steadily now, turning the earth to mud, but it seemed like nobody cared about the cold or the wet. Some had their heads in their hands. The winch that lowered food and coffee to the men down in the caisson was standing idle, and the old Italian man who ran it was slumped against the scaffolding, his arms draped over it, like a prize fighter who's only just made it to his corner. He looked to have been crying.

I collared a foreman who was bustling past, red-faced and urgent, and compelled him to stop. "See here, brother," I told him, "we're from the Harper's Weekly and we'd like to know what's going on here."

The yegg tried to pass us off with some mumble about asking the shift manager, but Dupin spoke up then, and either his gimlet eyes or his weird accent took the wind out of the foreman's sails. "What is your name?" He demanded.

"O'Reilly," the man mumbled, truculently.

"Your given name, as well as your family name," Dupin snapped, for all the world as though he had some kind of right to ask. "Come, come."

"John. John O'Reilly."

"*C'est ça.* Tell us what has happened, John. Be brief and precise, if you please."

The foreman didn't seem to know what to make of this strange little guy in the fancy clothes. But on the principle that most people he met were going to turn out to be more important than he was, he coughed it up. "We got twenty men dead. The whole night shift. I went away to sign in the morning crew, and when I got back they was all…" He faltered into silence and pointed down into the caisson, as if the period of his sentence might be found down there.

"Twenty men?" Dupin echoed, and O'Reilly nodded. "Twenty men is a full complement, then? A full workforce?"

"It depends what's going on," O'Reilly said. "There's less men on at night, on account of we just light the lanterns up in one half of the caisson. There's a fire hazard, see?"

"No," Dupin said, forcefully.

"What?"

"No, I do not see. Show me."

"Listen here, I got to…"

"Show me."

If the situation hadn't been so tragic, I might have laughed at the spectacle of this queer little foreigner taking charge so decisively. Dupin followed the foreman and I followed Dupin, my materials case clutched in my hand like a doctor's Gladstone bag – only there wasn't going to be any good I could do down there, I thought as we skirted round the wheezing steam pump. Not unless you count bearing witness.

The caisson was eighty feet long, sixty wide and forty deep. The last ten feet or so were under the bedrock of the East River, so the air had a hellish dampness to it. We went down through several successive chambers, each sealed off by greased tarpaulins laid out in overlapping sheets. You had to lift a corner of the tarpaulin each time, like turning the page of a massive book, to expose the trapdoor and carry on down to the next level. Below us, candle flames flickered fitfully like someone was keeping vigil down there. The bellows of the steam pump kept up a consumptive breathing from up over our heads, and from below us that sound was compounded by the muttered conversations you mostly get around the bedsides of dying men.

The floor of the caisson was one half packed earth and one half new-laid stone. There weren't any dying men there, only hale ones and dead ones. The dead ones were laid out in rows, like men sleeping in a dormitory. The living ones stood over them, candles in their hands, looking impotent and terrified as behoves men who are in the presence of such a disaster.

The shift manager – a clerkish-looking man of middle age, named Sittingbourne – introduced himself to us, and we returned the favour. I was vague about exactly who Dupin was, but emphasised our association with the Harper's Weekly. That put a woeful look on Sittingbourne's face, as well it might. This was the sort of thing he would probably have wanted to keep out of the papers until he'd talked to his bosses about what shape his future might likely take.

"See here," he said, "don't you go talking to none of my people without me being in on the conversation. Is that understood?"

"You got any people left for me to talk to?" I countered – and he deflated like a punctured soufflé.

"It was an accident," he said. "A terrible accident. I don't see how anyone could have foreseen this, or done anything to guard against it."

"Perhaps not," Dupin said acerbically. "But perhaps – yes. That is what we must ascertain. I wish to see the bodies."

This came as a surprise to all of us, but principally to Mr. Sittingbourne, who thought he was dealing with newspapermen and now wondered if he was maybe dealing with something even scarier than that. A state commissioner, maybe.

"The - - the bodies?" he temporised.

Dupin brushed past him, taking his candle out of the man's hand in an *en passant* move that made me wonder if he'd ever done any sword fencing. He squatted down beside the nearest body and brought the candle up close to its face.

I winced, but I didn't look away. I'm a sketch artist, and looking away isn't in my religion. The dead man's face was lividly pale, his lips blue rather than a healthy red. His face was twisted in a desperate travail, the eyes bulging half out of his head. All in all, it looked like death when it finally came for him might have been something of a relief.

"Poor bastard," I muttered.

"*Oui, le pauvre gosse,*" Dupin said. He moved the candle from face to face. "They all seem to have died in the same way. Or at least, they all display the same symptoms."

"It's known that working in the caissons is dangerous," Sittingbourne said. He was hovering at my elbow, nervously wringing his hands. "There's a condition…"

"Caisson sickness," I said.

"Caisson sickness, to be sure. And we've had our fair share of it. But nothing like this. Nothing on this scale. I honestly… I don't know what to say. I really don't."

He was talking to Dupin's back. Dupin was still examining the bodies, his mouth puckered into a grimace. "The light is inadequate," he commented.

Sittingbourne looked around, startled. "Get your candles over here!" he called out to the other men. They clustered round us looking like they were about to burst into a Christmas carol.

Dupin stood. "Who turned out the lanterns?"

"I don't know," Sittingbourne confessed.

"Then find out."

The Frenchman swept past us and headed back for the ladder, but he couldn't climb up because there was a whole posse coming down. It was hard to tell in the sepulchral light of the candles, but they looked to be in uniform. Once they touched down, I was able to identify them as New York City cops – the Eastside variety called spudpickers elsewhere in the City because they're bog Irish and Tammany men to a fault.

The two in the vanguard were sergeant Driscoll and his lackey, Flood. Driscoll looked as saintly as a christening cloth, and Flood looked like a nasty stain that somehow got smeared onto it, but I knew for a fact they were as bad as each other and a good deal worse than most.

"What are we having here?" Driscoll asked, mildly. "Mr. Nast, is it? You must have sneaked past us all quiet like, when we were quelling the angry mob."

"I'm sorry, sergeant," I lied emolliently. "I didn't realise you were restricting access. But I'm here as a representative of the press."

"A guy who draws funny pictures!" Flood sneered.

"My associate makes a cogent argument," Driscoll said. "You can't be painting pictures in the dark, Mr. Nast, so I'll thank you to bugger off out of this." To the room at large, he added. "These workings are hazardous, and they're not being properly maintained. I'm closing them down, herewith. You can apply at City Hall for a new license, subsequent to a complete overhaul of the safety procedures and a thorough inspection at the contractor's expense."

"But…" Sittingbourne protested. "Please, sergeant. If I can consult Mrs Roebling, I'm… I'm sure we can…"

"I'm sure you can't," Driscoll told him, deadpan. "Not unless you want go around Boss Tweed."

That shut Sittingbourne up, *instanter*. You could go around William Tweed, of course. Topographically speaking, I mean. He was a mighty obstacle, but you could do it. The trouble was, you'd need to be properly provisioned for a journey like that, and your troubles would set in as soon as you were out of sight of the high road, as it were. I knew men who'd tried it. I even knew where some of them were buried.

"Might I inquire why this is being done?" The voice was Dupin's, the tone was sharp, and nobody was more surprised to hear it than I was. Well, maybe I was runner-up. Driscoll's face was a picture. He made a show of peering around on his own eye level for a little while before he looked down and found

Dupin a foot or so below.

"Who the hell are you?" he demanded.

"*Le Chevalier* Auguste Dupin, at your service. I repeat, why is this being done?"

Driscoll didn't seem inclined to dignify that question with an answer, so Flood obliged us instead. "He already told you, you moron. These workings ain't safe. Twenty men died here."

"Twenty men died here," Dupin agreed. "But not because of the presence or absence of adequate building standards."

"And you'd know?"

"Yes. I would know. They were murdered."

Flood's face went through a series of discrete states, like a slide show. Astonishment, then a sort of ghastly dismay, then anger. "You fuck!" he spluttered. He balled his hand into a fist and drew it back.

Driscoll caught it in mid-air and held onto it. He moved as quick as a snake, and he didn't seem to be exerting any particular effort to hold the constable immobile. "I think you should get your friend home, Mr. Nast," he said mildly. "Otherwise, I'll have to arrest him for breach of the peace."

"Breach of the peace?" The Frenchman glanced at me with an interrogatory expression.

"Means you're stirring up a riot," I translated. "Come on, Mr. Dupin, we're leaving."

"Yeah, you better," Flood spat. The sergeant gave him his hand back and he glared at us, rubbing his wrist, as I hauled Dupin over to the ladder.

"I have further questions for the gentleman in charge," Dupin protested.

"They'll have to keep," I muttered. "Trust me, these two will break your head as soon as look at you."

"They are agents and representatives of the law."

"Nope, of the city. Not the same thing at all."

I steered him ahead of me halfway up the ladder, but then he stopped – which meant I had to stop, too, since the only way up was through him. "Monsieur!" he called down to Sittingbourne. "Hola, Monsieur! Who put out the lanterns?"

Sergeant Driscoll slipped his nightstick out of his belt and tapped it meaningfully against his palm.

Sittingbourne made a helpless gesture. Dupin tutted, and carried on up. But he'd got the bit fairly between his teeth now, and he certainly didn't seem interested in leaving. He went over to the steam pump and started to walk around and around it, inspecting it from all angles. It looked a little beaten up here and there – especially around the protuberant valve assemblies to which the hoses were attached. A pump like this was like a heart in a human body, working mightily without cease. It was an amazing thing in its own right, that allowed even more amazing things to be done.

"You know how a caisson works?" I asked Dupin.

"Yes," he said. "I believe so. It is a hyperbaric environment, no?"

"It's a what?"

"It utilises air at higher than atmospheric pressure to create a dry working space below sea level. Or in this case, river level. Air is pumped in by artificial means to maintain the pressure, which may be two or three times greater than that in the ambient air outside the caisson."

"Well, yeah," I said. "That's more or less how it's done."

Actually, Dupin seemed to understand the process better than I did. He was starting to fiddle with the controls on the steam pump now, and the foreman came running over hell for leather.

"Say hey, now," he yelped. "You don't want to be messing with this. This is delicate equipment. And that outlet connection there is loose!"

Dupin gave him a withering glare. "Nonsense!" he snapped. "This is a Jacquard-Sevigny pump, made from a single moulding. You could take a hammer to it – and indeed, it looks as though someone has – but still it would not break."

O'Reilly faltered a little, but only for a moment. "It's private property," he said. "You keep your hands off it, or I'll sic the police on you, see?"

I felt like we'd had more than enough of that already, so I took Dupin by the arm with a view to getting him moving again, but he slipped out of my grip and went after O'Reilly like a terrier after a rat. "You found the bodies?" he demanded.

O'Reilly backed away. "Yeah, I did," he said. "So?"

"So. How did you find them? Tell me."

"I just… well, I went away, and I come back, and they was dead. I don't know how. I don't know anything about it."

"When was this?"

"It was eight o'clock. On the turn of the shift."

"Did you disturb the bodies?" The foreman was still moving backwards and Dupin was still following, almost stepping on his toes.

"No! I never touched them!"

"And yet they were arranged in rows. Was that how they died?"

"No. Yes. I moved them, obviously. But that was afterwards."

"And the lanterns?"

The foreman was looking a little bit desperate now. "The what?"

"The lanterns. Did you extinguish them?"

"No. They was already out."

Dupin stopped dead, and turned to me. "*Bien*," he said. "We are finished here."

That was news to me, since I was the one who was meant to be showing him the sights. But I guess we'd gone off that agenda a while before. "Okay," I said. "You want to go see the Equitable Life building? It's got a hydraulic elevator, made by Elisha Otis, and you can ride all the way up to the..."

"I want to see the lady you mentioned, Monsieur Nast," Dupin interrupted forcefully. I was a little mystified at this, and I must have looked it. "Madame Roebling, I think the name was? The lady who builds this bridge."

I tried to explain to him that we couldn't just walk in on the Roeblings, but Dupin wasn't having any of that. There's a thing called a New York minute, and inside of one of those we were pulling up at the door of the Roebling house in midtown in another cab that Curtis was going to get all sore about paying for. And Dupin was explaining to some sour old curmudgeon in a spiffy black and silver livery that he was the godson of Colonel Maximilian Roebling-Lefevre of the *Légion d'Honneur*, and on that basis would be delighted to pay his respects to the lady of the house.

The curmudgeon went away and came back with a different face on. Mrs Roebling would be delighted to see us in the morning room.

She didn't look all that delighted, though. It was like walking in on a funeral, which I guess in one sense we were. Mrs Roebling looked as pale as death, and though she rallied enough to greet us, she couldn't find a whole lot to say.

"You'll have to forgive me, gentlemen," she said. "I - - I've just had some very bad news. Twenty workers on one of our construction projects have died in the most tragic of circumstances. It appears that our working practices may be to blame. The caisson sickness has incapacitated a number of our masons and navigators, and laid my husband low. And now – now it seems it's taken a score of men at a single stroke!"

She started in to crying at this, which was a distressing thing to see. I made the usual *there, there* noises, but Dupin surprised me – surprised both of us – by laughing. Not the belly laugh, this time, but a little snort like a steam kettle saying it's ready. Mrs Roebling gave him a startled look.

"Pray, sir," she said, affronted, "what can you find in these awful facts to amuse you?"

Dupin made a dismissive gesture. "The facts, Madame," he said, "the facts are not amusing at all. What is amusing is the refusal of all parties concerned to acknowledge them. You feel responsible for the deaths of these men?"

Mrs Roebling blanched at the blunt question. "Why yes," she said. "To some extent, I do."

"Then calm yourself. You are not responsible at all, and I will prove it. But tell me, how was the news brought to you?"

"By a runner," Mrs Roebling said. "Sent by the foreman, Mr. O'Reilly, shortly after eight o'clock."

"And then?"

"And then, hard on his heels, an attorney came from the mayor's office to tell me that my building permits had been revoked. We now owe the city a great deal of money. We must pay for a full inspection, which will be expensive and onerous. There will be a fine, besides, for so serious a breach of safety regulations. And of course, compensation for the families of the dead men must also be found. I fear this may sink our project completely."

Dupin glanced at me. "The mayor's office?" he queried. Evidently I'd been appointed his personal perambulatory encyclopaedia.

"253 Broadway," I said. "Don't tell me you want to go see the mayor, Dupin. It's a long haul back the way we came, and a long haul west, and I let the cab go."

Dupin didn't seem to be listening. He'd turned his attention back to Mrs. Roebling again. "At what time, precisely, did these runners arrive?"

Mrs Roebling couldn't say – not precisely – but the butler (the gent in all the black and silver) was called and he knew the times to a nicety. See, that's what I mean about clothes and moral seriousness. The runner from the works had arrived at 8.27, and the clerk from city hall at 8.33.

Dupin absorbed this news in solemn silence, then turned to me again. There was a kind of a gleam in his eye. "I do not, Monsieur Nast, wish to see the mayor. But I think perhaps I would like to see the commissioner of police."

Mrs Roebling gasped. "Do you honestly believe, sir, that a crime has been committed?" she demanded, her face clouded with bewilderment.

"I believe, in fact," Dupin said, "that several crimes have been committed. But I will not speak of things I cannot prove. For this morning's events, I can speak with absolute certainty. Those men were murdered, and the culprit is already known to you." He turned to the lady again. "Madame," he said. "I request you to remain here, and to ignore for the moment any communications from the mayor's office or from city officials of whatever provenance. I will tell what I know, and we will see what we will see. But I assure you, you will pay for no inspections nor levies. The compensation, yes, since the men are dead and you would not wish to leave their families destitute. But that will be the limit of your exposure."

We left the lady in a pretty confused state – and to be honest, I was more than a little consternated myself. Otherwise, I think I would have put up more of a resistance. But Dupin had the hang of summoning cabs now, and that was a terrible power to put in a Frenchman's hands. He waved his cane like an orchestra conductor, and a two-horse rig rolled to a halt right in front of us. He was jumping up onto the running board even while I was explaining that this was a fool's errand. I had no choice but to jump up after him.

"You can't just walk into the police commissioner's office and make wild assertions, Dupin," I told him, in something of a panic. "Especially not in this city. It just won't wash."

"*Pourquoi ça*, Monsieur Nast?" Dupin snorted. "Why will it not wash?" He wasn't even looking at me. He'd taken out a fancy silver pocket watch and was consulting it with a look of deep deliberation.

Where to begin? "Well, for starters, you're not even armed."

"But yes. I am armed with the truth."

"Oh, jumping Jehosaphat!"

I carried on remonstrating with him, because I kind of felt like it was incumbent on me to be the voice of reason. But there wasn't any way of shifting him. I just got sucked along in his wake, and before I knew it we were walking up the steps of the police headquarters building.

Two officers standing up on the top step like bouncers at the door of a bar room looked us up and down and asked our business. Dupin was looking at his watch again, so I handled the introductions myself – with something of a sinking feeling in my stomach. I said we were from the Harper's Weekly and we'd love to talk to Commissioner Smith and maybe sketch his portrait for the papers.

One of the cops led us inside, leaving the other one to take care of the business of looking tough and surly by himself for a while. We got some curious glances from the flatfoots sitting in the bullpen, and the officers in their little working cupboards. Dupin looked neither left nor right, but when we finally approached the commissioner's door he put on a turn of speed and got there first.

"See here," our tutelary spirit said. "I got to announce you, is what."

"I am the chevalier Auguste Dupin," the Frenchman declaimed, with fine contempt, "and I will announce myself."

The door was already ajar. Dupin threw it wide with a thrust of his cane and walked inside. I followed him, into a fug of smoke chopped into lines of solid white and solid black by the sunlight filtering through the window blinds.

It looked like the men in that room had put the sun in jail, almost. Had thrown it behind bars. A fanciful notion, obviously, but they were the men to do it, if such a thing could be done.

There were six of them, but I only saw four of them out of the gate. Police Commissioner Hank Smith, whose office this was, his doughy face overshadowed by a massive brow like the ledge over a cave. James Kelso, his superintendent, who looked like a cardinal of the church of Rome, thinning hair swept back and thin lips pursed. Mayor Oakey Hall, with his pendulous, bifurcated moustache like the mandibles of a huge spider.

They were sitting around a big table, off to one side of Smith's desk. At the head of the table sat not Smith but Smith's boss and the boss of everyone else here.

William Magear Tweed rose slowly from his chair as we entered the room. He towered above us. The man was architectural in his build – well over six feet in height, three hundred pounds or more in avoirdupois. But he looked a whole lot bigger and a whole lot heavier than that. His tiny round eyes might have looked weak on another man. In his face, the eyes being the windows of the soul, they looked like pinholes pricked into a black inferno.

"Well, now," he said. His voice was a deep basso rumble like a trolley car going by. "It's Mr. Nast, and his friend with the dapper clothes and the funny accent. You going to introduce us?"

"Actually, Mr. Tweed," I said, "we just come here to sketch the commissioner's portrait. But since he's busy, we'll come back another time."

"Wouldn't hear of it," Tweed said. "Pull up a chair for Mr. Nast, and… I don't know, what do you say to a high stool for the little guy?"

He was talking to the two remaining men, who stepped out of the smoke and shadow then. Sergeant Driscoll closed the door. Constable Flood kicked two chairs in our general direction, his face suffused with a nasty grin as with a bruise.

That sinking feeling I was talking about sunk about another twelve storeys, quicker than any hydraulic elevator yet invented.

"Sit down, you yeggs," Flood sneered. I slumped down in one of the chairs, but Dupin didn't even acknowledge the loaded courtesy.

"You are Boss Tweed?" he demanded. "I have heard of you."

"Most people have," Tweed allowed. "As a humble servant of the city of New York, I hope. So you gents came here to paint a pretty picture?"

I opened my mouth to answer, but Dupin was in there a sight too fast for me. "No."

"No?"

"Not at all. We are here to report an act of mass murder."

Something like a soundless shockwave went through the room. The two cops and the three seated officials braced themselves against it, seemed to tremble slightly as it passed. Not Tweed. He just raised his eyebrows up a little and let it go by him.

"Mass murder," he ruminated. "I thought you ran a tighter ship than that, Hank. Any mass murderers you know of that you didn't put on payroll yet?"

The police commissioner gave a sickly grin. "Very droll, Bill," he muttered. "Very droll. You better watch what you say, Mr. Nast. Perjury's still a crime in this state."

"Although it's also somewhat of an industry," Tweed added. Everyone except Smith laughed at that, even the two cops.

Now I hadn't said a thing to the purpose, let alone under oath, so the perjury shot went wide. But then it wasn't a writ I was afraid of here. I took Dupin by the shoulder, hoping we could still steer a way out of these choppy waters, but he didn't budge an inch. And it probably wouldn't have mattered if he had, because Driscoll and Flood had taken up station at the door. Driscoll had his hand resting on the holster at his belt and Flood had his nightstick out, casually resting it athwart his shoulder. There wasn't any way out except forward.

"The murders I speak of," Dupin said, "were committed at eight o'clock this morning at the site of the bridge that is being constructed close to the Centre Street Pier. The principal agent and perpetrator is most likely the foreman at that site, a gentleman named O'Reilly, but I believe he had confederates whose names he might be made to divulge under questioning."

"Oh, you believe that?" Tweed asked politely.

"Yes."

"Those weren't murders," Jimmy Kelso said, all windy self-importance. "We already looked into that. Those men was killed by the caisson disease."

"That," said Dupin, "is an absurd conclusion. Every single observation that can be made says otherwise."

"And what observations are those?" Tweed asked. He was looking highly amused, which I didn't like at all.

Dupin seemed pretty happy too, and I realised he'd been building up to this. He struck a stance. "To begin with," he said "caisson sickness is a malady with a slow onset and a slow progression. The idea that it might afflict a score of people all at the same time, and kill them at a stroke, is absurd."

"Horse puckey!" Kelso said, with force. "Nobody even knows how the caisson disease even works, so nobody can say what it can and can't do."

Dupin's lip turned at the corner as he stared at the superintendent. "There is already a body of literature relating to hyperbaric environments," he said.

Kelso blinked. "There's a what?"

"There are essays, monsieur, and monographs, and longer studies, about the conditions in which these unfortunate men worked. The caisson sickness seems to be a side effect of those conditions – conditions which, though they may be imperfectly understood, are extremely well documented. I have myself visited le professeur Fontaine's hyperbaric chamber at the Sorbonne and studied its operation. Air from the outside world is excluded by welded seals and tight-fitting doors. Breathable air, under higher than atmospheric pressure, is injected into the caisson by means of a Jacquard-Sevigny steam-driven pumping apparatus. The same machine draws away exhaled air and expels it outside the caisson, so that the level of oxygen – that indispensable gas identified by Monsieur Lavoisier, another of my countrymen – remains constant."

"You talk beautifully," Boss Tweed said, every bit as easy as before. "But not to the purpose. Who cares how the pump works?"

"I do, monsieur," Dupin said. "I care very much. When I examined the bodies in the caisson, I found that they all had livid skin and blue lips."

"So?"

"*Alors.* If they had died from caisson sickness, their skin would be bright red. An urticuric rash, as from the touch of nettles, would have been visible on their faces and necks. This in itself was enough to arouse my suspicions. What confirmed them was the fact that the lamps in the caisson, essential to the continuing work there, had all been extinguished.

"And that, monsieur, could mean only one thing. A wind or breeze, in that space where air was so carefully rationed, was impossible. The only thing that could have put out those flames was the absence of the oxygen on which they fed. The lights died for the same reason that the men died. They had no oxygen to consume, and without it, had not the wherewithal to continue in existence."

Something like a frown passed across Tweed's big, heavy-featured face, but he rallied pretty quickly and managed a pained smile. "You're saying someone stole the air?"

"*Bien sûr que non.* Not the air. Only the oxygen from the air."

"And how does a man go about stealing that, exactly?"

"A man," Dupin said with grim emphasis, "attaches the outlet hose on the steam pump back into the inlet valve, creating in effect a closed system. A *boucle.* A loop. The men's exhaled air, depleted of the vital oxygen, is fed back to them, again and again, until they suffocate. Which does not take long at all."

There was a deathly silence in the room. The men at the table looked to

Tweed, as if they weren't willing to venture an opinion on this subject until the boss had spoken. I kept quiet too, but for a different reason. I was thinking of those men's last moments, and my mind was reeling. I couldn't imagine a worse way to die – and I couldn't imagine the mind that could have cooked up something like that. At the same time, I was starting to put things together the way Dupin had, running along after his thought processes the way a dog runs after a fire tender.

"The marks on the pump," I said. "That outlet valve did look all beaten up. As though..."

"As though someone had levered it off, with a wrench or a crowbar," Dupin finished. "And then replaced it again, after it had served its purpose. Yes, I believe that to be the case."

"But whatever you believe," Boss Tweed said, with the calm of complete indifference, "you can't prove who did it."

"Ah, but I think I can," said Dupin, sealing our fate. "The runner who came from city hall to announce that the workings were unsafe and had to close arrived at thirty-three minutes past the hour. Let us assume that a message was sent from the worksite as soon as the deaths were discovered, and that the mayor – " he gave Oakey Hall a perfunctory bow " – delivered his decision immediately. The two journeys, cross-town and then north to Mrs Roebling's house, require a minimum of fifty minutes to complete. It can therefore be established by a very simple calculation that the messenger sent from city hall must have been dispatched before any notification could have arrived from the site."

Hall blanched as Boss Tweed shot him a cold, disapproving glance. "That true?" he demanded.

"I thought we wanted to shut them down fast," the mayor protested, with something of a whine in his voice. "I didn't think anyone was going to be standing on the street with a damn stopwatch."

"No," Tweed agreed. "You didn't think. You never do, Oakey. Maybe it's time I replaced you with someone who does." He gave a hitch of his shoulders, which was evidently a sign to Driscoll and Flood. Driscoll put his gun in my back, and Flood grabbed a hold of Dupin.

"But... but why?" I demanded. Given the extremity of the situation, talking back to the Boss didn't feel like quite as fearful a prospect as it would normally have been. "Why would you do something like this?"

Tweed seemed surprised to be asked. He shrugged his massive shoulders. "The usual reason," he said. "Come on, Nast. You're a newsman, not a babe in arms. The New York to Brooklyn bridge is the biggest building project this city has ever seen. All we wanted was a decent kickback. The old man was dragging his feet, so we arranged a little accident for him. We started leaning on the son, and he was just about to roll when he got sick. That left us with the lady, who's the toughest nut of the lot. Or maybe just the stupidest. She didn't seem to understand that when we said we could help her with her licenses and her on-site security, we were asking for a bribe. She just said thank you and goodnight. So we thought we'd move things along a little."

"By killing twenty men?" I asked, my throat dry.

Those tiny black eyes blinked slowly, the way a cat's eyes do. "Well, you know what they say about omelettes. If you're serious about making them, you can't afford to get sentimental about eggs."

"You murdering bastard," I said. "Some of those eggs had wives and kids."

"They'll break too," the Boss replied laconically. "Sooner or later makes no difference. It's not like eggs are built to last." He gave Driscoll a meaningful look. "Get rid of them," he said. "Somewhere real quiet. Say a few words over the bodies, then take the evening off."

That was the end of the interview. Driscoll and Flood hauled us out of there, and took us via the back door of the building to a paddy wagon. They pushed us inside and locked the door. We could hear Flood hitching up the horses, with a lot of cursing, while Driscoll berated him for his clumsiness.

It was a long, uncomfortable ride, all the way uptown to the northern tip of Manhattan island. The swampy ground around the Palisades was slowly being reclaimed, and the city was obviously going to head out that way in its own good time, but back then it was a wilderness. The few tracks there were petered out quickly, leaving you adrift in an endless expanse of couch grass and stunted trees.

"I'm real sorry, Mr. Dupin," I muttered.

"About what?" Dupin demanded.

"All this. Dying in a ditch is a poor sort of a way for your day of sightseeing to end. And I'm the native guide here. I should have headed this off before you got too far into it. Mind you," I added, "I didn't know you were going to be accusing Boss Tweed himself of multiple counts of homicide."

"*Je vous en prie,*" Dupin demurred, and since I had no clue what that meant the conversation ended there.

The paddy wagon slowed to a halt. We heard Driscoll and Flood jump down from the driver's seat, and a second later the doors were hauled open. Driscoll had a pistol levelled at us, and Flood had some kind of a sap – shorter than his nightstick but just as lethal-looking.

"Last stop, my buckos," the constable said cheerfully.

We climbed down out of the wagon into a desolate landscape. We were only a few miles outside the city limits, but there wasn't a building in sight. The sun was touching the horizon, and there was a sharp wind getting up, making the leafless trees lean over like they were hunching down against the cold.

Sergeant Driscoll chucked me on the chin with the barrel of the pistol, as though to coax a smile out of me. "Any last words, Mr. Nast?" he asked, mildly. "A prayer, perhaps? Or a confession? We're not in any hurry."

It was a thoughtful offer in the circumstances, but I couldn't think of anything either reverential or splenetic that was worth detaining him with. I'd sort of resigned myself to death, now, and I just wanted to get the unpleasant business over with. I shook my head.

Dupin seemed even more detached. He wandered over to a flowering bush and prodded it with his cane. Flood stood over him, sap in hand, guarding him until it was his turn to be dispatched.

"Right then," Driscoll said. "May the good lord have mercy. I can speak for my shooting, so your only worry's what happens afterwards."

He took aim at my forehead, and I braced myself for the world to come.

At that point, constable Flood gave a sudden, constricted gasp and sank to his knees. Driscoll turned, astonished.

"What's the matter with you, you idiot?" he demanded.

Flood opened his mouth, but nothing came out of it except a thin trickle of blood. He pitched forward onto his face.

Dupin swished the sword that had appeared from nowhere in his hand. "Direct your thoughts, monsieur," he suggested, "to what happens afterwards."

Driscoll was as fast as a snake, a trait I believe I've remarked on earlier in this narrative. He swung the pistol round in the blink of an eye, but Dupin's arm dipped and rose and intersected the other man's at some significant point in its arc. The gun went flying away through the air and Driscoll started back with a cry, nursing his hand.

The sword flashed again and the sergeant's legs buckled under him. A spurt of crimson from his severed throat splashed my sleeve as he fell. I stared at it stupidly, only decoding its meaning when Dupin slid the slender blade back into its housing in his cane. "*Voilà,*" he said.

"You - - you had - - " I stammered. "You were - - "

"Armed," Dupin agreed. "The truth is all very well, but sometimes one needs a little more. Come, Monsieur Nast. We have a carriage and horses, but not much daylight left. It would be a good idea, I think, to get back to the city before night is fully upon us."

In fact, he left me at the edge of town. He purposed to hire a boat or a berth at the tiny harbour on Spuyten Duyvil Creek, rather than risk buying a ticket home anywhere in New York City itself. He had a shrewd suspicion that Boss Tweed might be looking for him, once he realised that his two spudpicker assassins had misfired. The haulage men at Spuyten Duyvil would take him on up the coast to Bridgeport or Westhaven, and he could continue on his travels from there.

"My survival, Monsieur Nast," the Frenchman assured me, "will be the earnest and guarantor of yours. Tweed and his associates will want you dead, but they will not dare to move against you so long as I am free and able to speak of what I know. I cannot, of course, prove that he was involved in these murders, but I can embarrass and clog the machine of which he is a part. And I will do so, if he defies me."

We shook hands and parted company. Dupin rode away northwards and I hiked down to Morningside. There, I was able to prevail on a fisherman to give me a lift on the back of his cart when he took his day's catch down to Peck Slip, and I was home only an hour or so after sunset.

Dupin, I learned later, had put pen to paper before he embarked from Spuyten Duyvil. Whatever it was he wrote to Tweed, the Tammany machine rescinded its writs and remands against the Roebling family and their great construction project and withdrew any and all accusations of unsafe working practises. A warrant was issued for the arrest of the foreman, O'Reilly, on twenty counts of murder, but his room in a seedy boarding house at Red Hook was found to have been emptied of all moveable items. Verbal descriptions were issued, along with a promise of reward, but O'Reilly never turned up again, and I doubt he will now – not until the last trump brings the dead up out of their graves.

Dupin wrote to me, too, enclosing a letter for Mrs Emily Roebling but also a few lines for my own edification. *Your Mr. Tweed*, he wrote, *trades very strongly on the appearance of invulnerability. If you wish to harm him, you must first encourage the perception that he is susceptible to harm. I mention this, my dear friend, because your own trade of cartooning seems to me to be very admirably suited to this purpose. You asked me a question when we first met: what is your motive and your métier? What is the singular thing that you pursue? I ask you now to consider this very question yourself. I believe that your answer will be the same as mine – that you are a servant of truth. And you will know to what I am referring when I say she arms her servants well."*

Well, I chewed that over a while, and I saw clear enough that he was right. So I took up my sword (it was shaped somewhat like a Woodson & Penwick number 1 black sable paintbrush) and I went to war.

FOOTNOTE: From 1870 to 1873, Thomas Nast's editorial cartoons mercilessly lampooned the corrupt activities of the Tammany Ring, and its formidable front man, William "Boss" Tweed. Harper's Weekly rallied behind him, and one by one the other New York newspapers joined the crusade. In 1873, Tweed was arrested on multiple charges of fraud and racketeering. He died in prison five years later, having been convicted on all counts.

M. R. CAREY

M. R. Carey is a British writer whose work appears in comic books, novels, TV, film, and radio. His novel The Girl with All the Gifts is an international bestseller, and has been adapted by Carey for the 2016 Colm McCarthy-directed film.

He has written for DC and Marvel, including critically acclaimed runs on Ultimate Fantastic Four and X-Men, and with Peter Gross, Lucifer and The Unwritten. His books include The Girl with All the Gifts, Fellside, the Felix Castor series, The Steel Seraglio (with Linda and Louise Carey), and The Boy on The Bridge.

THE FANGLUR AND THE TWOOF
by Toby Litt

I asked my Mother, who is now dead, Are they shells or are they teeth? And she lied to me because she said, They are shells.

But I knew they were teeth like my teeth from the way they crunched under my feet – teeth crunch differently to shells, so I asked her, the Noma, when my mother was up ahead talking to Uncle Big.

They aren't shells, are they? I said, They are teeth.

The Noma said, What did your Mother say?

She told me teeth, I said. I wanted to test the Noma.

The Noma turned her head in my direction. She was wrapped in grey rags. There was a slit for her eyes and a hole for her mouth. Her head was much higher than mine because she was up on her mount, which was silvery blue like they say sea-water was.

Then these are teeth, she said.

My Mother said they were shells, I said.

The Noma looked away from me and out towards the horizon. I looked too.

I could see all five of us – my Mother, my Father, Uncle Big, Uncle Small walking and the Crone on her mount.

If your mother said these are shells, she said, then these are shells.

I reached down and picked a handful.

Look, I said, they are teeth. My mother lied to me so I wasn't scared. But I'm not scared.

The Noma made a sound which might have been a laugh.

I held all the teeth up in my hand, held them high towards the Noma.

Have a close look, I said.

She leaned down and to take them. And when she held out her palm, I saw a black drawing of an eye with a tail like a fish.

I knew if I asked about the eye-fish the Noma would stop talking so I kept going like I hadn't seen it.

I said, How can there be a whole desert of nothing but teeth?

The Noma said, Ask your Mother.

Then she kicked her mount in the sides and went much faster than I could.

I watched her ride and I knew it was the most perfect thing I had ever seen. Her mount was a beautiful creature but with the Noma on its back, it was complete.

When she did the deal with Uncle Big and Uncle Small and my Father, and they promised her one tenth of our herd if she got us safely to the jungle, the

Noma had been on her mount.

Noma always do business in the saddle, said my father. You must learn this.

But the way he said it made me think he had only just learned it.

He grew up in the mountains, like my mother, like me. This was the first time he had seen the desert, but he said we had no choice except to cross it.

My Father knew that in the jungle there were lakes and pools. For a long time, as he persuaded my Mother, that was what I heard him say, late at night, Lakes and pools.

*

The sun was the width of my fist above the horizon when the Noma stopped and said, Here.

We got our bedrolls out from our bundles. There was nothing to burn but the Noma put down a shape like four triangles on top of a square that glowed green and, after a few moments, was very hot.

Don't touch it, said Uncle Small.

He won't, said Uncle Big.

The Crone said nothing, just made her cooing sounds. She never ate anything, which was lucky because there was very little.

The Noma's mount was close to us but the Noma was standing on a dune, looking back the way we came. When I finished eating, I went to stroke the blue of the mount's neck.

I was watching the Noma when she fell to her knees. She covered her eyes with her hands and lifted them off, six times.

She hurried to my Father. I heard my Mother say, What? as the Noma dragged my Father to the top of the dune. The rest of us, except the Crone, stood up and ran to join them.

Who are they? asked Uncle Big.

I saw them – two dark shapes standing on a high dune, about a hundred paces away, looking at us.

Where? said my Mother, who is now dead.

And at that moment, the shape on the left raised an arm, or what it had instead of an arm.

What do they want? asked my Father.

The Noma said, Gift them your herd, and they will let you live.

Uncle Big said, Never. He had a weapon. Uncle Small had one, too, and my Father.

Who are they? I asked.

212

The Noma said, On the left, the one who signalled, that is the Twoof. On the right, that is the Fanglur.

Uncle Big laughed. Funny names, he said.

Do we have a choice? my Father asked the Noma, and the Noma said, No.

What? said Uncle Big. But this is a set-up. This woman is with them.

Be quiet, said Uncle Small. Then to the Noma he said, He did not mean it, blessings.

She said nothing.

We should give them the herd, said my Father.

Decide, said the Noma. But understand. If you do not gift them the herd and walk away, they will not accept the herd after. They will kill you, one before moonrise, every day. That is how they feed.

There are two of them, said Uncle Big. There are seven of us.

I was surprised he counted the Crone.

The Noma said, I am not one of you. And she walked away from us.

I vote we give them the herd, said my Father.

And I say no, said Uncle Big.

Uncle Small mumbled, I also say no.

My mother said, I vote with my Husband.

They looked at me.

I thought of the shells and the teeth and said, I vote with my Mother.

It is decided, said my Father, and started to walk toward the Noma.

The Crone, said Uncle Big, we must ask her.

But she has no part of the herd, said my Mother.

But she is one of us, Uncle Big said back.

We walked over to the Crone and my Mother explained the choice.

The Crone pointed to a nearby beast and shook her head.

We are split, said my Father.

This is our Grandmother's herd, said Uncle Small to my Mother. And you will give them away?

My Mother looked at my Father and said, I change my vote. Then she spat at Uncle Small and walked away.

My father went to the Noma and told her what we had decided, then went to my Mother.

Uncle Big and Uncle Small were looking toward the two.

I went across to the Noma. I stroked the mount's neck and it raised its head, then put its head down.

How many days to cross the desert? I asked.

Seven, said the Noma. Today was the first, she said. The moon has risen.

Six days left, seven people left.

*

Uncle Big died first. We had walked all morning. The herd was running faster than usual.

There had been a lot of talk, at first between Uncle Big and Uncle Small, then between them and my Father. They touched their guns.

I tried to talk to the Noma but she rode away from me.

The Fanglur and the Twoof, also riding fine animals, kept the same distance.

The sun was as high as it gets, when Uncle Big and Uncle Small and my Father began to charge back towards the two.

The Noma glanced back then carried on. She knew what was going to happen.

When the Twoof fired the harpoon it went through Uncle Big's neck.

Uncle Small kept charging. My father stopped by Uncle Big.

Uncle Small's shots flew past the Fanglur before it fired its harpoon. The bolt went through Uncle Small's weapon and took off two fingers.

Uncle Small ran back, grabbed my Father by the arm and pulled him away from Uncle Big.

When my Father and Uncle Small got back among the herd, we all looked to see what the two would do. The Twoof held up one of whatever it had instead of arms. Then it and the other climbed down off their mounts and fed upon Uncle Big.

My Mother cried. My Father swore. Uncle Small tied the finger-stumps up in rags.

I ran after the Noma.

Tell them they can have our herd, I said.

The Noma rode ahead.

Keeping up with the herd soon took us out of sight of Uncle Big. But by the time the moon rose, the shapes of the Fanglur and the Twoof were one hundred paces away.

Five days left, six people.

*

Soon as the sun rose, we moved. My Father had made a decision. We would cross the desert fast.

The sun was two fists above the horizon when Uncle Small charged toward the two. This time he had no weapon. Instead, he was shouting that if they let the rest of us live, they could have the Noma's mount.

Uncle Small was ten paces from the two when the Twoof's harpoon hit him. It went through his left shoulder. The two would feed straight away, I thought. But instead they kept Uncle Small alive, pulling him behind them as the sun set.

Idiot, said my father.

The Crone wept for Uncle Small as if he had been her grandson. I hadn't seen her cry for Uncle Big.

Uncle Small was killed just before the moon came up.

I went to the Noma and said, Can you speak to them?

The Noma said, Your Uncle should not have offered them my life.

It was your mount, I said.

He offered them my life, said the Noma.

Four days, five people.

*

The Crone would die next, I was sure. Her old mount was slow and, with the pace my father set, she often fell back from the herd. Sometimes she was even alongside the Fanglur and the Twoof, but they did not kill her. Perhaps they did not want to feed on her until they had to.

I often looked back. I wanted to see what the two were like, but they were as covered over as the Noma. Where she wore rags, they wore black material that looked newly woven.

My Mother died next. The day was almost gone, the sun had set and she had been muttering to herself as she walked.

Before my Father could stop her, she grabbed the reins of the Crone's mount and pulled it back towards the two. I could hear the Crone squealing in terror, but it was my Mother who was chosen. The two did not harpoon her. They just got down off their mounts and shooed the Crone's mount away, with the Crone still on it, then began to feed. I ran to stop them. My Father was not fast enough to catch me. I got very close before the Noma rode up and grabbed me. Before she had me over her saddle, I saw my Mother's exposed back. It was covered in perfect red circles where the thing that was not the Twoof's arm had touched her. There was a jagged chunk out of her side, where the Fanglur had bitten. His eyes, I saw, were not on the front of his head, but on either side.

The Noma carried me away from my Mother. The mount was an amazing thing to be riding upon. I wanted to stay there. I knew I would be safe there. But the Noma dropped me beside my Father.

As the Crone rode up to us, my Father said to her, It should have been you.

Why? she said. It was the only word I ever heard her speak.

Three days, four people.

*

Even before the sun rose, my Father forced us on. I heard him ask the Noma, How long to the edge?

Three days, she said.

That only made my Father push faster.

A furious wind hid the two from us. We kept going, teeth whipping our ankles. When the sky cleared to white, the Fanglur and the Twoof were one hundred paces behind us, and the Crone's mount trotted along without a rider. Instead it carried her bundle.

Two days, three people.

*

The last day of his life, my Father kept thinking he saw the edge.

It's there, he said, we're almost there.

The Noma tried to tell him he was wrong.

We will be there before moonrise, he shouted back at the two. Look! Look!

When the sun went down, he looked at me and said, Pools and lakes.

I tried to stop him but he hit me harder than he'd ever hit me before, and walked the hundred paces to offer himself to the two.

One day, two people.

*

That evening the Noma would not sit near me. I had plenty of food and water. Tomorrow, I could ride the Crone's mount.

I thought about escaping in the night. But I found I could not leave the herd.

I thought about my Father and my Mother, not the others.

*

The sun was high before we started.

'There it is,' the Noma said, and I saw a dark line of what I thought might be trees.

It would take us one day to get there. The moon would rise before we reached whatever it was.

Give me back the teeth I gave you, I said.

The Noma kept riding.

Why? asked the Noma. They're just the same as all the rest.

They're mine, I said. Give them back.

With her left hand, the Noma reached inside her rags, up near her chest, and pulled out the handful of teeth.

I said, You can keep them.

The Noma didn't speak.

I said, I just wanted to see if you'd give them back.

The Noma looked at me and this time she definitely did laugh.

Then she threw the teeth high in the air. I only caught one of them – this one, here, on this string.

As her hand opened, I saw the eye-fish on her other palm.

After I caught the tooth, and put it somewhere safe for the journey to the afterlife, I asked her what the eye-fish meant.

It is protection, she said, holding up both palms. Against the creatures of the sea.

The sun went lower. The edge seemed close. I could see trees.

Then the Fanglur and the Twoof sped up, and rode towards us. I thought Uncle Big had been right – the Noma was about to hand me and the herd over, for payment. I got off the old mount.

The Fanglur and the Twoof were a couple of paces away when I heard the Twoof say, Which?

Neither, said the Noma, and her hands came out from beneath the rags. I did not see what she had as she threw it, but it went through the left side of the Twoof. When the thing hit the ground, I saw the green glow and knew it had been our fire.

Go, said the Noma. I thought she meant run, but as she said it she was climbing down off her mount. Take her, she said, and gave me the reins.

The Fanglur had not even looked down at the Twoof.

The Noma walked across to the Fanglur.

I jumped onto the back of the mount and it carried me away.

I looked back and saw the Twoof had stood up again. I saw the Noma raise her hand. I was not close enough to see the eye-fish, which had not protected her.

The herd followed me. We reached the jungle before the sun was at its height.

The jungle was of hair and the pools were of blood. There were no lakes.

TOBY LITT

Toby Litt is the author of nine novels and four books of short stories. He is currently writing Wrestliana, a memoir about his relationship to his great-great-great grandfather, William Litt – a champion wrestler, poet, smuggler and exile. Toby's most recent book is Lilian's Spell Book. Toby teaches creative writing at Birkbeck College. His website is at www.tobylitt.com.

Lilian's Spell Book is a paranormal adventure novel about an ordinary English family – mother, father, pre-teen son, baby daughter – who inherit an extraordinary house. They move to this vast Elizabethan mansion in rural Sussex and away from their small South London maisonette. Very soon, they all find out their new home is haunted. But it is the mother of the family, Jeane Jonson, who begins to suspect that the secret to the house lies in the Elizabethan portrait that hangs in a room just off the vast entrance hall – a glittering, gorgeous oil painting showing the proud, red-haired Lilian holding in her hand a small leather-bound book. But the real wonders start when the narrator discovers that book itself, in the secret library of the mansion. You see, Lilian's father was an alchemist... *Lilian's Spell* Book was the #1 Paranormal novel on wattpad and has had over 750,000 reads.

SIX MONTH ANNIVERSARY
by James Miller

The flight

Just before we get on the plane Emily wants another picture of herself for her 'followers.' She hands me her I-phone 6 and strikes a pose, one leg slightly forward, a three quarters view, tilting her head towards the camera at an angle that could be called 'coquettish' with her golden blonde hair falling over her left shoulder. She fixes her perfect smile for the camera, the whiteness of her teeth matching her knee length hold ups and contrasting with her red jacket, skirt, shoe and bag combination. She holds out her boarding pass and makes sure there's enough 'background' for everyone who sees the picture to know we're at the airport. No sooner have I snapped the shot than she whisks the phone from my hands and with admirable dexterity adds tags and adjusts the filters before uploading it to Instagram.

We're flying Easyjet to the Greek island of Kos so obviously there's no Wi-Fi on the plane and Emily is agitated the whole time, looking at her phone even though it's on 'flight mode' taking it out, putting it away again and sighing. I try to read the guide book but it's hard to concentrate. This is our six-month anniversary. Emily is by far and away the most beautiful girl I have ever dated. I love her and just wish there was more I could do to keep her happy. Whenever I tell her I love her she smiles and says "me too" but that's okay, I don't want to push her. We don't need to rush things.

The moment the plane touches down Emily switches her phone back on. I can feel the tension radiating off her as she waits for it to re-connect with the network and for the 'Welcome to Greece' texts to arrive.

"You'll need to buy an internet booster pack to check Instagram," I tell her.

"I know. Thanks."

The pilot warns us that the plane is still moving and we must remain seated.

"You know the hotel has wi-fi?" I add.

She knows.

The arrival

If Emily is sad that her airport picture only garnered 563 likes in the four hours since she was last on-line she tries not to show it. Instead, she compensates by having me take a whole sequence of photos of her at the Aquaublu Boutique Hotel and Spa: Emily lying on the king sized double bed facing the camera with another winning smile, her hands propping up her chin; Emily on the balcony, gesturing at the view of the beach and the setting sun; Emily sipping a cocktail at the poolside bar; Emily in the bathroom (it's dark now) in some red lingerie. I take all the photos. She then spends an hour or so selecting which ones to upload. Certain times of day are better than others for getting likes. The morning is good, as is late afternoon. Some of it has to do with when people are getting up or perhaps coming home from work and have time to idly scroll through their feed. Some of it has to do with when America comes on-line. It's important not to upload too many pictures but at the same time it's important to upload at least one picture every day. Emily is very worried that her followers might forget about her. "The moment you're not there, you're gone," she says.

As she does this I go and sit on the balcony with my notepad and the guidebook. The hotel is located a couple miles from Kos town. Tomorrow, when it's light, there should be a wonderful view. All the same, I have an uneasy feeling as I gaze out into the darkness. I see a couple of lights in the blackness, blinking on and off. It's very quiet and there's a cool breeze and a faint, sweet smell. I spend a bit of time reading about the history of the island. Under Alexander the Great Kos became an important centre. There are numerous ruins, an Odeon and a gymnasium – I glance over the photographs of white stone pillars and amphitheatres, the remains of a 'healing temple' where they worshipped the God Asclepius – it seems like there is quite a lot to see. But I guess it's okay if we don't do anything. I know Emily wants to work on her tan and get some treatments at the spa. I wonder if I can write a story about the trip, perhaps weaving the ancient history of the island into the narrative?

"What do you think about this?" Emily comes out onto the balcony in an outfit I haven't seen before, a flowing dress made of thin lace and gauze and woven with silk flowers and a matching lace headband.

"Wow, you look amazing."

"Do you like it?"

"I love it."

"I thought perhaps we could take some photos tomorrow in the old town. Proper ones, with the camera."

Emily isn't actually a model. Well, she's had some interest. She's on the books of a small agency but it hasn't happened for her yet. One problem is that she's quite petite – only five four – so she's too small for high fashion modelling. She says her figure, which is curvy but not glamour model curvy is more suited to underwear, swim suits and certain types of street fashion or lifestyle. She knows she'll never be marching down the catwalks of Milan or Paris in the latest Praha or Versace and at twenty four she's probably too old anyway, but there are plenty of other options. That's why she's working hard on her social media profile. Lots of agencies won't even consider a girl unless she has ten thousand followers on Instagram and they have to be real ones not fake bought ones. To my eyes, Emily is the most beautiful girl in the world but as she says there are a lot of beautiful girls out there, in magazines, on social media, and she's right. There are a lot of beautiful girls.

The past

Please don't think that Emily is some sort of looks-obsessed bimbo. She's not like that at all. She's a fashion student but we met at a poetry slam in Brixton. I was one of the performers. At the time I was producing cut-ups based on fashion and celebrity magazines, reconstructing the words to make a sort of 'found poetry.' I think maybe that's why Emily was attracted to me, because I kind of understood where she was coming from but also had a bit of an ironic distance to it as well. I admit these things – fashion, beauty, celebrity – fascinate me a great deal even if I act like I don't care that much. But that's the good thing about being a writer. We can be contradictory, we can like and dislike something at the same time. It's allowed. We're not saints or politicians. After the reading she came up to me, I would have never approached her, I mean, seriously, you should see her and then you should see me. Talk about out of my league. But she came over – she was wearing, and I'll never forget, a fetching grey beret, a silk scarf, a very tight grey pullover and a little tartan kilt, her hair neatly bound in a single pony tail - and she told me that she liked my poems "the best." We went for some drinks after the others left. It was clear we had a connection. I kissed her that very night outside the tube and we started dating soon after. Now, I know Emily has dated lots of guys. Beautiful girls always do, always have. She went out with her last boyfriend for two years, her longest ever relationship. He was a banker called Jack McKinsey but she says he was "always working." Between him and me she had a fling with a personal trainer called Dave and there are times when I torment myself thinking about Dave but at least Emily says Dave was "stupid" (although I imagine he had what Emily calls "a fit bod"). But it's okay, I think Emily wants someone who can see beneath the surface, someone who doesn't just judge her for her looks. I dated a girl called Susan while I was at university, for three years we were inseparable – then it all went to pieces. We don't speak to each other anymore although we used to have lots of friends in common. Most took Susan's side after the breakup which, when I think about what happened, is fair, I suppose. Between Susan and Emily my history is barren apart from a humiliating one night stand with one of Susan's old friends, Helen, who doesn't speak to me anymore either. Anyway, I don't talk to Emily about this stuff. She wouldn't be interested and things have moved on.

The night

It's late so we go to bed. The hotel is costing me a fortune but at least the bed is huge and comfortable. It might be the nicest place I've ever stayed. Emily snuggles up to me and I run my hand across her smooth legs. She's changed out of the red lingerie and is wearing nothing but a pair of plain white panties that manage to be completely ordinary and amazingly sexy at the same time. I let my fingers drift over them, circling around. She sighs and reaches for my hand. "I'm sorry, James," she says.

"What is it?"

"I forgot to take my pill. I think my period is starting."

"Oh... but... we're only here for four days!"

"I'm sorry."

"I thought we were going to have lots of hot wild sex in our amazing hotel!" I want to shout. Instead I swallow my disappointment and say, "Okay, I guess we can still have fun."

"I'm sorry I'm such a muddle head," she sighs and snuggles closer. I tell myself it doesn't matter. We have sex all the time and it's not like this is the only holiday we will take together. Emily falls asleep almost immediately but I'm restless. I think I might be too horny to sleep. I try and think about other things but the tingle in my penis won't go away. I lie there for a bit longer and then decide to get up and go into the bathroom with my phone. I get onto Emily's Instagram. She uploaded the photo of her having a cocktail in the bar by the pool. I'm not quite sure why she went for that one as the pictures I took of her on the balcony were much better and this one has only gathered three hundred and twelve 'likes' so far. The pre-flight picture isn't doing too badly, with nine hundred and thirty two 'likes.' I scroll down until I find a set of six pictures. These were taken by a professional glamour photographer shortly before we met and Emily says they are the most liked photos on her Instagram, averaging about two thousand 'likes' each. She's modelling sexy black underwear in some shots, in others she's naked, a well-placed hand or leg preserving her modesty, except for one where she's stretching upwards, breasts revealed but nipples airbrushed out so that Instagram won't block the pictures. Nipples, it seems, are unacceptable. In another she has her bum raised in the air and she's giving the camera her best 'fuck me' look, all heavy lashes and intense red lipstick. I scroll between them and try to jerk off. When we started dating I asked her how she felt about guys looking at these pictures. "Don't you think they wank off to them?" I'd asked. Emily gave me an "ew" expression and said, "Guys wank off to anything. It's hardly my problem." I'm still trying when my phone vibrates with some breaking news. Two hundred and fifty migrants feared dead off Sicily after their boat capsized says the *Guardian*. Rescue operation underway. A picture pops up of women and children being pulled out of the water. This news interferes with my mood and my desire withers. I give up and go back to bed. Eventually, Emily's gentle breathing sends me to sleep.

The Pool

We sleep late and after breakfast Emily wants to hang out by the hotel pool. I put on my swimming trunks and a white T shirt but it takes Emily a while to decide what to wear. She unpacks the enormous suitcase she brought with us and starts going through her outfits. I discover she packed six different bikinis and five swimsuits not to mention eight pairs of shoes, from white high heels to flip flops made of cork and customised Converse trainers. No wonder she had to pay a £60 surcharge when they weighed her luggage at Stansted.

"We're only here for three more nights," I tell her, "You can't wear them all."

"Oh but I can," she laughs, "And I will," passing me her Canon camera. I take a few of her pondering what to wear. She's good at these sorts of shots, my Emily, pulling goofy (but charming) expressions and making an amusing pantomime of her indecision. She knows when she's being ridiculous and that's one of the things I like most about her. For her first outfit she settles for a plain white bikini, the top embossed and styled in such a way that it resembles two sea shells. "I'll be like Aphrodite," she says as I snap away.

It's almost noon by the time we reach the pool. The sky is a fearless bright blue, the sun very hot. The pool area is busy, lots of families hanging around, their kids splashing about in the water, playing and laughing as their parents look on. Emily frets about getting her hair wet as she spent so long straightening and styling it this morning for the pictures she wants me to take so for the first set I snap her hanging around the pool, reclining on a sun lounger, Gucci glasses hiding her eyes, then standing under a sun shade – she wears her three inch heels for this one - then sitting at the edge of the pool (no heels for this!) her legs dipped in the emerald water as she beams and blows kisses at the camera. We end this sequence with a couple of shots of her turning away wearing a large straw sun hat, her thoughtful mood indicated by the slight downturn of her lips.

Then she goes back to the room and changes into a red one piece that was sent to her by a company called Aqua-Swimwear. It's not nearly as sexy as the bikini but each year Aqua-Swimwear select a couple of girls to be the face of the brand and that means lots of potential opportunities for exposure, sponsorship, tours, all sorts of cool things. As a result, I can tell she's a little tense about these pictures being good and we spend ages getting it right. I feel bad I'm not a better photographer, not a professional. It's really hot out now, so hot that most of the families have quit the pool and we have to keep putting on sun cream. It's difficult because the cream conflicts with Emily's make-up combo and although she tans nicely we can't risk her getting burned as that would be a disaster. I manage to get sun cream on the camera lens and that upsets her. After we sort that out Emily dives into the pool (three times, in fact, to get it right) for some "water shots" and I photograph her pulling herself out the pool, the water running down and glistening off her body. I photograph her running her hands through her wet hair. I photograph her at the edge of the pool, resting her arms on the side and her head in her arms with an expression that says 'this is just me, just Emily, just chilling.' It's very bright though and I worry about whether I've got the right exposure on the camera. As we've been doing this for a couple of hours we've attracted a bit of attention. I can sense the men all looking at her, especially the Dad's with their families, the lust in their eyes; I know they wish they were me and Emily was their girlfriend. The women too, they check her out – I can tell they don't approve - and I'm reminded why Emily says she doesn't have many "girlfriends."

Finally, Emily is satisfied. "How's your period?" I ask.

"It's hurting," she says, touching her belly. "Cramps."

"You're doing really well."

She goes back to the room to get changed, to wash and dry her hair and sort out her make-up. She doesn't like to eat lunch but I sit down in the restaurant area adjacent to the pool and order a Greek salad. "Your wife is very beautiful" the waiter tells me as he brings a bottle of chilled water and some retsina.

"Oh, we're not married" I say, showing him my ring-free fingers, "But thanks."

He gives a smile that might be a little closer to a smirk and wanders off.

The town

Emily comes down an hour and a half later wearing the lacy dress she modelled for me last night and the large sunhat we used by the pool. I kept an eye on Instagram as she got ready and saw that she has uploaded two pictures in quick succession. The first is of her in the white bikini lying back on a sun lounger. Something about the pose, one leg bent, the other pointing a little too the left seems to extenuate her flat stomach and the swell of her breasts. She has the hat tilted over her face in such a way that we can just see her pert chin and lips – it adds a hint of mystery and allure to the picture. I think she's used the Reyes filter as it bleaches out the colours a bit and she's upped the contrast and structure levels to emphasise the shadows around her body. For the second picture she's wearing the red swimsuit. She's using the Mayfair filter – her favourite – and it's from behind with her arms outstretched embracing the view of the sea. It's a picture that says, 'here I am, here is life, the world is beautiful, let's dive in.' I refresh the pictures, watching the likes accumulate.

It's too hot to walk so we hire a moped and ride into Kos town. I go slow as Emily won't wear a helmet in case it messes up her hair and she won't let me go fast for the same reason. She's happy though. She tells me that she's gained nearly a hundred followers since last night including a Russian glamour model she's long admired. I point out that the Russian has had loads of surgery and her breasts look ridiculous but Emily says that's obvious and who cares because the Russian has a quarter of million followers.

We park near the remains of some sort of castle by the harbour. Emily says it's the perfect backdrop and I can tell she's right – the white dress, the blue sea and sky, the pale stone of the battlements, boats in the background – it's going to look amazing. There's even a little breeze, the wind wafting through her hair and dress and adding a dynamic quality to her poses as I snap away.

After a while Emily sighs and says, "I think that's enough, let's get a coffee or something."

She takes my hand and I feel a surge of desire for her. "It's so annoying about your period," I moan.

"I'm sorry babe, you know how forgetful I am." She strokes my arm, "I'll give you a little something later, because you've been so nice and patient with me today."

I kiss her cheek. She smells faintly of peach. I hope the "something later" might be a blow-job as this is a favour Emily dispenses very rarely. She's very fussy about what she puts in her mouth.

"I'm sorry darling, you just make me really horny" I whisper in her ear, "You're just so hot, I can't get over it."

"Silly," she blushes and moves closer to me.

As we're doing this I notice a few people – women and children as well as men – gathered in the shade of the buildings opposite the harbour. There are various bags, rucksacks and the like piled around them, as well as bedding, bits of cardboard and newspapers. I see a little girl with a dirty face, fast asleep on her mother's lap. One of the men looks at me and holds out his hand but we walk past. I guess maybe they are gypsies or something. A little further along is an upmarket café, tables and chairs set out under some awnings, chilled-out dance music playing. The proprietor beams at Emily as we sit down and presents us with a couple of menus. I order a frappe, Emily goes for a glass of white wine but after a couple of sips she pushes it away. "I should never drink on my period," she sighs, touching her tummy and frowning.

"Do you want to go back?"

"No, it's okay. Let's sit here for a bit. It's nice."

We sit for a bit. It must be the heat but I can't think of a thing to say. A few more people wandering past. I don't think they are tourists or locals, they seem sort of aimless and lost. Most of the women have headscarves. "I didn't expect to see so many gypsies here. Do you think they're from Turkey?"

"No," Emily shakes her head. "They aren't gypsies. Do you have any money?" Obviously, she didn't come out with her purse. I feel a spur of annoyance. I mean, I'm paying for the hotel – nearly two hundred Euros a night – and I've paid for all the food and drink so far. The only thing Emily paid for is her flight and her luggage surcharge.

"I've only got ten Euro notes," I say.

"Well, that's money," she answers, taking a note, getting up and walking over to one of the other women lurking on the other side of the street. I know I shouldn't be annoyed by this – it's a sign of Emily's good heart – but I'm surprised to see her talk with the woman for so long. Can't she give her the money, if she must and then go? I don't know, it seems a bit much. What is she trying to prove here? I check my phone, I sip my frappe. It's far too hot. Emily continues to talk with the woman. For the first time I notice there's a small child with the woman and Emily pats the toddlers head.

When Emily comes back, ten minutes later, she seems preoccupied.

"You really shouldn't really encourage them like that," I snap at her.

"Oh do shut up. I'm not encouraging anyone."

The dinner

I'm not sure why but the mood has soured. Maybe it's Emily, or maybe it's me, it's hard to tell. Emily hardly spoke on the ride back to the hotel. I keep asking her what's wrong but she just says "nothing" in a passive aggressive way that adds to my irritation. "Is it me?" I want to ask, but I don't dare to in case she says "yes." For dinner she changes into a pretty flowery dress but it's a very expensive designer label and I'm convinced her ex Jack the banker must have bought it for her. This fuels my anxieties. I tell myself to get a grip, it's probably just sexual frustration that explains the tension I feel between us. If we could just make love everything would be better, I'm certain. I offer to take a few pictures of her in the dress but Emily says she's "had enough" pictures for the day.

We go for dinner at the hotel. Emily is pensive and sullen. I order lamb chops, she orders prawns. When they come the prawns are magnificent but still have their heads and tails attached.

"I can't eat this."

"Why not?"

"Look at them. I just can't."

"They look amazing."

"You eat them then." She signals to the waiter. "I'm sorry," she says, handing him the plate. "I'll just get a salad."

The prawns cost 18 Euros but I know mentioning that will make me seem petty and cheap. I hate seeing good food going to waste but try to rise above the incident. I do my best to come up with topics Emily likes to talk about. I even ask her about her mother – she has a complicated relationship with her mother – but she just shrugs.

"Perhaps we can go see the ruins tomorrow?"

"Sure."

Emily doesn't want any desert. Finally, she apologies and says that her period is really hurting. "I don't mean to be a bitch," she gives me a weak smile and squeezes my hand.

We go back to the room. I sense a blow-job is probably out of the question and, indeed, Emily gets into bed hugging a pillow to her tummy and asks if I mind "turning out the light".

"Okay."

I don't feel very tired but don't really feel like reading or doing anything. I lie in the dark next to her. Emily is also restless, turning and sighing and I wish she'd tell me what was bothering her. I lie there thinking about how much this is going to cost me, all of it racking up on my credit card and wishing I'd gone for the cheaper place that Emily said she liked the look of when we were booking online. I always try too hard, that's my problem.

The morning

I check the time on my phone. Half past five. Careful so as not to wake Emily, I slip out of bed and open the doors to the balcony. First light. The sea is a like a pool of pale milk, the sun behind us, a sweet freshness to the morning air and the sound of birdsong. Somewhere, on the road into town, I hear a motorbike pottering along. It's all very beautiful and I decide to go down to the beach for a walk. I'm restless, angry at being unable to sleep, my head hurts and the room feels stifling.

Quiet as possible I slip on some clothes and put on my flip-flops. I wonder if I should leave Emily a note but she probably won't wake up. I won't be long. I decide to take my phone instead, just in case.

At this time the hotel is deserted and I walk out of reception, the night porter dozing at the desk, past the pool and the restaurant and down through gardens leading onto the beach. Several gulls, perhaps disturbed by my presence, circle overhead calling to one another. On the beach the soft sand is still warm from the day before and the waves lap gently. It's all very calm and peaceful. Using my phone I take a couple of pictures of the sea blending into the sky. There's a faint haze in the distance. Since I've been dating Emily I created my own Instagram account but I've only managed to gain about fifty followers. Emily is nice about it and says my pictures are very "artistic" but she won't let me post any photos of her. She doesn't put any pictures of me up either – or of us doing things together. I suppose she's worried it might dilute her brand. She always says it's better if people don't know about her private life. My guess is that if people think she's single then she gets more followers, more likes, especially from men. Now and then guys leave creepy or pervy comments under the pictures, but she just blocks them. It doesn't seem to bother her as much as it bothers me.

A little further along and this section of the beach isn't so pristine. There's a fair bit of rubbish mixed with tangles of dark green sea weed and driftwood. I see plastic bags, a waterlogged rucksack its straps broken and bedraggled, a pair of bright pink plastic sandals for a child, a man's leather shoe, a length of rope, what might be an old scarf, plastic bottles, a paddle for a canoe or a small boat, bits of net, another rucksack, what might be a nappy, food wrappers and other things. I see a large black rubber object that I realise must have been a dinghy, now punctured and deflated, lying half in the water like dead whale. Mess in the wet sand, scattered footprints leading towards the land, marks suggesting something has been dragged along the beach. I stop for a moment. Somewhere I can hear a small child, wailing with distress.

The Return

When I get back to the hotel Emily is awake and I can tell she's been crying. "I just went for a walk," I say, "I couldn't sleep." But she won't tell me why she's upset and I don't think it has anything to do with waking up to find me gone. I wonder if it's something to do with her mother but she just wipes her eyes and says, "You don't get it, do you?"

"Get what?" I say. "What are you talking about?"

I try to make the best of it but the rest of the holiday doesn't go as well as I had hoped. We never make it to the ruins. Emily spends a lot of time having treatments in the hotel spa. She doesn't even bother to wear all the different bikinis and swimsuits she packed.

Two days later, as we sit together on the Stansted Express heading back towards London, Emily tells me things have been very "intense" between us and she needs some "space." "Okay," I say, trying not to look upset. "I understand," but that's not really true because try as I might I don't understand at all.

For the next week Emily continues to post pictures – one a day – from our holiday onto her Instagram account. Of course I like them all. Then she doesn't post anything for quite some time.

JAMES MILLER

James Miller was born in London. He is the author of the novels
LOST BOYS, SUNSHINE STATE and UNAMERICAN ACTIVITIES
as well as numerous short stories.
He has a PhD in American literature and is currently senior
lecturer in Creative Writing at Kingston University. You can
read an extract from UNAMERICAN ACTIVITIES here:
http://www.dodoink.com/pour-out-the-vials
More of James Miller's short fiction can be read here:
https://thepigeonhole.com/books/sexstaves and here
https://www.litro.co.uk/2014/09/area-52/.
For more info please visit www.jamesmillerauthor.com
Or Follow James on Twitter: @jmlostboys

Unamerican Activities explores the conspiracy theories and violence
of modern America through a series of interlocking stories told by deranged
and desperate narrators. Populated by meth addicts, vampire hunters,
porn stars, fanatical evangelists, disgraced academics and zombified hipsters,
James Miller's third novel is a crazy homage to American pop culture
and genre fiction, an unforgettable road trip through through the
dark heart of the United States.

DARK MATTERS
by Courttia Newland

The world beyond his room had grown mysterious, untrustworthy. He spent whole days alone, his parents' downstairs, lying belly-down on the carpet, sketching and colouring images. At first, during his early years, Max responded to the graffiti everywhere he went, the characters and wild styles and throw ups, the improbable mix of colours that seldom met in the natural world. When he grew older he searched above, towards the light saturated night sky. His canvas became larger, moving from school notebooks to A3 sheets. He began to conjure nebulae, solar systems, distant dwarf stars that shone pale milk blue, the lifeless glow of dead planets. His parents began to grow worried. To them his pictures were of nothingness, empty, dead space, cold and isolated. His mother complained to Aunt Lina that he'd lock himself away for hours, rarely coming down to eat, and even when he did he wouldn't speak. His father eyed him with sullen concern, mouth opening and closing fish-like, cigarette poised by his lips, grasping for a language never caught.

Max knew what he feared most; the foreign looks, that slow creep away, and in strange, laughable contrast, the trailing six steps behind him in every shop, his newfound size met with awe and some distress. The previous summer he felt people thought him charming, possibly lovable. Without warning all that had changed. Now he was a foreign body causing panic. A threat.

He lay stretched on his stomach painting a watercolour cloud of blue in red when Noel knocked for him. His neighbour lived two streets away, so their mothers made sure they walked to school together, hoping to deter rougher neighbourhood youths. When the boys reached their school gates they split like torn paper, staying apart until it was time to go home. Max didn't blame him. He liked Noel. He was short, not self-conscious, confident and popular with girls, boys, and teachers, humorous and knowledgeable without seeming quirky. Once, at lunch, Noel spent ten minutes stabbing every chip on his plate onto a fork with intent precision, while the entire population of the school hall watched, applauding as he crammed the soft-spiked bunch into his mouth.

At the knock, Max half-rolled over, knowing who it was. There was nobody else it could be.

'Come!'

The door eased open, stopped. Noel's head appeared.

'Yes Maximillian!'

'Bruv. I told you not to call me that.'

Noel pursed his lips in a closed-mouth smile. 'Yes Max. You good?'

'Yeah. Come.'

Noel entered. Sagging skinny jeans, fresh black Adidas, a matching t-shirt and black hoodie. Noel always had the manners to remove his snapback when he came in the house, which Max's mum never stopped going on about. His haircut was barbershop fresh, a day old at the latest, making his small head gleam like a water chestnut. Max, in contrast, had on worn trackies from last year, a fraying polo short, and his Afro hadn't seen a barbershop in months. His cheeks warmed as Noel looked for somewhere to sit, opting for the single bed. The room was small, barely room enough for the thin bed. A single wooden chair was filled with a pile of folded clean clothes. Posters of street murals, Hubble photographs and rap stars surrounded them.

'Why you lyin on the floor?'

'It's comfortable. Plus it's the best place to draw.'

'Don't you hurt your back an shit?'

'Sometimes. I haven't got a desk, so...'

Noel craned his neck, tracking the walls.

'Man can draw fam.'

'Thanks. It's just practice.'

'Nah, it ain practice. I could practice years and not draw like that.'

'Everybody's got their thing innit?'

Noel wrinkled his nose.

'You reckon?'

'Blatant.'

A wait, the distance between them more apparent with every second. Downstairs, a clang of kitchen utensils. The aroma of melting coconut oil. Frying onions.

'Bruv, I see something you know.'

Max rolled onto his back. Noel was staring out of his window at the underground tracks beyond his garden.

'What?'

'I dunno.'

He laughed, stopped. There was a thin shadow of hair along Noel's jaw Max hadn't noticed before.

'You dunno?'

'Yep.'

'Where?'

'The industrial estate. It's proper mad. As soon as I see it I thought, that's Max. He'll know what to do. It's peak.'

His skin began to tingle. It came from nothing, nowhere. He felt pressure in his veins, the sparkling sensation of a dead arm and realised he was leaning on his elbows. He sat up. The barricade lifted, blood rushed back where it belonged.

'What is it?'

'I can't explain. You gotta come, trust. You're the only man I'll let see this ting, believe me. Everyone else's too stupid. They'll ruin it.'

'Is this a joke?'

Noel stared. His eyes were dark marbles.

'Bruv. Do I joke?'

They held each other's gaze, and burst into spluttered laughter.

'Nah, but really,' Noel said. 'Do I joke about seriousness?'

Max was already on his feet, easing into trainers that were blackened like plantains, a sweatshirt lined with creases and over that, a gilet vomiting cotton from the loose jagged teeth of torn seams.

'Come then,' he said, avoiding Noel's smile.

They rode single file, in silence. Past the small park used by Amberley Aggy more than anyone else, beneath the quiet thunder of the underpass and onto the busy main road that for some reason was called a lane. Even their bikes were nothing alike, Noel's a gleaming thoroughbred, bright red with thin black tyres, Max's a lumbering matt black no-name, thick boned with a wide snakeskin tread, rusting and creaking as its wheels turned slow. They cruised at medium pace, Noel seemingly in no hurry, traffic snarled up this close to rush hour, granting the ability to ride single and double yellows in lieu of bike lanes, ignoring the momentary panic on passenger's faces, unaware of their relaxed, guilt-ridden calm once they were gone. The day was bright, the breeze chilled as the sun began to fall, Max grateful for his mild sweat as he bore down on the pedals. When Noel turned left immediately after the overhead railway bridge, he followed.

Traffic sounds lowered. The rolling shush of car tyres became soothing, momentary. There was even the sound of chattering birds. He closed his eyes, enjoying the sensation. His tyres whirred beneath him.

The warehouse had once been some kind of factory but that seemed like decades ago. On the upper floors, steps ascended into thin air and crumbling window frames. The only intact ceilings were on floors one and two, which were dark even though the sun was bright, foreboding even from outside. Noel glanced over his shoulder as he wheeled his bike towards the dusty steps; other than that, he hardly noticed Max. He lifted the bike up, towards the blue factory doors. A spider web of tags was etched on wooden boards that replaced the broken glass. Max thought the doors were closed, locked, as both were straight-backed and rigid, but when Noel pushed there was just enough space to squeeze themselves and the bikes through their attentive resistance. Inside, he kicked one semi-closed. It barked splintering protest, stuck. Noel wheeled his bike further inside and so Max left it be, trailing after him.

The ground floor went on forever. He couldn't see the far end, as it was consumed by shadow, the walls disappearing into gloom much as the stairs above their heads evaporated into sky. Everywhere was dust and rubble, as though an earthquake had taken place, leaving the outside untouched. He saw repeated mounds of white plaster embedded with red brick that reminded him of strawberry meringue. Some mounds touched the pocked and cracked white ceiling. Cathedral arch windows beamed stunted blocks of daylight on either side of the boys, but the centre of the hall was dark, difficult to make out.

Max found himself stumbling every few steps, on what, he dared not guess. The smell was of mould, damp earth. It clogged his nose and made his eyes feel heavy. The scrape of their feet caused a sea of dust to foam around their ankles. Every now and then there was a downpour of debris as showers of plaster fell from the floors above, thankfully nowhere near them. He stopped pushing the bike to rub his fingers together. They were rough, powdery, and he could taste a crackle of grit between his teeth. In front of him, the dust fog settled. He could just make out Noel's shadow in the gloom. He angled his handlebars in that direction and only knew he'd reached him when he bumped the back of his legs.

'Oi,' Noel said, softer than usual.

'Sorry,' Max whispered, following his lead.

'It's sleeping,' Noel said. Max was just about to ask what, but he stepped out from behind him, and saw.

Beyond the boys, there was a small pile of rubble as high as Max's waist. On, or spread across the crumbled plaster, it was difficult to tell which, was nothing. Or rather it was something as far as Max could see, although exactly what he didn't know. A black patch, dark ooze where there should have been sand-like plaster. The absence of light, not above and surrounding them, in the misted air where it should have been, but on the ground before them, a hole-like rip in the earth that led into... an abyss. It was empty space, the substance he'd stared up at night after night. It was the vision before his eyes when the lids were closed. The deepest part of the night when he lay in bed, roused from dreams. To see it where it shouldn't be made Max dizzy with uncertainty and he stepped back with a yelp of surprise. He stumbled on an unseen half brick, which escaped his foot and made him fall, the bike clattering to the dust in a clatter of gears and wheels.

He blanked out for a moment, trying to collect himself. The far away blue sky spun in slow motion. A wisp of cloud travelled on the wind. Noel whispered, 'Shit,' and Max only just heard him, thinking he might be in trouble, so he tried to get up; only when he'd pulled himself into a sitting position, he froze. Everything left him. Body heat, voice, his breath.

The dark ooze had moved. It wasn't spread out on the floor, it was sitting up like him. It wasn't sitting up, it was pushing itself onto hollow haunches. He could see that what he'd first thought of as a random spread of substance was actually man-like – arms, legs, torso, head, all midnight black, all devoid of features. Humanoid. The creature got to its feet, spreading its arms out wide. A man-shaped silhouette three inches taller than he, around six-feet four, a cut out patch of blank shape and inside that, dark void. Max tried to peer into the depths. For a moment there was the glitter of distant stars. Galaxies perhaps? The nothing was so deep it almost gave off its own light. Maybe that was what he was seeing? He leant forwards, yearning for more, so captivated he barely registered Noel say; 'See? It's beautiful.'

The being seemed to hear him. It extended a pitch black hand, fingers reaching, strained for contact. It didn't move. Noel stepped forwards.

'*No*,' Max whispered from the rubble floor.

He ignored him, inching closer, an exhalation of dust at his feet. He touched the darkened fingers and immediately, instead of grasping them, Noel's fingers began to disappear. It was as though they'd been immersed into a glittering pool of thick oil. He made a terrible noise, moaning fear and revulsion, deep throated, growing louder as he fell deeper into the creature's body, the darkness covering more of him, his knuckles, wrist, forearm, his elbow and up one shoulder, Noel's feet beginning to slide closer into the creature, sending roiling dust puffing high, some of which also vanished into the dark form. Half Noel's torso, his leg, his face, which turned towards Max and let out a roaring scream, until it covered his shaven head and the substance filled his mouth, cutting off his voice as though a plug had been pulled inside him.

Max yelled something that wasn't even a word, his throat raw.

It sucked Noel in. Took his whole body until there was only a flailing arm, a bent elbow, fingers writhing like wind-blown leaves, sliding inside the creature with a dull plop. Immersion.

The creature was still. The void became auditory. It turned towards Max, opening its arms.

He picked up his bike, pushing it a metre before him and leapt on, pedalling hard and fast. He only looked behind once, against his will, believing the creature would come after him, but it stood in the same spot, arms wide, turned in his direction. He made it to the graffiti-stained doors, jumped from the bike, wrenched the doors open (breaking three nails so his fingers bled), and pushed himself outside without a care for bumps or scrapes, threw himself back onto the bike and sprinted hard. His breathing was a harsh, ragged, quiet scream, ripping his chest like smoke, his expression a wide-eyed mask of shocked fear. He rode so frantically cars veered out of his path to avoid collision, and buses sighed to a stop.

At the small park his muscles could do no more and his legs gave out. He fell onto the grass, bones jarring as they met earth, lucky to have the bike roll away and not collapse on top of him, the whine of his breath like the sawing rasp of an asthma attack, sweat pouring from his face and body, soaking his clothes. Old Man Taylor and Ms Emmes saw him as they returned from the parade of shops, and assumed he'd been smoking, or possibly injecting, forcing a wide space between themselves and the boy, storing the image of him splayed and panting to recreate for his parents.

Max's chest rose and fell, looking painful, possibly dangerous. By the time it returned to an even pace, daylight had dimmed. The Amberley Road teenagers arrived, sauntering in no clear direction only to pivot on the spot, palms slapping, barking laughter, passing lighters and curses, heads nodding to smart-phone music until they noticed Max; then whispering among themselves as they saw him on his back, motionless. They tried to pretend he wasn't there, yet his presence muted their voices. The strange kid, even stranger now, possibly drugged or the victim of an attack. Unable to tell which, they left Max alone. When he rose to his feet some time later, the youngsters were a darting swarm of burning orange sparks. Max lifted his fallen bike and walked it home, ignorant of their hush as he stumbled past, group suspicion clouded by nightfall.

To his room, marching away from the calls of his parents, the shrillness of mum's voice, the not quite panicked enough to remove their sagging flesh from the television and see if anything was actually wrong. With his bike safely stored in the shed at the bottom of their garden, he tried to treat himself similarly, locking his door, collapsing on the bed, energy spent, head revolving slowly as a park roundabout, throbbing angrily. He was cold, and so he climbed beneath his covers fully clothed, teeth transmitting code for his ears alone, the image of Noel absorbed into the void of the creature returning like a DVD glitch; repeat, repeat.

Beyond his room, the garden and the untidy jungle of overgrown slope beyond his father's greenhouse, the underground tracks that caught Noel's attention; the Central Line to Ealing Broadway or Ruislip going west, Hainult or Epping to the east. Every five minutes there was a mechanical shudder, a rattle and roar of trains, the glow of carriage windows creating a cinema reel of lights, illuminating gloom. Hours passed. The darkness gained depth, thickened. His mother knocked on his bedroom door, tentative, though it was easy to feign sleep, closing his eyes to cement purpose, wait until she went downstairs, the soft thud of her footsteps on carpet matching the pulse of his fear, which although slowed by then was faster than normal, more rapid than at any other time. He opened his eyes only when he felt safe, tracing the patterns of rattling trains on the white screen of his ceiling, absorbing their flow without meaning, lips moving as though in conversation with himself, or his consumed friend, a whispered dialect that perhaps only they understood.

He tried to imagine himself doing more. Instead of freezing on the spot mute and powerless, reaching for Noel and pulling with all his strength. Picking up a half-shard of brick, pitching it at the creature with all his power. Maybe rushing it with a broad shoulder, forcing it to the floor, away. And yet as much as he tried to conjure images of himself in action, they were solemn fragments, still, unfocused photographic lives at best, patchy and unclear. Whenever he attempted to force them into motion they fell apart, or resisted, so he couldn't see the results. And yet he continued to try, eyes red and stinging, a snail's trail of tears leaking from the corners, running from his temples and onto the pillow as the dark grew stronger, and the cat's eye lights of the trains flickered against his poster-lined four walls, and his body gave in and slept, plunging Max into a subconscious well of nightmares and ether.

Something woke him. He kept his eyes closed. Sound had become rare, outside or inside the house. The trains had stopped, which meant midnight had passed. His parents had gone to bed. Floorboards and walls ticked, creaked. Max felt no physical sensation. His body had seemingly dissipated, leaving nothing physical behind, only spirit, the invisible void.

He heard night workmen, their noisy clink of metal, and with that, sensation returned. He'd seen them sometimes, guiding a battered flat-bed carriage along tracks, mustard yellow, mottled with vitiligo rust. He laid still, eyes closed, absorbing sounds, imagining slow progress. High points of conversation caught his ears, snatches of swearing, and the beam of their mounted spotlight flooded the room, turning the dark behind his eyelids red. He opened his eyes.

The thing from the warehouse rose at the foot of his bed, reaching, arms wide, seemingly bigger this close, pure emptiness within. Max tried to scream and nothing came out but a strangled whine. He wanted to move only for his limbs to resist, the thing stretching its arms like dark honey, creeping closer until each encircled the bed, and the thing grew taller, spreading up and out until it was a dark, giant mass above and around him. Max's heart pounded so hard, his skin was so cold, and his fear so paralysing he thought he might die.

And yet inside the body, he saw something. Now he was closer and the creature stretched out like canvas, he could make out a powdered white terrain, the purple glow of something that resembled sky. The curving glow of moons, the shadow of a planet and on what he assumed was the ground, a series of blocked shapes that looked liked plateaus, or cliff tops. There were marks in the sand, a trail of some kind. Curiosity broke paralysis, although a residue of fear still caused him to shake, gasp breath, as he sat up in bed, leaning closer. Yes. Yes, it could be. He knelt before the creature as if he were about to pray, reaching, touching, feeling the ooze creep along his arm, not the sensation of contact he usually associated with touch, but something else, a warmth that transformed his whole body, stilled his heart, and he wasn't afraid he was relieved, filling with joy. He released a monotone groan, understanding *this* was the sound Noel had made upon contact, it was release not resistance, letting it wash over him until that warm feeling was everywhere, seeing nothing more of his bedroom, only the thick absence of light that embraced him.

A temporary floating sensation, the pop of air pressure, soft, hardly noticeable. Solid ground beneath shoeless feet. Warmth against his soles. The glowing white land. A purple sky, closer now, everywhere, the spray of stars and the planet, heavy and low, half dark half red, bursting with its own weight. Beyond that, far-away moons, twin ice crystals, tiny and bright. The trail he'd seen was footprints, climbing from where he stood, a dual pattern on the sand, the reversed imprint of trainer soles. They rose, disappearing behind dunes to reappear further, towards what he'd thought were flat mountaintops from the unimaginable distance of his bedroom, but were actually looming structures, white as the sand. Turrets or towers, Max couldn't tell. He turned to look behind himself. The creature's silhouette; inside the body, a distant view of posters, the dull wooden foot of his bed, the night workmen's spotlight reflecting on his white ceiling. Home.

He relocated the trail of footprints, eyes rising upwards. The structures shimmered in half-light, piercing the velvet atmosphere, blinking silent reprieve.

COURTTIA NEWLAND

Courttia Newland is the author of seven works of fiction that include his debut, The Scholar. His latest novel, The Gospel According to Cane, was published in 2013 and has been optioned by Cowboy Films.
He was nominated for the Impac Dublin Literary Award, The Frank O' Conner award, The CWA Dagger in the Library Award, The Hurston/Wright Legacy Award and The Theatre 503 Award for playwriting as well as numerous others.
His short stories have appeared in many anthologies and broadcast on BBC Radio 4. In 2016 he was awarded the Tayner Barbers Award for science fiction writing and the Roland Rees Bursary for playwriting.
He is associate lecturer in creative writing at the University of Westminster and is completing a PhD in creative writing.

THE BIRDS, THE BEES
by David James Poissant

So, then, the birds disappeared. First, it had been the bees, now the birds. Which became a joke, in headlines, between parents, in the not-so-clever opening monologues of weary late-night talk show hosts. The birds and the bees! Ha! Hilarious.

But, without the birds and the bees, other things started dying, and suddenly it wasn't all that funny anymore.

Turns out, a lot of things need pollinating to survive. Bird poop too. Birds eat seeds, seeds get pooped out, and a tree sprouts where seed smacks earth. No birds, no poop; no poop, no trees. Flowers too: No bees, no pollination; no pollination, no flowers.

Some flowers, of course. Some trees. Because birds and bees aren't the only ways that things get grown. There are insects aplenty. There's wind. Any number of Johnny Appleseeds scouring the globe, making a difference, or trying to.

But the big two were gone. Leastways, the bees. Birds were still around, but they were on what newscasters called the decline.

Little birds were the first to go: the nuthatch, the finch, the helpless chickadee. As with the bees, we didn't know where the birds were going. No bird flu to account for all this loss. No mass migration. No plague. One day the birds were among us, the next they weren't, were just...gone. And not gone as in dead. Gone as in gone. No carcasses to account for. No feathers. Zero unhatched eggs.

Without little birds to feed on, big birds' flocks thinned. Bald eagle sightings, already rare, turned rarer. California condors were right out. And, at 927 Fifth Avenue, to the disappointment of New Yorkers and birders everywhere, no more Pale Male.

At supermarkets, the price of chicken skyrocketed, while, at pet stores, parakeets went for several grand apiece.

Thanksgiving became kind of a bummer.

We hoped the flightless birds might go unaffected. After all, they couldn't fly. Where could they go? But reports arrived from Antarctica that even the penguins had disappeared.

Which isn't to say this was, like, the bird rapture. Birds didn't vanish, didn't rise into the sky in a heavenly choir, all birdsong and warble. Zoos stayed stocked, aviaries remained safely birded. But any bird not zooed or caught or caged was liable to leave, to join whatever subterranean or stratospheric congregation all birds had lately been flocking to.

A few holdouts remained. Pigeons, mostly. With their grizzled, fuck-you attitudes, pigeons clogged sidewalks and gutters. They shat from overhangs onto our unsuspecting heads. Was it possible there were more of them? Were other birds not disappearing but turning into pigeons? No, that was just our imaginations.

There were also woodpeckers, for whatever reason. Now, the woods were knocks and taps and rat-a-tat-tats in place of the music songbirds used to make. Even the screech of an owl would have been welcome, but no. Just wood-pecking all the livelong day.

So, the plants that were dying kept dying, and the flowers that were going unpollinated kept going unpollinated, and so we learned to live without honey and without featherbeds and without turkey sandwiches and without down jackets and without duck ponds (which were now just ponds that sad children hurled bread into only to watch the breadcrumbs sink or, occasionally, get gobbled up by fish, which, can't we all agree, isn't nearly as satisfying, seeing as fish are, like, cold and slimy and soulless, plus kind of hard to look in the eye for long, gills flapping, mouths opening and closing like asthmatics desperate for breath, fish being, after all, no glorious masters of sparkle and flight and grace, but nature's shut-ins, basement dwellers, evolution's rejects, those weird, scaled, godforsaken creatures of the deep).

These thoughts we kept to ourselves, though, silence a charm against another vanishing. After all, we'd taken our birds for granted, our bees. If fish were next, we'd run out of things to eat. "We love you fish!" we shouted at koi ponds and mountain streams and at the beach.

We did not love the fish, but we loved to catch them, to eat them, to hang their airbrushed bodies on our walls. For, if things were not sacred in and of themselves, they were sacred to us to the degree to which we found them useful. And we were only just now registering how useful things outside ourselves, beyond ourselves, apart from ourselves, could be. In that, if nothing else, these things beyond ourselves became ourselves. How this food became that fat. How a cell becomes a cell. How the water you drink is the same water a dinosaur drank before, only, now, with more birth control hormones in it, and also mercury and arsenic and barium and copper and nitrates and cyanide and lead and vinyl—not from LPs but from the PVC that carries water into your home—and radium and uranium and what's left of the Xanax after you pee it out.

A hundred years later, not one of us would be left. Even given advances in medicine, in science and engineering, in robot arms and robot legs, no matter how many people WD-40ed their future joints, we, all of us, would die. In a world minus birds and bees, we were dead meat. And, by then, who knew? Maybe the world would be fishless. Perhaps cowless. Rabbitless, almost certainly, for what rabbit could survive this brave, new, inhospitable world? No rabbit you'd want to put in a petting zoo or in your belly, that's for sure.

A hundred years go by in the blink of an eye.

But we beat on, boats going right along with the current. Like, totally with the birdless, beeless current. The current carrying us along faster than some of us would have liked, shepherding us with our robot arms and our robot knees, carrying us—kicking and screaming, some of us—into the future we'd given to ourselves.

We would not change. We would not curtail.

This was us. This is how we lived.

DAVID JAMES POISSANT

David James Poissant's stories have appeared in The Atlantic, Playboy,
One Story, The Southern Review, Ploughshares, Glimmer Train, and in the
New Stories from the South, and Best New American Voices anthologies.
His writing has been awarded the Matt Clark Prize, the George Garrett Fiction
Award, the RopeWalk Fiction Chapbook Prize, and the Alice White Reeves
Memorial Award from the National Society of Arts & Letters, as well as
awards from The Chicago Tribune and The Atlantic and Playboy magazines.
He teaches in the MFA program at the University of Central Florida and
lives in Orlando with his wife and daughters.

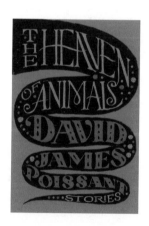

ARTICLE ELECT
by Tomek Dzido

When *Black Shirts* stormed St. Andrew *Bobola* Polish Church in Shepherd's Bush and slaughtered over three hundred innocent people, I knew no God could save us. Where politics had failed before, I prayed it might rescue us from this nightmare, but I was misguided in my belief, the ferocity of their rage so brutal I swore to never kneel again.

What began as a rebellion against the government born from deep-rooted resentment at the elite political class and a determination to reverse mass migration rapidly spiraled in to a full-blown uprising; riots and protests further rousing the spite of an enraged electorate. Anger and bitterness consumed the country as *Black Shirts* stormed the streets, their crusade of carnage gaining momentum with each newly recruited member. When the Home Secretary announced a delay in withdrawing from the EU the public protested. The people had voted. They wanted out *–NOW!*

In the space of three weeks every embassy in London was looted by members of the newly formed *British Defence Front*, an army of fanatics fiercer than their bottled bombs. By the time we learnt of their acquired expertise in military organisation it was too late, their loathing of immigrants a uniting force of frenzied aggression. This was when *he* re-surfaced, organised rallies and protests the perfect setting for his vile doctrine, his words resonating with a disgruntled populace. *He* was back.

The last time I saw him was six months ago when he flaunted his false pity at our loss, the grin on his wretched face so vile I struggled to suppress the urge to strike him. He straightened his tie and informed me of his decision to leave the opposition and run for Prime Minister, and in that ghastly second of full disclosure, it all made sense. As I stood frozen with fear an activist surged through security and hurled a missile through the air, its target hiding behind the Head of his Security. 'Don't just stand there Sid, you *dumb fuck*, get me out of here.'

Sid glowered at his harrier, nostrils flaring and masseters flickering. Hesitantly he forced a footpath through the crowd, a smile flashing across his face as an egg shattered on the suit of his employer. Watching them slip inside a waiting limousine, I commenced to hatch a plan, my own fangs craving bigot blood.

My decision to leave England was called into question, but despite the mêlée within Parliament, I could not ignore the ongoing humanitarian crisis at the Grande-Synthe Camp near Dunkirk. These refugees were human - like the rest of us - and deserved to be treated as such, political squabbles and power struggles be damned. If history taught us anything, we remained ignorant of its lesson, perpetually repeating our barbaric behaviour, again and again repeating our mistakes, our failings, much as we continue to fail each other now. But we *can* change. We *must* change. We owe it to our children, and *their* children, and every future child untainted by the wasteful world we've fostered. We owe *everything* to them, if only to prove we were human too. We can *choose* to change.

I was on my way to meet European Socialist Leaders in Paris to discuss the refugee crisis when my car was accosted by anti-immigrant activists, their rage so fierce I shuddered in my seat. As they pummeled the car with signs and placards I looked through the windscreen mirror at my appointed chauffeur. He shook his head, fingers curling tight around the steering wheel. 'Fous racistes'. I leaned forward and placed my hand on his shoulder, 'One day they will learn, Gilen.'

He looked up and held my gaze, his dark brown eyes probing my reflection, a flood of eggs exploding on the windshield.

'Maybe we should teach them.'

That evening, alone in my hotel room, I collapsed on the bed and cried. The visit to the camp destroyed me. I could not believe we were capable of such ignorance and neglect, our fruity Frappuccinos more central to our concerns than the misery of our dispossessed. As I lay atop my scented sheets all I could see was that little boy from Egypt, sitting dejected in the mud as orange vests dismantled his tarpaulin tent and snarling bulldozers devoured his home, human faeces floating in a murky puddle beside him, his tiny hands clutching the last of his possessions; a misshapen cricket ball and a crumpled piece of paper which verified his pained existence, a person with a name, *Hossam*.

My brain was broken. I couldn't shut it down. I couldn't stop thinking and crying and thinking and crying, so I did the only thing I could. I rose from the bed and stumbled across the room, opened the fridge, and gulped down miniatures until I passed out.

I was awoken by the incessant ringing of my phone but I ignored it and lurched to the bathroom. Within seconds I was hunched over the toilet, my stomach convulsing as I spluttered and gagged and vomited; the stench of bile and alcohol making my eyes water as ashen tiles shifted in and out of focus. When I finally finished vomiting I twisted the tap and stepped into the shower, my clothes soaking through as I clung to the riser rail and trembled in my stupor.

Back in the room I collapsed on the bed and stared at the muted television, subtitles blinking across the screen, my mind drifting back to England. No one envisioned we would fight such a vicious battle on home soil, least of all wage war against British people – *our* people – but they were furious at the failure of democracy. They were fed up, and the only one who seemed to listen, was *him*. He was growing stronger by the day, his army of *Black Shirts* rising through the rubble of discontent. When options were few and far between, the zeal of his beliefs united them, an army of aggressors high on hate.

Just when I thought things couldn't get any worse; I witnessed a bulletin so shocking it ripped the air from my lungs;

Explosion in England - emergency services struggling - thousands feared dead.

The BDL detonated seventeen pounds of semtex in the Sports Direct Warehouse in Shirebrook, all 1,500 of its foreign staff slaughtered and entombed within the walls of this gargantuan gulag.

I fell to my knees and wept, a fresh wave of nausea twisting at my guts and blurring my vision, flames and smoke engulfing me in a shroud of sorrow and despair. I clutched my throat and gagged and choked and heaved, but there was nothing left; I was empty.

So this was it; hell on earth, aflame. I dragged myself to the fridge, unscrewed the remaining bottle of Jack, and threw it down my throat.

The devil was *real*.

I took leave from office and said I was visiting family, a distant uncle suffering from an unknown illness, and without further explanation, I disappeared. The one thing I knew for sure; no one could be trusted, not even those I once called friends. I knew that *he* could trace my every move, so once on land I travelled by train and coach, using only cash and a prepaid Sim as my sole means of communication. The meeting point was established by co-ordinates hidden within an unremarkable phishing email, and whilst I was unfamiliar with the language or layout of the land, I travelled like any tourist; pale-skinned and anonymous. When I arrived at my hotel I was greeted by the commissionaire and immediately introduced to the manager, who waved the porter away and accompanied me to my room.

'My name is Claudia', she said, and held out her hand. We shook and smiled. 'If you need help with anything during your stay, please call me.' She pulled a card from her pocket and placed it on the desk beside the door, a sealed and unmarked envelope resting against the unlit lamp. '*Anything.*'

I stood there staring at the envelope on the table. The letter was unexpected, and unexpected was unsafe.

Trembling, I ripped the seal and read…

"THE REVOLUTION IS NOT AN APPLE THAT FALLS WHEN IT IS RIPE. YOU HAVE TO MAKE IT FALL."

I recognised the quote immediately, but the motive behind its presence puzzled me. It must be from *Them*, I thought, and examined the room for clues. One of the paintings on the far wall was somewhat askew, and upon closer inspection I observed that it was fixed to the wall by hidden hinges. Pulling it towards me revealed a safe imbedded in the stucco brick behind. I stared at the digital display and considered what the code might be, or how I might unearth it. I rummaged through hotel brochures and instruction manuals but could find nothing concerning access to the safe, until my eyes fell on the piece of paper in my hand. Without hesitation I entered; 1 4 0 6 2 8. Che Guevara. Of course.

Inside the safe was a large manila envelope within which I found a fake ID, passport, bank cards, and a full employment history, together with references, dating back to 1969. So this was my new identity. This was who I would become when the time was right and each component was in place to execute our plan. I slipped the documents back in the envelope and returned it to the safe. It was time for me to go, so I slid my sunglasses on, pulled down my hat, and exited the building. The streets were bustling with tourists enjoying the pleasures of their vacation, sipping aperitifs and staring at menus, lost in their little worlds as I set off to save the only one I knew.

I boarded the bus and kept my head down, not wanting to draw attention to myself. I got off at my stop and quickly disappeared down a slip road. Walking through the fields I spotted the rusty caravan beneath a canopy of eucalyptus trees, the murmur of distant voices winding through the stirring branches. As I neared the caravan I couldn't help but admire the beauty of this secret spot, so finely attuned to allay suspicion. Surrounding the caravan were slashed cane limbs supporting streams of vegetation and growth, tomatoes and corn and courgettes shooting out from the centre. I stopped and stood on decking made of aged pallet wood, rot and woodworm gnarling at the grains, pots of thymus, rosemary, basil and laurel running along the perimeter, tyres and shoes and ruined furnishings scattered across the dry soil, a single solar panel pointed up towards the cloudless sky and a plastic wind dial purring beside me. It was perfect.

I inhaled deeply, took one last look around, and knocked on the door. After several seconds I was ushered into the darkness by a figure cast in shadow and I was stunned by the emptiness within, the walls stripped of furnishing and the floor a bare carcass of stained lino, the windows blacked out, a solitary table sitting in the centre, an empty chair waiting for me. There was no need for introductions; the nature of our meeting determining the speed at which we agreed upon our course of action. Despite the precision of our plan and the meticulous care we had taken to consider every eventuality, we were nervous. The events of recent months merely affirmed the unpredictability of our people, now even further fixed on loyalty to *him*. If we could pull it off, humanity might yet stand a chance. We might somehow, still, survive. We shook hands and wished each other well. From here on in, I was on my own. "We don't say, 'See you later,'" the shadow whispered. "We say instead: 'See you there.'"

The walk to the main road was burdened with doubt and dread, sweat soaking through my clothes as I traipsed through the brush beneath the setting sun, a faint explosion echoing in the distance as the caravan burst aflame and crumbled beneath a shroud of rising smoke. Once aboard the bus I sat atop the rumble of its groaning engine, and for the first time in months, I *believed*. I watched the winding roads snake by, little houses lost amid oleander and prickly pear, false olives and citrus groves and endless rows of grapevines. It was stunning, and beside this sinuous stream of beauty, I drifted off to sleep. When I awoke I was alone on the bus, and conscious of the driver I rose to my feet, thanked him, and stepped down onto the pavement. I didn't know where I was, and for once, I didn't care. My flight wasn't until tomorrow afternoon so I decided to enjoy what little pleasure I could seize and explore the town. The scattered shops were closed for lunch and in the distance I spotted the spire of a church, so I headed in that direction hoping to discover a square in which I might enjoy a coffee, or better yet, a beer.

My prediction was correct and as I reached the end of the street I spotted the square, little cafes and bars lining the perimeter beneath the spire. I took a seat in the quietest bar and waited for the waitress, but as I examined the menu I became concerned about whether my presence in such a populated place was too great a risk. I had taken numerous precautions to ensure my whereabouts were unknown and despite my disguise there remained the possibility that someone might recognise me. I knew I should return to the hotel and remain in my room until it was time to journey back to England, but I also wanted to forget about my mission, even for one solitary evening of abandon. I distracted myself with the spectacle before me; luxurious ensembles and expensive jewels and designer shirts and shoes and soft brown skin. Before I could act on my concerns the waitress was upon me, standing beside my table with her hazel eyes and auburn hair. I was stunned to silence by her beauty, the sparse scarring on her face a magnificent imperfection amid the extravagance exhibited around us. 'Preggo', she asked.

'Ichnusa, per favor.'

She slipped the order book in her back pocket and turned to walk away, lifting empty glasses from adjacent tables and disappearing inside the bar. I sat and thought of nothing; no computer, no phone, no schedule. Tonight I was free. Within minutes she was back at my table, placing my ice cold beer before me, together with a bowl of crisps. 'Grazie,' I said, and stared up at her broad smile, once again muted in my seat. She didn't speak or move, and neither did I, both of us caught in some acute moment of calm. Fearing she might have recognised me I lifted my glass and saluted her speedy service, the smile flashing across her face once more. I sat there drinking beer, eating crisps, watching kids glide by on hoverboards as hand in hand parents tailed together, their pace unhurried and free from household difficulties or dilemmas. As I gazed upon the steady flow of pedestrians it dawned on me just how very different lives we lead, defined by wealth or work or pedigree, all of us struggling to survive, to see our dreams delivered, starving for some meaning in a world sickened by endless wars and violence.

I was thinking again.

Stop it.

To distract myself I watched the waitress, her movement fluid and precise, and despite the vast array of splendor on display, I was deeply drawn to her alone. Perhaps the perfection of our companions made her all the more alluring, her natural beauty matchless in this realm of makeup and veneer. She noticed me staring and promptly approached my table. 'Birra?' She asked.

'Yes – I mean, *si*.' And without thinking I offered her a drink. She returned moments later with a tray and two beers. Handing me my glass she lifted hers and held it out towards me, 'salute.' We clinked and sipped. I was immediately embarrassed, an old codger like me buying a beautiful girl like her a drink. What was I doing? What was I thinking? And then it hit me; I *wasn't* thinking.

'I like your ring', I said, gazing at the fabulous decoration wrapped around her finger. She looked down at the ring and fell silent. 'Are you okay?' I asked.

'L'anello della mia nonna…my…grandma ring…'

Her eyes began to water and I could tell this was a wound not yet healed by time. I didn't know what to do. I didn't know what to say. I was never good with tears, no matter what the cause. I could submerge myself in sense and logic but present me with the pain of raw emotion and I flap and drift and drown. But I couldn't stand to see her so upset, so I reached out and seized her hand, gently squeezing to confirm my tender contact. Caressing the ring with my thumb I directed it towards the light, 'Bellisimo'.

The focus of her stare returned to me and my absurd Italian tongue and I could sense something shift, the stiffness of her muscles slackening in my hand. She cleared her throat and blinked, lowering herself into the seat beside me. I watched as she rummaged in her pocket and pulled out a pack of cigarettes, her trembling fingers struggling to place the stick between her lips. I picked up the lighter and flicked the spark wheel, holding the flame steady as she sucked in her vital hit of nicotine. She shook her head and sighed. 'Scusa.'

'It's okay', I replied. 'Don't worry.'

She flicked her cigarette above the ashtray. 'English?'

'Si.'

'I love England...I move London.'

'Really? When?'

'Two week...a month, maybe.'

'To study?'

'Work. Per familia. *Money.*'

I could see the sadness in her eyes; a million buried fears swimming in her glass of golden beer. 'You okay?' I asked again, wondering if there was anything I could do make her feel better, if only for the time she stole to sit with me. Before she could answer the manager of the bar appeared, 'Alessandra.' She stubbed her cigarette out and rose to her feet, and with her back to the waiting manager, downed her beer.

'Grazie,' she said, and for the first time since sitting down, she smiled. 'Grazie mille.'

I remained at the bar for a little while longer, saluting Alessandra and pulling funny faces whenever she walked past my table to serve another customer. Every so often she surprised me with a fresh beer and further supplies of salty nourishment, the tiny portions appreciated by my alcohol -infused stomach. During this time I absent-mindedly enjoyed the peaceful patter of transient feet and let myself soak in the tranquil ambience so unlike the anarchy back home. When I attempted to get up and use the restroom I realised just how many beers I had consumed, and so seating myself back down, I counted a hundred Euros and slipped the notes beneath my empty glass. I sat for a further ten minutes waiting for an opportunity to say my farewells to Alessandra, but when she failed to re-appear, I decided to leave.

As I stumbled down the road from which I had arrived, I heard a voice call out behind me, and almost tripping as I turned I saw Alessandra, her hair floating in the air as she ran towards me. I steadied myself on a lamppost and waited, a beaming grin plastered on my drunken face.

'Per que no goodbye?' she spluttered, doubled over and panting.

'I...'

Slapping me on the arm, she whispered, 'Idiota.'

I stood there like the old fool I was; self-conscious and shy, fingers fumbling as Alessandra stepped forward and hugged me, her body so small and frail. Placing her hands on my flushed cheeks, she looked deep into my eyes and kissed me gently on the lips. 'Grazie', she repeated, before she spun round and bound back up the street. 'See you in London', she waved. And just like that, she was gone.

In a drunken daze I found my way aboard the bus and stared at the stars above as I journeyed back to my hotel. Tomorrow would bring a new beginning, and I lay in bed thinking about how vastly things would change. I thought about the citizens of each nation and their assorted sense of hope, and as I drifted off to sleep, I thought about the bar, the beer, and Alessandra, the taste of tears still lingering on my lips.

To quell the insurrection the Prime Minister called for an emergency General Election, which was precisely what *he* wanted. The Prime Minster and her parliament devised a plan to pacify the BDL and offered *him* the position of Vice Chancellor, naively believing they could control him, but he refused and demanded the role of Chancellor, his troops marching through Downing Street in a show of support that was impossible to ignore. As the House debated how to proceed, armed forces thundered through plumes of endless smoke, Molotov cocktails flying through the air as bullets tore through bricks and Banksy. The Metropolitan Police were soon outnumbered and we had no choice but to recall our armed forces to establish order, armoured personnel carriers and combat vehicles strategically stationed around the country as infantrymen patrolled the streets.

The General Election and discussions with our new Chancellor resulted in a fragile truce, the violence momentarily abated as we sought a way to end this war. Whilst the BDL ceased their acts of aggression foreign citizens from across the country relocated to the capital, abandoning their homes and setting up camp in London's largest open spaces. Hyde Park, Kensington Gardens, Richmond Park, St. James Park, Regent's Park and Bushy Park, transformed into 'safe zones' for millions of native refugees, banding together despite their creed or customs, constructing homes with nails and hammers and hands of countless colour. Despite the endless miles of fences and police on patrol and guards on rolling duty, it was a disaster waiting to happen, waiting for *him* to happen. If the BDL wanted to kill - which they certainly did, now they knew precisely where to strike. An attack on any one of these safe zones would destroy all hope of peace, the EU and NATO's forces watching and waiting, armed and ready to intervene regardless of our membership status, a Humanitarian crisis unfolding on home soil, the home of abandoned beds, the one we built, together.

As the housing market crashed and interest rates sky rocketed and sterling tumbled and industry struggled to stay afloat amid a drowning workforce, the time to act had come. My contact at *Shred it Safe* confirmed the location of their meeting, the leaders of each neighbouring land gathering to calculate and concur how *they* could win the war and ensure the safety of their status as rulers of a new world order; *The Grave New World*. I explained that the sick Uncle I recently visited had died, and as might be expected, my presence was urgently required. Despite the chaos gripping our country it was a request they could not reject. Hiding out at home I counted down the days until the meeting, not knowing if my partners were in place, but trusting them as they hoped to trust in me. Meanwhile, I spent the week on sunbeds, shaved and dyed my hair, rehearsed my Italian accent, and became, in time, Lorenzo.

I arrived at the Wolf's Lair early in the morning, dressed appropriately and in accordance with house rules. As I stood outside the door awaiting permission to enter, I glanced over my shoulder and noted the delivery van parked outside; *Gousto Gilen*. The package was delivered. Phase one complete. Now it was up to me.

I was a new member of staff and as such, security checks were required to ensure I was not a threat to *him* or his allies. As I waited for them to complete my clearance, hands hovering over loaded weapons, I assured them they would find no cause to fire. They did not speak or seek to engage with me. I was a foreigner trespassing on their land. I was the enemy. Without a word they led me to the kitchen and ordered me to wait for the House Manager. As I stood between the guards in silence, I knew there was no going back. The day of reckoning had come.

She entered the kitchen and immediately approached me. 'So you are Lorenzo?'

'Yes', I answered.

'I'm Claudia.' She held out her hand and we shook, not for the first time. 'The guests will arrive at four o'clock. You have two hours to set the table in the conference room.' She pointed at the serving trolley. 'Everything you need is in there.'

'Grazie.' The guards gripped their guns and watched me closely as I wheeled the trolley towards the door. 'Conference room, per favore?' Reluctantly, they led the way. So far, so good. Security was tight, but the plan was working. I was inside, and very soon, he would be too. Him and all his cronies. All of them in one room. Plotting and scheming and perishing together. We reached the end of the hall and stood outside the conference room as one of the guards rapped on the door and waited. We stared at each other coldly as from within the security system disarmed. Access was granted solely to those in possession of verified pass cards and as the door swung open I could not be sure if the following phase of our plan would work. We knew what we had to do, but we were human too, and it was possible we had made mistakes. It was possible we had missed a detail that might put us all in danger. But we were *already* in danger. The whole *world* was in danger, and it was up to us to save it.

The door opened and before I could register what was happening I was confronted by the barrel of a gun pointed squarely at my face. 'Sir, this is Lorenzo Gregorio. He is here to prepare the conference room.'

'Have you patted him down?' The voice answered from within the shadows. The two guards looked at one another and lied.

'Yes. He has been thoroughly checked and cleared.'

'Very well.' The gun lowered and from behind the door a figure stepped out. 'I'm Syd; Head of Security.' He ushered me inside and turned towards the guards. 'That will be all.'

'But' –

'I said, that will be all.'

Without further delay he closed the door and re-activated security, sealing us safely within the room. Following a final check of our surroundings he pulled the receiver from his ear and switched his communication devices off. It was him and me, exactly where we wanted to be. 'Do you have everything?' he asked.

'Claudia said it's ready to go.'

He nodded. 'We have one hour.'

I pulled the cloth from the cart to reveal its true contents, and after a moment of silent meditation, we unloaded the explosives from the trolley, carefully positioning them in hidden points around the room. Claus Von Stauffenberg made the error of leaving the bomb to do his work for him. We would not repeat such a mistake. There was only one way to activate the explosives. There was only one trigger. Me. I would remain in the room and when he and all his guests were seated; BANG. Inevitably I would perish too, but the truth is; I deserved to die. I deserved this fate, unlike the innocent people I condemned to slaughter. I *had* the chance to save them, but I failed. I failed to fight for the conservation of humanity, the morals of mortality, the very principles I promised to uphold. Their blood is on my hands, the plight of our nation prompted by my inability to act accordingly, my failure to represent – but not today. Today – too many days too late, I will represent them all, hope for humanity, home.

As Syd finished with the explosives I did the best I could to set the table, if only to make it appear that Lorenzo had completed his job. When we were both ready he re-started his communication devices and handed me the detonator, his phone immediately ringing with dozens of missed calls. I placed the empty wine boxes on the trolley and gathered the residual evidence of our mission into the waste compartment beneath. Conducting a final check of the room I satisfied myself that everything looked precisely as it should; a display of fine dining perfect for dictators. They would never know this was their last meal, their saviour first to lurch for pleasure, high on praise and power but built from flesh and bone and brittle like the rest of us. This is where their world would end, and ours would finally prosper in peace.

Syd's telephone rang and as soon as he answered I knew it was *him*. He was screaming and shouting and swearing, Syd's eyes slamming shut and his fist clenching beside his hip. 'Sorry, sir, there was a problem with one of the waiters – yes – I know – I know that's what I'm paid to – no...It's under control. I've sorted it. Everything is on schedule. Okay...' He hung up and exhaled heavily.

'You ready?' He asked.

'As ready as I'll ever be.'

Lifting the hidden hatch beneath the table he lowered me in and nodded. 'They will start arriving in the next hour. Won't be long now.' He held out his hand and we shook firmly. 'Good luck.'

'Thank you,' I replied as the hatch door sealed shut above me. So this is where I would die, beneath a roof of floorboards like the millions who could not escape the Fuhrer's rule. Different dictator, same delusions. But was *I* any different? I would murder for *my* beliefs and dreams. I would kill those I deemed responsible, but what right did I have to play judge and jury and executioner? Did they not kill by definitions of what was right and wrong, regardless of the reason? Was I as bad as them? Did killing to save a life make it any better? Would it even make a difference? Would it really change the future? Might it not inspire others to fight in their place? Despite my desire to begin a better world, it was entirely possible things could still get worse. I could open the gates of hell and welcome different devils. Was I a devil too?

I heard voices at the door and instantly realised I had let myself lose focus. I could not be sure how much time had passed, but they were here. One by one they entered the conference room, laughing and joking and praising each other's accomplishments. I gritted my teeth and listened for their names, recalling the attendance list from memory and noting who was here and who was yet to enter. Eventually the only missing name was his, and as I struggled not to move, my muscles trembling and skin enclosed in sweat, the vast applause igniting up above signalled *his* arrival. Finally, *he* was here. They cheered and stamped their feet and roared with joy, the leaders of every major nationalist and right wing party gathered in one room, united in their merciless pursuit for power. It wasn't long before the business of their assembly was addressed, the room silent as *he* spoke, his words carefully selected and his tone convincing in conviction. His power of persuasion was astounding, his assurances calculated towards each ally, the promise of power precisely what they craved to hear. He worked the room superbly, their agreement and applause confirming his position as their leader, the rightful King to rule them all.

I couldn't believe what I was hearing. The reality of their dream far worse than anything I had imagined.

World War III.

All those meetings with the President of America made sense now. They had been planning this for years; the riots and rage and slaughter. Like the Twin Towers collapsed to give credence to their calls for war in the Middle East, the issue of migration was a means by which to build their army of radicals devoted to complete annihilation. Britain was merely the testing ground, his path to parliament already set in motion, and once officially elected as the new Prime Minister he would reign supreme. He would abolish 'safe zones' and squash their spirit and send them *home* to fall in line and fight the *real* enemy: Kim Jong-un. A Europe bound by hate and fear and armed for endless wars and genocide, soldiers and sufferers disciplined to die together, the powerless and poor eradicated from existence. Europe *and* America, missiles aimed at global domination.

Enough was enough.

I closed my eyes and thought of Alessandra, the beauty of a better life, a better world, and strengthened by her smile, I made a choice.

I chose to change.

You will too, eventually.

TOMEK DZIDO

MANAGING DIRECTOR & EDITOR IN CHIEF

Tomek Dzido is a London-based writer. He is the author of two novels, *Anamnesis* and *Spit and Polish*, and a short story collection *Soapsuds Island*. He holds an MA in Creative Writing from Kingston University and is presently working on his third novel, *Mind The Gap*. In 2013, his short story Ya Get Me was a semi finalist in The *New Guard Literary Review Machigonne* Fiction Contest. Further short stories have been published in *The Alarmist* and *Front & Centre*.

DAYLIGHT BREAKS THROUGH
by Ross Jeffery

The dust whips up again, stinging my eyes. I have made this journey countless times this year without any headway. I glance down at the footprints in the dust, the only marker to tell me I'm heading in the right direction.

The sun-scorched plants offer no signposts. Each day they are withered, burnt up, then blown away by the heat of the breeze. The dust out here clings to you; it bites into your flesh.

The heat of the day enables me to move undetected; no one in their right mind would be out here during peak *heat* hours, but who said I was sane? Shadows seem to have scurried away, hidden directly below their casters, giving the path an unnerving bleakness. I stop, shielding my eyes from the sun and dust, stare heavenward, stand there looking for the signs of a drone; the metal glinting in the searing heat, like noticing a star out in the middle of the day. It is the only thing that gives them away. I turn and peer down the winding path; from what I can make out there is someone a way off, shuffling along the path, their body dancing like a mirage.

Next minute, they're gone.

Am I going mad? Am I hallucinating? I turn back into the wind and continue along the path, trying to put as much distance between us as possible.

Over the peak of this dune I can see the top of the wall, red lights signalling the entrance ports, with its sentries armed and swivelling, motion trackers pick up anything moving over a two-hundred-meter distance. Whether that be a rodent, Mexican, or Alien, it's all cannon fodder. Unless, that is, you can pay the fees or find a sponsor to secure you entry. The soldiers are small dots on its structure, moving around like ants on a hive, all armed and ready to protect the dream of a lunatic.

I must be close.

The wind makes me stop in my tracks. I drop to one knee to shield myself from the dust being thrown into my face. I grab a water can from my belt. Sliding my breathing apparatus down, I take small sips of water; I feel the grit from the breeze in my mouth, reminding me of sandy sandwiches and picnics on the beach. A time when there used to be beaches to have picnics on. I swill the water and spit it on the path. Looking ahead from the low vantage point, I see the path more clearly. I only notice now the strange littering of animal corpses along the way. Various insects, rodents and other small creatures, impaled on thorny bushes and cactus trees. It must be a shrike; a small white bird with a bandit black streak across its eyes. It uses various sharp barbs to pin its pray, returning at a later point to eat them. It reminds me briefly of our history lessons, about the Romans and Spartans. How they would display their enemies on sharpened sticks, their heads on huge spikes to show that those who oppose them what happens when you mess with the establishment.

I had heard the rumours of what hangs on the wall here, but no one can verify the rumours, no one can turn those rumours into facts without being killed by the security systems, so we are left with the Chinese whispers and idol scaremongering. The wall portrayed in the media is a lot different from the actual wall we see first-hand. Was the bird sending me a warning?

A shrike flies past, making me jump; movement out on the trail is a rare thing. It lands ahead of me on a thorny branch, a small frog in its beak. I watch in abject horror as it thrusts its prey down onto a thorn. Impaling the defenceless creature, it's high-pitched squeal soon wiped out by the winds howling.

Up ahead I locate my target. Well hidden, as always, sitting between three large boulders. One each side and another forming a lintel across the top a poor man's Stonehenge; it was built this way to stop it being picked up by the constant sweeping of drones in the area. Nervousness rises in me. Every day it could be '*the*' day. I swallow the nerves back down, but can't quench the fear that comes along for the ride. My body breaks out in a chill although it is twenty-eight degrees. I turn a corner marked by two large flowering cacti. Littered with tiny animal shish kababs, snack sized horrors. The car, my marker, is wedged between the three rocks. I take one last look at the blue sky; who knows when I'll get another chance to see it. I disappear under the large hanging boulder and into the first piece of shade I've encountered for what must be hours. Pools of sweat have built up around my armpits, chest and back now running cold as my body reacts to the change in temperature. The car is an old, rusted out Mini Cooper, the remnants of a broken Mexican number plate hangs loosely from a remaining screw. Yellow paint chippings lie shredded and curled on the ground, like a discarded snakeskin. The back wheels are missing, so the rear of the car sits snugly on the sand. I search the path for the person following me, but they are lost in within the haze.. I turn back to the car and prepare myself.

I take my backpack off. Reach into my shirt; I locate the leather strap that has a key on the end. The leather damp to touch and the key slippery in my hand, I think of the fishing trips with my father before the incident, holding an oily fish in my hands, trying to hold it, but failing. I take one deep breath, turn the key in the lock and climb inside.

X

The heat below ground is worse than that above, a heat that bakes you. Sweat doesn't even have time to trickle before it's evaporated. I reach into my backpack and pull out a torch. There's a light up ahead but too far off to distinguish what's in front of me; familiar sounds of talking, singing and the sound of shovel on dirt. SHIKT, SHIKT, SHIKT echo around me.

I click the torch on and descend the carved steps, torch lighting the way. I head towards the noise. Although what we are working on is highly secret, we do not like to work in silence and depending on who is working, there are different songs each shift. Mondays bring songs of the resistance, rebel songs of the fight against the regime. Tuesdays are Hispanic folk. Wednesdays, the perfection of hymns. Thursdays, I'm not sure, I have never worked on a Thursday. Friday is whistling like Snow Whites' bloody dwarfs. Saturday is the only day that changes. Sundays, well, Sundays are considered holy and those involved in the tunnel don't work. They spend the day praying for the safety of the tunnel, the workers and for protection from the forces against our entry.

Today is Wednesday and the sound of hymns fill my ears.

Up ahead the torch reveals a table and chain linked-fence. An odd sight when you're underground but a familiar one to me. Pablo is seated at the table. Flanked by Nunez and James; AK47's draped over their shoulders. They raise their guns.

"Please lower your light." Pablo's voice bounces off the walls. I do as he says.

"Hernandez?" he continues.

"Yes…" They know me but his voice is uncertain.

"Hernandez…it *is* you!" With this exclamation, Pablo stands and moves around the table towards me, arms outstretched. We embrace in a soggy coming together, kiss each other's wet and bristly cheeks. Pablo pats me hard across the back and escorts me to the table.

"We thought you were one of the dead."

"One of the dead? Pablo, I don't understand."

"We had a cave-in two days ago…we'd not seen you for a few days so assumed you were still in there?"

"In where?"

"We were digging another route, an offshoot of the main tunnel and, well, we must be right near the wall; the weight broke the support beams like toothpicks…" Pablo gesticulates with his hands on the table, his fingers bowing, and then slams his hand down. "…Boom. All dead. We'll be digging out those poor souls for burials all week." Pablo sits back down, his elbows rest on the table and his fingers bridge in front of his mouth.

"Where were you, Hernandez?"

"My mother, she's not been very well…"

"Your mother? I thought she was dead?"

"It was Isabella, my wife's mother that died last year. My mother is bedbound, I get her groceries and medication on Tuesdays."

Pablo looks up, with his hand motions Nunez towards me. Nunez reaches around and pulls a contraption off his belt, the size of a mobile phone. Grabbing my shirt, he forcefully pulls me toward him, as a blue laser emits from the box.

"What are you doing?" I try in vain to pull away but he's too strong.

"It's not going to hurt…" He pushes my head down to the table, my forehead cracking on steel. He pulls my shirt collar down, revealing my tag. The laser scans it and something beeps on the table. Nunez releases his grip. I stand nursing my face. My name now displayed on a screen, a small green dot next to it.

"What the hell is that about? Why are we scanning people? We haven't had to do that since the wall went up."

Pablo raises his hands trying to placate me

"Do you know how many people are working on this project, Hernandez? Do you?" I shrug. "I have roughly three hundred people digging this tunnel, and do you know what kills me?"

I feel like a petulant child scolded by his headmaster.

"Those men and women who died in the collapse, I don't even know who they were. I don't even know if any single parents were down there or if they have children starving at home. I don't know if they have sick relatives that need looking after. I'm tasked with getting these tunnels built, but that doesn't mean we don't have structures in place. I need to know who's down here at what time so if we have another cave-in I know who needs our help. So *that*, Hernandez, is why you will consent to getting scanned. In and out. If you don't like it…" Pablo gestures with his hands "…there are ten more men willing to take your place. Do we have an agreement?"

I look at the three of them, weighing options.

"Yes. We have an agreement."

Pablo clasps his hands together and makes a strange wheezing sound. Nunez turns and opens the lock on the chain fence. I step into the darkness and turn on my torch. I'm led by a rhythmic hum as the fence is locked behind me. When I turn the corner I am aware that the humming sound is in fact the far off singing of John Newton's 'Amazing Grace'.

"My chains are gone, I've been set free…"

X

It started on the 20th January 2017.

That's what became known as first wave. It brought with it the wall.

The wall was shipped in from China (what isn't these days?), each part of the wall built with the efficiency and industry we've all come to know that makes China the go-to for everything we own and covet. Each segment of the wall was fifty meters wide and 40 meters tall. Each piece connects like a series of Lego pieces meaning that within a month the wall separating our countries was built; the dream of a lunatic had been accomplished. It wasn't until what we call the second wave that things got decidedly worse for all, outside and inside the wall.

The second wave brought with it the Transition Squads, deployed to remove all families who resided in America who had a connection with what the establishment labeled sojourners, anyone that wasn't a pure blood American: mothers, fathers, uncles, sisters and brothers overnight declared enemies of the state. They began shipping people outside the walls, leaving them deserted in a country that wasn't their own. As you can guess this did not go down too well and so people rebelled, initially via peaceful protests. Nevertheless, it soon escalated. Authorities initiated program ID, which meant all those living in the United States and Mexico had to have barcodes printed on their necks. An identification mark. Had we not learned our lessons from Auschwitz? Scanners were set up on the walls, on street corners, underground stations, buses, churches, the few remaining mosques. Everyone's movements recorded and tracked, with the scanners nowhere was safe. People had nowhere to hide.

The protests died down, paving the way for riots, then the home-grown terror began. Every night, for eight months, there was bloodshed and devastation. If you were identified on a scanner, you were over the wall by nightfall. Families ripped like trees from their roots. There were orchestrated explosions either side of the wall, weakening it in designated spots. An uprising took place, people rebelled; a resistance was born on both sides of the wall. Those that managed to break into America were normally rounded up and sent back as quickly as they arrived. The ID scanners reduced the population of non-essential personnel by 25% within the first two months of its inception. A wasteland soon developed either side of the wall. Two-hundred meters each side, a four-hundred meter no go zone, patrolled by soldiers, gun turrets and ID scanners. Anyone caught in these restricted zones were an example of. Usually executed where they stood.

The problem with all elections is that those in the spotlight fling a lot of shit, the problem is that some of that shit tends stick and snowball out of control. If people get behind an idea, take it to heart, it is enough to topple nations. It takes a strong presidential candidate to go back on his promises, to go back on the very things that incited a nation to vote him into office, however much he tried. Which is what we are dealing with now. The wall, just one big stain on humanity.

You may be wondering why so many Mexicans still want to get into America?

The reason as always is for a better life and financial gain; the same old story. All the trade routes Mexico had with America were cut off, all roads blocked, paths destroyed. Even air space is now cut off, denied to any alien of the state. America is now its own fortified bastion with a big white prince sitting at its helm. Mexicans could only be granted access to the United States with a travel permit. Dignitaries mainly held these and they could only pass through designated, heavily fortified areas of the wall, these were often the targets of bombers. The path towards the wall is narrow, the width of two cars. If you wander out of the demarcated zone, the guns or the drones shoot on sight and ask questions later. The road in was more akin to a battle zone, soldiers stationed in bunkers. Think Northern Ireland during the troubles, staggered road checkpoints over the two-hundred-meter approach to the wall and the subsequent two-hundred meters on the other side. They were truly fighting a war against terror both foreign and domestic.

That's when we took the fight underground.

X

So here I am. Hundreds of feet below the ground. Getting ready to join my chain gang, digging our way to freedom. I pass the collapsed tunnel, walk towards the singing. The torch offers enough light that I see small pinkish worms in the soft mud, jutting out between the rocks, rubble and splintered timber. Only when I get within touching distance I notice they are in fact fingers.

I pass three people huddled around a LED lamp eating a meal of rice, chicken and peppers, stuffed inside a taco. I nod. Place my rucksack down on the floor with the other bags. The smell of their food is enchanting and makes such a pleasant change from the damp, earthy smell we all have become accustomed too. My stomach aches for the taste of their food but I trudge on up to the line. I pick up a shovel. A woman old enough to be my mother turns to me, her body hunched, her face covered in terracotta mud. Her knuckles that grip the shovel appear arthritic. She wobbles towards me on unsteady legs. I drop my shovel and hold her up, she mutters something in Spanish to me but it is unclear what she is trying to say. The only word I can make out is 'Agua'. One of the men drops his taco, food spilling into the mud. Trampled underfoot as he rushes to our aid. He helps me carry her to their rustic picnic. She collapses to the floor and the men shoo me away as they pull out a bottle of water and give it to the woman.

I reclaim my discarded shovel and start digging.

Sometime later, someone taps me on the shoulder. A mustachioed, rotund man. Face jet-black, I can only assume mine is just as filthy, offers me his water. I take it, not realising how thirsty I am. I have almost drunk the whole bottle when I remember my manners. I stop my guzzling, spilling some down my vest top. It's cool and brings some comfort. I offer him the dregs of his bottle; he waves me away defiantly, so I assume its ok to drink the rest.

'¿Por qué estás cavando el túnel?' His hot breath spills into my face.

I struggle working out what he said: I think back to the lessons my mother used to give me, but they seem like a lifetime ago. I was more interested in learning lyrics to 90's rap songs than learning my mother tongue. I open my mouth to tell him *I don't understand*, but words just spill out.

'Lo siento, no entiendo.'

My Spanish momentarily stuns him, and me. 'Sorry, I don't understand,' I offer again. He then begins to fire off Spanish trying to establish why I am here.

'Familia…?'

'Dinero…?'

'El empleo…?' His hands grip his shovel harder, even in this light I can see his knuckles turning white.

'El medicamento, el medicamento!' I say, trying to stop his flow.

His face contorts, frown lines deepen, it appears he may attack me. He suddenly smiles. Leans in and hugs me. I awkwardly hug him back in the darkness. We detach and head back to our work. He joins me in the digging line, muttering to me occasionally in Spanish. I let him.

A woman joins us, wearing cut-off denim shorts, a checked shirt tied around her waist, hair scooped out of her filthy face with what appears to be a yellow bandana.

'Are you American?' she manages to pant out as we dig.

'Yep…'

'My name's Jasmine…' she offers

I nod, not wanting to get into a conversation.

'Not much of a talker huh…I was just trying to…'

'Look Jasmine, I came here to work, not to make friends...'

We settle down into an awkward silence; I feel her look at me after every few scrapes at the wall.

'I'm digging for my son...he's got diabetes.' I don't know what she expects me to do here, break down crying and offer her my sympathies; just when I think it was just a statement she starts up again.

'I need to get him insulin but can't afford the prices here anymore. His father died in the cave-in last week, I'm all he's got. I've heard there is a medicine man that can help...but he's on the other side of the wall.'

She stops talking. Silence. I stop digging. Lean on my shovel.

'...I'm digging for my mother.'

I feel her turn to continue the conversation but I pick up the shovel and continue digging.

x

I take a break; leaving the woman at the wall, two men take my place. I pick up my bag and move to the side of the tunnel. Placing the bag under my head, I close my eyes.

'Hernandez...Hernandez...'

I awake, with the feeling that I've been falling. I'm at home. The television playing some Spanish chat show, the audience finding whatever the presenter is saying hilarious. The laughter all-consuming. I stand, the remote falls to the ground. I pick it up and turn it off. The sounds of birds replaces the cackling audience. Light cascades into the living room, sounds of children playing baseball in the street creeps through the house on the breeze from the open window.

'Hernandez...' this time cut off by coughing. Emanating from upstairs. Instinctively I move into the kitchen and fill up a glass of water, empty pills from prescription bottles into my hand. I look out the kitchen window and in the distance, I see the wall.

I walk past the fridge. I stop. My gaze held by a picture I'd not noticed before. It's a picture of me at High School with my class. It was a summer full of hope and wonderment as we set off to our college campuses that summer. But my mother, it would appear had used this photo to keep track of who was still here; still with the living. We were, are a close-knit community. My mother knew most of the children in my class knew their families; that was until she got sick and became somewhat of a recluse. Big red crosses etched deep into the photo removed my friends of their faces. There were some I knew about,

Jane, Samphire and Jed; they were rounded up in the second wave by the Transition Squads. The others. Now faceless, I'd be hard pressed to remember their names.

I trudge up the stairs, follow the coughing. Pushing open my mother's door to reveal a room shrouded in darkness, machines beep and chime within. An emaciated arm beckons me over, a rosary entwined around her fingers like weeds around a plant. She coughs as I approach. Above her bed is a picture of Jesus looking down on her. Her bedside table cluttered with other Catholic paraphernalia, burnt out candles, incense sticks, pictures of saints and a well-worn bible.

'Hernandez mi hijo hermoso! Mira cuanto has crecido...'

'Mami en ingles por favor...'

'Why do you always insist we talk in this filthy language?'

'Mama this is where I was born, this is all I know...you shouldn't let anyone else here you talk like that, people have been...'

'Enough Hernandez...' cough. '...give me the medication and agua.'

I hand them over and watch as she swallows the tablets, her neck so thin I swear I see the tablets working their way down.

'Mama I've got to go, but I'll be back in a few days with your new meds and check on you, ok?'

'You are good to me, Hernandez, I don't know what I'd do without you.'

A whistling wakes me.

A whistle blows in the tunnel. One of the fail-safes the team has in place. If you hear a whistle everyone stops. It's for numerous reasons, intelligence regarding drones overhead, listening devices deployed above ground. Today it would appear it's more a directional change. Pablo approaches with his two guards in tow, carrying a device that sits atop a long metallic tube. When he reaches the wall we've been digging, the device begins to flash; a green light is emitted into the cave. He presses a button on the side of the device, six tubes shoot out diagonally from its base, making the bottom of the device more tripod than staff. He clicks another button on the side and the top of the staff lowers. A red laser scans the wall. Pablo rubs his stubble-covered chin, his face flushes with excitement.

'We now go up. Ahora subimos.'

Everyone shouts, singing breaks out, the old woman who sat down to recover leaps to her feet, rejuvenated. She shouts 'Halleluiah' and charges towards the wall with her shovel.

'Now get back to work...con rapidez.' Pablo shouts, his voice swallowed up by the commotion around him.

Everyone grabs their shovels, the laser now leading us up to the salvation we have all hoped for since the wall's inception. A chance to get in, a chance to get away from a life that has been forced on us. Oppression only lasts if those that can make a difference choose not to. I get up and begin to dig with the others. We dig for what could be hours or days, taking it in turns to sleep, unbeknownst to us if it's day or night, time passes as unnoticed as the first green leaf of spring.

X

Bodies ache and blood issued. I the only remaining person digging. I touch the soil. I cradle some of it in my palm; it's orange. I dig my shovel into the dirt where it sticks. I begin to feel the soil with both my hands. I reach out like a preacher praying for his congregation. It is then I feel what I could only see before. My hands touch the wall. The soil has changed consistency, warm to touch, dustier and dry. My hands dig into the soil; it falls away in large clumps.

We must be close. We must almost be through. I glance behind me; the rest of the diggers are sleeping or eating, unaware that we are so close to a breakthrough. I carry on digging in silence, each shovel bringing down more dirt, small cave-ins at a time. A cloud of fallen dirt clears and a pinprick of light breaks through; daylight enters this cavern. Plumes of dust dance in the enchanting light. Particles held within its beam shimmer; I ruminate for a moment, imagining each particle of dust is a planet, rotating some invisible orbit; a galaxy suspended in time.

I stand dumbstruck, the shovel falls from my hands to the floor, clanking against the rubble at my feet. The other workers realise, hushed excitement and exclamations sound as whispers in the wind. I'm nudged from behind. I turn to see black faces staring back at me all white-eyed and red-lipped looking like a group of minstrel singers. They usher me forwards with their hands. I creep forwards, the soil making the sound of virgin snow being trampled underfoot. I look down as my boot enters the beam of light; I must imagine it but as my foot breaks the beam, my body flushes with the heat of the sun. I reach out a grazed, bloodied hand towards the pinhole of light. I force my finger into the hole. Momentarily plunging us all into darkness. I wiggle my finger like a caterpillar exiting an apple and feel the heat of the ground above. I make the hole bigger. Suddenly the cave is washed in sunlight. I guess it's down to me. I move gingerly towards the hole. I place the shovel through the hole. I notice my hands shaking. I hope no one else can see my fear. I don't want my head blown off if we've come up short of the two-hundred-meter mark. I hold the shovel there for a few seconds, waiting for it to be shot out of my hands. Nothing. Of course, that doesn't necessarily mean it's safe. The scanners are looking for barcodes, not tools.

Fuck it.

I drop the shovel, reach forwards, pulling at the earth. The dust floods the tunnel. Choking, I thrust my head up through the hole, from the womb of the earth. The dust clears.

Inches from my nose, a pair of shiny boots. Four pairs, in fact. I glance up, the sun causing me to squint. The boots belong to soldiers, each silhouetted against the sun. They point guns at my face. Someone is shouting at me in Spanish.

'¿Eres americano?'

I can't work out what they are saying in the chaos of this situation. I look for the words to say in my limited Spanish. *What is the word for I don't understand?*

'¿No entiendo?'

'Are you American?' they spit back at me with an Hispanic twang.

'Si...Yes, American!'

I hear the click, but I don't see what happens next. It would appear when shot in the face everything moves in slow motion; my legs give way and I fall back into what has now become my grave. The last thing I hear before blackout.

'This is a Gringo-free Mexico... you built the wall, you live with the consequences!'

ROSS JEFFERY

EXECUTIVE DIRECTOR, HEAD OF BOOKS

Ross Jeffery is a Bristol based writer and Executive Director of Fiction /
Head of Book Reviews at STORGY Magazine. Most often than not to be found
collaborating with Tomek Dzido and Anthony Self with either a pen or a
camera. He is an avid reader of an eclecting mix of fiction, a lover of the short
story genre; and has been hard at work on his own collection of short stories
and a novel for publication in the near future. Ross has been published in
STORGY Magazine and 13 Dark. Follow him on Twitter @Ross1982

RED
by Alice Kouzmenko

My mother didn't understand why none of us touched the Eton Mess she'd made for Sunday dessert.

'There's homemade jam too. And a bowl of fresh ones just at the end there. Go on, Lily. Strawberry season doesn't last long enough, eat them while they're sweet.'

I sat stiff between my daughter Lily and husband Jeff. Meringue crumbs spilled from my mother's mouth to fill the silence; a minute or two before Lily reached over. I noticed her nails were painted coral as she grabbed the top berry by its stalk. Each was a little thing; could fit in the palm of a hand. But it's all relative, isn't it? One person's little thing is another's whole world. She took a small, slow bite; her first in years. Jeff's widened eyes met mine.

'Come round next week and I'll let you in on some baking secrets only grandmas know,' my mother winked at Lily. 'Bye dear,' her sweet breath lingered as she planted a sticky kiss on my cheek.

***

Sweet and sticky like that June morning. The late spring sky was a patchwork of blue and white, outside air cooler than it appeared from the window. Nick insisted on wearing his favourite ripped shorts, those that exposed his scarred knees, seeded with grass stains and blood patches and flakes of dry mud from his weekend adventures. That boy had climbed and fallen out of every tree in the local park. Our evenings were spent bandaging bloodied limbs and picking pebbles out of fresh wounds with tweezers.

'How do you do it?' I'd ask mums on the playground. Mums whose sons lingered in sight, while mine would return brown and bruised, shoes soggy with soil.

'You're lucky he's never broken a bone.'

'Hospitals are a nightmare.'

I was lucky. I just didn't realise quite how much.

We ignored the grey clouds that multiplied as we drove.

'Are we there yet?' The kids asked in unison. Although Nick was seven years older than his sister, I was often tempted to say I had two nine year-olds. Their crooked smiles were almost identical. The same rosy, freckled cheeks, same light blonde, unbrushed hair.

'Almost, guys, almost.'

A few wrong turns and impatient sighs later, the sign appeared: Redberry Farm. *An experience you won't forget!*

'We're here.'

'Don't forget the sun cream, kids,' Jeff said. British optimism; by that point, our sun was almost gone. Within seconds, my two nine year-olds sent squirts of thick cream flying. At least it was the outside of the car they splattered.

'That's enough, guys.' Since that day, the smell of cream makes me sick.

Within ten minutes the tips of Lily's fingers were stained a colour you could mistake for blood. Her and Nick made a maze of the fields, buckets clutched between chubby fingers.

'Competition time! Whoever picks more strawberries gets two scoops of ice cream with dessert,' Nick said. Competitions were serious business for him. I spent every school sports day awaiting a call: 'Mrs. Freer? There's been an incident. Nothing to worry about – your son just got a little overexcited about the relay race.'

'Me and Nick versus you two!' Lily's posture was a crooked attempt to mirror her brother's. Chin up, chest out, he'd taught her. While his torso was toned, hers was plump.

'Three, two, one,' Jeff said.

'We're gonna beat you, Mummy.'

A blink and they were gone. Instead of running after them, Jeff and I linked arms and strolled like we had through Italian vineyards, reliving our honeymoon like twenty years, grey streaks and stretch marks hadn't happened. We stomped on our responsibilities and let them trickle away like fruit juice. Clouds hurried but our time stilled.

We wandered directionless, woken from our daydream by ripples of ripe laughter. Through a narrow clearing, we saw our kids sitting cross-legged beneath low-hanging green vines. Each spot of surrounding sunlight was shrinking, except for theirs. We crouched down on the other side of the bush, but they were oblivious to all but each other and their bright berries: gooseberries, raspberries, strawberries, ripe and unripe, big and small. It would be wrong to call that day my favourite family outing. But, for some time, it was.

'Have you got any strawberries left? I've finished mine,' Lily said with her mouth still full. Juice dribbled down her chin like syrup, her white top already stained.

'We'll never win,' Nick's own mouth was crimson. He giggled and passed her another handful. 'Smell them, they smell so sweet. Like springtime and grandma's house.'

I inhaled myself: freshly-picked fruit drifted somewhere between crisp grass, sweaty children and lurking rain.

'Spring's the best season. Shame it's so short,' Nick said.

Lily licked every last sliver of fruit as if it were forbidden, as if time was running out. I almost warned her about choking, but that would give us away. She pulled a vine of redcurrant from her bucket and tucked it behind her ear.

'Do you like my new look?' Blades of grass beat together in applause. A butterfly danced past.

'You need a real flower in your hair,' Nick said. 'A lily.'

'I don't think lilies grow around here.'

'Maybe not. But do you know what does?'

'Lots and lots and lots of strawberries!' The kids erupted into high-pitched screams at the sound of Jeff's voice. 'While you guys are stuffing yourselves silly, looks like mum and I are winning.'

He towered over the bush then ran across the field. While the kids followed in Jeff's footsteps, knees buckling and laughs growing, I lingered behind to find the vine of redcurrant that had fallen from Lily's hair. I picked it up and tiptoed my fingers over each silky berry: fat and red, the colour of my ruby ring and Jeff's favourite Christmas baubles and the lipstick Nick used to scribble over Lily's face while she was sleeping.

'Come on, Mummy,' Lily's voice echoed from across the field. Jeff was a few paces in front of her, while Nick was nowhere to be seen. I dropped the redcurrant.

Soon we were lost, feet greased with mud. As we wandered, ignorant of signs, each footpath narrowed, became a minefield of stinging nettles and rabbit holes.

'Nick?' Lily called.

'Nick, that's enough now.' Leaves wrestled in the strengthening breeze. 'You've won,' I said.

'Maybe he's hiding by the river.'

River was a strong word. A stream of razor rocks, more like, positioned with careful deliberation. The water was an afterthought, a sly attempt to disguise what lay beneath.

'Hold my hand, Lily. It's quite slippery.' Her palm was moist. 'Come on, Nick, it looks like it'll rain soon.'

'Mummy, is that an owl?'

'Owls only really come out at night, love,' I said in time to a wild bird call: shrill, but cracked, like a train untested, driver eager but unprepared. 'Maybe I was wrong. Nick? This isn't funny anymore.'

'I'm by the pond,' We turned in the direction of his voice. The pond was across the stream. 'Come here, Lil, I've got a surprise for you,' he said between broken, panting breaths. Nick's shorts were covered with the same duckweed as the pond. He stood barefoot on a sloped stone, forehead glossed, cheeks blushed.

'Look,' he raised one hand and, as he did, the other half of his body skewed sideways. While his balance swayed, his gaze locked on Lily. Her smile widened, not shy about the red remains trapped between her teeth.

'Go around, Nick. Follow the path,' I said a second too late. He followed the rocks instead, around the pond, over the stream, hop, hop, hop before his foot slipped, legs stolen from under him, flung head-first into the water, except it wasn't water, it was rocks, rocks sharp as knives, cruel and cunning. They'd had it planned all along. The water lily he'd held drifted down the stream, its white petals striped scarlet with his blood.

'Nick!' Lily spat half-chewed slivers: muscle, skin, flesh.

Jeff lunged forward. 'Ring 999!' He meant me, but I stood still, body independent from my brain. I can't remember how long before I rang, or what I said on the phone, or when the ambulance sirens sounded.

I remember red. Thick patches bleeding into shallow water. The fallen bucket of berries: splattered skin, sad seeds buried beneath sad earth. Drifting in and out of consciousness, snippets of Nick's life. His climb to reach a stranger's red kite trapped between high tree branches. A flash of his crimson swimming cap as he dived into the deep end before I'd even noticed that Lily had fallen into the pool. My daughter's blotched face and swollen eyes. My son, his head smudged with blood, mouth open, saliva fresh on his cheek. The scars on his knees gleaming in the last streaks of sunlight. Hospital screens, scarlet lights and zigzag lines tracking the progress of a little red heart that refused to keep beating. Roses brought to the funeral, wilting before they even had a chance to thrive.

For months afterwards, driving was hard; I accelerated through towns to avoid every red light. Raced to escape suburban existence, all the lives lived with no regard for those unlived: dog-walkers, smitten couples, children running carefree. A blonde boy skateboarding on the road, hair messy on his forehead, big eyes burning with big dreams.

Today, I watched the green fade and amber flicker. Unlike that June morning, I knew what was coming. I pressed my foot down, down, down into the brake. It was the first time in a long time that the car came to a halt just as the colour changed.

'Mum, you stopped,' Lily said. I glanced in the rear-view mirror and, in her ripe, crooked smile, caught a glimpse of him. When I turned, Nick was gone. A moment short, intense, but enough.

'Yes, darling. It's okay. It'll be okay.'

ALICE KOUZMENKO

EDITORIAL DIRECTOR – ALICE KOUZMENKO

Alice Kouzmenko is an English Literature with Creative Writing student currently based in Norwich. First published at the age of nine, Alice has been writing ever since. She loves the work of Zadie Smith and Toni Morrison and aims to, one day, capture the human experience as accurately and brilliantly as they have. Alice's stories have received gold keys in the Scholastic Art and Writing Awards and she has performed her poetry on the radio. Her publication on the STORGY website encouraged her to reach out to Tony and become a part of the team. Alice dreams of becoming a full-time writer and is currently working on an idea for a novel.

THE RECKONING
by Tabitha Potts

The same day they burned our mother I told my brother I was going hunting. Tuin understands that I venture into the Dead Forest to be alone among the ancient sequoias. I wish they were still living; the bushes that creep across the forest floor now are no substitute.

Sometimes I climb the giant trees but this evening I lay beneath them, drinking the water I had brought with me. It was dark but the moon was high in the sky and I could see the stars shining above me, the Big Dipper pointing to the North Star. Far away to the West, I could see the Skylands glimmering above the clouds, light streaming from its vast towers. Below the Skylands there was nothing, just a wall of blackness.

I heard a noise behind me and when I turned I saw a boy with thin lips, pale eyes and hair like smoke before it drifts away. You can never be sure but I thought he was a Skylander, not a bot. If the bots do not choose a human face based on one they have seen they can look too perfect, disturbingly so. Because they can travel through the air, Skylanders and their bots can surprise us easily, and for that reason we Earth people rarely travel alone.

I glanced around to check if he had his bot with him, perhaps in the shape of a wolf or a bird, but could see nothing. When he put his hands on me I knew what he wanted, not that there had been much doubt.

Afterwards I returned to our camp. There was a lot of preparation to be done for the Reckonin, and everyone was busy readying their canoes and packing their provisions for the journey. I found Tuin sitting next to Erilea by the campfire.

'How's he been?' I asked her.

She shrugged.

'No different from usual. What happened to you, Tatara?'

She was peering at me in the glow of the firelight.

'I fell over when I was night hunting'.

'You should be careful in the Dead Forest at night. It's not a safe place for a girl – especially on her own'.

'I can take care of myself, Erilea'.

'Maybe it's a good thing. The bots probably won't take you with that black eye'.

'Hope you're right. Come on, Tuin'.

Tuin followed me to our tepee and we lay down on our mats.

'Did you see anything tonight?' I asked him, quietly so no one could hear. 'Anything I need to worry about tomorrow?'

He shook his head.

'That's good'.

Sometimes Tuin spends hours drawing with charcoal sticks or clay paint. The drawings are based on dreams that make him scream in the night and often during daylight too. He drew many pictures before our father went to the Shadowlands and our mother shortly followed. I used to find him crying when he drew, but when our mother's body burned on the pyre next to the Great Tree, just as he had drawn it, there were no tears. It was as though something inside him died with her.

'I wish you could talk', I said.

His eyes were wide open, watching me.

'It's the Reckoning tomorrow'.

I reached out and touched his hand.

'Mother always thought they'd take you, but now I'm afraid...'

I broke off. He's only ten, I told myself, a little boy who lost his mother.

'Do you want me to tell you a story?'

He nodded.

We still have songs, stories and poetry. The Skylanders never saw their worth and left them with us. Erilea, our wise woman, tells us that they are the secret weapons of the oppressed, because they can travel to inaccessible places, like a seed carried by a bird.

I told Tuin how the Skylanders escaped the Great Flood in their flying machines, taking their bots with them to serve them, and seeking refuge in the Skylands, believing that the rest of the human race would succumb to war, flood and the poisonous air and sea. Then I told him how the first wise woman of our tribe helped people survive by hunting in the Dead Forest and fishing in the ocean and how we've lived here ever since, just as Erilea told me by the campfire when I was little.

When I finished the familiar story, Tuin was asleep. I put my hunting pouch and knife under my pillow and closed my eyes, but sleep eluded me.

We don't know why the Skylanders carry out the Reckoning by the Sunken City but apparently it was an important place once.

The little ones spent the day diving and playing near the great orange bridge, most of which is underwater, while us elders dove by the City to search for anything useful we could find. A few people salvaged oxygen tanks but you can't free dive very deep, because it's dangerous. I wore a pair of goggles and stayed near the surface.

It was strange to look down upon the City, as though you were a bird. I could see how beautiful it must have been once. It's hard to believe the City was once inhabited if you look at it now.

As I hauled myself into the canoe I felt a hand grasp mine and without thinking, I slapped it away, reaching for the knife hanging from my belt, the Skylander boy's face etched in my mind, lips twisted in a grimace, eyes closed.

I was preparing to strike when I realised that the face I was looking at was my brother's. He was huddled at the back of the canoe, staring at me. I spat out sea water, put my knife away and climbed into the boat.

'I'm sorry, Tuin. You startled me'. I grabbed the paddle. For a second I'd thought of him as an enemy. It scared me.

Erilea was carrying the lists, telling who had been born into our tribe and who had gone to the Shadowlands. The bots would take them from her to carry them to their masters. The Skylanders like to know how many of us there are, and where we live, even though we are of little consequence to them. She stood apart from the rest of us, holding the lists, her head bowed. I think she is ashamed when the time of Reckoning comes, even though there is no way we can fight against the bots.

They arrived among us as they always do, as swift as lightning. We tried not to look at their sinisterly flawless faces. They never spend long choosing and I kept my head down and held tight to Tuin's hand.

A bot with ruby eyes pointed at Rayan, tall and handsome, who was betrothed to Maya. They wept and clung to each other but there was nothing they could do. Eventually Rayan stepped forward into the bot's arms and they disappeared together. I looked West at the Skylands to where he was being taken.

The Skylanders are human just like us, descendants of those who left Earth to escape the wars and Flood, but because they are so inbred we have heard rumours of madness, their Emperor holding banquets in a torture chamber.

Maybe it is because of this they started taking us. Only one in maybe fifty is taken, with no warning, but they are usually the special ones - clever, quick, beautiful or strong.

I heard a gasp from Erilea and when I looked back I saw a bot with silver skin pointing at me. There was no doubt. I reached into my leather pouch for the crystal I had been hiding and held it against my forehead. As I had hoped, it melted through my skin deep into my skull.

I remembered how it glimmered on the Skylander boy's forehead as he drew his last breath. He struck me several times without noticing my knife and the moment he dropped his guard, I twisted it in under his left rib. It was a clean kill. I snatched the crystal and hid his body in a giant pit where a tree had fallen, hoping scavenging animals would discover it before the bots or Skylanders.

A strange calm possessed me as the crystal entered my mind. I could sense the bots around me and somehow access their infinite knowledge. I knew, with sudden confidence, that I could command the bot who summoned me. I could have the same power as a Skylander. I also realised something else – these beings were angry. They weren't happy at being controlled by creatures they saw as inferior and expected to do their bidding. This was something I could use.

But first, I looked at Tuin.

That was when I realised. the creature standing next to me was not the little boy whom I had loved and protected for so many years, but a perfect replica of Tuin, right down to the freckles on his face, his gentle smile, his bitten fingernails and his long brown hair. We foolishly believed no one knew about his visions – only our family and Erilea - but the Skylanders took him, in secret, without waiting for the Reckoning.

I let go of his - its - hand and walked towards the silver bot and as every atom of my body dissolved into the air and I left Earth forever, I promised myself I would find my brother again, wherever he was now.

TABITHA POTTS

MARKETING DIRECTOR

Tabitha Potts grew up in East London and much of her work is inspired
by this fascinating and unique city. She studied English Language and
Literature at university and went on to work on TV and radio dramas and
documentaries, reading, script editing, researching and producing.
More recently she's been helping UK charities grow their online presence as
a digital manager and marketer. She has published four short stories
(two in anthologies) and some poetry and is currently working on a novel,
when she isn't kickboxing and walking the dog.
Find out more on www.tabithapotts.com.

BIRTHDAY TREAT
by Anthony Self

George Bryant is hunkered behind a pillar when he witnesses the man in the orange boiler suit throw the girl from the platform.

He'd first seen the man skulking around the entrance of Turnham Green station.

Everyone has to be careful of the Boilers.

George's daily ritual for the past twenty years hadn't been interrupted on this particular morning – the flicker of anticipation as he enters the living room to kiss his wife Elspeth goodbye is there; it's always there. He usually takes a moment in the hallway to put on his *'mask'* – his layer of feigned nonchalance. It had taken years to practice the look, so it comes naturally to him now. The disguise of someone who's been shamed so many times, he's simply adapted to never showing his genuine appearance. He slips into his mask effortlessly. He never knows if he's about to be on the receiving end of some trivial rebuke or emasculated in some condescending way before leaving the house, so when he pokes his head into the living room he can measure the way the conversation is about to go. It usually plunges.

He can see that this morning she's already settled into her morning TV shows - her *stories* as she lovingly calls them, but the cackle of her laughter at the TV is a good sign. Today it's something about evictions, so Big Brother. He knows this is usually on in the evening so she's playing catch-up.

That's good, he thinks. *She's in a good mood.*

She usually clips her toenails as she watches her shows. George shudders at the thought of the sickle cell-shaped bullets sniping the picture of his mother on the mantelpiece and picks up his briefcase that's always left beside the sofa. He thinks that she has another three episodes to get through until she's into her afternoon regime. Sure enough, she's already nestled in, enveloped in her dressing gown, the flab around her middle spilling out. He swiftly plants a kiss on her forehead, turning to leave. He's almost free, when she starts imploring him in a mechanical voice to eat some fruit at the office, so he leaves her with the fake people on TV, passing the framed photograph of his beloved pet corgi in the hallway, absently reaching out with the tips of his fingers and trailing them over the immaculately polished glass.

Yip, yip, yip…

He answers from the hallway that yes, he *will* get a banana from the shop, then he's out. Free for a while, at least.

Soon he's ordering an Americano from the coffee shop with the pretty girl that always smiles at him as she hands over his coffee. She's got a nose ring - George once complimented her on it. He said it looked nice. She gave him a wan smile, as though she'd heard that a thousand times.

'There you go, Gary. Have a good day.'

George just smiles and nods appreciatively. It's easier to be polite. He wonders if she has a boyfriend...maybe a musician in a rock band. She has the kind of look that screams alt crowd. She has teardrop eyes, which makes him think that one of her parents is oriental. He's thinking this as he takes a slurp from the coffee. He also contemplates her legs...whether she has thick, muscular calves. He's always been one for athletic legs. He can never see them from behind the counter, but he thinks she has.

He's at the entrance to the station now and sees the man in the boiler suit, lurking; pacing up and down slowly with a cigarette dangling out of his mouth. He has dark hair slicked back into a ponytail. George notes his long face, accentuating an aquiline nose and gaunt cheeks. His lips are a crimson red, as if he's applied lipstick to them.

But it's the eyes.

The eyes always give it away.

Yip, yip, yip...Tallulah goes pip!

Those wide, grey orbs beginning to glaze over. The eyes of someone with a birthday treat surprise in mind. George keeps his distance as he enters the station, managing to glimpse over his shoulder as he taps through the turnstile. The man in the boiler suit with the unnatural red lips still paces, smoking. Smirking.

He usually stands for the train at the end of the platform - he doesn't like to sit on benches as he's read somewhere that older gentlemen...older and *overweight* gentlemen shouldn't sit down for too long. He counts the hours in the day that he sits behind a desk. Imagining the blood clots forming behind the kneecap. He multiplies the hours of a week. He thinks about those TV shows, like in *House* or *NCIS*, when the camera zooms inside the victim's body to see a perforated lung or a heart as it stops beating and now he's viewing himself standing, releasing the clot, letting it zip straight to the heart. He's got a whole day of sitting, so he likes to take the opportunity to stand.

"Passengers are reminded that smoking tobacco, marijuana and opiate cigarettes is prohibited at all stations and on all train services," a clipped voice announces over the PA system.

He notices something odd as the people nearest to him start flittering, like a school of fish darting away from a predatory shark. George has worked for Lombard and Wilkinson, an insurance firm in central London for the past thirty-three years, so he knows the signs of impending danger. That's his job - recognising, evaluating and judging people on their lifestyles, their habits and their vices. George instinctively follows the anxious glances being thrown at the stairwell and looks below the railing to view the man in the brightly coloured boiler suit, trudging up the stairs with a mirthless, rictus grin.

The man is going to take his birthday treat early, it would seem.

Being the cautious type, George slinks behind one of the pillars of the platform, careful not to spill his coffee. Last thing he needs right now is a stain on his white cotton shirt. Elspeth would be livid if he came home with a stained shirt. But then a rebellious thought crosses his mind.

Let her fucking take care of it.

But she won't. He will. He always takes care of everything. She's the kind of person who thinks 'fine' sorts out all of life's problems. Tell her to *clean the dishes* after he's cooked a meal and she says *fine.* Then you come home the next day and they're piled up in the sink. You say, *please do a wash so I have a clean shirt for the next day* and she says *fine.* But when you check the wash basket that evening all the dirty clothes are still there.

He notices other commuters eying the man with the ponytail with scrutiny and move quickly away from his general proximity. George glances down the track to see the approaching train; he reckons it will be about ten seconds before it stops at the platform. The man in the orange boiler suit is at the top of the stairs now, scanning the crowd of people like an automated turret. George keeps his body against the pillar and manages to swig some coffee without making a sound.

Damn, that's good.

Furtively peeping his head round the pillar, he can see the man with the red lips pick someone from the crowded platform: a girl precariously close to the platform edge, eyes closed, tapping her foot by the thick yellow safety line with massive headphones wrapped around her teenage head, presumably to block out the bustle of the morning travel.

"May I have your attention please," the PA announcement squawks. *"The train now approaching platform 2 will not be stopping, due to legislation policies. Please stand well clear of the edge."*

George glances at the cameras mounted on the station ceiling, pointed and following the gaunt man with the long ponytail swishing past the nape of his neck. Yeah, thinks George, *they know what's about to happen. Probably happens once a week. Definitely going to be late now. Have to finish the Mitchell case. Can't be late.*

The man in the orange boiler suit seems galvanised, marching over to the girl, those big headphones blocking everything out around her. He walks with purpose and George notices his hefty gait as he zeroes in on his prey. Many of the other people on the platform are practically tripping over themselves to get out of the way, because you never really know what's going through a Boiler's mind.

George watches with rapturous awe as the pony-tailed man clamps a hand down on the girl's shoulder.

The girl's eyes snap open. Half a second passes before she registers what's happening. *Stupid really,* George thinks, *you should never let your guard down in public.*

Because you never know when you might bump into a Boiler. They're everywhere. And they're here, every day. The girl sharply turns to run but the man is far too quick, securing his hand firmly on her satchel and pulling her into him. The sound of the approaching train is building to a crescendo. His vice-like arms wrap around her and he brings his face down close to hers. He lifts one of the massive ear cushions and deferentially whispers something into her ear.

At this moment George wonders what he's saying. It looks reverent, as if he's unburdening himself to her.

He takes another sip from his coffee cup. The train is almost on top of them; he can hear the taut coiled wires whipping and feels electricity in the air. In a moment he will feel the rush of air as the train whizzes by.

"I've always wondered if you bitches could fly!" the Boiler with the ruby lips suddenly screams, pushing her towards the edge. George's eyes drop to the stenciled *'Mind the Gap'* moniker etched along the beige line. He speculates why in this day and age a warning so perfunctory and arbitrary should still exist.

Struggling to be free of the man's grasp, the girl kicks out with her legs and screams for help at the morning commuters, huddled like sheep at the other end of the platform. She knows it's useless though; most of them have already turned their heads and are looking away, pretending not to hear the wails and ear-piercing shrieks.

The Boiler throws her onto the track.

From his spot behind the pillar, he doesn't see the intensity of what twenty-seven tonnes of metal travelling at over forty miles an hour can do to human flesh. He doesn't think about the way her skull smashes against the front of the carriage as she's launched from the platform edge, her legs flailing wildly in the air. He doesn't think about the way she twists after the initial impact, her feet trying to find purchase on anything to prevent her body being pulled violently under the carriage. He doesn't think about the sound of her thrashing legs snapping like twigs as they touch the track, her hands momentarily struggling to grip on anything in order to save herself from going fully under – the way her body is dragged like a rag doll under the plethora of wired pipework and tubes, under the grease-stained cables and jagged edges. He doesn't think about the way that she'll try to grapple the undercarriage of the train in panic with her outstretched arms, the way the momentum of the train will rip these appendages from her body like a petulant child cleaving a doll's plastic torso in glee – he doesn't think about the way that the remaining limbs will be caught like a silk scarf in a fan and shredded beyond recognition.

He doesn't think about these things.

George shivers as her cry is abruptly cut off. He observes the headphones, left on the platform floor. *They must have fallen from her as she flew,* he thinks. He hears several other people mumble under their breath, a few even shake their heads, but they know better than to linger on it. For them, and George – the moment is over. Like the few seconds of guilt that pass after walking past a homeless person on the street, they go on about their daily lives.

George keeps the Boiler in his periphery vision. He watches the gaunt man exhale sharply, as if he's kept the last ten seconds of air trapped in his lungs. The Boiler rips off a strip at his breast pocket. A bright light starts flashing in recurrent intervals. As the pale man with striking red lips takes a seat on one of the benches, holding his head in his hands, George likens the flashing light to the life jackets worn by plane crash survivors, lost at sea. Soon the proper authorities will arrive and the Boiler will be taken home. He will resume his job tomorrow like a normal person and colleagues will nod and talk to him like nothing has ever happened. Safe in the knowledge that this man has not targeted them. Because today is his birthday, and now he's had his treat. George will later learn that the man is a caretaker of a local comprehensive All Girl's school.

No one looks at the track once the train whistles by.

*

George is forty-five minutes late for work. As the automatic doors swish open, he can already see Sebastian Faulkner peering down at him with contemptuous, reptilian eyes from the balcony. Muttering crude and incomprehensible words under his breath, he passes the security guard with the buzz-cut hair at the turnstile, reaches the lifts and punches the UP button multiple times with a podgy digit. The wall-mounted TV is showing Trump Jr's inauguration party as the new World President.

He should really take the cement stairs up to the fourth floor, to burn off some calories and make a point of tackling the paunch issue that has now become a gut, but he's not in the mood.

When the lift pings open on the fourth floor, he finds himself staring at the bulky shape of Sebastian Faulkner.

'George!'

Faulkner is the kind of guy that laughs after every thing he says, a staccato *yuk-yuk-yuk* that drills into the brain and is forever lodged. George nods his head and starts walking towards the doors of the large office space, wondering what this uncharacteristic morning greeting actually conceals.

'How's it going?' Sebastian asks. Yuk-yuk-yuk.

George hesitates for a moment. He hasn't mentioned anything about his lateness, which means that he's after something.

'Oh, just fine,' George replies, not breaking stride. George notices Sebastian's elegant suit and his shoes that are buffed to distraction and he unconsciously looks down at his own scuffed shoes. For a split second his mind hurtles back to the man on the platform, the man with the red ruby lips and the ponytail – the way he calmly and proficiently lifted the girl's headphones to whisper something sweetly into her ear before throwing her in front of the train. He questions now whether *he* is the girl with the headphones, about to be thrown under the train.

'Yes, let's walk and talk. I know you're a busy man,' Faulkner says, coolly turning on his heels and keeping pace. 'George, something's come up that we need to discuss,' he whispers, leaning in and staring with those black, dead eyes. 'Something very important.'

George pushes through the doors and into the office space. He's not in the mood for Faulkner's games.

'What is it, Sebastian?'

George notes Sebastian's eyelid twitch at this – *probably had a whole speech ready for me,* he thinks, *the officious little prick doesn't like to be hurried on.* Within a microsecond of the thrombotic twitch, his mouth twists cruelly into a leer.

'Well, it's Parker.' *Yuk-yuk-yuk.*

Like a dial-up modem, George's brain starts screeching noises as his brain tries to connect to the worldwide web of forewarning. Every office had a 'Parker,' the kind of guy that's never really given any worthwhile tasks to complete, as he can't thoroughly comprehend them. Slow of reaction, he's not particularly agile on his feet in a mental capacity.

'What about him?'

'Well...the higher uppers want him to take on a more...substantial role. It's quite an embarrassing situation really. I'm mortified. Ha-ha. But we've got to keep the cog turning, so to speak.'

George's places his briefcase at his desk, snapping the latches open.

George's mind is still whirring as he takes out his laptop. Faulkner continues: 'They want him to front the Mitchell case.'

George slowly closes the lid on his briefcase.

'But I'm leading the Mitchell case.'

'Yeah. As I said, I'm *mortified.*'

George looks at Faulkner. An uncomfortable moment passes, and George thinks: *A certain frequency of silence makes a guy want to scream,* but marshals this to the back of his mind. Something is definitely up. He wonders about his own role, and what has prompted this act of blatant destabilisation.

'Parker?' George says, as if he hasn't heard properly.

Faulkner claps a heavy, sausage fingered hand on his shoulder. 'Yeah. I need you to get him up to speed and ready for a presentation with the managers within the week. That okay, George?'

Adding substantial salt to the wound, Parker saunters around the corner just at that moment and provides Sebastian and George a churlish two-fingered wave.

'All right, fucktards?' he says, unburdening his Hello Kitty backpack from his shoulders onto the desk.

Faulkner grimaces at this and for a moment George takes child-like glee in watching the twitch returning to his eyelid, but the moment is short lived. Faulkner looks at George for so long that he thinks he may have suffered a sudden embolism.

'Remember ,George,' he says, eyeing him with weary, sad eyes, 'management will be looking at *all* of of us with this presentation.'

The veiled threat does not pass over George's head.

'Well, it's a good thing that management doesn't hate *all* of us,' Parker says, nonchalantly.

George has to hand it to the kid, he may be simple in the ways of the world, but he says what he thinks. Faulkner snaps his lizard-like head to Parker and hisses quickly, 'Mr. Parker, I may remind you that you're talking to your superiors.'

Parker nods, indicating something behind George and Faulkner. 'And I may remind you, *Mr. Faulkner* – that it's George's birthday this week.'

George and Faulkner simultaneously swivel their heads round to see a whiteboard on the wall. In crude red lettering, a few names have been scrawled against dates. George notices the following:

HOLLY LUCAS: 25th
GEORGE BRYANT: 26th
ALFRED JUBB: 29th

Faulkner takes a moment to absorb this information. Parker switches on his laptop, humming a listless tune, which George thinks may be *Ode to Joy*.

'I…I didn't know it was…your…your birthday this week, George,' Faulkner stutters. His face is turning beetroot. Faulkner takes an imperceptible step back from George. 'You've not had your birthday treat yet?'

George shakes his head.

'Well…maybe this year, eh?' He laughs after this, another *yuk-yuk-yuk*, but this time there's hollowness to it.

'Maybe,' George says, turning on his laptop. Faulkner soon retreats, saying something about an important meeting.

'I'd put that guy out of his misery,' Parker says matter-of-factly. 'If it was *my* birthday treat, I mean.'

He still can't believe that he's been dropped as the main lead for the Mitchell case. He realises that his hands are shaking.

'Are you not worried that I'd come after you?' George says.

Parker shrugs. 'Shit rolls downhill. What would be the point of you taking your treat out on me? I'm sure you'd prefer to go after your bosses.'

George gives a noncommittal nod. He's right. Again. *What is happening to the world?*

Parker looks up. 'Who's Holly Lucas, anyway?'

George shakes his head. 'No idea. But it's her birthday tomorrow,' he says desultorily, before getting on with the Mitchell handover notes.

At lunchtime, George meets Holly Lucas in an underwhelming, prosaic fashion. In the staff canteen he finds himself slowly chewing on a stale egg and cress sandwich when he realises a slender, redhead girl is sitting on the bench opposite him. He notes that she's staring him. George finds himself laughing nervously, trying not to make eye contact. He wonders how old she is; her face is strong, intelligent and sharp in a forbidding sort of way.

There's a tinny *ping* and George manages to slyly glance at the girl as she picks up her phone and taps a few buttons, before replacing it back on the table.

She catches his eyes. 'Do you mind picking that up for me?' she asks innocuously enough, pointing to a napkin on the floor. George's eyes flit from her pursed full lips to the discarded serviette. He has no idea how long it's been there. It's crumpled up, as though someone has already used it. He looks back up at her anticipating smile, a thousand thoughts dancing in his mind like a kaleidoscope.

'Sure,' he says finally, slowly standing from the bench.

George bends down, picking up the napkin with all the subtlety of a hippo tap dancing, the effort leaving him breathless and slightly dizzy. He saunters over to her bench in a hopefully nonchalant manner and places it delicately on the table. George notices that she's wearing a tortured expression; as if she was sucking on an incredibly sour sweet she dare not spit out.

He turns to go back to his seat, but she's not finished with him yet.

'Do you mind doing something else for me?' she asks, blinking a few times for dramatic effect. She clasps her hands together, as if in prayer.

George smiles weakly, raising his eyebrows.

'Do you mind getting it out for me?'

George tilts his head to the side. 'Excuse me?'

She points a finger at his crotch. 'Your penis,' she says, matter-of-factly. 'I'd like to see it.'

George feels his head suddenly swell alarmingly. Heat rushes to his cheeks and there is a slight buzzing noise in his ears. He can no longer hear her voice. The day had started on a bum note and it was getting procedurally worse. For a moment he wonders if he's still asleep, and this is all a dream. He mentally pinches himself and realises that this is in fact real life.

He snaps out of his reverie and realises that the red head is expecting some kind of response from him.

'I said: I don't have all day,' she says, those luscious lips twisting into a grimace of animal hate.

'Who are you?' he asks in a tiny voice. At that moment, her phone *pings* again and she holds out a palm, picking up the mobile with the other and checking the latest message. George stands there, feeling like a fifth wheel while the girl checks her message. She lets out a guttural snort of laughter, muttering something as she taps away. George remains still, watching her finish. Finally she puts the mobile down.

She stretches out a hand. George observes that her nails are painted a brilliant vermillion. For some reason he thinks of Elspeth. 'Holly Lucas. Tomorrow it's my birthday.' She stares at him with a piercing gaze as he takes her hand and she starts pumping it with suspicious eagerness. 'If you don't get your wing-wang out right now I will *crush* you. If you don't get your honkey-doodle out right now and I get my birthday treat tomorrow, I will personally come round to your home and I will crush your testicles under my heels like overripe plums. I will fucking *end* you.'

She lets his hand go.

'I get a picture,' she says, indicating the pink mobile phone on the bench. 'My friend and I have our birthday on the same day, so we're trying to get the most amount of dick pics.' She says all this without any humour in her voice.

George takes a moment to absorb this information. He opens his mouth to say something, anything, but his throat simply emits a small clicking noise. He doesn't look down at her heels.

Softly, almost purring, Holly says, 'Listen…just whip it out. It'll be over in a moment. Then I get to make an ass out of another suit.'

There's another *ping* and Holly retrieves her phone. That mobile announcement is starting to sound like a death knell to George. He stands there, indecisive. Reflexively, his hand wavers towards his zipper, but then his brain kicks into gear and he starts thinking: *She might not get her birthday treat tomorrow. She's young…it may be another twenty years until she gets her treat.*

Fear is creeping into the pit of his stomach, churning and coagulating like thick, spoiled stew. Holly's smile is wide now, almost voluptuous as she returns the text. She's looking at the canteen entrance, as if already planning her next target.

But what if you defy her? What if she gets her treat and comes in tomorrow, in her bright orange boiler suit and stabs your testicles with those sharp, pointy heels? No one will stop her and she'll be well within her means to do it. She'll kill you and come in the next day all smiles and red nails. What then?

'C'mon, just let the birdy fly,' she says, getting the camera ready on her mobile.

Suddenly, out of the dark recesses of his mind, a single image appears before George Bryant. His beloved Corgi.

Tallulah.

Something inside George snaps. He holds up the hand that moments ago were so near to unzipping his flies. 'Let me stop you there, Holly, just for a second. Where do you actually work?' he asks this in a voice that is not his own. Without even realising it, his arms start to fold in front of his chest in a defiant gesture, his whole posture changing from fearful wretch into business power-point mode.

'What?' Holly asks hoarsely, surprised at this sudden dynamic shift. *Yip, yip,*

yip…Tallulah goes pip!

'What department do you work in?' George asks, in an eager voice that has lain dormant for years. A voice that makes George Bryant somehow taller.

Holly takes a small step back, her venomous expression retreating in on itself, her brow creasing into a puzzled look. 'Admin,' she says.

'Uh-huh,' George says vaguely, looking up now, authority swelling within him, 'do you know that I saw a caretaker throw a school girl in front of a train this morning?'

This seems to stump Holly. George can see that she's looking for a witty retort, but he doesn't give her the opportunity to answer. 'It doesn't matter now, Holly. You know why it doesn't matter? Because she's dead, Holly. That's right. Dead. They'll likely be scraping her brains off from the track for the next couple of days.'

Holly visibly shrinks and George is unaware that his own voice is rising, shifting a few octaves higher to a point that could be considered loud.

'Yeah, that's right, Holly,' he presses on, 'threw her out on the track like rubbish. You think it's a coincidence that the lower waged workers get their birthday treats before their thirties and the *'suits,'* as you call them, don't seem to get them at all?'

Holly's eyes are darting left to right, her face screwing up in bewilderment and disbelief as her brain tries to process this information.

'You don't have a grievance with me, Holly. Not really. You have a gripe with what this place means to you, how it holds you back. Hell, maybe you have a boyfriend or a husband who's pissed you off for so many years that you take pleasure in this kind of shit now, isn't that right?'

He can see tears welling up in her eyes now. He pushes on. 'Is that it? You fucking idiot? Is there a guy involved? Holly, you cretin…are you *that* fucking transparent that you project all your insecurities onto the people you work with, rather than direct them at the bastard buggery dipshit boyfriend that's causing all this?' George doesn't realise it, but he's screeching at Holly now. 'You shithead. You fucking idiot shithead. He doesn't treat you right? He doesn't appreciate you, Holly? Is that it?'

Another *ping.* George dives forward and grabs the phone from her hand roughly. The raw power generated by his massive bulk and momentum astonishes them both, inadvertently sending Holly crashing back so that her ass bumps against the table, sending her sprawling. But George doesn't stop there – something buried deep has been awakened and he'll be damned if he doesn't follow through on this almost animalistic impulse. He dashes the mobile hard against the far wall; where it impacts with a severe and satisfying crack before dropping to the floor in a broken, limp fashion.

'How does it feel, Holly?' he screams, flailing his arms in the air like one of those wacky, flapping tube streamers from car lots, 'how does it feel to be useless?'

Something flashes in his peripheral vision and he manages to blurt out a feeble, 'what are yoooooou–' before the security guard with the buzz-cut leaps and knocks the wind out of him, hurling them both to the floor. Before he knows what's happening, the burly security guard is on top of him, applying some skillful pressure to his arm, causing a sharp pain to jolt through his entire body. He hears a noise that dubiously sounds like plastic ties being wrapped around his wrists and then he's pulled to his feet. For the second time in the last ten minutes after being so close to the floor, he feels breathless and dizzy.

Before he's escorted to the security room, he sees Holly kneeling over her broken phone, cradling the smashed pieces of plastic, sobbing pitifully.

**

The reprimand is swift and to the point. Faulkner stands by the doorway, eager to leave. Any mention of Holly's name during the meeting generates a spasmodic twitch to his face and any mention of George's upcoming birthday makes his body practically dance. He'd rather be anywhere else than in a cramped, sweaty security office filled with beige-coloured pullout filing units, but procedure dictates that George's Line Manager should be present for an official warning.

George sits languidly, nodding his head at all the right moments where a gap comes up in the conversation, muttering affirmations in all the right places when he is expected to confirm that he understands what's being said to him, but he isn't really listening as the head of security reels off all the Governmental terms and conditions frequented with prior birthday treat offences. After an hour, they wrap up and Faulkner bolts out of the room quicker than a coked-up party reveller.

He leaves early that day. On his way home he thinks about the girl on the platform, the way her legs danced swiftly in the air before her skull smashed against the driver's window. The way her headphones were left on the floor without anyone to listen to the music it produced. The way the Boiler sat down after he had received his treat and looked correctly drunk. He wonders whether Holly will come into work the next day wearing a brightly-coloured Boiler suit, armed with a Kalashnikov, spraying bullets in all directions. Don't be stupid, he chides. *Where would she get a Russian rifle? A snub-nosed*

Uzi though...

George thinks all of these things and many more before he opens the door to his house in Chiswick. As he takes his coat off and glances towards the kitchen he can see the pile of dishes from this morning stagnating in the sink. He sighs inwardly.

'Is that you, Georgie?' comes the voice from the living room.

'Hmm.' George grunts, walking down the hallway. He pauses in front of the picture of Tallulah. A vivid image of his dog springs into mind, broken and battered on the tarmac. He recounts the way he cradled Tallulah's broken skull in his arms, sobbing and sniffling in the same manner as Holly did over her phone. Just out of focus in this memory is a carroty blob, dancing wildly in the streets. A screeching voice chanting the same thing plays over and over, like a mantra: *'Yip, yip, yip, Tallulah goes pip! Yip, yip, yip, the bitch is finally zip! Yip, yip, yip...'*

George goes into the living room.

'You didn't do the dishes,' he says in a flat voice.

'Nah,' Elspeth replies, her eyes on the screen. 'Too many stories to catch up on.'

George counts his fingers, speculating the amount of times she's managed to lift her fat ass from the sofa today. He opens his briefcase, taking out a paper before placing it beside his chair and sitting. The tinny canned laughter from the television set is the only sound in the room.

'Oh, you had a phone call today,' Elspeth finally says, when an advert interrupts the monotony.

George looks up from his paper. 'Who was it?'

Has Holly filed a complaint against me? Have Lombard and Wilkinson terminated my contract? After all those years? How could they –

'Someone from the Government,' she says, turning her head to look at him. Her eyes narrow and scrutinise him for a moment. 'Wanting to know your chest measurements.'

George considers this.

'You know,' she continues, leaning in a way that makes her legs spill out on the sofa, 'we haven't done it for a while, have we? I mean, not in a long time.'

George thinks instantly of the girl in the coffee shop. He sees himself wearing a Boiler suit, issuing demands. Ordering clothes off. Forcibly grappling with the girl. He finds himself staring off at the wall. The nod is imperceptive, and whilst his wife thinks he's nodding at her, what he's really confirming is that he's ready to commit an atrocious act when his birthday treat arrives.

Still in a trance, he hardly notices as she takes his hand in hers and slinks off the sofa. Elspeth places herself against the doorway and the picture of the corgi, so that he doesn't see it and start thinking of the day several years ago when she'd finally had enough of all the yip, yip, yipping and took action when it was her own Birthday Treat.

She plans to give him the best night of his life in the bedroom. After a wild night between the sheets he'll forget all about the animal, about what she did a few years ago when she received her Government-issued boiler suit. She doesn't think that he still holds a grudge against the Tallulah incident - of course he'd been upset at the time and of course it had taken a while for him to finally admit that the dog was the cause of their problems and in the end it had all been worth it, because now they had established a status quo in the relationship.

But.

She wouldn't risk it. She'd read an article in *Women's Weekly* that proved, statistically, that most Boiler incidents occurred in the home. Daughters turning on mothers. Brothers turning on sisters. Husbands turning on wives. No sir, she was going to ride George Bryant so hard that he'd be too exhausted to even put on his boiler suit the day after next.

She'd make sure of it.

**

George Bryant has a dreamless sleep that night. He thinks about the next couple of days, specifically his birthday. The time may be approaching when he has all the power in the world.

George turns, thinking that tomorrow may be the first day that he's actually lived in his life.

ANTHONY SELF

EXECUTIVE DIRECTOR, HEAD OF FILM

Anthony Self is a London based writer. He Co-founded STORGY with Tomek Dzido in the hope of exploring the short story format and engaging with other artists and writers. He began writing theatre scripts and one of his short plays '*Maybe the moon didn't want Armstrong*' was performed at Hampstead Theatre. His love for prose was bolstered when he entered a short story competition and Margaret Atwood commented that his style was Kafka-esque. He has also directed several music videos and short films, one of which, *Anticipation* won an award judged by British film maker Shane Meadows. He is currently writing his first novel and hopes for a publication date some time before 2065.

INTERVIEWS

Interview with Rachel Connor

Author of How To Curate A Life

Tell us a little about your background and your earliest engagement with literature.

I was brought up in a working-class family where books were a rare thing. They were hidden in a cupboard in fact, and I was fascinated by them (no classics, but popular titles like Neville Shute's *A Town Called Alice*). I never saw my parents reading books (my dad would sometimes read the local rag). And yet, they encouraged my love of words. I learned to read, long before school, by decoding words on produce at the supermarket and sitting on my dad's knee to read the newspaper. At school, I raced through the primers and was put on 'free reading' at quite a young age. I have a very clear memory of reading aloud *The Mill on the Floss* to a teacher aged around 8 and being able to read the words but not having a clue what was happening in the story. So, in the early years it was my own curiosity and my parents' efforts that spurred me on. My mum took us to the library every week; I soon outgrew the children's section and moved onto adult fiction (much of it was completely age-inappropriate, though I don't think she or the librarians ever knew). After that, when I was a child and a young adult, it was dedicated teachers who encouraged my love of literature. I went on to do an English degree and a PhD in literature. I was the first in my extended family to go to university and I've always valued that, and tried not to take education or literature for granted. I think it's one of the reasons I now find myself teaching writing – paying it forward, so to speak.

What made you want to become a writer and how/when did this realisation occur?

I found real pleasure writing stories as a child and a teenager. My high points were 'The Day in the Life of a Penny' (aged about 8) for which I was sent to the head's office to read it aloud to him, and around the age of 17 my Woolf-ian phase (I was studying *Mrs Dalloway* for A level) – very intense and stream of consciousness. But after about 18, I wrote very little and I think what kicked in was fear (of not being good enough, of being judged. Just before I graduated, a friend challenged me about my decision to pursue academia and I remember feeling very defensive. It was only in my 30s that I came back to writing again. Doing a residential 'Starting to Write' course at Arvon was a high point – I always say I went in the door feeling I was an aspiring writer and left feeling like I absolutely was one. But in the end, it's the integration of practice that makes one a writer; a constellation of habits, a regular discipline, a growing body of work, the call of the story getting up in the morning. That has taken me a long time to properly inhabit, if I'm honest.

Where did the idea for 'How to Curate a Life?' come about?

The story comes from a fascination about identity and what it is in this era of online content and the selves we create and carve out of social media. I came across something that predicted what careers would look like in the future; one is that of a 'digital death manager'. I tried to imagine what that would be like, how that person would have a lot of power over the identity of the client in terms of the material that was collected and curated. A key question kept occurring: who are we when we're dead but still exist online? Can the 'soul' continue through the fragmented online traces we leave behind? I wouldn't class myself as a dystopian writer. But I had to project into a near future for the story's context. I like to think that the story explores a tension between the spiritual and the material, soul and body, between desire and duty. But ultimately, I suppose, the question is simple: who 'owns' us when we're no longer here? This question is much more complex in a digital age.

Tell us a little about your current writing habits. Where and when do you feel most productive, and why? Has this changed since your early writing career and following publication?

No doubt about it, I'm more productive in the morning. I'm quite haphazard as a writer. I don't have a rigid daily practice, though I constantly beat myself up that I 'should'. Like many people, I have to fit writing in to an otherwise busy life. Sometimes I'll snatch half an hour then on other days I can write most of the day. There's not much regularity to it. One thing I've realised is that I work better if I have a few projects on the go that are at different stages. One will be in the very early stages, sort of pre-writing phase; another I might be having to bash out a first draft (the stage I find most challenging). Editing is my favourite phase, and the one that requires least energy, so I will often save that for later in the day. All that makes it sound as though I'm constantly writing, which isn't true at all. I'm a full time academic, so writing always jostles with other things for priority. But I've found those other things (say, teaching a workshop or designing a new degree course) are all creative too, and feed into the writing in an important way. For me, in a busy life, it's about integration. So many things are creative, if you think about it. The writing comes out of those things, rather than being something separate that I must carve out time for.

When you need inspiration, which book of short stories or novel might you pick up? Aside from literature, which other art forms or artists might you draw inspiration from?

There are some favourites I go back to again and again, as though they were a comfort blanket. I never exhaust Virginia Woolf's *Mrs Dalloway*, for example. I think that's probably my desert island book. On the other hand, if I need inspiration I tend to pick up something that isn't fiction. Poetry is good for that – sometimes a line can dislodge something, or just provide a new avenue for exploration. Otherwise, I love a good mooch round an art gallery. But the main thing that inspires me is dancing. There's something about moving that can unlock the cognitive process of writing. I've come to respect a great deal the intelligence of the body, what it can tell us and the stories it holds. The writing comes from a better place when I can trust that and let it unfold.

What might you tell a fellow writer who was experiencing moments of self-doubts or creative sparseness? How might you inspire the continuation of creation?

Like everyone else, I've had my fair share of fallow times, when the doubt has been overwhelming. But now I realise that self-doubt is an intrinsic part of the process – it's the ego self tussling with the spiritual self that wants to create. The best advice I give to myself is to recognise its presence but press on regardless. Every day becomes a battle with fear and self-loathing, to a greater or lesser extent. What helps are the usual kinds of things: setting a timer to write against the clock; freewriting before the first draft; writing alongside other (carefully chosen!) people; having different projects at different stages so I'm not always just in 'first draft' mode all the time; writing in cafes (good for a sense of accountability); having good, honest but trustworthy companions on the artistic path who will mirror and respond.

I think there's something, too, about recognising that a piece has its own life cycle. In the past, I feel I've tried to force something into being when it's not ready. It can take a long time for something to distil down to what it needs to be. That's not always a conscious process. So, ultimately, and perhaps paradoxically, the best advice is not to be afraid to let go. If it's meant, it will come back to you.

What is the best advice you have received regarding your writing and/ or literary ambitions, and what advice would you offer our readers and other aspiring writers?

The best technical advice (in relation to writing fiction and drama): that old adage 'arrive late (to the scene) and get out early'. I learned that on my first course at Arvon, and it's always stuck with me as the key to good dramatisation (in fiction as well as scriptwriting). In a broader and more philosophical/ spiritual sense, I learned from my mentor Sara Maitland about decoupling the practice of writing from the external factors of success. When publishing something, you cross a line. It can be hard to hold on to the internal drivers of why we write in the first place in the face of the public stuff that goes with promoting a book and the 'glory' of getting it out there. It's distracting, and, in a way, not real. We all need an audience and validation. But the real stuff is what happens when you're engaged with the art, with that struggle, because it comes from within. The public stuff makes you feel wonderful but is somehow brittle and not that long-lasting.

Which authors influenced you and your writing, regarding the short story?

Oh my. So many: Raymond Carver, Alice Munro, Alison Macleod, A L Kennedy, Ali Smith, George Saunders, William Trevor. There will be loads I should mention here and have forgotten.

You're about to Exit Earth, but can only take one item from the planet. What do you take?

My heart would want to take my notebook and pens, while the logical part of me would be focused on survival. It would depend where I was going. But probably seeds, so I could plant vegetables. You can always write in your head, after all, but you can't conjure up food from thin air.

Finally, what's next for you?

The hard drive of my Mac is littered with stories of varying lengths, that are half finished and require redrafting. But the main thing I'm working on is another novel. It's a curious process. I'm trying not to overplan it, follow and see where it leads. I'd also love to do more radio drama – it was such a wonderful process to write the last one (my first). We'll see if that comes off! In the meantime, I'm very much looking forward to seeing *Exit Earth* come to life, reading the rest of the stories in it and celebrating its existence with the other contributors at the launch!

Interview with Duncan Abel

Author of Don't Go To The Flea Circus

Tell us a little about your background and your earliest engagement with literature.

I was late to the party. I was nineteen or twenty when I started reading children's books in my lunch breaks at the factory I worked in. I got a bit of stick from the other boys, but it was worth it, it really was.

What made you want to become a writer and how/when did this realisation occur?

I couldn't find stories about people I knew: pub-footballers, factory workers, lorry drivers, stay-at-home drinkers. All I could find were books about heroes overcoming the odds. I wanted stories about people who were, as Thoreau says, living lives of quiet desperation. They were the people I was interested in.

Where did the idea for 'Don't go to the Flea Circus?' come about?

It's about survival. I like to read metaphorically.

Tell us a little about your current writing habits. Where and when do you feel most productive, and why? Has this changed since your early writing career and following publication?

I used to set my alarm for 5 a.m. and write for two hours before I went to work. I did it for years. I was at my most honest. These days I write during the daytime – it's less romantic, but I'm more productive.

When you need inspiration, which book of short stories or novel might you pick up? Aside from literature, which other art forms or artists might you draw inspiration from?

The Tenants by Bernard Malamud. It's a beautiful and gritty portrayal of two writers and the sacrifices they make for their art.

What might you tell a fellow writer who was experiencing moments of self-doubts or creative sparseness? How might you inspire the continuation of creation?

That story that you can't quite explain, and you know no one will like, and certainly no one will publish, but which you can't get out of your mind – write that.

What is the best advice you have received regarding your writing and/ or literary ambitions, and what advice would you offer our readers and other aspiring writers?

Sit down and write – it's the only thing that works.

Which authors influenced you and your writing, regarding the short story?

Sherwood Anderson. Irvine Welsh. Sir Arthur Conan Doyle.

You're about to Exit Earth, but can only take one item from the planet. What do you take?

Please don't make me exit earth; I don't even like going on holiday.

Finally, what's next for you?

I'm writing a few things for the stage at the moment. But I've always got short stories on the go. I spend time with them when I should be writing other things. They're like mistresses!

Interview with Joseph Sale

Author of When The Tide Comes In

Tell us a little about your background and your earliest engagement with literature.

Wow. It's difficult to remember my earliest engagement with literature. I guess it was my father reading me, or more accurately inventing, stories at bedtime. He was a wonderful storyteller, the best anyone could ask for, and he used to tell these sprawling epic tales which mixed together all these different characters from so many worlds. One of the stories I remember best had Batman pitted against Frankenstein's monster. It was genius, really. And it's become an influence on my work even to this day, where I often play with the idea of different dimensions. It was hugely inspirational. And when I got older, we'd read together. He was very concerned. He didn't want to steer me too much, didn't want to force me to be like him, perhaps because that's what his own father had tried to do, but soon it just became obvious that some things are passed on whether consciously or not and I was already in love with books. He talks so passionately about literature, I guess it was inevitable that he would inspire it in his son. He used to challenge me with some quite weighty stuff – stuff no school would ever show an eight-year old: Macbeth, Homer's The Odyssey, Paradise Lost, Spenser's The Faerie Queene, The Lord of the Rings. It was all mind-blowing and changed me at some profound level, I think. One of the main things was that dad didn't at any point doubt I could handle it. We always have this idea that children are stupid, which is ridiculous. Children perceive things we barely notice. Of course they still are developing, but we patronise children in our society too often, and this limits them. If you tie a rope around an elephant's ankle, even when it grows up it cannot break the rope, despite having the requisite strength to do so. This is "learned helplessness", which is what carnivals use to train their animals. And we do it en masse as a society.

Dad never patronised me, so I never believed for a single second I wouldn't be able to read this stuff, and it was one of the most liberating things in the world. I'm so, so grateful for it.

My mother was no less influential. She is an avid reader and an incredible artist. She exposed me to 2000AD's comics and modern fantasy novelists such as Terry Pratchett, David Gemmel and Margaret Weiss & Tracy Hickman. Her artwork, and her eye for the striking image, later became something that would inform my writing just as much as what I was reading. My writing is very visual, which partly stems from those comics, her work, but also the grand poetry I read at a young age, which was just so audacious with its metaphor.

What made you want to become a writer and how/when did this realisation occur?
I've always wanted to be a writer, I think. Or at least, I've always wanted to tell stories. Stories are at the heart of us, it's how we understand everything. For millennia it's the way we've contextualised ourselves in the universe, tried to understand the way things are and how they might be in the future, and explained our purpose. Stories can be used for good and bad, of course. Suffice to say, I believe that to save our world we need to tell more stories, not abolish them.

There have been times in my life where I've wandered from this path and thought about becoming something else. At one point I went into amateur dramatics and took courses in drama, thinking I'd become an actor, but then I realised what I really loved were the words. I also tried to become a video-game developer, but again, when it got to it, what I cared about what the stories of writers like Hideo Kojima, Shinji Mikami and Hidetaka Miyezaki, who have brought these incredible worlds to life. I didn't really want to sit for hours and code, although learning a bit showed me that coding is really an art-form in itself.

If I had to isolate a specific moment where I realised that writing was where I wanted to be, it was probably when I first read The Nibelungenlied. It's a 9th century German epic, the author unknown. That story shook me to my bones. It's so surprising, menacing, intriguing, with such a rich cast of characters, and the ending is nothing short of earth-shattering. After reading it, I started writing my own 'sequel', drawing on my friends – the same ones I used to drink with down at Portman Ravine – to create some new heroes of my own. That was when I really knew I wanted to tell stories.

Where did the idea for 'When the Tide Comes In?' come about?
I grew up in Bournemouth, by the seaside. I was never more than ten minutes from the ocean. Me and a group of friends used to always go down to this place called Portman Ravine, drink God-awful cans of K cider (eight or nine percent strength if I recall) until the sun started to set behind the cliffs, and there was no light at all. We'd just talk about everything and nothing. They are such

amazing human beings and it's a privilege to know them. I think those visits to the beech were some of the most humanising experiences of my life. I learned so much just listening to them talk and laugh. We still meet up and have the best time, and I'm so grateful for that, but there was a certain magic to those cliff-side outings which we miss now. It was spiritual, I think. I feel very lucky to have had those experiences. And so, when I sat down the write Exit Earth, after an initial failure of a story which was overly intellectual and trying too hard to make political points, I went back to those memories.

Let's be honest, we've all imagined the end of the world. It's impossible not to, especially in our current climate. The wonderful thing is that despite all that's going wrong with the hierachy, people – real people working and surviving – are still just going on being people: eclectic, wonderful, talented, foolish, confused, hypocritical, sexual and a-sexual. Everything. And nothing.

I wanted to write a story about this brilliant side to us, and I knew that the true beauty wouldn't lie in scenes of us fighting off aliens with gung-ho machine gun antics, but in those quiet talks on the beach as the sun's reflection on the water began to fade away, and the night and the cold drew on, and we felt we might be the last people alive in the universe. I could never have gotten to this revelation without the advice of my wonderful partner, Michelle, who sometimes knows who I am better than I do myself.

Tell us a little about your current writing habits. Where and when do you feel most productive, and why? Has this changed since your early writing career and following publication?

I've always preferred to write first thing in the morning. There's nothing better than just getting up, having a nice cup of tea, and sitting down to smash out one or two thousand words. However, right now, it's not an option, as I'm working around some pretty heavy office work, most of which is obscenely early-morning start. So, I write when I can. Evenings after everyone else has gone to sleep (until my eyes go crusty and turn red). Mornings on the weekend (before anyone else has woken up). In the brief minutes of a lunch break. I jot down ideas all the time. That's a key part of the creative process. Never go anywhere without a notepad.

Karen S. Weisner talks about only sitting down to write a story when it is "ripe and ready to drop", i.e. when it's reached a point when you can't not write it, and I think that's great advice. You need to let the seed germinate, growing and growing, and only when it's bursting should you set pen to paper/finger to keyboard. When you start writing, you should do a little bit every day. That's the best way to get through it. Don't wait for the weekends and start smashing out four or five thousand words, that's a quick way to get bored, lose interest, or just burn out. Four hundred to one thousand words a day, that's the ticket. You'll be done in no time.

When you need inspiration, which book of short stories or novel might you pick up? Aside from literature, which other art forms or artists might you draw inspiration from?

Great question, because, I believe we all have one story which resonates with us most deeply. That story is the story that forms us as a person, that most profoundly connects to our personality and our life-myth, the kind of story we tell everyone (including ourselves) about ourselves. We always go back to that story when we need it most. For me, The Lord of the Rings will always be that story. The Nibelungenlied made me realise I wanted to be a writer, but The Lord of the Rings reminds me of what writing is. There are so many fine, fine stories in the world, many of which have moved me to tears or made me rage and laugh and jump out of my seat, but nothing, nothing, feels as much a part of me as that book. Every time I read it, the deeper it gets. The films have much the same effect too. I think Peter Jackson really captured the spirit of the books very profoundly, with some minor quibbles here and there perhaps, but overall rather magically. So, when I am out of ideas, I re-read or re-watch it, and remind myself of what real storytelling is, and what my myth is.

The works of Stephen King also deserve a mention. You can pick up almost any book or story by him and just find something so utterly profound and human there. So, when I'm flagging, I will often just pick up one of his books, one I haven't read yet, and just start reading. His short story collection Night Shift is still as monumental as it ever was. The Stand, perhaps his most epic work, is just packed with spine-tingling moments.

In terms of other forms, I often turn to video-games. The Metal Gear Solid series is just one of the greatest stories ever told. Kojima is a genius, and should be regarded as an epic poet really for creating such an iconic hero in Solid Snake. Dark Souls is another masterpiece. The art and design for that delves so deep into the human psyche, what lies beneath all of us. I'd also like to shoutout Darkest Dungeon. This little masterpiece is one of the most incredible examples of procedural storytelling ever made. It's gobsmacking what Red Hook Studios achieved here. And there's a wealth of Lovecraftian influence for those who love the Weird Mythos.

What might you tell a fellow writer who was experiencing moments of self-doubts or creative sparseness? How might you inspire the continuation of creation?

All writers experience doubt. Don't be afraid of it. It's natural. There've been times I've wanted to burn every word I've ever written, that I've felt I could never step out from under the shadow of better writers. But it's not about that. We all have our own story to tell. And if that story reaches even one person, yes just one, you've changed someone, changed history even, and that matters. Doubt is part and parcel of what we do. To be a writer is to at once be connected to everyone and also cut off. We are eyes, watching the world, observing, but also, to be truly good writers, we must be part of the world and feel empathy for people. My recommendation, if you are flagging, is to live. Recharge your batteries by going out for a drink with friends, a walk in the woods, throwing yourself into exorcise, or perhaps even picking up another art project. I always find music is a key initiator for me in terms of inspiration, so if that's your jam, return to that. Be amongst the world and it will fuel you up: with characters, settings, poetry, life. Then, you can use that fuel to put stuff on the page.

But, having said that, don't think you can be a writer who never writes. Writing is a craft, like any other. If you wanted to be a carpenter but never practised, you wouldn't be able to make a table. Writing is no different. To write a novel, and write it well, you have to practise. There's a fallacy I encounter in a lot of young writers. They say: "I have this amazing idea, but I'm not good enough to write it yet, so I'm going to wait and write it when I'm older and more experienced." This is ridiculous. You will not be any better at writing when you are older if you don't write, and in fact you may be less connected to your "amazing" idea than when you first conceived it. The thing is, if you are really meant to write, you will always get another idea. Your best ideas aren't going to come at seventeen or eighteen. You think they are, but they aren't. The ideas are going to keep coming so long as you remain open to them. Ideas are also cheap. We have an obsession in this culture for innovation, bold strides, "original thinking", but the truth is there is nothing we can come up with that hasn't already been come up with. Shakespeare, one of the greatest writers of all time if not the greatest, only came up with perhaps one or two of his own plots, and even then they are not strikingly original. There are no new ideas, not really. What matters is the execution of that idea. The greatest tales live on because of how they were told, how true they are to human thought, feeling, nature, how they make us see the deeper reality behind reality. That is the true power of writers and what all writers should strive towards.

So, work on your craft. Practice. If you can't work on the project you're currently working on, why not try short stories or poetry as a break, or even just coming up with incidental images and dialogue? Read. Read a fuck-ton. Just keep reading the works of contemporaries, classics, the whole spectrum. Try genres you don't normally like, and find yourself surprised. If you are really blocked, take a step back, live life, pay attention to those around you: friends, family, lovers, colleagues, creatures. Learn from them listen, then internalise it all. The story will come. Trust me. Some people say we're all born with a story in us and I believe in that wholeheartedly. Maybe not all of us are born to be legendary writers of the stature of King or Tolkien or George R. R. Martin, but all of us have a story, and that story must be fed, shaped, and allowed to burn.

What is the best advice you have received regarding your writing and/ or literary ambitions, and what advice would you offer our readers and other aspiring writers?

Wow, this is a tough question. I've received so much good input over the years. From my English and Drama teachers at St Peter's Sixth Form, Rachel Dixon & Steven Pyburn, to my lecturers at Birmingham University: Richard House, Luke Kennard, Elsa Braekkan Payne, Philippa Semper, Huge Adlington, and many more. Then there's Richard Thomas, whose online class Advanced Creative Writing I took later this year. That was transformational. There's also some stellar 'craft books' out there such as Stephen King's On Writing and Karen S. Weisner's Bring Your Fiction To Life and Tristine Rainer's Your Life As Story. All of my teachers, however, have echoed one idea, which I think is at the heart of my writing, and the one piece of advice that has helped me the most with saving stories I didn't think I could finish. The advice is this: when you think about your ending, think about it like this. Something is lost; something is gained. It's that simple. But, surprisingly hard to pull off. The loss needs to feel significant enough to justify the end, but not so colossal that it overshadows any resolution. It's a tough balance, and there's certainly a lot of variations that are possible, but I think it's the key to nailing your ending. And to be honest, the ending is the story.

Which authors influenced you and your writing, regarding the short story?

So many! A lot of Japanese writers. I've been reading Ryu Murakami recently, specifically In the Miso Soup, and was just blown away by the concision of his storytelling, the electricity of his prose, and the acute observations of people and our fallibility. I also am a big fan of Haruki Murakami, and I've mentioned Kojima already... So, though I was drawing on my own experience of the coast, I actually found myself tapping into these Japanese authors for the setting and characters of 'When the Tide Comes In', which I think allowed me to do some different things with the story.

You're about to Exit Earth, but can only take one item from the planet. What do you take?

This is tough, but I think if it was literally one it would have to be my crucifix. It's a small silver thing, quite delicate, with some Celtic spirals on it. I wear it all the time. It has great symbolic meaning for me not just in the religious sense. It was a gift from my mother, after I'd been through an incredibly distressing experience. That crucifix became a kind of symbol of endurance for me, and remains so. It's proof I could weather the storm. However, given I could just put the crucifix round my neck, in that situation I'd take Lord of the Rings. Then I'd teach it to future generations as the actual history of the earth. Fiction is the lie that tells the truth, after all.

Finally, what's next for you?

Only God knows, really. I have dreams, and big ideas, and thoughts of world domination. I have two novels I'm working on. One is about video-games, and how beautiful they are, and how they can change your life forever. That's already written and has been sent a few places. The other, I'm still playing around with ideas, but it's scope is kind of difficult to grasp – and I'm writing the bloody thing! I'm very excited about it though, it's going to draw together a lot of genres and stories that I love into one being. Both these projects kind of mark a new phase of my writing that's hopefully a little more mature, literary, but still bristling with speculative and supernatural elements.

I'm also writing a lot more short stories and hoping to get them published in some wonderful homes. Especially after this competition. It's given me such a confidence boost. I can't say enough how staggered, grateful, overawed, joyous and tearful I am to have placed in Exit Earth. It's the most amazing thing, and I never anticipated it. In my heart, there was this nasty voice telling me I just wasn't good enough, and to have had destiny prove it wrong is kind of mind-blowing. Then, there's 13Dark. I hope that becomes an empire. We're going to release all 13 stories (plus a few extras) if it kills me. We may also be publishing some novels if things go as well as they are. It's so exciting. I want this work to reach everyone in the speculative writing community: readers, writers, artists, publishers, editors, and for people to get as excited about the work as I am. Those authors are so talented, it's an honour to publish them.

Look out for my work, and reach out to me if you ever need help. I'm always up for helping new writers or just being someone to talk to about writing and publishing and films and games and all the wonderful things that make this world worth living in. You can find me on Twitter @josephwordsmith and my website is themindflayer.com.

Until then, adios.

ILLUSTRATORS

AMIE DEARLOVE

London based tooth fairy and monster enthusiast Amie Dearlove,
works in a sweet shop by day and creates creatures by night.
When not making tiny toothy jewellery Amie can be found keeping
sketchbooks and live drawing with her fellow artists.

Find out more about Amie and her artwork on Instagram:
https://www.instagram.com/amiedearlove/

Visit Amie's shop on *Big Cartel*:
http://amiedearlove.bigcartel.com/

HARLOTVONCHARLOTTE

HarlotVonCharlotte is an artist living and working in London.
She graduated from the University of Plymouth in 2009 with a BA(Hons)
in illustration, subsequently discovering that the years spent there were
a complete waste of time. She primarily focuses on figurative illustrative
artwork of the slightly odd and macabre persuasion and has also used
sculpting, painting, figure drawing and graphic design to create new styles
and unique works of art. She is currently experimenting with laser cut acrylic
collages. She collaborates with other artists for live drawing events.
Her client list ranges from corporate to personal commissions.

Discover more about HarlotVonCharlotte and her
artwork via the following links:

http://www.harlotvoncharlotte.com/
https://instagram.com/harvonchar/

Visit HarlotVonCharlotte's shop on *Big Cartel*:
http://harlotvoncharlotte.bigcartel.com/

CRAP PANTHER

Carrie South is an illustrator and painter from Oklahoma City, OK who creates delightfully brutal illustrations.

Discover more about Crap Panther on to her Instagram page: https://www.instagram.com/crap_panther/

Visit Crap Panther's shop on *Etsy*: https://www.etsy.com/shop/warmachineink

COVER DESIGN

ROB PEARCE

Rob is a Graphic Designer from London who has worked with clients ranging from Nike & The British Film Institute to The Churches Conservation Trust. He recently designed the cover for the novel The Boy From Aleppo Who Painted The War, which was serialised for BBC Radio 4.

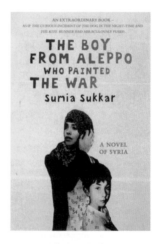

JUDGE PROFILE

DIANE COOK

Diane Cook is the author of the story collection Man V. Nature, and was formerly a producer for the radio show, This American Life. Man V. Nature was a finalist for the Guardian First Book Award, Believer Book Award and the Los Angeles Times Art Seidenbaum Award for First Fiction, and received Honorable Mention for the PEN/Hemingway award. Her stories have appeared in Harper's, Tin House, Granta, and elsewhere and anthologized in Best American Short Stories. She is the recipient of a 2016 fellowship from the National Endowment for the Arts. She lives in Brooklyn, NY.

http://dianemariecook.com/

Interview with Diane Cook

You Produced *'This American Life,'* for six years – did any of the stories for the radio/podcast initially influence you for the final stories that were written in *Man V. Nature*?

In general, my time working at This American Life had a great influence on the kinds of stories I wrote. TAL is nonfiction and often a story would get killed because it just wasn't laying out the way it needed to. We worked with facts we couldn't play around with. With fiction I have freedom to make something work to my advantage. Writing my stories was a kind of therapy to recover from all the stories that didn't work for TAL. As for specific stories, for years I never thought any of the stories directly were influenced. Then I heard a rerun of a story I'd worked on about a guy who gets stranded in the bay that is surrounded by the burroughs of Queens and Brooklyn, and incredibly busy waterway, the least isolated place on earth. And I realized that idea had in some way led to the story "Man V. Nature," about three friends who get lost on a lake they have no business getting lost on.

There's a 'strange-normal' landscape in each of your stories and each could be read like a *Twilight Zone* episode – without sounding like asking the arbitrary question of 'where do you get your ideas from?' do you tend to find a setting which characters are thrust into and proceed from there?

Most of my stories start differently. With a voice, or a character or a place, a set of rules I make for myself, but a few of them start with a *What if* question. Like, what if our babies were as vulnerable to predators as baby animals in the wild are? A question like that leads me down a path that eventually produces a story like "Somebody's Baby." I had a series of stories that began with that *What if* question. But it is only a jumping off point. It doesn't dictate where the story goes or what the story ends up attempting to say.

You mentioned in an interview with *'FlavorWire'* that the next novel you're working on 'is a speculative novel, so it's a future world where things are bleak, but it's not post-apocalyptic yet. It's extreme survival, but they do it because they think it's worth it.' With our EXIT EARTH competition, we're aiming to read stories that don't have to be dystopian in nature, but comment on the society that we live in today (or in the future, or in the past!) – Why do you think readers are drawn to stories such as these?

Sometimes fiction can feel like the theory of parallel universes come to life. Perhaps that's why stories that begin with a premise that asks, *What if the world were wildly different than it is,* are enticing to people. The *what if* thought experiment is where great invention comes from. Whether it's dude being like, What if we could still see after the sun sets but without fire? Or whatever question led to google glasses. I guess invention is where *what if* meets *I wish.* I wonder how much *I wish* propels writers. I think it must compel readers in some way. Not that they want the lives of what they read. So many fictional lives are tough. But it might be more like, I wish I could live someone else's life for a few hours. I wish I could see where all these decisions are taking us.

Who are your literary influences and what are you reading at the moment? Do you have any writers you would recommend to our readers? What makes their words and work of particular interest to you and why might our readers enjoy them?
I really enjoy Alan Weisman's thought experiment in *The World Without Us.* And I imagine the Exit Earth participants would be into it as well. It's pretty self explanatory, but also totally mind melting (and alarming.)

A story collection coming out in the fall by Carmen Maria Machado is brazen, frightening and so confidently written that a couple of times I found myself standing up to applaud at the end of a story.

I've reread Steinbeck's *The Grapes of Wrath* a few times over the past few years. I loved it the first time I read it and every time since. It's inspired. I think a lot of people have bad memories of it though, because they read it in high school and thought the last scene was cheesy. But it's so good. So it should be given another chance. Especially in these political times.

STORGY promotes the short story form – we're always on the prowl like an anxious jaguar, pacing the literary meadow for a good read to devour. In your opinion, what makes a great short story and what advice would you give an aspiring author that would like to write a winning short?
I always like a story where something happens. Where a character goes through something. Narrative like this is surprisingly difficult to pull off. So if I feel like I've journeyed along with a character, physically or emotionally or intellectually, while reading a story that is a success in my opinion. The other important thing is voice. A story with a strong sense of itself coming through the voice will always seem more successful to me than a story that reads flat,

but has, say, a working plot or narrative. It's got to feel like there's something alive behind that plot of yours. In general though, it can be hard to pin down what works. I think you have to trust yourself as a writer, even if you're a new writer. Follow your instincts first, before you follow rules. You want to see what you're capable of and then work with that to shape your inherent knack into something readable to other people. I would figure out what you like about the books and stories you like. And then avoid thinking your writing should or is supposed to do something. At least in drafting. Let your brain have some fun before it has to work too too hard.

Please, please can you tell us what the monster is in 'It's Coming'?
You don't really want me to tell you, you just *think* you want me to tell you.

There's a reason they're making the series of Margaret Atwood's *'The Handmaid's Tale,'* today. We live in a world where the phrase 'Alternative Fact' is actually a thing. Truth is becoming malleable – what are your opinions on the current climate we find ourselves in?
I don't know how to answer this. First I'll say, facts are facts and it's merely propaganda to say otherwise. If we can be convinced that facts are malleable, then we are malleable. Moving on, I personally think things are really really really bad. But then I see or hear of or even meet people who are thrilled with how things are going, or at least with the parts I think are horrifying. It's easy for me to think of those people as duped or uninformed and I know they think the same of me. And they aren't wrong—I am deeply uninformed about some things, and I'm probably as knee jerk as they are, just in the other direction. It's maddening.

I'm always really fascinated by survival stories because deep down I don't think I'm much of a survivor. The futures in some of the stories for EXIT EARTH or in other apocalyptic books like *The Road*, make assume I'll be the first one with a knife to my own throat once something goes catastrophically wrong. Sorry to get so deeply macabre. But it's what I find so fascinating about the instinct to keep going. And why I write about it so much. Because to me it feels unfamiliar and I want so badly to test it and understand it. The most interesting thing to me is while I think I'll be the first self-sacrifice after the apocalypse, I could in fact turn out to have that survival instinct after all. I'm not sure which is the right option, frankly.

Can you talk us through the process of balancing between surrealism and realism that permeates throughout the collection of *Man V Nature?*
In these stories, I change the rules of the world so I can come to a better understanding of it. In a way I'm asking myself and the reader to take a second look, do a double take on the world that you thought you knew but on second look is quite strange. I feel this way about our world all the time. When I look a little closer at some aspect of someone's life I assume will be familiar, I'm often surprised, sometimes even shocked by how unlike my reality it is.

The Apocalypse has occurred. In a wildly unlikely and highly improbable event, chemical radiation has left you with a superpower to wander the barren wilderness. What is that superpower? How would you use it?
It's not so much a superpower, but I really hope someone invents dehydrated water so we can carry more with us as we roam the dry earth. Maybe chemical radiation could cause a reaction that allows water to exist in powder form? I think we really, really need this to happen. Can someone make this happen?

Do you have any writing routines or rituals? Do you have specific times or locations which help you focus and/or write? Does music help to inspire your imagination, and if so, which type/bands?
I walk a lot. And I listen to the same song on repeat. Three so far have made the cut. They have to be instrumental and emotional. One has a slight hopeful feel and another is ominous. I switch it up based on where I need to go or the scene I'm working on.

There seems to be a personification of fears and anxieties in *Man V Nature* – in 'Somebody's Baby,' a man kidnaps babies, in 'Man V. Nature' three men are stranded at sea on a boat, in 'The Mast Year' a woman is besieged by random people that watch her every move – one could argue that there is symbolism running deep throughout these particular selected stories (social media interfering with our lives, grief and parenting etc) are these anxieties you have felt at some point?
In a way. Maybe you could subtitle the book, Twitter makes Diane Cook Depressed, Or Diane Cook hates living in the city and yet SHE KEEPS LIVING IN THE CITY. I think most stories jump off of a feeling or question a writer is having about themselves or the world. I have these feelings to work through not necessarily because the feelings are happening to me but because I'm asking questions of the world around me and it's making me feel things. Which is different than stories being a kind of therapy for my personal feelings. But

also, the feelings and ideas are universal and you've most likely felt them. *What do you want? How will you feel if you don't get it? If you do get it?* Who hasn't grappled with this and its aftermath?

Writing Workshops: Good or Bad?

Personally, I love writing workshops and still rely on a version of them today. They can get a bad rap and some for good reasons, but a good writing workshop lets you connect with readers who really get you. And you can keep working with those people even after a formal class is over. A group of us kept meeting after grad school and they were essential for me in getting my stories ready for publication. We'd met through our grad school workshops and always really liked their work, liked how each person talked about stories in general, and found their critiques personally really helpful. In lots of ways, I think this is the point of a grad program—to find readers. Generally, though, I find it very important to show early work to readers to help me see what my work is doing. Ideally you share a piece with a writing workshop and you get valuable feedback. And you can make the story stronger with it. Sometimes workshops fail a writer, though I tend to think if you're not getting anything useful from a workshop the problem may begin with your expectations. As for whether you should get involved in writing workshops, I can't say. Some writers do well on their own. I'm not one of them. So for me, writing workshops: good.

Describe your early writing habits and how you sustained the motivation to write. Have you noticed any differences/changes over the years?

Writing short stories was, in general, fun for me. Writing a novel is, in general, hard for me. Each form has forced a different process on me. Both have their joys and hardships. Perhaps it's just that with my first book of stories, I was in a honeymoon period. Making out all the time, making goo-goo eyes, saying, "I can't believe we did it. I think we're the only people who've ever felt this way." Now, I've been married for a few years and someone asks, I look at my book and it looks at me. Earlier in the day we had the same fight we always have and even though we worked it out, we're exhausted. Our smiles are tight and small. I say, "Well you know, marriage is hard and it takes a lot of work…. It's worth it, though." I sound like I'm convincing myself. But then my book finds my hand and squeezes it in a way only the truly in love can.

Were there any stories from Man V. Nature that didn't make the cut? If so, what were they and why didn't they make it? Will we ever read them?
I have a couple of stories that I always imagined being in the book but they didn't work for one reason or another. They still exist, but so does the thing that wasn't working about them. Occasionally I look at them with an eye to figuring out how to get them to work, but if I'd known how to do that I would have done it in the first place and put them in the book. They are stories that still puzzle me. Which I'm not complaining about. It's kind of nice to have these obstinate worlds and characters that refuse to be known by me. I feel a little nostalgic for them. They came from a time that I've gone and published, and so in a way, put to bed. These keep that time of my life alive in a way and its comforting.

ACKNOWLEDGEMENTS

We would like to thank all the below people without whom EXIT EARTH would not have been possible.

Rosie Carroll, Andy Gallo, Steve Passey, Richard Martin, Gary Hartley, Carla Fantini, Jessica Anderson, Rebekah Hughes, Emma Brown, Mark Or, Corette Nel, Lisa Lambropoulos, Thomas Dedola, Stacey O'Brien, Ian Critchley, Sarah Courtauld, Samuel Parr, Leah Webber, Brian Kirk, Thomas Garcia, *Mark Mayes, Alice Kouzmenko,* Haroun Khan, Phil Breach, Sam Hanson, Jungmi Park, Gregory Cobb, Scott Minneman, *Matthew Blackwell,* Kathy Burrows, Alex Grasham, Taé Tran, Tracy Lee-Newman, Lauren Bergstrom, Fiona Gell, Michele Sheldon, Sam Mills, Sophie Hopesmith, Ben Salter, James Smith, Emilio Maldonado, Zola, Philip James Kirke - author~architect, James Frederick Walter Harrington, Matthew Brandenburg, Natasha R. Chisdes, Brian Zielinski, Tim Stroup, Justin Hale, Kaleigh Lindholm, Mario de la Cueva M., Ian Chung, Greg C Bowlin, Anon, Andrew Hatchell, Neil Shah, Scott J. Wilson, David Ginsburg w/Tales from the Fandom podcast, Isaac Chappell, Brea Baxter, Ryan Duan, *Kim Jeffery,* Ben Kenward, Lexi Vranick, Apola Kipso, julie Stirling, Sarah Tille, Christian Meyer, Cristina, Alex Sheldon Savva, Ryan Lambert, Janka Romero, *Neil Greybanks,* Dan Coxon, Francoise Harvey, Francoise Harvey, Lizzie Huxley-Jones, Jamie Thunder, *Matt Hollas,* Laura Harris, Richard Sheehan, *Harry Gallon,* Bobbi Boyd, *Adam Heffernan*, Maggie Jones, Ian Dacre, Paul Marcantonio, *Joseph Sale,* Mike Scott Thomson, *Daniel Soule,* Rashers Tierney, Jamie D Kosmin, David Golightly, *Issiah Marley, Thomas M. Davy,* Luc Soudain, Paul Hancock, *Joseph Surtees,* Charlie Rodgers, *Tabitha Potts,* Paula Marcantonio, Chris Beckwith, *Gemip, Lawrence Pratt, Robin Griffiths, Tomas Marcantonio, Richard Lee-Graham,* Jacinda Buker, James Sykes, Michael H Bullington, Briony G, *Lisa Self,* Huw Davies, *Rhett Coxhill,* Benjamin Yeoh, Sam Rae, Claire Turner, Finbarr Farragher, Anthony Brown, theyoungdaydreamer, *Robert Dzido, Richard Thomas.*

DEDICATIONS

Sincere thanks to **David Self** for his spectacular support
and exquisite genes. You are a legend of a man.

Thank you to **Joshua Cooper** for your incredible
contribution and belief in us and EXIT EARTH.

Brendan Horgan
Thank you for all your words of encouragement throughout our voyage
into EXIT EARTH. Your support was invaluable and shall remain forever
cherished in our hearts. We could not have done it without you.
Thank you, brother.

Thank you to **Cristina Mameli Dzido**, **Sharlotka Voicheck**, and **Anna,
Eva** and **Sophie Jeffery**. Thank you for your unwavering faith in us and
STORGY. During our darkest days of doubt you remained a constant source
of solace and strength. Thank you for your love and kindness.

Thank you to **Rob Pearce** for your patience and understanding
during the design of the cover art for EXIT EARTH.
Your work continues to inspire and amaze.

Thank you to **Steven Pyke** and **Louise Culling** from *Page Bros Group*
and **James Cook** from *Firelabel Merchandising.*
Your advice and patience was invaluable throughout the design
and delivery of the EXIT EARTH book and our Kickstarter perks.

Thank you to everyone who helped us publish and promote EXIT EARTH.
Thank you to all our authors and artists and thank you to you, our readers.
We hope you enjoyed EXIT EARTH.
Thank you.

STORGY

MAGAZINE

ONLINE ARTS & ENTERTAINMENT MAGAZINE

BOOKS - FILMS - ART - MUSIC
INTERVIEWS - REVIEWS - SHORT STORIES

For more information about STORGY Magazine visit our website.

STORGY
www.storgy.com

 @fb.me/morest0rgy  @morestorgy  morestorgy

www.storgy.com